Munshi Premchand's

GABAN

A Timeless Classic

Cedar books

Published by:
Cedar books

An Imprint of
Pustak Mahal®, Delhi

Administrative and Sales Centre
J-3/16, Daryaganj, New Delhi-110002
☎ 011-23276539, 23272783, 23272784, 23260518
E-mail: info@pustakmahal.com • *Website:* www.pustakmahal.com

Branches
Bengaluru: ☎ 080-22234025, 40912845
E-mail: pustakmahalblr@gmail.com
Mumbai: ☎ 022-22010941, 22053387
E-mail: unicornbooksmumbai@gmail.com

ISBN 978-81-223-1196-9
संस्करण : 2023

Printed at : Glorious Printers, Delhi

1

It is the rainy season – *Savan*, the fifth month of the Hindu calendar. Golden clouds are gathered in the sky. It keeps drizzling now and then. It is afternoon, but it seems as though it were evening already. Swings have been placed in the mango orchards. Girls and their mothers enjoy using them. Two or four of them are on the swings, while another two or four are assisting them, pushing their swings. Some sing the *kaljli,* a song of the rainy season, and some sing *barahmasi* songs, sung all round the year. In this season, the women's childhood memories are aroused. It seems as if it washes away the worries of their hearts, and revives and greens the wilted soul. Everybody's hearts are filled with ecstasy. The green coloured saris of the women seem to develop a relationship with the greenery around.

At this moment, a peddler came and stood close to the swing. The swinging stopped, and everyone, whether young or old, surrounded him. The peddler opened his box and started taking out glittering objects to show them. There were ornaments of pearls, unfinished laces and gold and silver spangles, coloured socks, beautiful dolls and their ornaments, tops and rattles for children. They picked up one or other thing. A girl with big eyes chose the most beautiful amongst all those glittering things. It was a turquoise coloured necklace, a *Chandrahar*. She said to her mother, "Amma, I will take this necklace."

The mother asked the peddler, "*Baba*, how much is this necklace for?"

Wiping the necklace with his handkerchief, the peddler said, "The purchase is for twenty *anna*s, but my lady may give whatever she likes."

Mother said, "This is very expensive. All its shine will fade away in a few days."

Nodding in a warmly sympathetic manner, the peddlar said, "Bahuji, your daughter will get a real *Chandrahar* in a few days."

These words of sympathy touched the mother's heart. The necklace was purchased.

There was no limit to the little girl's happiness. Perhaps she would not have been so pleased with a diamond necklace. Wearing the necklace she roamed around the entire village. This crystal necklace was the dearest and the most precious of all the childhood treasures that she possessed.

The girl's name was Jalpa; her mother's, Manaki.

2

Mister Dindayal lived in a small village in Prayag. He was not a farmer, but practised farming. Neither was he a landlord, but acted like a landlord. He was not a police officer, but behaved like one. He was the landlord's attorney. He was known for his grandeur in the village. He had four peons, one horse and many cows and buffaloes. He got a salary of just five rupees, which was not even enough to meet his tobacco expenses. Who knew what other means of income he had. Jalpa was his daughter. Jalpa had three other brothers, but now she was alone. If anyone asked her what had happened to her brothers, she would say with great simplicity, "They have gone far away to play." It was said that the attorney once had beaten a poor man so badly that he died. Within three years of this incident, all his three sons also died. Since then, the poor fellow was extra cautious about each step he took; as they say, once bitten, twice shy. After all, what other support is there in a mother and father's life?

Whenever Dindayal went to Prayag, he would definitely get some ornament for Jalpa. So habituated was he to thinking this way, it never entered his mind that Jalpa could be happier with anything else. He considered dolls and toys worthless, and that is why Jalpa played only with ornaments. These were her only toys. The crystal necklace that she had purchased from the peddler was now her dearest toy. Till now, the desire for a real necklace had not risen in her mind. She would wear the same necklace for any occasion or festival in the village. In her view, no other ornament seemed suitable!

One day, Dindayal came back with a necklace for his wife. This was a long-cherished wish of Manaki. She was enchanted upon getting the necklace.

Now, Jalpa did not like her own necklace anymore. She said to her father, "Babuji, get me a necklace like this too."

Dindayal smiled and said, "Beti, I'll bring one for you also."

"When will you get it?"

"Very soon!"

Her father's words did not satisfy Jalpa. She went to her mother and said, "Ammaji, get a necklace like yours made for me."

Her mother replied, "Beti, that will cost a lot of money."

"You have got it made for yourself, why not for me?"

With a smile, her mother said, "Yours will come from your in-laws."

The necklace had been made for six hundred rupees. It was not easy for Dindayal to collect such an amount. Which high rank did he hold? After many years, the possibility of getting this necklace made had appeared. He doubted if he would ever get such an amount of money again in his life.

Jalpa felt **ashamed** and ran away, but her mother's words were branded in her **heart**. The in-laws' house no longer held much terror for her. She would get a *Chandrahar* from that house and the people there would love her more than her mother and father did. She thought, 'That is why, the thing that these people cannot make, will come from there.'

'What if there is no necklace from there?' she thought. Three girls had got married before her, but none of them got a necklace from their in-laws. She wondered, 'If it doesn't come from my in-laws house also, then? Then will Mataji give her necklace to me? Certainly, she would.'

In this way, seven years passed away in enjoyment. Finally the day arrived, when her long-held desire would be fulfilled.

3

Amongst the people with whom Munshi Dindayal was acquainted was Mister Dayanath – a thorough gentleman and kind-hearted person. Mister Dayanath was working in the court and was paid a salary of fifty rupees. Dindayal was a lowly employee—a worm—of the court. Dayanath had asked him for favours on innumerable occasions. If he had wanted, he could have got thousands of rupees in return, but he never saw a single paisa. This behaviour was not an act for Dindayal – this was his nature. He was also not a man of very high ideals. However, he considered bribes as immoral. Perhaps he had seen its bad results with his own eyes. He had seen someone going to jail, others losing their children and yet others, falling into the clutches of terrible addictions. He could not find any examples where anyone was at ease after taking a bribe. It had now become his conviction that earnings through immoral means go to immoral destinations. He always remembered this.

What wordly happiness can fifty rupees provide in today's time? Taking care of a family of five persons was very difficult. Children hankered for good clothes and the wife longed for jewellery, but Dayanath would never lose his patience. His eldest son stopped his studies after staying in college for just two months. The father said clearly, "I cannot keep all the others hungry and naked just to pay for your degree. If you want to study, then you should do so through your own efforts. Many people have done it. You can also do it."

However, Ramanath did not have the required dedication. For the last two years, he had been totally idle. He would play chess, wander around and awe his mother and younger brothers. Through his friends, his desires were fulfilled. He would borrow someone else's overcoat and go out for a stroll in the evening. He would use someone else's pump shoes and strap on someone else's wrist watch. Sometimes he moved out in the *Banarasi* fashion and sometimes, the *Lakhnavi*. If ten friends made one set of clothes each, then he got ten different suits to wear! This was an innovative utilisation of cooperation. This was the same young man whom Dindayal had selected for Jalpa. Dayanath was not prepared for the marriage. He did not have the money or courage to take up the burden of a new family. Rameshwari had her way through sheer feminine obstinacy, and the man had to succumb to this power. Rameshwari had been extremely restless to get a daughter-in-law for years. The women she had seen as new brides were now playing with their grandsons, then how could the poor lady be patient? She was now gradually growing slightly disappointed. She would pray to God that proposals would come from somewhere or the other. When this proposal was sent by Dindayal, she saw a ray of hope. If this unsuspecting person also escaped, then she had no idea how long she would have to wait.... She knew that hardly anyone would approach them. They had neither money nor property. Who was attracted to the boy? People looked at wealth; therefore, she put all her efforts into this alliance and succeeded.

Dayanath said, "You are responsible for what you do. I do not have the capacity. It seems immoral to marry off someone who doesn't even bother about his livelihood. Then there is botheration for money, also. At least a thousand would be needed for all the glitter and show, the rest for the clothes and jewellery!" Putting his hands over his ears, he said, "No dear! I cannot handle the burden."

These arguments had no effect on Rameshwari. She said, "He will also give something."

"I will not go to ask him for anything."

"You will not need to go to him. He will give by himself. No one gives a second thought to money when it comes to a daughter's marriage. Yes, indeed! If you need some financial support, then Dindayal is a dependable fellow. And then, this is our child. If we save it, who shall we keep it for?"

Dayanath, now, could not think of anything, and just said, "He may give lakhs, but he might also give nothing. I will neither request to give nor will refuse to accept. I don't want to take on a debt. And if I did take one, then from whose house will I pay it back?"

Rameshwari, as if blowing this obstacle to the winds, said, "I'm sure he will give not less than a thousand as a nuptial gift. It is enough for your show. Arrange the ornaments from some jeweller! If he gives a thousand for the engagement, then won't he give a thousand for receiving the bride at the door? Give that money to the jeweler. The remaining two-four hundred will be paid off gradually. Some or the other door will open for our child.

Dayanath sighed and sarcastically said, "And the doors have opened! One who doesn't get time from playing chess and loitering around – he will find all the doors closed."

Rameshwari recalled an incident from her marriage. Dayanath had also spent his youthful days in pleasure, but as soon as she came into his life, how obsessed he had become with the worry of earning even a little money. Hardly a year had passed before he got a job. She said, "Once our daughter-in-law comes, he will also realise. Recall your own days. This merrymaking will continue till the yoke of responsibility fastens over the throat. The yoke will fall and the intoxication will flee. There is no better way to get such idlers back on track."

Whenever Dayanath was defeated, he would start reading the newspaper. This was the only means with which to hide his defeat.

4

Munshi Dindayal was one of those men who was good to good people, but would be the devil himself, not just crooked, with crooked persons. If Dayanath would have been overambitious and talked about thousands, then Dindayal would have bluffed him in a way he would not have forgotten all his life. However, he was overpowered by the goodness of Dayanath. He had thought of giving a thousand rupees in all, but had already given one thousand as a nuptial gift. Manaki said, "When one thousand is given as a nuptial gift, then the same amount must also be given at home. From where will it come?"

Dindayal fretfully said, "God is the master. When they have shown kindness by bestowing their son to me, then I also want to show that we are equally decent and that we know the worth of such behaviour. If they had been forceful, I would have certainly told him off!"

Though Dindayal gave one thousand rupees, instead of making Dayanath's burden lighter, it made it heavier. Dayanath had kept himself far away from debt. He had decided to follow the policy of 'giving back to where it came from' in this marriage, but the kindness of Dindayal had shattered his self-restraint. All the pomp and show, dance and music, the imagination of which he had suppressed till now, rose up before him, taking on gigantic forms. Now the tied horse had broken loose. Who could stop it now? It was resolved that the marriage would be a grand affair. Previously, the question of jewels was trivial to him, but now it had become the most important thing. The marriage gifts should be such that the spectators present would be completely thrilled. Everybody's eyes should open wide! Around three thousand rupees worth of goods were made. One thousand rupees in cash was given to the jeweller. The jeweller did not object when asked for a week's time to pay another thousand. The jeweller thought he would get two thousand rupees straight away, and the remaining balance of five to seven hundred would be left; this would go nowhere but to him. If a business person gets his initial outlay, he does not insist on getting his profit immediately. 'Still, there was no *Chandrahar* –a good, gem-encrusted *Chandrahar* would not be for less than a thousand,' thought Dayanath. He was making up his mind to get the *Chandrahar* along with the rest, as he had gone so far. He did not want anyone wrinkling their noses at its absence, but Rameshwari did not give her consent.

The tables had turned now.

Dayanath agitatedly said, "How will you be affected? You will be sitting at home. I'll be the one who will die, when people from there will be displeased."

Rameshwari said, "From where will we get money? Have you thought about that?"

Dayanath, "We will get at least one thousand from there."

Rameshwari, "What, have you tasted blood?"

Ashamed, Dayanath said, "No, no. But we will get something from there, won't we?"

Rameshwari said, "If we get something, then there will be equal expenditure, too. Reputation is not gained by show of jewels and ornaments, but by gifts and donations."

In this manner, the proposal for acquiring the *Chandrahar* was cancelled.

Even if Dayanath considered the marriage pomp and show as worthless expense, Ramanath considered it to be the most essential. He wanted the marriage procession to be so grand and splendid that there would be a great uproar in the entire village. Initially, it was thought that the bridegroom would travel in a palanquin. Ramanath insisted on going by motorcar. His friends encouraged him and the proposal was accepted. Dayanath was a solitary creature, he neither had friends nor was he social and outgoing. Ramanath was a friendly youth; at this moment his friends were taking the initiative. Whatever work they did, they did wholeheartedly. Fireworks were arranged; these were of excellent quality. The dancers were excellent, the band, too – there was no mention of any second-rate arrangements. Seeing his uncontrolled desire for excellent things, Dayanath worried, but could not utter a word. What would he say?

A drama is 'passed' when a passionate society likes it. The drama of a wedding procession is admirable when the passers-by like it. A drama is tested over four to five hours, whereas a wedding procession has only four to five minutes to be judged. The effect of the entire arrangement, decoration, scurrying about and final touches is over in five minutes. If everybody admires it, the act is passed, otherwise it fails. Money, effort, worries – all in vain. Dayanath's show was passed. It would have stood third in the city, but it stood first in the village. Some people were enjoying the various 'gho gho po po' sounds of the musical instruments; some were staring at the motor car. Some were astonished at the majestic, flowery throne. The fireworks were the major entertainment for everyone. When rockets hissed upwards and red, green, blue, yellow crocus flower-like fireworks scattered in the sky, when the Catherine wheels went off and dancing peacocks shot forth, people were mesmerised. People exclaimed at the workmanship displayed.

For Jalpa, these things did not even hold the slightest attraction. Yes, she wanted to catch a glimpse of the bridegroom, that too, secretly, but in the crowd, she got no such opportunity. At the time of the bridegroom's entrance (*dwarchaar*) ceremony, her friends dragged her to the roof and there she saw Ramnath. All her indifference, all her detachment, all her heartfelt turmoil disappeared in a moment. Her face flushed with happiness. Love is such a storehouse of energy.

After the *dwarchaar* ceremony, the bridegroom's party went away from the bridal residence (*janwasa*). The preparation of food began. Some ate *puri*s while others cooked *khichari* over a fire of dried cowdung cakes. Dancing and singing began for the entertainment of spectators from the village.

5

At about ten o'clock, the band suddenly started playing again. Everyone came to know that the ornaments for the bride were being brought, that each ceremony was held in the proper manner – when it came to be known that the bridegroom was approaching for the *kaleva,* the music started playing. When it was known that the fathers-in-law were meeting each other, then the band played. As soon as the bridegroom's gifts (*charava*) reached, great commotion ensued in the bride's house. Ladies and gentlemen—elderly and young—all were curious to see the ornaments. As soon as the trays of gifts reached the marriage pavilion, everyone left their work and ran to see what had come. People pushed and pulled each other to get a better view. Manaki was almost senseless from thirst; her throat had dried up, but as soon as she heard about the *charava* her thirst fled. Dindayal was lying almost lifeless from hunger and thirst, but sprang to life on hearing about the *charava* and came running. Manaki started taking out each item to see and to show. Everyone present there was a specialist in this field. Men had got jewellery made and women had worn them; everyone began to comment.

"How pretty is the gold-wire bracelet (*chuhedanti*); it must weigh about ten *tolas*. Wow! If it turns out to be a *ratti* under eleven-and-a-half, I will lose, making the wrong guess."

"Look at this tiger-faced (*sherdahan*) jewel, how superbly it has been made! I feel like kissing the hands of the artisan. This will also not be less than twelve *tola*s. Wow! Have you ever seen anything like this? If it ends up less than sixteen *tola*s, I will not show my face."

"Yes, but the stuff is not all that good."

"Look at this bangle, how perfectly it is joined. It's such fine workmanship that you can't make out. How much it glitters! It is made of real gems. Where would you find this glitter in counterfeit stones?"

"What a beautiful thing this *guloband* is! It has such beautiful flowers . . . and those diamonds in their centres . . . how they shine! Some Bengali goldsmith must have made it!"

"Have the Bengalis taken all the contracts for workmanship? Our land has such good artisans – how can the poor Bengali goldsmiths compete with them?"

In this manner, one by one, each piece of jewellery was being assessed. Suddenly someone said, "Is there no *Chandrahar*?"

Manaki looked tearful and said, "No, the *Chandrahar* did not come'.

One woman said, "Oh! There is no *Chandrahar*."

Dindayal gravely said, "Everything else is here, only the *Chandrahar* is not there."

The same woman made a face and said, "The *Chandrahar* is something special."

Manaki took away the *charava* and said, "There is no *Chandrahar* in this poor girl's fate."

Behind this circle of people, Jalpa stood still in the darkness, like a statue full of hope and expectations. The names of different kinds of jewellery floated into her ears, but there was no mention of the *Chandrahar*. Her heart pounded heavily. She wondered, 'Is the *Chandrahar* not there? Maybe it was under everything else.' In this way, she consoled herself. When she was certain that the *Chandrahar* was not there, her heart felt bruised. It seemed as if there was not a drop of blood left in her body – and as though she would faint. In this frenzied condition, she came to her room and burst into tears and kept sobbing. The longing that had germinated in her heart for the last seven years, and was a fully flowering desire, was dashed to pieces by this thunderbolt. The luxuriant waving green plant was now completely burnt and only its ashes remained. All her desires had centred on this particular day. Today, misfortune had snatched even this from her. In a frenzy of disappointment, she felt as though she might scratch her own face. She thought if she could have had her way, she would have thrown the *charava* into the fire. A statue of Lord Shiv was placed in a niche in the room. She took that statue and threw on the ground. It broke into several pieces, just like her hopes. She resolved that she would not wear any ornaments. She thought, 'What happens if one wears ornaments? Those devoid of beauty may decorate themselves with the ornaments, but God had already made me beautiful. I will not look unsightly without jewellery. They picked cheap things. What would have required spending money upon was not even named. If it was a matter of counting costs, then for the same cost, they could have bought double the amount of jewellery!'

She was sitting, filled with rage, when three of her friends came in and stood before her. Her friends thought that Jalpa was not aware of the *charava.* On seeing them, Jalpa wiped her tears and began to smile.

Radha smiled and said, "Jalpa, it appears that you must have done fervent penance. I've never seen such a *charava* before. Now, all your wishes have come true."

Raising her long eyelids, Jalpa looked at her with such sad eyes that it seemed there was no hope left in life, "Yes, sister! All my wishes have come true."

The heartfelt painful emotions expressed by uttering these words were not understood by any of the women. The three of them, surprised, began to look at her face as if they could not understand what she meant.

Basanti said, "I feel like kissing the hands of the goldsmith."

Shehzadi said, "The *charava* should be so fabulous that whoever sees it is thrilled."

Basanti said, "Your mother-in-law seems to be a wise lady who did not leave anything out."

Jalpa turned her face and said, "It must be so."

Radha said, "Each and every ornament is there, just the *Chandrahar* is not."

Shehzadi said, "How does it matter if the *Chandrahar* isn't there, sister, the *Guloband* is there instead."

Jalpa sarcastically said, "Yes, what difference does it make if an eye is missing from the body? Other parts of body are there. If there is no eye, how will it make any difference?"

Just as we laugh at children when they utter something serious, similarly Radha and Basanti could not stop their laughter when they heard these words from Jalpa. However, Shehzadi did not find it funny. This lust for ornaments was not a matter of laughter for her, but a subject to cry over. Displaying artificial sympathy for Jalpa, she said, "All these uncultured people! They brought each and every other ornament except the *Chandrahar*, which is the king of all the jewels. Lala should be here any minute. I shall ask him which tradition he has followed. Does anyone act so senselessly?"

Radha and Basanti were afraid lest Jalpa should sense their real intention. They would have told Shehzadi to be quiet, if they could. They both gestured to Shehzadi to be silent; but this sarcasm of Shehzadi's was misconstrued as empathy by Jalpa. With teary eyes, she said, "What will you do by asking, sister? Whatever had to happen has happened."

Shehzadi replied, "You are talking about asking, I would make them weep. When the bangle was missing in my *charava*, that moment I was so upset that I felt like kicking all the jewellery. I didn't sleep a wink till the bangle was made."

Radha queried, "So do you know that Jalpa's *Chandrahar* won't be made?"

Shehzadi answered, "It will be made when it is made; however, it is not here on this occasion. It is not a thing worth ten or five rupees that can be made whenever you want to. It is an expense of hundreds of rupees. And then, isn't it difficult to always find a good craftsman?"

Jalpa's broken heart seemed to revive on hearing Shehzadi's words. With a voice choked with emotions, she said, "That's just what I think too, sister. If I didn't get it today, then will I get it later?"

Radha and Basanti were cursing Shehzadi in their hearts, and threatening her with feigned slaps. However, at this moment, Shehzadi was enjoying the drama. She spoke, "No, I really don't mean that, everything is possible if insisted upon soon. Keep on reminding your father- and mother-in-law. A lot can be attained if you remain displeased with your husband for two-four days. Just understand that the family members should not be at ease. This matter should always be there in their minds. They must understand that without getting a *Chandrahar* made, all won't be well. If you relax even a little, then all is lost."

Withholding her laughter, Radha said, "If you won't be able to do so, then she will be called, isn't it? Now will you get up or keep on giving advice the whole night!"

Shehzadi replied, "I'm just leaving, what is the hurry? Oh! I remember well, Jalli, your mother has a very good *Chandrahar*. Won't she give it to you?"

Jalpa heaved a long sigh and said, "What should I say sister, I have no hopes."

Shehzadi said, "Just try and ask her once. Which of her dressing-up days await her anymore?"

Jalpa said, "I will not be able to say it."

Shehzadi said, "I will say so."

Jalpa said, "No, no, I beg you. I want to test my mother's love, for once."

Basanti caught hold of Shehzadi's hand and said, "Now will you please get up or keep giving advice the whole night?"

Shehzadi got up, but Jalpa stood up and blocked her way. "No, sit for some time, I implore you."

Shehzadi replied, "I will sit when these two witches let me sit. Here I am teaching you tricks, and these two are infuriated with me. Are you not listening? I am quite a knot of poison."

Basanti said, "Yes, you are indeed a poisonous knot."

Shehzadi retorted, "You have also returned from your in-law's home after one year. What new things did you get made there?"

Basanti retorted, "And what did you get made in three years?"

Shehzadi said, "Forget about me. My husband takes no notice of me."

Radha said, "Jewellery is worthless when compared with love."

Shehzadi said, "Then, may this dry love be fruitful for you."

Just then Manaki came in and said, "What are the three of you doing here? Come along. People are coming to eat over there."

The three young women left. Jalpa, seeing the splendour of the *Chandrahar* around her mother's neck thought, 'She is yet to tire of wearing her jewellery.'

6

The degree of excitement with which Mister Dayanath had gone to attend the marriage was matched by the degree of dejection he returned with. Dindayal had given a lot, but all had been spent in the dance and music and presents for relatives. He repented again and again as to why he had spent so much in the dance, pomp and show. Where was the need? At the most, people would have called him a big miser. What was the harm in hearing that? He had not taken any contract to entertain the villagers. All this happened due to Rama's rashness. 'He was the one who increased the expenses and made me bankrupt,' thought Dayanath. Other promises could be delayed for four to five days, but the jeweller would not agree. He had promised to give one thousand rupees on the seventh day after the marriage. The jeweller came on the seventh day, but where was the money? Dayanath was not an expert in fooling others with words, but today he tried his level best to bluff him. He promised to repay the entire money in instalments within six months. Then he reduced this period to three months, but the jeweller stood his ground, and went only when Dayanath promised to return items worth the remaining amount on the third day. This, too, was the jeweller's generosity. Those three days passed, and now Dayanath had no way left to maintain his self-respect. A cunning man perhaps would not have been so disturbed; he could have bluffed the jeweller with excuses for months, but Dayanath was ignorant in this respect.

Rameshwari came and said, "The food has been prepared long back. It is getting cold. Eat and then sit."

Dayanath raised his head as though there were several tons loaded on it. He said, "You go and eat. I am not hungry."

Rameshwari said, "Why aren't you hungry? You did not eat last night, either. By leaving your food this way, will you be able to repay the jeweller's money?"

Dayanath, "I am thinking about what I will say to him today. I am badly trapped by this wedding. Will our daughter-in-law return some of jewellery?"

Rameshwari said, "You are fully aware of our daughter-in-law's state. Yet you have such expectations from her? She insists she will not touch any of the jewellery until she gets a *Chandrahar*. All her jewellery is locked inside her box. She has just worn the crystal necklace around her neck. I have seen many daughter-in-laws, but none like her. Think, how terrible it will look, to snatch the jewels of the daughter-in-law who has just entered the house!"

Dayanath irritatedly said, "You are sprinkling salt on the wound. If you do not like it, then get a thousand rupees, I will give it to the jeweller. Are you giving me the money? I, myself, am feeling terrible, but what is the solution? How will I save my neck?"

Rameshwari said, "Have you married off your son or conducted a joke? Everybody takes loans for weddings; you have not done anything new. Whoever gets into debt for clothes? Shouldn't you get some reward being a saint? Satyadev is of the same rank as you, and he has built a *pukka* house, has purchased a *zamindari*. For his daughter's marriage, he must have spent nothing less than five thousand rupees."

Dayanath said, "Is that why both his sons also passed away?"

Rameshwari spoke, "Death and life constitute the routine of this world. Those who take bribes will die, those who don't, also die. If you want to, you can repay the entire money in six months."

Dayanath frowned and said, "I cannot do something I have never done throughout my life, in my last moments. Tell Bahu everything clearly. Where is the need to hide and then, for how long can you keep it a secret? She will come to know everything tomorrow, if not today. She needs to return only three-four things, and it is done. Just tell her once."

Rameshwari flared up, "You tell her. I won't be able to."

A frightened Ramanath came in carrying a tennis racket. He had worn a white tennis shirt, white pants, and canvas shoes. This dress, added to his fair complexion and handsome features, had dignified the grandee. He had kept a garland of jasmine flowers in his handkerchief. Fragrance wafted from it. He was intending to quietly go up the stairs, without his mother and father noticing him, when Rameshwari stopped him.

"He has sown the thorns, why don't you take advice from him?"

Turning to Ramanath, she said, "You have blown away twelve to thirteen hundred rupees in dance and shows. Now tell us, what answer should we give to the jeweller? With great difficulty, he has agreed to take back some of the jewels, but who will ask Bahu for this? This is all your doing!"

Not accepting this allegation, Ramanath said, "What did I spend? Whatever was done was done by Babuji. Yes, I did what I was told."

There was some truth in what Ramanath said. If Dayanath would not have wished it, then what could Rama have done? Everything happened with Dayanath's permission. The problem would not be settled by putting the blame on Ramanath. Dayanath said, "I am not blaming you. I have done it, but somehow this problem has to be got rid of. The jeweller is demanding and tomorrow his man will come. What will our reply be? To me, the only way out appears to be returning jewellery equal in worth to the money still owed. He will create difficulties when we return the jewellery, but will agree to it in his greed for more value than money we could pay. What is your advice?"

Ramanath said in embarassment, "What can I suggest in this matter? All I can say is that she will not agree to this proposal happily. Amma knows how bad she felt because she did not get a *chandrahar* in the *charava*. She has vowed not to wear any of the jewellery till the *chandrahar* is made."

Seeing her argument being supported, Rameshwari said happily, "This is what I have been telling him."

Ramanath said, "There will be much hue and cry and with this the family's secret will also be disclosed."

Wrinkling his brow, Dayanath said, "Why is there a need to hide things from her? The sooner she understands the real situation, the better it is."

Ramanath, in accordance with his youthful temperament, had boasted a lot to Jalpa. He had exaggerated greatly – that there is a *zamindari* that gives a profit of many thousands; that there is money in the bank which gives interest. Now, If Jalpa was told about the jewellery, she would consider him to be a complete liar. He said, "The secret will be revealed one day, but if revealed so early the result will be that she will consider us to be mean. Perhaps she may even write to her family. We will be defamed all over."

Dayanath said, "We never told Dindayal that we possess lakhs."

Ramanath said, "Then why did you say that we have brought jewellery on loan and will return them in three-four days? Was all this drama for making an impression or something else?"

Dayanath said, "Then you will have to ask for the jewellery using an excuse. It will not work without asking. We will either have to pay the money or return the jewellery tomorrow. There is no other way."

Ramanath did not reply. Rameshwari spoke, "What other excuse can we make? If we say that we have to give the jewellery to someone for an occasion, perhaps she won't agree. Even if she gives it, how will we return them after two-four days?

An idea struck Dayanath. He said. "If we give her gold-plated ornaments in place of the real ones...." Immediately he realised that it was a poor idea, and opposing it said, "Yes, later, when the plating will disappear after a few days, then humiliation will follow. My senses have stopped working. The only thing that occurs to me is that the whole situation should be explained to her. She will be disappointed for a while, but the path ahead will be clear."

Dayanath thought that after a bout of wailing Jalpa would calm down, but it was a matter of disrespect for Rama. He wondered, 'When she will question me where the *zamindari* has gone and what has happened to the money in the bank, what will I say in reply?' He spoke in an indifferent manner, "There is nothing but ill-repute in this. Can't you delay the jeweller's payment by two-four-six months? If you want, you can give thousand or twelve hundred easily."

Dayanath asked, "How?"

Ramanath suggested, "The same way that your brothers do."

Dayanath said, "I can't do that."

All three kept sitting silently for some time. Dayanath announced his decision. Rameshwari and Ramanath did not agree with it. Thus, the burden of settling this knotty problem rested on them now. Rameshwari, too, had made up her mind. Dayanath would have to succumb and break his own rules. She thought, 'What kind of principle was it that we insist upon following our rules when a calamity falls on us?' Ramanath was badly caught. He knew well that his father would never do something now which he had never done in his lifetime. He was repenting why he had exaggerated and boasted to Jalpa – who he might have to ask for jewellery, now. Now it rested upon him to find a way to keep his respect.

Jalpa's beauty had charmed him the very first day. He was overjoyed at being so fortunate – was this house worthy of this unique, beautiful lady? Jalpa's father was a salaried servant for five rupees, but Jalpa had never swept her house. She had never washed her own saris. She had never made her own bed, not even repaired small holes in her clothes. Dayanath got a salary of fifty rupees per month and here there was just one maid for washing the dishes. The rest of the work had to be done by oneself. What did Jalpa know about the difference of the urban and rural life-styles? She had never got an occasion to stay in a city. She had asked her husband and mother-in-law, many times in astonishment, "Are there no servants here?" There was no scarcity of milk, butter and ghee in Jalpa's house. Here, the milk was not even enough for small children. To fill these deficiencies, what else could Ramanath had done other than talk sweetly and boast greatly? The rent of the house was five rupees, but Ramanath said it was fifteen. There was hardly an expense of ten rupees on the childrens' education, but Rama said it was forty. At that time he did not have faintest doubt that one day these illusions would be shattered. Illusion is not farsighted, but who knew that the day would arrive so soon? If he had not boasted so much, then like Rameshwari, he would have left everything to Dayanath and remained unbothered. Right now, he was entrapped in a web of his own making. How would he get out?

He thought about many solutions, but none of them would not put him in some trouble or trap him in a quagmire. All of a sudden, a certain trick occurred to him. His heart jumped, but he was unable to voice it. Oh! How mean it was! What deceit, what unkindness! Such cunningness with his beloved! His heart cursed him. If, at that time, someone would have given him a thousand rupees, he would have become his slave for life.

Dayanath asked, “Did you think anything?”

“Nothing occurs to me.”

“Some solution has to be thought of.”

“You think. I am unable to think of anything.”

“Why not ask her for two or three ornaments? You could get them if you wanted. It is difficult for us.”

“I feel ashamed.”

“You are a strange man! Neither will you ask yourself, nor let us ask. Then how shall this boat move ahead? I have said not once, but thousands of times, don’t except me to pay for it. I can’t spend my last days in jail. I don’t understand what there is to be ashamed of in this matter. Who does not come across bad times like this in their life? You may ask your mother.”

Rameshwari supported him. “I could not see my husband remain plunged in worry, while I sat there wearing ornaments. Otherwise wouldn’t I have jewellery today? One by one, all were sold. Not less than five thousand worth of jewellery had gone in my *charava*, but in just five years, everything was sacrificed. Since then I did not have the good luck to get even a plain ring made.”

Dayanath insisted, “This is not the time to feel ashamed. We will have to ask for them.”

Ramanath said hesitantly, “I cannot ask. Say, should I just pick them up?” Saying this, his eyes filled with tears of shame and distress at realisation of his own meanness.

Dayanath, stunned, said, “You will pick them up, hiding them from her?”

Ramanath said sharply, “What else are you thinking?

Dayanath put his hand on his forehead and after a few moments, said in a hurt voice, “No, I will not let you do such a thing. I’ve never deceived anyone and I never will. And that too with my own daughter-in-law! Shame! Shame! Why commit a fraud for something that can be done properly? If somehow she sees it, you understand what she’d think of you in her heart? It is much better to ask.”

Ramanath said, “What have you got to do with this? Take these things from me, but when you knew this all would happen, then where was the need to take so much jewellery? You have uselessly invited the problem. It was a million times better to have taken whatever could have been easily managed. What is the use of eating a meal which causes a stomach ache? I thought that you must have devised some solution. Had I known that you would dump this basket of troubles over my head, I’d never have let you take those things!”

Dayanath, a little ashamed, said, “Even then, there was a lot of fuss over the missing *chandrahar*.”

Ramanath said, "How could that fuss have harmed us? There was such an outcry after having done so much, and yet our purpose isn't fulfilled! There we faced disrepute; here, we face this insurmountable problem. I don't want to show that we are so wretched. After the theft, we will have to be patient."

Dayanath remained silent. In his rage, Rama had bluntly said a lot to him while he stood, listening. At last when he was unable to take it anymore, he stood up and went into his library. This was his daily routine. His food would not get digested till he read three or four letters and magazines. On reaching that secure den, he was safe from the worries and difficulties of home.

Rama also got up, but instead of going to Jalpa's room, he went to his own. He did not have a separate room of his own; there was only an anteroom for gentlemen. In that room, only Dayanath chatted with his friends. Here, the two younger boys were playing cards. Gopi was thirteen years old and Vishwambhar, nine. They were terrified of Rama and trembled. Though Rama himself played a lot of cards and chess, but on seeing his younger brothers playing cards, his hands started itching. He himself strolled around all day if he liked, but dare his brothers go for a ramble anywhere! Dayanath himself never hit the boys. Whenever he got a chance he played with them. When he saw them flying kites, his childish nature would revive. He would have a few tries at bringing down someone's kite. Sometimes he would even play *gulli-danda* with the children. Hence, the boys loved their father as much as they feared Rama.

As soon as they noticed Rama, the boys hid their cards under the mat and began to study. With bowed heads, they awaited his slaps, but Ramanath did not slap them. Sitting on a stool, he said to Gopinath, "You've seen the *bhang* shop at the corner?"

Pleased, Gopinath said, "Yes, of course, I have seen it."

"Go and buy *majun* for four paise. Come back quickly. Yes, also bring half a kilogram of sweets from the sweet shop. Here, take this rupee."

Some fifteen minutes later, Rama went to Jalpa's room with these two things.

7

It was ten o'clock at night and Jalpa was lying on the open terrace. In the golden moonlight of May, the domes, pinnacles and trees of the city spread before her like dream-pictures. Jalpa's eyes were fixed on the moon. She felt as if she were flying towards the moon. Her nose felt dry, her eyes burned and her head spun. As soon as something came to her mind, she would forget it and try as she might, would not be able to remember however hard she tried. Once she recalled memories of her home and started crying. A moment later, she remembered her friends and began to laugh. Suddenly, Ramanath came in smiling with a packet in his hand, and sat near her on the cot.

Jalpa got up and asked, "What is there in the packet?"

Ramanath teased, "Let me see if you can guess."

Jalpa laughingly said, "A ball of laughter!"

Ramanath replied, "Wrong!"

Jalpa said, "A bundle of sleep!"

Ramanath said, "Wrong!"

Jalpa concluded, "Then it must be a basket of love."

Ramanath admitted, "Right! Today I'll make you the goddess of flowers."

Jalpa was delighted. With intense love, Rama began to decorate her with ornaments made of flowers. She felt a tingling sensation all over her tender body as the soft, cool flowers touched her. Every part of her being was in ecstasy.

Rama said with a smile, "Any present?"

Jalpa did not reply. She felt embarrassed to even gaze at her husband in this apparel. She had an intense desire to see herself in the mirror. A lamp was lit in the opposite room. She got up and went into the room and stood before the mirror. In her rapturous mood, it seemed to her that she was really the goddess of flowers. She picked up the betel-leaf box, came out and began preparing *paan*.

Now, Rama was remorseful over his deceitful behaviour. Returning from the room, Jalpa looked at him with love and pleasure-seeking eyes; he turned his face away. He was unable to face her innocent, trusting eyes. He thought, 'I am such a coward. Could I not have answered my father clearly? Why did I agree? Was it not my duty to tell Jalpa clearly about the family conditions?' His eyes filled with tears. He went and stood near the parapet. In that pure light of love, his emotions seemed to glare at him like some fearful creature. He started hating himself so much that for a moment he thought of disclosing the whole wretched business, but soon regained his composure. He wondered, 'How dreadful will the result be?' The thought of losing respect in Jalpa's eyes was unbearable to him.

Jalpa looked at him with intense love in her eyes and said, "My grandfather went back after seeing you and started praising you in front of my mother. I used to wonder how you would be. Different kinds of pictures came to my mind."

Ramanath drew a deep breath and did not reply.

Jalpa continued, "My friends were fascinated when they saw you. Shehzadi wouldn't move away from the window. She was very keen to talk to you. When you went inside, it was she who gave you *paan*, do you remember?"

Rama did not reply.

Jalpa said, "Oh, the one who was the most attractive, and who had a mole on her cheek? You looked at her very affectionately, and the poor girl was so overcome by shyness, she almost went through the ground! She told me that Jijaji seems to be a passionate man. Her friends teased her so much that the poor girl was literally in tears. Remember?"

Rama said, as if drowning in a river, "I really don't remember."

Jalpa, "Alright, this time when we go, I will show you. Did you go towards the market today or not?"

Rama said, bowing his head, "I did not have time today."

Jalpa said, "Go, I will not talk to you. You make excuses daily. Alright, will you get it tomorrow?"

Ramanath's heart quivered. 'She is so eager for the *chandrahar*. Little does she know that misfortune has come to snatch all that she possesses,' he thought. He was ready to rob everything from the innocent girl for whom he should have sacrificed his life. He felt so confounded that he wanted to take his own life by jumping from the roof.

It was past midnight. The moon was peeping from behind a tree like a thief. Jalpa was carelessly asleep with her arms around her husband's neck. Rama got up slowly with grim resolve in his heart, but seeing her flowery radiance resting in the lap of sleep made him unsteady. For a moment, he watched, entranced, her smiling face in sleep. He did not have the courage to go into the room. Then he lay down again.

Jalpa, startled from her sleep, asked, "Where are you going? Is it morning?"

Ramanath said, "It is still late night."

Jalpa said, "Then, why are you sitting up?"

Ramanath, "It's nothing! I just got up to drink some water."

Jalpa lovingly put her arms around Rama's neck and made him lie down, saying, "If you keep casting a spell on me like this, I'll run away. I don't know how you stare, or what you do or which chant you read to make me so restless! Basanti was right in saying that there in magic in men's eyes."

Rama said, in a broken voice, "I am not casting a spell. I am quenching my eye's thirst."

Both went to sleep again; one, plunged into rapture, the other, drowned in worry.

Three hours passed. The nearly-full moon extinguished its universal lamp. The cool dawn breeze gave forth its intoxication to nature. Even the late night *bazar* had gone to sleep. Only Rama was still awake. The contradictory arguments in his mind made him get up again and again, and then lie down. At last, when he heard the watchmen sounding four o'clock, he got up in panic and went to Jalpa's room. The jewellery box was kept in the cupboard. Rama picked it up and went downstairs, trembling. In this anxious state, he could not even find the time to select and take out a few pieces of jewellery.

Dayanath was sleeping downstairs, in the veranda. Rama woke him up gently. Confusedly he asked, "Who…?"

Putting his finger on his lips, Rama said, "It is me. I have brought this box. Keep it."

Dayanath sat up, now alert. Till now his eyes were awake, but now his consciousness also awoke. When Rama had said about taking away the jewellery, Dayanath thought that he had spoken in the heat of the moment. He did not believe that Rama would actually do what he proposed. He really wanted to stay away from these lowly, mean tricks. His soul could not accept aiding and abetting his son in such sordid work. He asked, "Why did you bring this?"

Rama said, shamelessly, "It was on your order."

Dayanath said, "You are lying."

Ramanath said, "So, should I then keep it back?"

Rama's question plunged Dayanath in a terrible dilemma. Abashed, he said, "How will you put it back now? If you are seen, it would be disastrous. You would do something that will invite mockery! Why are you standing there? Put this casket inside my box and go and lie down. If, she wakes up, then…."

Dayanath's room was behind the veranda. An old cedar chest was kept there. Rama put the casket inside the chest and quickly went upstairs. He stopped when he reached the roof and saw that Jalpa was in deep, sound sleep of the pre-dawn hours.

Just as Rama sat down on the cot, it startled Jalpa out of sleep and she clung to him. Rama asked, "What is it? Why did you get startled?"

Jalpa looked around with pleased eyes and said, "Nothing! I was having a dream. Why are you sitting up? How much time is left?

Lying down, Rama said, "It is almost morning. What were you dreaming about?"

Jalpa said, "I saw some thief carrying away my jewellery casket."

Rama's heart began pounding hard as if hammer blows were raining down on it. His blood ran cold, and he suspected that that she might have actually seen him. He burst into a shout, "Thief! Thief!"

Jalpa got up, panic stricken. She rushed into her room and flung the cupboard doors open. The casket was not there! She fainted and fell down.

8

As soon as it was morning, Dayanath took the jewellery to the jeweller and the calculations began. The jeweller had to receive his fifteen hundred, but he was not contented with jewellery worth that sum. He said he would take the jewellery back on commission only – who takes back sold articles? Had it been conditional, it would have been a different matter. These things had already been purchased. The jeweller spoke of business principles, and so neatly trapped Dayanath that the poor man could do nothing but acquiesce. How could an office clerk stand his ground before a clever shopkeeper? Jewellery worth twenty-five hundred had gone for fifteen hundred and on top of that, fifty remained. This became the reason for long arguments and counter arguments between father and son for many days. Both were holding each other responsible. They didn't talk to each other for many days, but the theft was kept a secret. If the police were informed, then the screen would be shattered. Jalpa was told that they would probably not recover the jewellery, but there would be needless hassle. Jalpa also thought there was no use in reporting the theft, when they would not get the articles back.

Jalpa loved jewellery, perhaps more than anything else in the world, and what was surprising in this? When she was an innocent child of three years, gold bangles had been made for her. When her grandmother used to play with her in her lap, she would talk only about the jewels, "Your bridegroom will bring very beautiful jewels for you. You will walk gracefully wearing them."

Jalpa would ask, "Will they be of gold or silver, Grandmother?"

Grandmother would say, "They will be of gold, *beti*, why will he bring silver? If he brings silver ornaments, then throw them back on his face."

Manaki would then say, "He will bring silver ones. Where will he get gold ones?"

Jalpa would then start crying and thereupon the old grandmother, Manaki, the housemaids, the neighbours and Dindayal – all would laugh. This was an inexhaustible store of amusement for these people. When the girl grew a little older, she began to perform marriages among her dolls. The *charava* would go from the boy's side; she decked the bride with jewels, and bid her farewell in a *doli*. Sometimes the bride-doll would demand jewellery from her groom-doll, and the poor groom would bring them from somewhere to please his wife. It was during these days, that the peddler gave her the *chandrahar*, which was safe with her even now.

When she grew up a little more, she used to sit among the elders and listen to them talking about jewellery. In that circumscribed world of women there was nothing else to talk about, except about this. Who made what kind of jewellery; for how much; whether they were solid or hollow;

studded with gems or plain; in which girl's wedding how many jewels had been given – on all these important subjects there was constant criticism and counter criticism, commentaries and counter commentaries. No other subject could have been so interesting, so agreeable.

Brought up in this jewellery-saturated world, Jalpa's love for ornaments was natural. One month had passed. Her condition was as it was. Neither did she eat or drink, nor laugh or talk to anyone. Lying on the cot, she kept staring into the empty sky with empty eyes. Everyone in the house was tired of explaining to her; the women in the neighbourhood also gave up. Dindayal came to console her, but Jalpa did not give up her sick bed. Now, she had lost faith in every member of the family. She was even dejected with Rama. She felt as if the entire family was ignoring her. She thought everyone was after her life. She wondered, 'When they have so much wealth, then why aren't they making my jewels?' We are angriest with those whom we love the most. Jalpa was very angry with Rama. 'If he would talk forcefully with his mother and father, then no one could ignore what he said, but only when he would say something. It seemed as though their mouths were glued tight. If he loved me, he would not sit, so unconcerned. He would not even sleep at night, till he would have got everything made. His love is only a show. How will he say anything to his parents, he will go their way as they are his own; who am I after all?' and so she raged on.

She not only remained tense with Rama, but whenever Rama would ask her anything, she would say something hurtful. The poor fellow remained shamefaced. He was burning in a fire of his own making. If he had only known that this would be the result of his long and exaggerated boasting, he would have sealed his mouth. Worry and shame crushed his heart. Gone were the days spent in laughter and jokes from morning till evening, the walking and strolling around; now he was stumbling around looking for a job. All the fun had disappeared. Time and again, he would be angry with his father, 'If he wanted to, he could have paid off the whole amount in three-four months, but why should he worry? Even if I die, he will not give up his obstinacy.' His loving heart, free of deceit, would burn all the time. Seeing Jalpa's wilted face, he drew cold, sobering breaths. He wondered, 'Now that the pleasant love-dream has faded away so soon, will these days ever come back again? How will jewellery worth three thousand be made? Even if I get a job, then which high position will I get? I may not be able to save three thousand in three lifetimes!' He wanted to find a way through which he could become the owner of immense wealth in a short time. He wished that he would somehow win the lottery. Then he would cover Jalpa with jewels. First and foremost, he would have a *chandrahar* made. It would be studded with diamonds. If he knew how to make counterfeit notes, he would have certainly made them and spent them on her.

One day he had wandered around in search of a job until the evening. Due to his playing chess, he was acquainted with many prominent people. However, out of fear and embarrassment he could not reveal his true situation to any one of them. He also knew that this respect would last only till he opened his hand to take help from others. After the respect had gone, nobody would ask about his whereabouts. He could not see any gentleman, who would understand everything without being told and arrange some good position for him. Today, he was very depressed. He was angry with his friends; he would scold them, one by one, and if they came to his door he would turn them out with a curse. He thought, 'Now, if anyone calls to play chess, I will scold them in such a way that they will remember it throughout their life.' If he pondered a bit, he would have realised that in this regard he was more to blame than his friends. There was not even one of his friends to whom he had not boasted and bragged. This was his habit. He concealed the true condition of his house like one avoids disrepute, and the result was that despite having so many friends, he was still idle. He could not share his mental agony with anybody, and the agony became unbearably suffocating. He came home and sat down, with a long, sad face.

Rameshwari gave him water and asked, "Where have you been all day, today? Take this and wash your face and hands."

Rama had just picked the jug when Jalpa came in and said scornfully, "Take me to my house right now!"

Rama put the jug on the floor and began staring at her, as if he could not understand what she meant to say.

Rameshwari said, "Are daughters-in-law sent from their homes like this? What are you saying, Bahu?"

Jalpa said, "I am not amongst those daughters-in-law. Whenever I feel like going, I'll go and whenever I feel like coming, I'll come. I am not afraid of anyone. Here, when no one asks about me, then I also don't consider anyone my own. I lie all day like an orphan. Nobody even bothers to look at me. I am not a bird whose cage you close after giving it food and water. I am also a human being. Now, I will not stay in this home even for a second longer. If nobody accompanies me home, then I will go alone. There is no wolf sitting on the way to carry me off, and even if it does, who would be sad? What kind of happiness am I enjoying here anyway?"

Rama cautiously said, "After all, one should know what the matter is?"

Jalpa said, "Nothing has happened. It is just my wish. I don't wish to stay here anymore."

Ramanath said, "If you will leave like this, then what will your family say? Just think about it."

Jalpa said, "I have thought about everything and I don't want to think about it anymore. I will go to pack my clothes and leave by this vehicle."

Having said this, Jalpa went upstairs. Rama also followed her, thinking of how he could pacify her.

Jalpa went into her room and began folding her bedding, when Rama caught her by the hand and said, "Swear by me that you won't talk about leaving now."

Raising her eyebrows scornfully, Jalpa said, "I don't care about swearing by you."

She wrenched her hand free and began folding her bedding again. Rama stood sheepishly in a corner. Jalpa tied up her bedroll and then began to clean her trunk. However, the earlier urgency had slackened; she opened and shut her trunk repeatedly. The rain had stopped, only the water caught on the roof was dripping.

At last, she sat on the bedroll and said, "Why did you make me swear?"

There was a tingle of hope in Rama's heart and he said, "Did I have any other way to stop you, except this?"

Jalpa said, "Do you want me to suffocate and die here?"

Ramanath said, "Why do you say such ill-omened words? I am ready to go with you. If you will not agree, then I'll be forced to take you to your home. Go, God is my master, but at least ask my mother and father."

He had added fuel to a dying fire. Jalpa said tormented, "Who are they to me that I should ask them?"

Ramanath said, "Aren't they anyone to you?"

"Not at all! If they were, they wouldn't have left me like this. Anybody possessing money cannot see their dear ones suffering. Couldn't they wipe my tears? I just lie here throughout the day, does anyone just ask after me? The women from neighbourhood come to meet me; but who should I meet? I cannot show them my face. Neither can I go anywhere, nor do I speak to anyone, how long can one live like this? Now, I have stopped hoping that your parents will give me anything. After all, there are two more boys. Will they save something for them, or just give it all to you?"

Rama got one more opportunity to brag again. He was happy that he got a chance to please her after so many days. He said, "Dearest, you think correctly. Most certainly, it is like this. Otherwise was two-three thousand a big issue for them? He has many thousands deposited in banks. He simply goes to the office to entertain himself."

Jalpa said, "But he is a miser from head to toe!"

Rama.said, "If he weren't a miser, where would all that money have come from?"

Jalpa said, "I don't care about anything. There is nothing lacking in our house. I can get *dal* and *roti* there also. There are three-four friends, fields and crops, gardens and orchards which would amuse me."

Ramanath said, "And what will my condition be? Do you know? I will weaken and die. Ever since the robbery, only my heart knows what it is going through. I have told my mother and father not once, but thousands of times, to have three or four things made, but nobody listened at all. I don't know why they have turned away from me."

Jalpa said, "When you get a job somewhere, then call me."

Ramanath said, "I'm searching. I will get it very soon. I know many thousands of important people, so will it take me time to get a job? Yes, but I want to work in a good place."

Jalpa said, "I understand these people. I will also stay here with full rights. Why don't you say something about a job to someone?"

Ramanath said, "So then, are you really going? Grief stricken, will I sit and cry at parting from you or look for a job? No, drop the idea of going for now. Otherwise, I tell you this truthfully, I will also run away somewhere. I've seen the state of this house. Who else is here besides you for whom I'd lie here and rot? Move away, let me open the bedding."

Jalpa moved a little off the bedroll and said, "I will come back very soon. As soon as you'll go, I'll come back."

Unfastening the bedroll, Rama said, "No, dear, excuse me! I am not going to fall into this trap. You will enjoy yourself with your friends, and will not even ask about me. Here, it will become a matter of life and death for me. How will I then set foot inside this house?"

Jalpa said, as though she were obliging him, "You have opened my fastened bedding. Otherwise, today I would have blissfully reached my house. Shehzadi was right in saying that the men are great magicians. Today, I had sternly made up my mind, that even if Brahma himself descended, I wouldn't listen to him, but in just two minutes you have spoilt all my plans. Do write the letter tomorrow. We cannot carry on without you earning something."

Ramanath said, "Not tomorrow. I'll write two-three letters right now."

Jalpa said, "Eat the *paan* at least."

Ramanath ate the *paan* and came into the anteroom and sat down to write letters.

However, after thinking about something, he stood up and walked away in one direction. Obeying the loving request of a woman, what is there that a man cannot do?

9

Amongst Ramanath's acquaintances was Ramesh Babu, a head clerk in the Municipal Board. Though, he was over forty years of age, he was quite a pleasure-seeking man. When he sat down to play chess, he would get up in the morning; he would even forget his office. He was like a bullock with no nose-rope in the front or tether from behind to restrain him. His wife had died when he was quite young, but he had not married again. What other support did he have in this lonely life except such entertainment? If he wanted, he could have made thousands, but he considered every paisa taken in bribe contemptible. He had developed a deep affection for Rama – who else was there who would play chess the entire night with him? He had been upset for several days now; he had not played even a single game in chess. For how long could he read the newspaper? Though Rama had visited him once or twice during these days, he did not sit to play chess. Ramesh Babu had set out the pieces and made him sit him down, but he would not sit. 'Why would he play chess? A new bride had come, he would rather talk to her rather than play chess with this old man,' thought Ramesh Babu. Several times in the recent past Ramesh Babu had thought of inviting Rama, but had to drop the idea after thinking that he had no reason to come. He wondered where he could go – to the cinema? At least, in some way the time would pass. He was not fond of the cinema, but this time nothing occurred to him. He wore his clothes and was about to leave when Rama stepped into the room.

Seeing him, Ramesh went quickly to the door, and holding his hand said, "Welcome! Babu Ramanath Sahab Bahadur! You have completely forgotten this old fellow! Yes, dear, why will you come now? Here, where will you get the pleasure of your beloved's sweet talk? Did you get any information about the theft?"

Ramanath said, "Nothing at all."

Ramesh said, "It was good that you did not complain at the police station. Otherwise you would have lost a hundred or two there as well. Bahu must have felt very sad?"

Ramanath said, "Please don't ask. She does not eat or drink after that. I am completely hassled. I feel like running away somewhere. Babuji doesn't listen at all."

Ramesh said, "Does Babuji have Karu's treasure kept somewhere? He has just spent four to five thousand. From where can he get the jewellery made? Even if he has ten or twenty thousand, there are the two boys to think of and how much can the job be trusted? What is fifty rupees anyway?"

Ramanath said, "I'm in a really problematic situation. Now it seems that I will have to work. I was busy enjoying a peaceful and merry life. But now, for no reason, I have been trapped in this problem. Now can you tell me, if there is a possibility of job somewhere?"

Ramesh took the chess board and pieces from the niche and said, "Come, let's play one game. Then we'll think about this problem. It is not as easy as it looks. Well-deserving people are suffering blows."

Ramanath said, "I don't feel like playing right now. Until this matter is resolved, I won't regain my senses."

Placing the chess pieces on the board, Ramesh Babu said, "Come, sit. Just play once, then we'll think what can be done."

Ramanath said. "I don't feel like playing in the slightest. I feel like hailstones fell on my head, as soon as I got it shaved . . . if I had only known, I would have gone nowhere near marriage."

Ramesh said, "Just come and play two-four moves and you will automatically start taking interest in the game. The knotted senses will open a bit."

The game started. After a few ordinary moves, Ramesh Babu struck down one of Rama's rooks.

Ramanath exclaimed, "Oh! What mistake did I make?"

Ramesh Babu's eyes began to turn red, like those of someone intoxicated. For him, chess was no less intoxicating than liquor. He said, "The beginning was good. I am thinking of a job for you, but the pay is very little – only thirty rupees. You know Khan Saheb, the one with a coloured beard? He is not able to work now. I have saved him many times. I thought that as long as it worked, let him remain. He is a man with children. He has asked me several times to let him go. The position is certainly not suitable for you, but if you want to, you can take it."

Saying this, he killed one of Rama's bishops.

Making an attempt to reinstate the bishop, Rama said, "You are taking away my pieces while keeping me busy with talk. That's not fair, put my bishop back."

Ramesh said, "Look, brother! Don't cheat. I didn't take your bishop by force. Alright, so do you accept the position?"

Ramanath said, "The salary is just thirty."

Ramesh said, "Yes, the salary is less, but it might increase later. My opinion is you should do it."

Ramanath said, "That is all right, if it is your advice, then I'll do it."

Ramesh said, "The position is such that you can earn. In that position, Mian was able to make his sons complete an M.A. and an LLB. Two of them are studying in college. His daughters have been married in good families. Yes, it is necessary to work with intelligence."

Ramanath said, "I'm not bothered about the income. Bribery is not a good thing."

Ramesh said, "Very bad, but what can a man with a family do? You cannot make both ends meet in thirty rupees. I am alone. For me one hundred and fifty is enough, I can manage to save some, but a house with many members, many sons to educate, daughters to marry – what can that person do? Unless the salary of the people on low income increases to a level that they are able to manage living an ordinary man's life, his practice of bribery will not stop. They also consume *roti-dal*, *ghee* and milk. Then why is one paid thirty rupees and the other three hundred?"

Rama's queen was also struck down. Ramesh Babu laughed uproariously.

Rama said with anger, "If you can play silently then play, otherwise I'll leave. You took away all my pieces engaging me in talk."

Ramesh said, "Alright, Sir! If I talk now, grab my tongue! Take this. Check. So, you put in the application tomorrow. I hope you'll get the post, but the day you get the job you will have to play chess with me the whole night."

Ramanath said, "You start crying after only two losses."

Ramesh said, "Gone are the days when you used to defeat me. The moon is powerful these days and I have achieved a powerful mantra. Who would dare to defeat me now? Check, again!"

Ramanath said, "I want to go only after beating you in the next game, but I'll be very late."

Ramesh said, "How will it be late? It is only nine o'clock. Play one more game to satisfy your heart's craving. Checkmate!"

Ramanath said, "Alright, I will see tomorrow. If I don't defeat you in five challenges, then you should talk."

Ramesh said, "Oh, go away! You defeat me? If you have the courage, the right time is now."

Ramanath said, "All right. Come on, I'll show you! But I will not play less than five games."

Ramesh said, "Not five; play ten games. The night is ours. Come, first let us eat food. Then we will play without worry. I'll send a message to your house that you are staying here, and they should not wait for you."

Both of them ate food and sat down to play chess. The first game went on till eleven o'clock. Ramesh Babu had won. The next round was also won by him. When the third game got over, it was two o'clock.

Ramanath said, "I'm feeling sleepy now."

Ramesh said, "Then go and wash your face. Ice is kept over there. I will not let you sleep without playing five games."

Ramesh Babu had full faith that his luck was strong and would hold. Otherwise it was not easy to defeat Rama three times, consecutively. He was sure that at present, no matter how many games he played, victory would be his. However, when he was defeated in the fourth round, his confidence began to waver. In fact, he was afraid of being defeated continuously. He said, "We should sleep now."

Ramanath said, "Why won't you complete five games?"

Ramesh said, "I have to go to the office tomorrow." Rama did not insist too much. Both of them went to sleep.

Rama usually did not get up before eight, and today, he had slept at three. Today, he had the right to sleep till ten. Ramesh, as per his usual routine, got up at five, bathed, meditated, went for a walk, and returned by eight, but Rama was still asleep. Finally, at nine-thirty, he woke him up.

In a temper, Rama said, "You have no right to wake me up. I was sleeping so soundly."

Ramesh said, "Are you going to submit that application or not?"

Rama said, "You submit it."

Ramesh said, "And if the Sahab calls for the applicant, then will I go?"

Rama said, "Oh! Do whatever you want. I'm going to sleep."

Rama lay down again. Ramesh ate his food, wore clothes and got ready to leave for office. Just them, Rama got up in a panic and rubbing his eyes said, "I'll also go."

Ramesh said, "Oh! Be a gentleman and at least wash your hand and face first."

Ramanath said, "But you're leaving."

Ramesh said, "No. I can wait for another fifteen or twenty minutes. You get ready."

Ramanath said, "I am ready. I will eat after returning from there."

Ramesh said, "I said that I am waiting for half an hour."

Rama washed his face in one minute, ate his food in five minutes and quickly went to the office with Ramesh.

On the way, Ramesh smiled and said, "Have you thought of what excuse you will make at home?"

Ramanath said, "I will say that Ramesh Babu didn't let me go."

Ramesh said, "Yes, you will have her rebukeed me, won't you? Then you won't be permitted to go to my house any longer."

Ramanath said, “I’m not so devoted to my wife that I won’t come. Yes, tell me, won’t I have to take that application to Sahab?”

Ramesh said, “So, what do you think? That you will get a position by sitting at home? You’ll have to run around for several months. You will have to bring scores of recommendations. You will have to dance attendance, morning and evening. You think it’s easy to get a job?”

Ramanath said, “Then I will be fed up of such a job! I’m ashamed to take the application, how can I think about flattering others? I used to laugh at the clerks, but now this calamity has fallen on my head. I hope Sahab won’t scold me?”

Ramesh said, “He scolds very badly. People tremble in front of him.”

Ramanath said, “Then I am going home. I won’t be able to tolerate it all.”

Ramesh said, “Everyone gets scared like this, but you get habituated to it after bearing it for a while. Your heart must be beating heavily thinking what may happen. When I started working, I was just of your age and had been married just for three months. On the day of my interview, I was so terrified – as if I was going to be hanged. But you needn’t worry about anything. I will take care of everything!”

Ramanath said, “You must be working for the past twenty or twenty two years now?”

Ramesh said, “A full twenty-five years, Sir. Twenty years have passed since my wife died. I joined service on a salary of just ten rupees.”

Ramanath said, “Why didn’t you marry again? You couldn’t have been more than twenty-five years then.”

Ramesh laughed and said, “Who feels like eating *gur* after *barfi*? Who would find pleasure in a hut after enjoying the pleasure of a palace? Love satisfies the soul. You know me closely. Though I am an old man now, I tell you the truth. Throughout my life as widower, I haven’t even looked at a woman. I had seen many beautiful ladies, and many times people tried to persuade me to get married, but I never even had the desire. For me, the fond memories of that love are full of lifelong bliss.”

Talking about such matters, both of them reached the office.

10

When Rama reached home from office, it was four o'clock. When he was still in the office, clouds had gathered in the sky. It was about to rain, but Rama was so anxious to go home that he could not wait. He had not even stepped out of the office compound when it started pouring heavily. It was the first rain of June and he got drenched in a moment. Even then he didn't stop. How could he be bothered by heavy rains when he was overjoyed at the thought of passing on the news of getting a job? The job brought in just thirty rupees, but it was a position in which he can earn. He had calculated mentally how much he could save monthly to make a *chandrahar* for Jalpa. If he could save even fifty to sixty rupees per month, Jalpa would be laden with ornaments in just five years. He had also gauged what kinds of ornament would cost how much. On reaching home, he did not even stop to change and went, drenched, to Jalpa's room.

Seeing him, Jalpa said, "Where were you that you got so wet? Where did you disappear to last night?"

Ramanath said, "I was worried about getting a job. Right now, I have come from office. I have got a post at the Municipal office."

Jalpa jumped up and said, "Really! How much is the job for?

Rama hesitated to tell the truth. He was feeling ashamed at disclosing a post of thirty rupees. Who wants to look contemptible in his wife's eyes? He said, "For now, I'll get forty, but soon I will be promoted. The post is one of earning."

Jalpa had imagined some high ranked post for him. She said, "What will happen in forty? It should be at least sixty to seventy rupees."

Ramanath replied, "I could get a job paying one hundred per month, but this post has respect and comfort. I will get fifty to sixty over the salary."

Jalpa said, "So you will take bribes and cut the throats of poor people?"

Rama said laughing, "No darling, it is not a job where poor people's throats are cut. I will be getting payments from big moneylenders who would happily embrace me. Whomsoever I want, I can make him wait throughout the day in the office. Each minute of the moneylenders is as costly as a gold coin. They would coax me to get their work done urgently, and would pay for this."

Jalpa, satisfied, said, "Alright, then it's fine. Do the work of the poor without taking anything."

Ramanath, "That I'll definitely do."

Jalpa said, "Have you not told Ammaji yet? Go and tell her. My biggest pleasure will be that I would feel that I also have some right in this house."

Ramanath, "Yes, I am going, but I will tell them I am getting only twenty rupees."

Jalpa said excitedly, "Yes! You may say it's fifteen, instead. It's useless to discuss the remaining earning. They may ask for an account of our income. I will first get the *chandrahar* made!"

Just then the postman called. Rama went to the door; there was a parcel for him. Dindayal had sent it. Feeling very happy, he brought it in and placing it in Jalpa's hands, said, "It has come from your home. See what is in it."

Rama quickly brought a pair of scissors and opened the parcel. He took out a box made of deodar. There was a *chandrahar* inside. Taking it out, Rama looked at it and laughed, "God has heard you. It seems to be a very nice thing."

Jalpa said, in a humiliated tone, "What did Ammaji think of? It is hers. I will not take it. Send it back if there is still a time for posting it."

Rama said, astonished, "What is need of sending it back? Will she not be angry?"

Jalpa said with displeasure, "I don't care. If Her Majesty gets offended, she can take pleasure in the fact that her husband is alive. I can live without their pity. After all these days she has taken pity on me. She didn't pity me when I was leaving her house. She should keep her jewellery with herself. I don't wish to be obliged to anyone. This is her time of life to dress up. Why should I be a hindrance? If you are there for me, I will get the jewels. I want to show Ammaji that Jalpa is not hungry for her jewellery."

Consoling her, Rama said, "According to me, you should keep the necklace. Just think how bad they will feel. It was good that she did not give it during your farewell. Otherwise, it would have also gone with the other jewellery."

Jalpa said, "I will not take it and that's final."

Rama asked why.

Jalpa said, "It's my wish."

Rama said, "There must be some reason for your wish."

In a choked voice, Jalpa said, "The reason is that she is not giving it to me willingly. It is quite possible that she might have wept, while sending it to me. And there no doubt that she will be very pleased when she gets it back. You must look into the heart of someone who is giving. If she gives me just a plain ring with affection, I would accept it with both hands. If she has given it by hurting her own feelings or for fear of a bad reputation or of being denounced by someone, then what is the point in giving? Charity is given to beggars. I wouldn't accept any charity from anybody, even if it is my mother."

Seeing Jalpa's hostility towards her mother, Rama could not say anything. Hostility does not listen to reason and logic. Rama took the necklace and getting up from the cot, said, "Let me show it to Amma and Babuji. We should at least ask them."

Jalpa snatched the necklace from his hand and said, "Who are they to me that I should take their consent? The only relation there exists is that of living in the same house. When they do not consider me anything, then I also think the same about them."

Saying this, she put the necklace back into the same box it came in, and began sewing the cloth she had wrapped around it. Rama said once more, a little fearfully, "What is the hurry? Send it back in five to ten days. That way, they will also feel honoured."

Hearing this, Jalpa, with a stern expression, said, "If I do not return it, I won't have any peace of mind. It'll rankle like a thorn in my heart. As soon as the parcel is ready, return it right away."

The parcel was ready in a moment. Rama, in a pensive mood, took the parcel and went downstairs.

11

When Mister Dayanath came to know about Rama getting a job, he was very happy. He had never hoped that Rama would become sensible so soon after his marriage. He said, "It's a good position. If you work honestly, you'll rise to a high post. It is my sincere advice; always consider other's money as ill-gotten."

Rama felt like saying outright, "Keep your advice to yourself, it is not suitable for me." However, he kept silent as he could not be that shameless.

Dayanath spoke again, "This post is worth thirty rupees, why would you get paid only twenty?"

Rama said, "Why would they give the full salary to a newcomer? It might increase in a year or six months. There is plenty of work."

Dayanath said, "You are a young man; you shouldn't be nervous of work."

The next day Rama had a new suit made, and purchased lots of fashionable things. There was some money left over from the money he had received from his in-laws; some he had borrowed from his friends. He wanted to make an impression in the whole office by dressing in an aristocratic style. Nobody would dare to ask his salary and the landlords would be intimidated by looking at his splendour. He knew he could earn well only when he maintained that high degree of splendour. An ordinary watchman is considered worthy of one penny only, but if it were a sergeant nobody dares to show him a single penny. For a beggar with tattered clothes, a pinch is considered adequate, but one feels ashamed to give only a rupee to a sadhu in ochre coloured robes. There is customary friendship between alms and appearance.

The third day, when Rama moved around in his pant, coat and hat, his dignity grew still further. The peons bowed and saluted him. When he went to meet Ramesh Babu and to take charge of his work, he found a Muslim gentleman sitting on the verandah, on a torn, dirty carpet with an open register kept on the trunk, and all the businessmen standing around him. In front of him was a veritable *bazar* of wagons, pushcarts and *ekka*s. Everyone was noisily trying to get his work quickly. Some were using rough language among themselves, while some peons were laughing and joking. The entire work operated without any system. Rama felt insulted to sit on that torn and dirty carpet. He went straight to Ramesh Babu and asked, "Do you want me also to sit on this torn and dirty carpet? Please have a nice table and some chairs sent for me, and instruct the peons to allow only one person at a time to meet me." Ramesh Babu smiled and sent a table and a few chairs. Rama sat on the chair with dignity. The old

Munshiji was laughing silently at Rama's high standards. He understood that it was a new zeal and a new craze. He handed over the charge. What was there in the charge – he simply had to give an account of the income of the day. There was a printed table with how much duty was levied on which kind of good. Rama understood the job within half an hour. Though the old Munshiji had left the job on his own account, he was now feeling sad at leaving. He had been sitting in this place for the last thirty years. It was through this place that he had earned both money and fame. Why would he not feel sad while leaving it? After handing over the charge, when he departed Rama went with him till the end of the stairs. Khan Sahib was happy at this kindness. He smiled and said, "It is an open secret that one *anna* is taken for each receipt. People pay happily. You are a rich person, but do not spoil this custom. Custom, if not followed, it is not easily established again. The peons have a right to half the *anna*. The former head clerk would take twenty-five rupees a month, but this one does not take anything."

Showing his disinterest, Rama said, "It's dirty work. I want to work cleanly."

The old gentleman said, "It looks dirty right now, but you will start enjoying it."

After bidding farewell to Khan Sahab, Rama sat on his chair and said to a peon, "Tell these people, they should stand below the verandah. Let them come one by one, in order. Write down everyone's name on a piece of paper, and let them approach me in that order."

One of the merchants, who had been standing there for more than two hours, said happily, "Yes Sir, this will be really nice."

Ramanath said, "Whosoever is here first should get their work done first. It won't do that people who come later and make a lot of noise, will get ahead, while the ones who came first, should stand, gawking at them."

Several merchants said, "Yes, *Babuji*, it will be good if this arrangement is made. This kind of uproar wastes a lot of time."

This control adequately established a good impression of Rama's all around. From this day onwards, the business community started praising and criticising his style. No professor of a reputed college could have gained this reputation throughout his life.

Rama was able to understand all the tricks of this trade in a few days. He thought of such plans that Khan Sahab would have never thought of in his dreams, also. There was so much chicanery in weighing, counting, and inspecting various goods that it had no limits. When merchants gulped hundreds of rupees from this chicanery, then why should Rama be contented with only an *anna* per transaction, half of which was for the peons? By weighing and inspecting goods strictly according to the rules, he could easily earn both money and fame. Why would he let this opportunity pass – especially when the head clerk was his close friend? Ramesh Babu was enthralled by the new recruit's adroitness in his work. Patting his back, he said, "Follow the rules and then do whatever you want. You will not be harmed in the least."

Rama's income began to increase, day by day. With the income, his influence also grew. Clerks who did not have much work to do in the office, would go to Rama whenever they wanted cigarettes, *paan*, tea or other refreshments. Everybody could make use of the flowing river of opportunity. There were praises all round, for Rama in the office.

'He regards money as a worthless object.'

'What a heart he has!'

'His speech is as good as his heart.'

'It appears as if honesty is filled in every nerve of his body.'

When the state of clerks was such, then what about the *peon*s and junior clerks? All of them had become Rama's slaves without payment. Not only their income, but even their prestige had grown greatly. Where earlier, even the cart-owners scolded them, now they could even send even the high and mighty down the steps, to wait in line. Ramanath's voice was being heard clearly.

However, Jalpa's desires had not been fulfilled, yet. On the occasion of *Nagpanchami,* several young ladies from the neighbourhood came to play *Kajli* with Jalpa, but she did not stir from her room. In August, the festival of *Janmastami* came around. The event was celebrated by a wealthy merchant who lived in the neighbourhood with great pomp. Jalpa and her mother-in-law were invited. Rameshwari went, but Jalpa refused to go. In these three months, she did not speak to Rama about the ornaments, but her love for solitude was even more provocative than her behaviour. Even more provocative was an old list of ornaments, which Rama had picked up from somewhere. It bore different types of ornament designs. Their prices were also given. Jalpa used to see the list carefully in seclusion. On seeing Rama, she would hide the list. She did not want to make a mockery of herself by disclosing her heartfelt wishes.

When Rama returned after midnight, he found Jalpa lying on the cot. He smiled and said, "A very good song was being sung. You did not go. You made a big mistake." Jalpa turned her face and did not reply.

Rama spoke again, "Were you not afraid, lying here all alone?"

Jalpa said in a sharp tone, "You say I made a mistake, I think I made a good decision. By going there, whose reputation would have been at stake?"

Jalpa did not want to taunt him, but she was provoked by what Rama had said. Another reason for her resentment was that the whole family her left her alone and gone to see the festival. 'If they had hearts, then could they not have refused to go there?' she thought.

Rama said, shamefacedly, "There is no question of being defamed; everyone knows there was a theft. And getting ornaments worth two to four thousands of rupees made these days is no small matter."

As soon as Rama uttered the world 'theft', his heart began to pound. Jalpa kept on staring sharply at her husband. There was fear that matters might get worse by speaking further, but Rama felt from her look, that she knew the secret of the theft and was not revealing it, due to some hesitation. He also recalled the dream that Jalpa had seen on the night of the theft. Her gaze started piercing his heart, like an arrow. He thought that perhaps it was misconception. The gaze had no emotion other than resentment, but then why was she not saying anything? Why was she silent? Her silence itself was most disturbing. To clear the doubt in his own mind and test the depth of Jalpa's feeling, he took a chance, "Who knew that as soon as you stepped down from the *doli,* this disaster would greet you?"

With eyes filled with tears, Jalpa said, "I do not cry for them in front of you. Whatever was written in my fate has occurred. What is written will occur in future, too. Women who don't wear jewels—don't they also pass their days?"

These words did remove Rama's doubts, but the acute suffering that was hidden behind these words could not be concealed. In these three months, he was not able to collect more than one hundred rupees. He had also spent a lot to keep the clerks happy, but then it wouldn't work without spending on their food and drink. All of them would have become his enemies and would start scheming to uproot him. He was fully aware that ill-gotten wealth could not be swallowed up by oneself, alone. He did not waste even a single penny himself. Like a clever businessman, he spent money in order to earn more money. Assuring her, he said, "If God wishes it, something will be made in a month or two."

Jalpa said, "I am not like those ladies, who die for jewellery. But, yes, I feel ashamed visiting someone's house like this."

Rama grew restless and felt guilty. Each word spoken by Jalpa was indicating disappointment. He thought, 'Who was responsible for this immense misery? Was he not to blame for not talking about jewellery in all these three months? If Jalpa was not talking about jewellery, due to hesitation, then did he have no other option with which to wipe her tears and gratify her, other than by keeping silent? Everyday there was one or another festival in the neighbourhood, everyday the women from nearby came to meet her and every day someone or the other came to invite her – how long would poor Jalpa keep on suppressing her spirit and suffer silently? Who does not like to laugh and talk? Who likes to be confined in the house like a convict? She has to face this horrendous punishment all because of me.'

He wondered whether it was possible to get some jewellery on credit from a jeweller? He knew a number of jewellers, but how would he say this to them? Suppose they refused, then what? It was quite possible that they would make some excuse. He decided that right now it was not right to take credit. If he wasn't able to return the money on time, then he would face many insults. He would be shamed. He decided that he would remain silent for a few days more.

Suddenly, he thought that he should consult Jalpa for her opinion on this issue. 'Let's see, what she says? If she wishes, then some jewellery might be taken from a jeweller on credit. I will bear this humiliation and embarrassment.' In order to satisfy Jalpa that he was, indeed, concerned about her jewellery, he said, "I want some advice from you, should I ask you now?"

Jalpa was feeling sleepy. With her eyes still closed, she said, "Now let me sleep, I have to get up in the morning."

Ramanath said, "If you agree, then, shall I get some jewellery made on credit from a jeweler? Is there any harm in it?"

Jalpa's eyes opened. How difficult a question was that? To ask a guest; should I get you some food? It was so ill-mannered. It simply means that we are unwilling to feed the guest. Rama should have brought the things and put them before her. On her repeated asking, he should have answered, "I have paid for them." Then, probably, she would be happy. To ask for her advice on this matter was like sprinkling salt on her wounds. She looked at Rama in disbelief and said, "I am not that keen on jewellery."

Ramanath, "No, it is not like that at all. I was thinking what is the harm if I obtain jewellery on credit? Gradually, I'll pay off the money."

Jalpa said sternly, "No, there is no need to take credit for me. I am not a prostitute who would snatch and scrape everything from you and walk away. I have to live and die with you. Even if I were to live without ornaments throughout my life, then, also I wouldn't ask you to get into debt for me. Women are not that hungry for jewellery. I am not one of those who would put the whole family into trouble just to wear jewellery. But you had said earlier that the position brought in a good income, but I am unable to see any specific saving."

Ramanath, "Certainly there is saving and it would be good, but only when one didn't have so many senior clerks to please. All those devils are sitting on my head. I didn't know I had to worship so many ghosts."

Jalpa said, "So what is the haste now? They can be made slowly."

Ramanath said, "Well, if that is your advice, then I'll keep quiet for one or two months more. I'll get bangles made first of all."

A visibly elated Jalpa said, “But you won’t have so much money now.”

Ramanath said, “I have a way out. Which type of bangle do you like?”

Jalpa could no longer maintain her forced composure. She took out the list of ornaments from the cupboard and showed it to Rama. At this moment, she was so eager – as though the gold had been bought, the jeweller was waiting; the design had to be chosen. She chose two designs from the list; both were really very beautiful, but Rama was stunned into silence at seeing their prices. One was worth a thousand and the other was for eight hundred.

Ramanath said, “Such things probably won’t be made here. But tomorrow, I will visit all the jewellers.”

Closing the book, Jalpa said with tenderness, “I don’t know, when you will have this much money? Oh, if they are made, they will be – otherwise, who is dying without jewellery?”

Rama had tense and confused thoughts and could not sleep till late at night. How beautiful those gem-encrusted bangles would look on those fair arms – he lost himself in this alluring dream and drifted off to sleep.

12

The next morning, Rama took the path that led to Ramesh Babu's house. He, too, had a tableau for *Janmastami* at his house. He did not have a great fondness for it, but since his wife had celebrated the occasion, he simply continued to do so in her memory. On seeing Rama, he said, "Come on, why didn't you come last night? Why would you come here to a poor man's house? How could you leave Sethji's tableau? It must have been really splendid?"

Ramanath said, "It was not decorated like the one in your house, but, yes, it was better than those of other years. Several Kathak dancers and prostitutes had also come. I had left by then, but heard that singing and dancing went on throughout the night."

Ramesh said, "Sethji had promised that prostitutes won't be allowed, then, what happened? At the hands of such fools, Hindu religion will be ruined. Prostitutes anyway do not have a good name, then, their presence in a temple! Shame, Shame! I don't know when these idiots will gain some sense."

Ramanath said, "If there are no prostitutes, who would go to see the tableaus? Everyone is not a yogi and ascetic like you."

Ramesh said, "If I had my way, I would put an end to this immoral act through legal action. Anyway, if you have time we may sit to play one or more games."

Ramanath said, "What else am I here for? But today, you'll have to accompany me to the jewellers' shop. Though I am acquainted to many big businessmen, yet your presence would make a difference."

Ramesh said, "If you say so, I will go with you, but I am really ignorant in this matter. Neither have I ever got anything made, nor purchased anything. What do you want to buy?"

Ramanath said, "Who's thinking about buying or selling? I will check the rates."

Ramesh said, "It seems you've been scolded at home."

Ramanath said, "No, not at all. She doesn't even mention ornaments. If I ask her, she refuses, but my responsibility also counts for something. Since all her ornaments were stolen, nothing has been made."

Ramesh said, "It appears you have learnt how to earn. Why won't it be, after all you are the son of a Kayasth. How much have you saved?"

Ramanath said, "Who has got money? I would take on credit."

Ramesh said, "Don't fall into this craze. Don't go towards the market until you have money in your hand. Old men keep their new wives happy with jewellery. What else do those poor fellows have, besides jewellery? Young men have lots of other tricks to resort to. If I want, I could arrange for you to get things worth two or four thousand, but the addiction to debt is bad."

Ramanath said, "I'll pay off everything in two or three months. If I weren't sure of this, I wouldn't have mentioned it."

Ramesh said, "Why not wait for two-three months more? There is nothing as sinful as debt. Nor is any trouble worse than this. You overcome this fear and you shall see yourself standing at the jewellers' shop, almost every day. Don't misunderstand me. I know that your income is good, but do anything trusting the future, except taking a loan. I don't know how this sickness, the desire for jewellery has spread throughout this wretched country? Those who don't have enough for food, they also die for jewellery. Each year, crores of rupees are spent on buying gold and silver. No other country of the world has such a high consumption of these metals. Why is it so? In developed countries, money is invested on business, which is utilised for people's welfare and brings further prosperity. Here money is wasted on decoration, which puts an end to both of two of its great strengths – progress and philanthropy. Just understand this – the more fools there are in a country, the more propaganda there'll be for jewellery. Here, at least, people stop after piercing their noses and ears, but there are several countries where people pierce their lips to wear ornaments."

Rama asked with great curiosity, "Which country is that?"

Ramesh said, "I can't recall properly just now, but perhaps it is Africa. It seems surprising to us when we hear this, but it would be no less surprising to people in other countries to hear of piercing noses and ears. It's a bad addiction; very bad. The money which ought to be spent on food goes towards purchasing jewellery and the children starve. Let the children not have milk, that's alright. Let them not smell ghee in their houses, that's still alright. It is no concern if they don't get fruits and nuts, but the Deviji must wear ornaments and husbands must get the ornaments made for her! I see poor clerks, earning just ten or twenty rupees and living like animals in small rooms, who are unable to afford a simple breakfast. They, too, have this madness for ornaments. We are being destroyed because of this custom. I say this is worse than slavery and subjugation. Even Brahman cannot guess how much we are declining spiritually, morally, physically, economically and spiritually because of this.

Ramanath objected, "I suppose there is not a single country where women don't wear ornaments. Isn't this custom prevalent in Europe also?"

Ramesh countered, "But your country is not Europe. There people are wealthy. Let them squander their money – it suits them. We are poor and we should not squander even a paisa."

Ramesh Babu forgot all about chess in this discussion. It was a holiday, so some more people came to see Ramesh Babu. Ramanath sneaked away quietly. After this discussion, there was one thing that impressed itself in his mind. He gave up the idea of taking the jewellery on loan. If he failed to pay the amount quickly; he would be defamed. Though he walked up to the jeweller's market, he had not dared enter any of them. He decided that he won't even talk about jewellery for three-four months. When he reached his home, it was nine o'clock. When Dayanath saw him, he said, "Where have you been since morning?"

Ramanath said, "I had just gone to see Ramesh Babu."

Dayanath said, "Why don't you go to the library for an hour or so? You waste the whole day gossiping. You are at an age where you can learn something. Though not for any examination, but you can add to your qualification. If a simple letter has to be written, you look around. Real education starts after leaving school and that is what is helpful in our lives. I have heard a few things about you; these caused me deep sorrow. Therefore, I consider it my duty to explain it to you. I will never tolerate a single wrongly earned paisa makes its way into my house. It has been thirty years now that I have been working. If I wanted, I could have saved thousands of rupees, but I swear I have never accepted a single paisa, dishonestly. From where you got this habit, I cannot understand?"

Displaying feigned anger, Rama said, "Who told you this? Tell me his name and I would pluck his moustache."

Dayanath said, "Whoever told me about this, it does not concern you. You would pluck his moustache, therefore I wouldn't tell you. But I definitely want to know whether it is true or false."

Ramanath said, "Absolutely false!"

Dayanath said, "Absolutely false."

Ramanath said, "Yes, Sir, absolutely false."

Dayanath said, "You don't take any commissions?"

Ramanath said, "Commissions are not bribes. Everybody takes them and takes them openly. People give these on their own. I don't ask them to."

Dayanath said, "Just because everybody takes them openly and people give them without asking does not lessen its immorality."

Ramanath said, "It is not in my hands to put an end to this practice. Even if I don't take it myself, I can't prevent the peons and clerks from doing so. People who earn only eight or nine rupees a month cannot make both ends meet, if they don't take it. I may not take it, but I can't stop them."

Sadly, Dayanath said, "I have explained it to you. It's up to you to agree or disagree with it."

Saying this, Dayanath left for office. It occurred to Rama to ask him clearly that by being so ideological, what had he achieved, he was blaming him. He had always had to count every paisa, and could even educate his sons – he couldn't even provide them with clothes and shoes. His high-minded talk would have graced him, when his disposition would have also been spotless and life would have been spent contentedly.

As Rama entered the house, his mother said, "Son, where had you gone? Your father was getting annoyed over it."

Ramanath said, "No, he was not getting upset about this, but yes, he was giving me a sermon on not taking any commissions. It weakens your soul and also causes defamation."

Rameshwari said, "You didn't say what was so special in your great honesty? All our lives we have lived hand-to-mouth."

Ramanath said, "I wanted to, but it would have irritated him. He wants me to also live earning paisa by paisa, like he did. He didn't have the courage to accept the money. When he saw it wouldn't work, then he decided to become a saint. There aren't such complete fools here. You need plenty of sense to squeeze money out of merchants; it's not the lighthearted matter or a joke. When someone starts acting saintly, I understand immediately that he is a fool. He does not know how to take. What will the poor souls do? Somehow, they will assuage their tears."

Rameshwari said, "Yes, yes, it is just the case, son. Whosoever knows how to take will certainly do so. He only knows to sit at home and expound the law, and he cannot speak before anyone else. For him, extracting money from anyone will be most difficult."

Just before leaving for office, Rama went upstairs to change his clothes, and Jalpa gave him three envelopes to post. He took the envelopes and put them in his pocket, but on the way, he began to read the letters. What were in the letters? A long, pathetic wait of hardship and pain shared with her three friends. All three letters had the same subject – only the emotions differed. 'My life has become a mountain; neither can I sleep at night nor rest during the day. I laugh and play sometimes simply to please my husband, but my heart weeps endlessly. Neither do I go to anyone's home, nor let anyone else visit me. It seems this endless sorrow will leave after taking my life. Promises are made every day: the money is being gathered, the goldsmith is being engaged, the design is being decided, but it is just a bluff and nothing more.'

Rama put all the letters into his pocket. He passed the post office, but did not post them. His thoughts haunted him, 'Does she still think that I am bluffing her? What shall I do, how should I convince her? If I had the capacity, I would have put a basketful of jewellery in front of her, or taken her to a big jewellery shop, and asked to pick whatever she wanted. What endless grief this is that it caused her to lose trust in me!' Now, Rama realised the true extent of her injury, which he had caused in order to keep his false dignity intact. If he knew that the act would bear such a result, then he would have revealed the truth about his boasts. Did he still have the scope to hesitate in taking a loan, when today Jalpa was being consumed by her intense grief? His heart was rented by distress. For the first time he prayed to God with a true heart, 'God, punish me, but do not snatch my Jalpa from me. Before that, take my life.' Each pore of his body started echoing: 'God...God...take pity on my wretched condition.'

Concurrently, he was also getting very angry with Jalpa, 'Why didn't Jalpa say this to me? Why did she hide it from me and express her pain to her friends?'

Goods were being weighed on the veranda. Notes and coins were being kept on the table, and Rama sat lost in his worry. Who should he take advice from? Why had he got married? The fault was entirely his. When he was aware of the condition of his family, why did he not refuse to marry? Today, he was not interested in his work, so he left the office early.

As soon as Jalpa saw him, she said, "You didn't post my letters, did you?"

Rama made an excuse, "Oh! I completely forgot about them. They kept lying in my pocket."

Jalpa said, "That is good. Give them to me. Now, I will not send them."

Rama said, "Why? I will send them tomorrow."

Jalpa said, "No, I don't want to send these letters now. I had written certain things that I shouldn't have. If you would have posted them, I would've felt sad. I had been critical of you."

Saying this, she smiled.

Ramanath said, "Whosoever is bad, deceitful and cunning ought to be criticised."

Jalpa said, fearfully, "You had read the letters?"

Rama said, unhesitatingly, "Yes, is it any inexcusable crime?"

In a timid voice, Jalpa said, "Then you must be really angry with me?"

A surge of tears choked Jalpa's voice. Her head hung down and tears fell on to the edge of her sari. In a moment, steadying her voice, she said, "I have made a big mistake. Punish me the way you want, but do not be displeased with me. God knows how sad I was after you left. I don't know how I wrote such words."

Jalpa knew Rama was as worried about the ornaments as she was, but while expressing one's distress to friends one usually exaggerates. The discussion of things considered most intimate is regarded as a kind of insult. Friends develop sympathy when they think that nothing is concealed from them. Women have a stronger tendency to display intimacy amongst each other.

Rama, wiping Jalpa's tears said, "Dearest, I am not displeased with you. There is nothing to be displeased about. If delayed, hopes turn into disappointment, don't I know this much? If you wouldn't have refused, I'd certainly have had a couple of things made for you somehow. It was a mistake on my part to ask for your opinion. This was just like offering food to a guest by asking him again and again what he wanted. I didn't realise that a person refuses in hesitation also. God willingly, now you won't have to wait for long."

Looking at him anxiously, Jalpa said, "Then are you going to take a loan?"

Rama said, "Yes! There is nothing wrong in taking a loan. When there is no interest, then it is just like making a payment in cash! The whole world works through loans. Who doesn't take loans? Once you have money, it is spent so easily. But if you are feeling the burden of dept, that worry keeps your spending in control."

Jalpa said, "I don't want to put you in worrisome situation. Now I will not mention the jewels, even by mistake."

Ramanath said, "You never mentioned it before also, but that does not mean my responsibility has ended. I needlessly fear debt. If I sit and wait till I collect money, then probably they will never be saved. We can get three or four things made in a year by taking a loan and repaying it."

Jalpa said, "But first get something small."

Rama said, "Yes, that's what I'll do."

When Rama left for market, it was quite dark. In the day, it was quite possible that his friends would see him. Even Munshi Dindayal could have seen him. He wanted to keep this matter a secret.

13

In the jeweller's market, Gangu's shop was famous. Although Gangu was a Brahmin, he was an adept businessman. His shop was always crowded with customers. His dedication towards his work developed confidence in customers. There was a fear of being cheated in other shops. Here, there was no deceit whatsoever. Gangu smiled as soon as he saw Rama and said, "Come in, Babuji, let's go upstairs. It is very kind of you. Munshiji, get some *paan* for the gentleman. What is your order, Babuji, it seems as if you are annoyed with me. You never visit my shop; show some mercy on us poor people, too."

Gangu's affability gave Rama courage to try. If he hadn't invited him so enthusiastically, Rama would not have gathered courage to enter the shop. He had not yet experienced the effect of his own good reputation. As he entered the shop, he said, "How can labourers like us enter your shop, Maharaj? There should be some money in the pocket, also."

Gangu said, "What are you saying, Sir? This is your shop. Take whatever you want – payment will be made sooner or later. Babu Sahab! It is not how you think, we recognise the worth of people. It is our good fortune that you, at least, came to our shop. Should I show you some inlaid work? Some bracelets or a necklace? We have just recently got some new stock from Delhi!"

Rama said, "Show me a less costly necklace."

Gangu said, "Around seven to eight hundred worth?"

Rama said, "Oh no! At the most, till four hundred."

Gangu, "I'll show you both. Take the one you like, Babu Sahab. We don't play any dirty tricks here. You must not worry a bit about this. Whether a boy of five years or an old man of one hundred years – we treat everyone in the same way. Babuji, one day we all have to show our faces to the Almighty."

The big box of ornaments came. Gangu started showing him the necklaces, one by one. Rama's eyes opened wide and he was delighted. What beautiful work! How beautifully they were decorated with gems! What lustre! Their sparkle would have put the lamplight to shame. Rama had thought to himself that he would not take a loan for more than a hundred, but the necklace worth four hundred did not please his eyes. He had only three hundred rupees in his pocket. He thought if he took the necklace and Jalpa did not like it, then it was of no use. 'I should take something that will thrill her. How beautiful this inlaid necklace will look on her neck?' he thought. The necklace with its thousand bejewelled eyes began to charm Rama. He stared at it mesmerised, but did not have the courage to express it in words. He thought how humiliated he would be if Gangu refused to give a loan of three hundred. Gangu, perceiving Rama's uncertainty, said, "Babuji, this necklace is suitable for you. In a dark home, it will light up everything."

Ramanath said, "Even I like it, but you should understand that I have only three hundred rupees."

Rama, embarrassed, started blushing. With his heart pounding, he looked at Gangu.

Gangu said honestly, "Babu Sahab, do not discuss money. If you say so, I'll send stuff worth ten thousand with you. This is your shop, how could you say such a thing? If you order, I'll show you a few more things. We have just received a newly made *shashiphool*. It seems as if a rose has really bloomed. Looking at it will make you happy. Munimji, could you just show us that *shashiphool*? It is not very costly, also. I'll give it to you for two hundred and fifty rupees."

Rama said with a smile, "Maharaj, I hope I am not being deceived with this smooth talks. I am totally ignorant in matters of jewellery."

Gangu said, "Babuji, don't say that. Take it and show it to persons in the market. If anybody says it costs a paisa less than two hundred and fifty, I'll give it to you free."

The *shashiphool* was brought in – it was truly like a rose on which diamond buds glistened like dewdrops. Rama stared spellbound as if something celestial was in sight.

Gangu said, "Babuji, the two hundred and fifty is simply the reward of excellent craftsmanship. This is one such piece."

Rama said, "Yes, the piece is immensely beautiful, but Bhai Sahab, don't start asking for payment right from tomorrow. I'll pay it back myself, as soon as I can."

Gangu put both items in beautiful velvet cases and gave them to Rama. Then Munimji recorded Rama's name, and offered him *paan* before he took leave.

At this moment, there was no limit to Rama's delight, but it was not pure delight, as some doubt had also gathered in his mind. This was not like the delight of a child who had purchased sweets after receiving money from its mother, but one who had stolen the money. Such a child likes sweets, but in his heart he fears that he might be beaten when he reaches home. He was not specifically worried about how he would be able to make a payment of six hundred and fifty rupees; if luck favoured him he would be able to pay off the entire amount in just six months. His fear was that his father would hear of this and be angry. However, as he advanced towards his house, he was filled with growing delight and his eager desire to see

Jalpa decorated with these ornaments gradually triumphed over his doubt. In a haste to reach home, he left the street and entered into a narrow lane. The darkness was intense. The sky had already been overcast when he left home, and as he entered the lane, raindrops began to fall on his head like buckshot. By the time he opened the umbrella, he was drenched. He began to worry that someone might come in the dark and snatch the two things, and in the continuous downpour, it was impossible to hear anyone call out. Even murders were committed in these dark lanes. He regretted needlessly taking this route. There would have been no disaster had he reached a few minutes later. This untimely rain hindered his pleasant fantasies. Somehow, the lane came to an end and he found a street. Lanterns came into sight. Today he truly experienced how light had the power to inspire feelings of confidence and security.

When he reached home, Dayanath was sitting and smoking his *hukka*. Rama did not enter that room. He wanted to go straight inside, without being seen by his father, when he sharply said, "Where did you go at this hour?"

Rama did not answer him. If he began to read out the newspaper, then he would take hours. He went straight inside. Jalpa was standing at the gate waiting for him. She immediately took the umbrella from his hand and said, "You're completely soaked. Why didn't you take shelter somewhere?"

Ramanath said, "There's no trusting the rain. It could rain all night."

Having said this, he went upstairs. He thought Jalpa must be following, but she remained downstairs talking to his brothers as if she had completely removed the idea of jewellery from her mind. It looked as if she had even forgotten that Rama had come from jeweller's shop.

Rama changed his clothes and came downstairs, irritated. Just then, Dayanath came to eat his meal. Everyone sat to eat. Jalpa was controlling herself, but because of her suppressed longing, she was unable to eat anything. When she went upstairs, Rama was lying on the cot. As he saw her, he said excitedly, "It was useless going to the jeweller's today. The necklace wasn't ready anywhere. I told them to make it."

Jalpa's lovely face, which had been shining expectantly, faded. She said, "I knew this from before. It may take five to six months to make it."

Ramanath said, "Certainly not, he was swearing that it would be ready very soon."

Jalpa said, "Uh! He can give it whenever he wishes."

Disappointment is the extreme limit of intense longing. Jalpa was about to lie down, turning her face away from Rama, when he burst out laughing. Jalpa was startled. She understood that Rama had played a trick. Smiling she said, "You're also very naughty. What have you brought?"

Ramanath said, "See, how did I deceive you?"

Jalpa said, "This is a habit that men have. What new thing have you done?"

Jalpa was happy and content when she saw the two ornaments. Her heart was filled with waves of happiness. She wanted to hide her feelings so that Rama would not consider her shallow, but she was so thrilled that each part of her body was radiant. All her feelings were expressed by her smiling face, glowing cheek and open lips. She wore the necklace round her neck, stuck the *shashifool* in her hair and intoxicated with joy, said, "I bless you. May God fulfill all your desires."

Today Jalpa's long awaited desire was fulfilled. This had been the dream of her imaginations and the playground of her hopes since her childhood. Today that craving of her's was satisfied. If Manaki would have been here today, she would be the first one to see the necklace and she would say, "Keep your necklace with you."

Rama was greatly intoxicated with all this. Today he felt that his life was successful. For the first time today in his life he tasted the joy of victory.

Jalpa said, "Should I go and show this to Ammaji?"

Rama said tenderly, "What is there to show to Mother? What's so special about these things?"

Jalpa said, "Now I won't ask for anything else for a year. I will feel light only after the payment is done."

Rama said proudly, "Why worry about money? It is hardly anything."

Jalpa said, "Should I go to show it to Ammaji? Let's see what she has to say."

Rama said, "But don't tell her that it's on credit."

Jalpa went running downstairs as if she would find a treasure there.

It was past midnight. Rama was sleeping peacefully. Jalpa came to the roof and glanced at the sky. There was clear moonlight everywhere – it was October moonlight which had the music of peace, the sweetness of peace and the passion of sweetness. Jalpa went into her room, opened her little box and took out the glass *chandrahar* which she had worn once and felt so lucky. Now when she put the new *chandrahar* next to the old one, she noticed the lustre of the old one had dimmed, like the light of stars next to the radiance of the moon. She broke the glass necklace and threw the beads into the lane below, in the same way as the devotee submerges the earthen statues in water after the *puja* is over.

14

From that day onwards, the Jalpa's heartfelt desire to serve her husband mingled with the love she felt for him. When he went to bathe, he found his *dhoti* crisply folded; the oil and soap kept in the niche. When he got ready for office, Jalpa would bring his clothes and place them before him. Earlier he had got *paan* on request, now he was forced to eat it. Jalpa would look at his face and sense what he wanted – he did not need to speak out his desire. When he sat down to eat, she fanned him. Previously, she would not cook willingly and would try to evade this duty. Now she went lovingly to the kitchen – the same dishes were cooked, but now they tasted much better. Rama considered the two ornaments, mere trifles, in the face of such sweet affection.

On the other hand, from the day Rama had purchased ornaments from Gangu's shop – that day onwards, the other jewellers learnt of Rama's fondness for jewellery. Whenever Rama happened to pass that way, the shopkeepers, on both sides of the street would stand up and salute him. They would say, "Come in, Sir. Please take some *paan.* At least, look at a few things in our shop."

Rama's self-restraint increased his reputation still further. This carried on till one day, an agent reached Rama's house. In spite of his repeated refusal, he opened his box.

To get rid of him, Rama said, "Right now, I don't wish to take anything just now. Why will you waste your time and mine also." The agent very politely said, "At least take a look, Sir. If you like something, take it, otherwise don't. There is no harm in looking! After all, where should I go, if not to the wealthy? Others have taken large amounts from you, and if my luck favours, I will also earn a little from you. Show it to Bahuji and Maji. My heart says that today my first sale is going to come from you!"

Ramanath said, "Don't talk about the choice of women – the things are bound to be good. It does not take any time to like something, but brother, this time I am empty handed."

The agent laughed and said, "Babuji, why do you say such a thing? If you order me, I will freely give you five to ten thousand. Babuji, we look at a man's temperament. God willing, today I'll get up only after striking a bargain."

The agent took out two things from his box: an inlaid bracelet after a new fashion and a pair of earrings. Both were flawless. They sparkled like lighted lamps. It was then ten o'clock in the morning and Dayanath had already left for office, and Rama was just going in to eat his meal. He was, therefore, in haste, but as soon as he saw these things, he completely forgot about everything and took both cases inside the house. On seeing the cases in Rama's hand, both the women practically snatched them from him, and looked at the jewellery again and again. The radiant jewellery so enthralled them that they neither criticised its shortcomings nor praise it.

Rameshwari said, "Old fashioned things seem nothing when compared with things made these days."

Rama smiled and said, "So both things fit with your choice, isn't it?"

Jalpa said, "Why should she not like them? Ammaji, you take them."

Rameshwari bowed her head to hide her turmoil. How could someone whose whole life had been spent in domestic worries even dream of hoping to wear this jewellery! Ah! The poor woman had never had any of her lifelong yearnings gratified. Her husband's income had been adequate for bringing up the children; nothing was left after these expenses. Her penance began as soon as she had become the mistress of the house, and all her longings had turned to dust, one by one. She averted her gaze from the ornaments. They attracted her so much that she was afraid to look at them, lest her feigned indifference be betrayed. She said, "What would I do with them, child? My days for dressing up have passed. Who has brought this, son? What are their prices?"

Ramanath said, "A jeweller brought them for us to see. I haven't asked the price yet. They must be costly. I had no intention of buying them, so what was the use of asking the price?"

Jalpa said, "If you didn't intend to buy them, then why did you bring them here?"

Jalpa spoke in such an agitated tone that Rama got irritated. There was so much vehemence and scorn in her voice that he did not dare return the jewels now. He asked, "So, should I buy them?"

Jalpa said, "If Amma says not to buy them, what will you do by buying them? Is he giving them free?"

Ramanath said, "Well, you could say we are getting them free."

Jalpa said, "Do you hear what he says, Ammaji? Please go and return them now. When we have money in our hands, we'll get plenty of jewellery."

Rameshwari said, in a voice suffused with desire, "I hope he isn't asking for money now?"

Jalpa said, "If he gives it on credit, he will charge interest, too."

Ramanath said, "Then should I return them to him? Decide quickly one way or the other. If you're going to take them, take them, if not, give them back. Don't get confused and dither."

Just then, this plain talk seemed very harsh to Jalpa. She had not expected to hear such words from Rama. It was her prerogative to refuse, his, to insist that she should buy it. She looked towards Rameshwari eagerly and said, "Return them. Who can bear being pestered for payment, day and night?"

She was about to shut the cases when Rameshwari put on the bracelet, as if wearing it, just for a moment, would satisfy her longing. Then, ashamed of her frivolous behaviour, she was about to take it off when Rama said, "Now that you have put it on, Amma, keep it on. I'm giving it to you as a present." Rameshwari's eyes brimmed with tears. The craving which had never been fulfilled, was fulfilled today, because of Rama's devotion to her. However, would she place such a heavy burden of debt on her dear son? He was still just an immature young man, what capacity did he have? How could one know whether money would come quickly or slowly? He did not even know the price. If these were high, where would the poor boy get the money from? How many times would he have to face demands for payment; how many times be humiliated? In a dejected voice, she said, "No Son, I put it on just by chance. Take it away and return it."

Seeing his mother's sad face, Rama's heart trembled with love for her. He wondered whether he could not even do this much for his self-sacrificing mother just because he feared debt? Didn't he have a duty to his mother too? He said, "I'll get lots of money, Mother! You don't worry."

Rameshwari looked towards her daughter-in-law, as if she meant to convey, 'See, how outrageously he's behaving towards me?'

A melancholic Jalpa sat – perhaps she was afraid that her mother-in-law would really keep the bracelet. Rameshwari had no doubt that her daughter-in-law did not like her wearing the bracelet. She immediately took it off and offered it to Jalpa, saying, "I am giving this to you as a present, Daughter. I've already done all the dressing-up that I had to do. Now you put it on and let me take a look!"

Jalpa did not have the least doubt that her mother-in-law had plenty of money. She thought perhaps, today her heart had melted and she would pay for the bracelet. A moment ago, she had thought that Rama would have to pay, and so despite her own wishes she wanted to return the bracelet. However, when her mother-in-law was going to pay, then why should she object? Hiding her feelings she said, "If there is no money, then let it go, Amma! Now, what is the hurry?"

Rama said, with irritation clear in his tone, "So, are you taking this bracelet?"

Jalpa said, "Mother is insisting, so how can I refuse?"

Ramanath said, "These earrings, why don't you keep them, too?"

Jalpa said, "Go and ask how much these things are for."

Rama said impatiently, "Keep these things with you, what's the price to you?"

When Rama went outside and learnt about their prices, he fell silent. The bracelet was for seven hundred and the earrings for one hundred and fifty. He had estimated that the bracelet would, at the most, for three hundred rupees and the earrings, forty to fifty rupees. He repented not asking the price in the beginning, otherwise, there would have been no need to take them inside. He was feeling ashamed to return them, but no matter what happened, he simply had to return them. He was unable to bear such a huge debt on his head. He said to the agent, "It is very costly, brother. My estimate went up to three to four hundred only." The agent's name was Charandas. He said, "Sir, if its price proves to be a single paisa less, I won't show my face. It is from Dhaniram's house, you may come and verify it yourself. Of course, I get a very small amount as commission, which you can give or not give, as per your wish."

Ramanath said, "Then Brother, we don't want to buy such costly things right now."

Charandas said, "Please don't say such things, Babuji. How big a difference will this amount of money make to you? If you hold on to these things even for two months, you would get twice as much for them. Who could be a better connoisseur than you? These things are appreciated by wealthy people only. How can simple country folk respect their value?"

Ramanath said, "But eight hundred and fifty is a lot, Brother."

Charandas said, "Don't even think about money, Sir. When your wife will sit in all her finery, a glimpse of her shall restore all your money!"

Rama believed that when Jalpa would hear of the high prices of the ornaments, she would be herself be greatly shaken. Therefore, he did not speak any further with the agent. He went inside and laughed and said, "What was your estimate about this bracelet, Amma?"

Rameshwari did not want to appear foolish by replying, so she said, "These inlaid things are not counted by their weight, they are sold according to mutual settlement."

Rama said, "Well, you tell me, Jalpa, how much do you estimate this bracelet to be?"

Jalpa said, "Not less than six hundred rupees."

Rama's whole strategy was spoiled. He had wanted to scare Jalpa by showing his own misgivings about the price. However, there was not that much difference between six and seven hundred, and it was possible that Charandas would agree to six hundred. A little embarrassed, he said, "Are the stones not a little unfinished?"

Jalpa said, "In any case, it won't be more than six hundred!"

Rama said, "And what about the earrings?"

Jalpa said, "At the most, one hundred."

Rama said, "At the most, one hundred and fifty rupees."

Jalpa said, "Does he think us to be fools? We are not going to buy at these prices."

Rama's trick backfired – Jalpa had not been greatly confused about the price of these things. After all, although Rama's financial situation was not hidden from her, yet she sat, assenting clearly to seven hundred rupees worth of stuff. How could Rama know that Jalpa had understood the situation quite differently, therefore she had set her heart on getting on the bracelet. There was only one way to save his neck now, and that was the agent refusing to take six hundred rupees. He said, "The agent won't agree to take a paisa less than eight hundred and fifty rupees."

Jalpa said, "Then return them."

Ramanath said, "I am ashamed to return them, Amma. Could you please go to the veranda and tell him that we won't pay more than seven hundred? If he agrees, we would take, otherwise he may go?"

Rameshwari said, "Oh, yes! Why not? I should go and to talk to the agent!"

Jalpa said, "Why don't you go and tell him? There is nothing to be ashamed of."

Ramanath said, "I won't be able to give him a straight answer. He will flatter me thoroughly. Choice phrases – you are a big man, you are wealthy, you are a raja. What is one hundred and fifty rupees to you? And I'll be caught in his net of words."

Jalpa said, "All right, I'll tell him!"

Ramanath said, "Fine! That should really take care of everything."

Rama ducked behind Jalpa. She went out on to the veranda and said, "Come over, Oh Jeweller! Did you come here to rob us, or to sell us things?"

Charandas came up to the veranda and said, "What is your order, Mistress?"

Jalpa said, "Do you come to sell or to rob? You are asking seven hundred for this necklace?"

Charandas, "Huzur, it cost seven hundred just to have it made."

Jalpa, "So, take it and give to someone who wants to shower seven hundred on it. You are demanding one hundred and fifty for the earrings. Is this robbery? Will you take seven hundred for both?"

Charandas said, "Bahuji, you're seeking an unfair bargain. Where is eight hundred and fifty and where, seven hundred?"

Jalpa said, "As you wish. You may take your things back."

Charandas said, "You want me to take back my things from your magnificent court? You may keep them just like that. If it were only a matter of just five or ten rupees, then I wouldn't have refused you. I'm not lying to you, Bahuji, there is very little profit in these things. And, that very small profit is consumed in shop rent, bad debt, dues and commissions. Now understanding this so that I also get four paise profit, give me your final price. This early in the morning, don't let me return empty handed."

Jalpa said, "I have told you. Seven hundred only."

Charandas made a face, giving the impression that he was caught in a dilemma, and then said, "Sir, it is certainly a loss for me, yet I am unable to refuse you. When shall I get the money?"

Jalpa said, "You will get it very soon."

Going inside, Jalpa said, "After all, he did give it to me for seven hundred, didn't he? He was trying to rob one hundred and fifty rupees. I am regretting why I didn't lessen it some more? That's how these people overcharge their customers."

Rama was anxious about the possibility of bearing such a heavy burden, but the situation had suddenly turned so that the burden had fallen on him, willy-nilly.

An excited and delighted Jalpa had taken both ornaments upstairs, but Rama remained standing, head bent, worrying about the heavy debt. 'When she knew his situation, why hadn't she spurned those things? Why hadn't she said forcefully that she won't take them? Why had she been so indecisive? It was going to be hard enough to pay off five hundred and fifty rupees he already owed; where was so much more going to come from? The fault was really his. He should have driven the agent away from the door,' these thoughts flashed through his mind.

However, he reasoned with his mind, 'This was atonement for his sins. Then, men earn for this reason only. We are not exactly starving for rotis.'

When Rama went upstairs to change his clothes after eating, Jalpa was standing in front of the mirror wearing the earrings. As soon as she saw him she said, "When I got up this morning, seeing the face of someone good must have brought me this fortune. I got two things free."

Rama was astonished and asked, "Free! How come? We won't have to pay for these?"

Jalpa said, "Mother is paying, isn't she?"

Rama queried, "Did she say anything about this?"

Jalpa said, "She has given them as a gift to me, who else would pay for them?"

Rama smiling at her simplicity, said, "This is what you thought when you took these things? If Amma was going to give these things to you, she'd have given it just after your jewellery was stolen. Didn't she have money then?"

Jalpa felt caught in a dilemma and said, “So how would I know this? You can still give them back now. Just say that the person you got them for didn't like them.”

As she said this, she immediately took off the earrings and the bracelet, too and, putting both things in their cases, offered them to Rama in the same way as a cat plays with a mouse. Even while letting go of it, she never lets it out of her grasp. She did not have the courage to stretch out her hands. Was her heart not in the same condition? Her face was turning pale. Why was she looking at the ground instead of Rama? Why was she not lifting her face? Where was the heartfelt joy that comes from escaping some great misfortune? Her emotional state was exactly like that of a mother who was consenting to letting her child go abroad – the same helplessness, distress and tenderness were appearing on Jalpa's face.

Rama did not have that firm self-control, which was necessary to take the cases from her hands. He was ready to bear everything – to endure the worrying demands for payment, to be humiliated, to hide his face, to burn up with worry. However, he was not ready to do anything which would break Jalpa's heart, or that which would make her feel wretched. All his knowledge, all his impulses, all his conscience opposed giving her such a shock. In the struggle between love and the force of circumstances, love, ultimately, was more powerful.

He smiled and said, “Let it be. Now that we have got them so why return them? Mother would laugh at us, too.”

With feigned trembling in her voice, Jalpa said, “Don't stretch yourself beyond your means. What's the need to take on a new trouble?”

Rama sounded as if were drowning, when he replied, “God is the master,” and immediately went downstairs.

How we destroy the happiness and tranquility of our lives through momentary embarrassment and allurements! If Jalpa had been able to steady herself against the gusts of her cravings; if Rama had not yielded to his hesitation; if both had the pure light of love in their hearts, then they wouldn't have strayed off their real path and headed towards their ruin.

It was eleven o'clock. Rama was getting late for office, but he was walking as if he were just returning from the last rites of a dear friend.

15

Jalpa was no longer a solitary young woman who hid her face, feeling sad. Now she did not like to sit at home. Till this day, she had been helpless, unable to move freely. Now God had also graced her with ornaments. Then why should she suppress her desire and remain sitting at home? After all, ornaments were not like sweets that should be eaten alone? What was the advantage in keeping the ornaments in a closed box? If invited by anybody in the neighbourhood, she would certainly go with her mother-in-law. Then, after a few days, she felt no need for her mother-in-law's company to visit anywhere – she started going alone. She was also not restrained because of housework and related duties. Her beauty and charm, her attire, her courtesy and conduct, very soon gave her a place of honour among the woman in the neighbourhood. Without her, their gatherings were empty. Her voice was so soft, her speech so sweet, her grace so incomparable, that she seemed to be the queen of the group. Her arrival would breathe new life into the lives of the women of the neighbourhood. Everyday there was a gathering somewhere or the other. An hour or two of singing or dancing or gossiping had become popular entertainment among the young ladies. This gathering took place in turns, in someone's house; this singing and dancing went on for fifteen days continuously, in the month of March. Jalpa's heart was as generous as she was beautiful. She usually paid for the *paan.* Sometimes singers were called to perform and the burden of their care also fell on her. Sometimes she went with the women to bathe in the Ganges, and the cost of the *tonga* and refreshments at the river bank would also fall on her. Thus, two or three rupees were spent daily by her. Rama was an ideal husband. If Jalpa were to ask, he would have sacrificed his life at her feet, so really, how much did money matter then? He longed to see her face. Jalpa talked about these gatherings everyday – how much she was honoured and respected in the ladies' circles. It gave him immense pleasure. One day, this group of ladies felt compelled to go to the cinema. Each one of them was entranced by the delights they experienced there. Now they went to watch a film every second day. Rama, till now, had not been fond of the cinema. Even if he had been, what could he have done? Now, he was getting money and Jalpa wanted him to watch films with her, then why would he not go? There were lots of young women at the cinema hall, who were not in the least embarrassed to talk and laugh openly without covering their faces. Their freedom was secretly beginning to work its magic on Jalpa, too. As soon as she left home, she would uncover her face, but in the cinema hall, out of embarrassment, she would sit in the section meant for the veiled women. How she wished that Rama, too, would sit with her! 'After all, how was she inferior to those fashionable ladies? Her face and complexion were no disgrace to her. She was as well dressed as anyone else. She was competent in speech, too. So why should she sit with veiled women?' she thought. Even though Rama was not highly educated, yet the influence of place and time had made him broadminded.

Previously, he so strongly believed that women should be veiled, outside their houses, that when he took his mother to bathe in the Ganges, he would not even let her talk to the Brahmin *pandas*. If his mother's laughter was heard in the men's section of the house, he would tell her angrily, "You have no sense of shame, Mother! People are sitting out there and you are laughing over here!" His mother would then be ashamed. As he grew older, this attitude of his gradually disappeared. Added to this, Jalpa's beauty emboldened him further. If Jalpa had been devoid of beauty, coal-black or boorish, he would have forced her to remain behind the veil. He would have been ashamed to be seen sitting or strolling with her. To go out with a matchless beauty like Jalpa gave him pleasure and pride. No other woman in the entire society in which they moved could equal Jalpa in features, figure, or dress. Despite being a girl from the village, she had taken to the ways of the city as if she had been born there. Her English was poor, but here too, Rama stood in to fill that deficiency.

How could he break this tradition of veils? There were so many friends, so many acquaintances of his to be seen sitting in the cinema hall. How they would laugh on seeing him sitting with Jalpa. At last, one day he decided to openly challenge this society. He said to Jalpa, "Today you and I will sit together in the cinema hall."

Jalpa's heart began to throb and her face glowed with delight. She said, "Really? Oh no! My friends won't stop teasing me."

Ramanath said, "Nothing will ever come of being afraid like this. What kind of farce is it that women have to hide their faces and sit behind screens?"

Thus the matter was settled. On the first day they both shrank with embarrassment, but from the second day onwards, their courage blossomed. A time came, when, after a few days, Rama and Jalpa could be seen strolling together in the park in the evening.

Jalpa smiled and said, "If your father should see us . . . then what will happen?"

Rama retorted, "Then what? Nothing!"

Jalpa said, "But I'd just sink into the ground with shame!"

Rama said, "I'd be embarrassed too, but Father won't come here!"

Jalpa said, "And if your mother should see us?"

Rama said, "Who is afraid of Mother? I'd set her straight with a few chosen words."

Within five to ten days, Jalpa had made an impression on her new circle of friends. She entered in to this society much as some skilled orator first comes on to the stage before an assembly. Even learned people, in spite of their wish to belittle him, bow their heads before his grace. Jalpa too 'came, saw and conquered'. Her beauty had that dignity, austerity, splendour and brilliance that are the hallmarks of women of good descent. On the very first day, one woman gave Jalpa an invitation to tea, which she was unable to refuse, even though she had no desire to go.

When both of them returned from the function, Rama said in a worried voice, "So we'll have to go to her tea party tomorrow?"

Jalpa said, "What could I do? I could not think of how to refuse her."

Ramanath said, "So should I bring a nice sari for you tomorrow morning?"

Jalpa said, "Why? Don't I already have saris? What is use of spending fifty to sixty rupees for such a small occasion!"

Ramanath said, "You don't have any really nice saris. Did you see her sari? I will bring one just like that for you."

Expressing helplessness, Jalpa said, "I ought to have clearly told her that we had no time."

Ramanath said, "And then we'll have to invite them over, too?"

Jalpa said, "What a lot of trouble we have got entangled in."

Ramanath said, "It is no trouble at all. I was just thinking that my house is not suitable for this. I'll borrow a table, some chairs, and a tea set from Ramesh, but what can I do about the house?"

Jalpa said, "Is it necessary that we should invite her?"

Rama gave no reply to such a mean remark. He now began to think about a new pair of shoes and a beautiful wristwatch for Jalpa. He had no money. His expenses were increasing day by day. Till now, he had not been able to pay off a single paisa to the jewellers. Once Gangu Maharaj had even indicated that a payment was due. However, it could not happen that Jalpa would attend a tea party in old, worn out clothes. No, he could be unfair to her. On this occasion, the impression of her beauty and glamour would be ruined. Everyone would be wearing their glittering saris. There would be no shortage of inlaid bracelets and pearl necklaces, but Jalpa, even plainly dressed, was miles ahead of them. None of them come up to the mark when compared to her. He thought that his beautiful wife was the fruit of his good deeds in his previous life. After all, these were the days for dining well, dressing well and enjoying life. If one did not enjoy oneself in one's youth, what would one do in one's old age? Even if one had wealth and respect in old age, what would it matter? After one's youth has passed, what is the point of marriage? He became obsessed with bringing the sari and wristwatch. He somehow kept his patience through the night, but the next day he did not rest until he had brought them.

Jalpa said, in an irritated tone, "I had told you that I don't need these things. They won't have cost less than a hundred and fifty?"

Ramanath replied, "A hundred and fifty! I am not that much of a spendthrift."

Jalpa said, "These things cannot be less than a hundred and fifty!"

Jalpa wore the watch on her wrist and unfolded the sari and was spellbound.

Ramanath said, "How beautiful the watch looks on your wrist! I have got my money's worth!"

Jalpa said, "Tell me the truth. How much did these things cost?"

Ramanath said, "Shall I tell you the truth? I have spent a total of one hundred and thirty five only – seventy five rupees for the *sari*, ten for the shoes and fifty for the watch."

Jalpa said, "It is around hundred and fifty. I didn't tell you an incorrect figure. But, how will you pay this big amount? That witch invited me, uselessly. Now, I will stop going outside."

Rama was also undergoing similar anxiety, but he did not want to dampen Jalpa's happiness by displaying his feelings. He said, "It'll all be paid off."

Jalpa asked, sarcastically, "May I also know where the money is going to come from? We are not saving a paisa, so where will it be paid from? Right now, Father is managing the home expenses, otherwise we would felt the pinch. Do you think I die for ornaments and saris? Go and return these things."

Rama looked at her lovingly and said, "Keep these things. I won't bring anything else, without asking you first."

That evening when Jalpa put on the new sari and shoes, strapped the watch on to her wrist, and looked at reflection in the mirror, her lovely face was radiant with pride and joy. She might have been sincere when she had earlier told Rama to take the things back, but just now, she was not prepared to make such a sacrifice. In the evening, Jalpa and Rama set out walking towards the cantonment. The woman had only given the number of her bungalow. It was easily located. At the gate of bungalow, the signboard read *Indu Bhushan. Advocate. High Court.* Now Rama came to know that this lady was the wife of Pandit Indu Bhushan, a renowned advocate of Kashi. Rama had seen him many times, but how would he have had the good fortune to make the acquaintance of such an important man? Six months ago, he could not have dreamed of one day having the honour of being invited to his house, but thanks to Jalpa, the impossible had happened today. He was the guest of Kashi's most important advocate.

Rama had thought that many people would be present there as invitees, but nobody else was there besides Vakil Sahab and his wife, Ratan. As soon as she saw them, she came out to the veranda, shook hands with them and took them inside and introduced them to her husband. Panditji shook hands with both guests without getting up from his armchair, smiled and said, "Excuse me, Babu Sahab, my health is not good. Are you working in some office here?"

Feeling embarrassed, Rama said, "Yes, Sir! I'm in the Municipal office. I have recently joined this office. I was thinking about studying law, but looking at what the junior lawyers were going through here, I lost my courage."

Rama did not think it improper to lie just a wee bit to inflate his own importance. Its effect was, naturally, very good. Had he directly said that he was a clerk, earning only twenty-five rupees a month, Vakil Sahab might have felt insulted in even talking to him. Panditji said, "You did well by not going this way. There you'll reach a good position after four to five years, while here, it is quite possible that you may not get even a single case for ten years."

Jalpa was still uncertain whether Ratan was Vakil Sahab's wife or daughter. Vakil Sahab's age was not less than sixty years. The smooth crown of his head gleamed like polished wood amid the surrounding white hairs. His moustache was immaculate, but the furrows on his brow and wrinkles on his cheeks told of a traveller who was weary of life's journey. As he lay on the armchair, he looked as if he had been unwell for years. His fair complexion had not faded even after having faced sixty years of sun and rain. He had a high nose and forehead and quite large, arrogant eyes. From his face it was evident that he did not like either talking to others or answering questions. Ratan, on the contrary, was a dark-complexioned, well-built young woman, warm, sociable and without a trace of pride. Her appearance had no feature that spoke of beauty; her nose was flat, her face, round and her eyes, small; nevertheless, she looked like a queen. Next to her, Jalpa seemed like a blossom of jasmine near a sunflower.

Tea was brought. Dried fruits, fresh fruits, sweets, ice-cream; everything was tastefully arranged on the tables. Ratan and Jalpa sat at one table; the other was for Rama and Vakil Sahab. Rama went and sat down, but Vakil Sahab was still sitting in the armchair.

Rama smiled and said to Vakil Sahab, "Please, won't you come, too?"

Vakil Sahab, still lying down, smiled and said, "You go ahead, please. I'll be there soon."

They had tea, ate fruits, but Rama and Jalpa both hesitated to laugh and speak in front of Vakil Sahab. Old people, who are full of life make enjoyable company, but, people who are cold and lifeless even when young, turn others into corpses. After much insistence, Vakil Sahab took two sips of tea. Sitting at a distance, he watched the drama. Thus, when Ratan said to Jalpa, "Come on, let us walk in the garden and let these two gentlemen critically discus society and morality," then Jalpa felt as if a noose had been removed from around her neck. Rama, like a caged bird, watched them leave the room and heaved a deep sigh. If he had known that this calamity was going to fall on his head here, he would not have even spoken of coming.

Vakil Sahab, screwing up his face, turned his side, and said, "I cannot say what has happened to my stomach. I can't digest anything. Even milk does not get digested. I don't know why people are so fond of taking tea, I fear even at looking at it. As soon as I drink tea, I feel spasms in my body and there are shooting sensations in my eyes."

Rama said, "You haven't taken any medicine for digestion?"

Expressing aversion, Vakil Sahab said, "I don't have the slightest faith in medicines. You won't find anyone with less sense than the *vaidyas* and doctors in this world. None of them has any capacity for diagnosis. The diagnosis of two *vaidyas* or two doctors will never agree. Symptoms would be same, but one will say it is deficiency in blood, the other as problems in the bile. One doctor says it is inflammation in lungs, another one says it is a problem of the stomach. There you have it! The treatment is based on guesswork and patients are slaughtered mercilessly. These doctors would have sent me to hell by now, but I have escaped their clutches. I have heard a lot about practice of yoga, but haven't met any practitioner as yet, from whom I could learn. I am afraid that more harm than good will come from doing anything on the basis of books alone."

While Vakil Sahab and Rama were engaged in denying the efficacy of medical science, the two women were engaged in discussing deeply felt love.

Ratan said, smiling, "You must have felt surprised to see my husband."

Jalpa was not only surprised, but also confused. She said, "It must be Vakil Sahab's second marriage."

Ratan said, "Yes. We have been married for five years now. His first wife died thirty-five years ago. Then he was only twenty-five year old. People urged him to marry again, but he had a son and refused to remarry. He lived alone for thirty years, but when his only son died in his prime, five years ago, it became necessary for him to remarry. I had lost my father as well as mother. My maternal uncle brought me up. I don't know whether my guardian took something from him or was captivated by his goodness. I think, it was all God's wish, but since the time I have come here I am becoming fatter, day by day. Doctors say I won't bear a baby. Sister, though I have no desire for bearing a baby, but my husband feels sad for me. I am the cause of all his illness. If God were to give me a baby today, all his illness would disappear in a trice. How much I like to become slim. I bathe in a tub of hot water, go for a walk daily. I drink very little milk, eat little ghee and only half of what I used to, and work as hard as I can. I am still getting fatter day by day. I simply don't understand it all. What should I do!"

Jalpa said, "Vakil Sahab must be getting annoyed with you?"

Ratan said, "No, Sister, not at all. He has never mentioned it to me even by mistake. He has never uttered a single word which would show his distress, but I know this worry is killing him. I am helpless to do anything. What can I do? I can spend whatever I like, I may live howsoever I wish – he never objects. Whatsoever he earns, he brings it and puts it in my hand. I tell him that there is now no need to practice law, why not take rest at home? But he cannot sit around at home. He eats only two *chapatti*s and if I insist, he eats a few grapes. I really feel sorry for him, and take care of him as much as I can. After all, he is ruining his life over me."

Jalpa said, "A man like this deserves to be revered like God. Here, as soon one wife dies, the second marriage takes place. Very few have the capacity to live alone for thirty years."

Ratan said, "Yes, Sister, he is God-like. Even today when somebody mentions his first wife, be begins to weep. I will show you her photograph. He is as soft-hearted inside, as he appears to be stern outside. He gives monthly payments to a number of orphans, widows and poor. By the way, your bracelet looks very pretty."

Jalpa said, "O yes! A very good craftsman has made it."

Ratan said, "I have no acquaintances over here. I don't want to trouble Vakil Sahab about jewellery. I'm afraid to have anything made by an ordinary goldsmith. Who knows what they might mix with the gold. All the jewellery of my husband's first wife are kept, but none of them appeal to me. Get Babu Ramanath to have a pair of bracelets just like yours made for me."

Jalpa said, "Let's see. I will ask him."

Ratan said, "Your coming here today has made me very happy. I remain alone here all day. I feel very anxious. Who should I visit? I am not acquainted with anybody nor do I feel like making friends with just anybody. I invited a couple of women over and even visited their homes. I thought we could be sisterly, but when I came to know how they thought and behaved, it seemed better to stay far away. They both wanted to fool me and rob me. They borrowed some money from me and are still paying it back. It makes me ashamed to say how much they loved all kinds of finery. You must come here for an hour or so every day, Sister."

Jalpa said, "Yes, what could be nicer than this?"

Ratan said, "I will send the car for you."

Jalpa said, "What is the need? *Tonga*s are easily available."

Ratan said, "I don't know why I don't feel like letting you go. Ramanathji must be feeling lucky to have got you."

Jalpa smiled and said, "He does not feel lucky any way. Rather, he keeps scolding me."

Ratan said, "Really? I don't believe it. Look, here he comes. Just ask him whether he would get another bracelet like this made for me."

Jalpa turned to Rama and said, "If we ask Charandas to make one more bracelet just like this, how much time will he take? Ratan wants to get a bracelet just like this, made for herself."

Rama replied immediately, "Yes, of course! He could have it made. He can make it even better than this."

Ratan said, "How much did he charge for this one?"

Jalpa said, "Eight hundred rupees."

Ratan said, "The price does not matter, but it must be exactly like this. An exact copy."

Ramamath said, "Yes, yes! I'll have it made."

Ratan said, "But, Brother, I don't have the money right now."

A man cannot say anything in the matter of money in front of women. Can he say that he does not have any money just now? He will die before making such an excuse. He will get into debt, he will flatter others, but he will never reveal his helplessness to a woman. He considers it contemptible to even mention money. Jalpa knew very well about her husbands' financial condition. However, if Rama had made some excuse just then, she would have found it very offensive. She was inwardly afraid of her husband saying that he would have to ask the jeweller first. Her heart was thudding, but Rama bravely said, "Yes, yes, don't worry about money. Pay me whenever you like." Jalpa was very pleased.

Ratan said, "So when should I hope to get it?"

Ramanath said, "I'll ask the jeweller today itself. Even then, it shall certainly take fifteen days."

Jalpa said, "Please come and have tea with us at our home this Sunday."

Ratan happily accepted the invitation, and both Rama and Jalpa took their leave. When they reached home, it was evening and Ramesh Babu was waiting there. Jalpa got down from the *tonga* and went straight inside the home. Rama went up to Ramesh Babu and asked, "Have you been waiting for me for a long time?"

Ramesh said, "No, I have just arrived. Are you coming from Vakil Sahab's residence?"

Rama said, "Yes. I am now poorer by three rupees."

Ramesh said, "Don't worry, you will soon recover it. It is not a bad thing to get acquainted with prominent people. Some important work might result from it. Invite them over one day."

Rama said, "We have invited them for tea this coming Sunday."

Ramesh said, "If you say, I'll also be here. Do you know one of Vakil Sahab's brothers is an engineer? One of my brothers-in-law is sitting around unemployed for a long time. If Vakil Sahab were to give him a recommendation, the poor fellow would get a place of gain. Just introduce me and I'll do all the rest. The party shall be so well arranged, by God's grace, that Memsahib will be very glad. I'll bring a tea set, painted glass flower vases, and lamps. Leave the tables and chairs, the flooring – everything to me. No need for coolies or labourers; my brother-in-law will be pleased to do the job."

Ramanath said, "Then it will be fun, otherwise I was greatly worried."

Ramesh said, "You don't worry at all. I will put the boy on the job. I'll tell him if he wants a place, he will have to look after the arrangements. Then you'll see how much he scurries around."

Ramanath said, "Didn't you arrange for a job for your brother-in-law, just two or three months ago?"

Ramesh said, "O yes! But there are six more left. There are seven in all. Let us sit down to prepare a list of important things. There will be a lot of running around to do today onwards, only then we will get everything together. How many more guests will be there?"

Ramanath said, "Memsahib will be here and perhaps, Vakil Sahab will also come."

Ramesh said, "That's good. If there are many people, there happens to be a lot of commotion. We have to focus on Memsahib. What is use of paying attention to useless people?"

Both men prepared the list. Ramesh Babu started gathering things from the very next day. He had access to many distinguished families, so he was able to get nice decorative items for the house, and the house shone. Dayanath, too, took part in these preparations. His task was to decorate the house in proper style. The three of them would argue for hours over issues like where which flower pot should be placed, where which picture should be hung or where which carpet should be spread. The three of them were fully absorbed in this task before leaving for office and after coming from office. One day the question over where a mirror ought to be put in one of the rooms, turned into an argument. Dayanath argued that this room did not need a mirror – it should be put in the rear room, instead. Ramesh opposed him. Rama stood by uncertainly, agreeing with neither of them.

Dayanath spoke, "I have seen hundreds of English men's drawing rooms, but there was no mirror in it. The mirror is really placed in the dressing room. Putting the mirror in this place makes no sense."

Ramesh said, "Though I haven't had the chance to look into hundreds of such Englishmen's rooms, but I have certainly seen three or four, and they all had a mirror. And then, is it necessary for us to copy the Englishmen in these very little things? We are not English, we are Indians. Well-to-do Indians place full length mirrors in their rooms. Here, you are talking like our spoilt babus, who take pride in copying the English in their clothes, decoration of their rooms, speech, tea and drinks and use of china tea cups. However, they have not been touched in the least by those things which have made English the English, and because of which they rule the world. Do you also harbour a fondness to become an Englishman in your old age?"

Dayanath also considered it very wrong to copy the English. He was also displeased with the tea party that was being organised. If he felt some satisfaction, it lay in the fact that this event would bring acquaintance with some distinguished persons. He had never worn a coat throughout his life. Though he drank tea, yet he would not use a china teas set. He did not object to drinking tea from anything – a *katora* or *katori*, a glass, a *lota* or a *tasla*. However, just now he was bent on seeing his side of the argument through. "Well-to-do Indians don't have tables and chairs in their rooms," he said. "They use the floor. When you placed tables and chairs in the room, you did things in the English style. But now, when it comes to the mirror, you're giving an Indian example. Keep it either Indian or English. As it is now, it's half quail and half partridge! It doesn't look good to wear a coat and pant along with an old-fashioned four-cornered hat!"

Ramesh had thought that Dayanath would be rendered speechless, but when he heard his reply his head reeled; victory was slipping from his grasp. "So you've never seen a mirror in an Englishman's room then?" he said. "Could you tell us the names of even five or ten such Englishmen? Besides that *Kiranta* head clerk of yours, you probably haven't even set foot in any Englishman's room. You consider this Christian an ideal example of those with a fancy for English ways? Very good, indeed! I must say!"

Dayanath said, "That's your language. Call him whatever you like – *Kiranta*, *Chamareshiyan*, or worm, but aside from his colour, he doesn't fall short of the English in any way. And before him, there was a European."

Ramesh was thinking of a reply to this when a motorcar pulled up at the door. Ratan bai got out and came on to the veranda! The three men came outside quickly. Rama found Ratan's coming at this time very disagreeable. He was afraid that she might come into the room and his pretence would be disclosed. He stepped forward, shook her hand, and said, "Please come this way. This is my father, and this is my friend Ramesh Babu." These two men, however, neither stretched out their hands nor stirred from the spot, but stood there rather discomfited. Neither did Ratan think it necessary to shake hands with them. She greeted them from a distance with a *namaskar* and said to Rama, "No, I won't sit down. I don't have any time right now. I need to speak to you."

She and Rama reached the motorcar, and she said in low voice, "You've told the jeweller, haven't you?"

Rama replied without hesitation, "Yes, he's making it."

"The other day I said that I couldn't give you anything just then, but I thought that it might be a bother for you, so I asked for some money. You need eight hundred, don't you?"

Jalpa had said that her bracelet had cost eight hundred. If Rama wished he could take that much. Ratan's simplicity and trust stopped him. He could not betray the confidence of such a generous, guileless young woman. He did not hesitate at all in taking three or four *anna*s from each businessman. He knew that all of them, too, hoodwinked their customers, and his conscience did not have the slightest twinge when he acted this way. To act treacherously towards this goddess would have required a hardened old sinner. Hesitating a little, he said, "Did Jalpa say the bracelet cost eight hundred? Perhaps, she didn't remember. Her bracelet was for six hundred. I can have one made for eight hundred, if you like."

"No," said Ratan. "I'd like one just like hers. Have one made for six hundred, please."

She took her bag out from the motorcar and took out six one hundred rupee notes. "There was no need to hurry," said Rama, "we could have settled when the bracelet was ready."

Ratan, "When I have money, it gets spent. That's why I thought I'd give it to you. My habit is to do whatever I want to as fast as possible. I get annoyed by delays."

She got into the car, and it vanished like the wind. When Rama went inside to put the money into a trunk, the two old men began to talk.

"Did you see that?" said Ramesh.

"Yes," said Dayanath. "My eyes were open. Now this breeze is blowing through my house, too. God save us!"

Ramesh said, "That's just the way it is, but these days, women like her are useful. If necessary, at least, they can help. If you get sick, they can send for the doctor. As for us, even if we should be dying, dare our wives set foot outside the house!"

Dayanath said. "I can't stand to see these western ways, Brother. But what can I do? I'm fond of my children, but sometimes I want to tell Rama straight out to go live somewhere else. But that would be like tearing out an eye to get rid of the pain. I get angry with husbands who spoil their wives like this. You'll see that woman will deceive Vakil Sahab one of these days."

"I don't agree with you there, my dear Sir," said Ramesh. "Why do you believe that a woman who comes and goes freely is bound to be frivolous? She thinks a great deal of Rama, though. Who knows why she gave him that money?"

Dayanath replied, "It seems to me there's something fishy here. Rama's not playing a trick on her, is he?"

Just then Rama came out and overheard the last sentence. He scowled and said, 'Yes Sir, I'm certainly tricking her. I'm deceiving her and extorting money from her. After all, that's my profession!"

"Why are you getting so annoyed?" said an embarrassed Dayanath. "I didn't say anything out of the ordinary."

Rama said, "You've as good as made me into a first-class forger. What else did you mean? Why did such a suspicion enter your mind? What did you seen in me that gave rise to such an idea? Besides the fact that I dress a little nattily and move with the times, what other bad quality did you see? Whatever I spend, I earn honestly. If the time comes when I have to lie and cheat, I'll take poison and die. Yes, it's true that some people have good sense about spending, and some don't. I have that good sense. If you consider this some kind of fraud, it's your privilege. When you've become so mistrustful of me, I might as well blacken my face and leave the house. Ramesh Babu is present here. You can ask him whatever you think about me. He won't lie out of any consideration for me."

Rama's statements sounded truthful enough to reassure Dayanath. He said, 'The day I find out that you have adopted this practice, I'll blacken my face and leave. I won't deny that when I saw your increasing expenditure, I had my doubts. But I'm content to hear you say that your intentions are pure. I just want that even if my boy remains poor, his intentions should always be pure. I pray to God to keep you on the right path."

"Well, this little story has come to an end," said Ramesh, smiling. "Now tell me, why did she give you money? I was counting. There were six notes, maybe hundred rupee ones."

"I cheated her," said Rama.

'If you play games with me, I'll thrash you. And if you've swindled her out of anything, I'll still pat your back and bless you. Swindle away, but don't let your reputation be harmed. Don't let anyone hear of it. I'm not afraid of God. I will answer whatever he asks of me. But I am afraid of people. Tell the truth, what did she give you the money for? If you're getting some kind of commission, then include me in it."

Rama said, “She asked me to get an inlaid bracelet made for her.”

Ramesh said, “Let’s go. I know a good jeweller. You’ve taken on a useless burden. You don’t know what women are like. They don’t trust anybody. If you spend three or four rupees of your own, they’ll think you’re robbing them. Yes, maybe you’ll add to your good reputation, but a bad reputation is standing hard by.”

“You’re repeating what foolish women say,” said Rama. “Educated women aren’t like that.”

After a little while Rama went inside and said to Jalpa, “Your friend Ratan came by.”

Jalpa said, “Really? Then things must have gone very wrong. Nothing was ready here.”

Rama said, “It’s lucky she didn’t come inside. She came to give me some money for the bracelet. You probably told her eight hundred. I took six hundred.”

“But I was only joking,’ said Jalpa, embarrassed.

In this way, she absolved herself from any blame, but her mind was in turmoil for a long time. If Rama had taken eight hundred instead, perhaps this turmoil would not have occurred. She was glad for her success, but Rama’s prudence had awakened her moral scruples. She was regretting her needless lies and thinking what a low opinion Rama must have of her, and how dishonourable Ratan must consider her to be, too.

16

Nothing special happened at the tea party. Ratan came with a sister, who was a distant relative, but Vakil Sahab did not come. Dayanath considered it quite appropriate to withdraw from the house for the duration of the party. Ramesh Babu stood on the veranda throughout, but although Rama entreated him several times to join the party, he could not summon the courage.

Jalpa introduced both guests to her mother-in-law. The young women struck her as rather frivolous. Their running all over the house, clattering up to the topmost room, jumping up and down here and there on the terrace, and laughing uproariously; all of it seemed wild and improper to her. According to her rules, daughters and daughters-in-law ought to be serious and bashful. What was particularly surprising was that even Jalpa joined in. Ratan did not even mention the bracelet today.

Rama had not found the time to visit Gangu's shop as he had been consumed with the party preparations. He thought that if he were to give six hundred to Gangu, it would be deducted from the previous account, and only two hundred and fifty would be left. With a credit of six hundred in the new account, only eight hundred and fifty would still be owed. This approach would give him an excellent opportunity to bolster his credit.

The next day, a happy Rama arrived at Gangu's shop and said in a commanding manner, "How are things, Maharaj? Anything new being made here?"

Gangu was so fed up with Rama's stalling that even the prospect of receiving some money did not please him. "How many things we've made and sold, Sahab!" he said in a complaining tone. "You've left coming here. We don't carry on business in this way. Eight months have gone by, and I haven't received a paisa from you."

"Brother, I am ashamed to come empty-handed to your shop. I'm not one of the people whom you have to pester to pay their debts. Enter this six hundred rupees against my account today and get a nice bracelet ready."

Gangu took the six hundred, put it into his money chest, and said, 'It'll be made. When will I get the rest of the money?'

"Very soon."

"Yes, Babuji. Pay off the previous bill."

Gangu promised to have the bracelet made very quickly, but having struck a bargain with Rama once before, he had learned that he would not collect his money quickly. The result was that Rama plagued him every day, and Gangu, with one excuse or other, made him wait. Sometimes the craftsman would fall sick, or sometimes he would go to arrange medical treatment for his wife at his in-laws, or sometimes his sons would become ill. One month passed and the bracelet had not been made. Rama stopped going to the park for fear of Ratan's insistent inquiries, but she had seen his house, and during that month she came several times to ask about it. At last, one day in July she said to him, "If that pig is not going to make it, then why don't you give it to some other jeweller?"

Rama said, "That rogue has misled me so badly that I don't even want to talk about it. Every day he says it will be ready today. I made a big mistake when I gave him an advance. It'll be hard to pry it out of him now."

Ratan said, "Just show me his shop, and I'll collect it from his father, plus the cost of damages separately. We ought to turn such a crook over to the police."

"Yes, what else?" said Jalpa. "All these goldsmiths delay, but not like this. Gulping down your money and making you run back and forth for something for months."

Rama, while scratching his head, said, "If you'll just be patient for ten more days, I'll get the money from him today and give it to some other jeweller."

"Why don't you show me this scoundrel's shop?" said Ratan. "I'll let my whip do the talking."

Rama said, "I'm telling you, you'll get your bracelet within ten days."

"You're stalling yourself. You must have fallen for his flattery. If you'd been harsh with him just once, would he have had the nerve to try this trickery?" said Ratan.

Finally, with great reluctance, Ratan took her leave. That same evening, Gangu gave an unequivocal answer to Rama's pleas. "Without half the money in advance, the bracelet will not be made, and in addition, the previous account has to be completely cleared."

Rama felt as though he had been shot. "But Maharaj," he said, 'that's no way for a gentleman to behave. It's something for a lady. She gave me an advance for it. Think about it, how can I face her? As for my money, have a promissory note written out in my name, and a stamp, too. What else will you do?'

Gangu said, "Am I supposed to put honey on the promissory note and lick it? Loans aren't given for eight months at a time. A month or two is plenty. You're a big shot. What's five or six hundred rupees to you? The bracelet is ready."

Through clenched teeth, Rama said, "If that was so, why didn't you tell me a month ago? Then I would have made arrangements for the money by now, wouldn't I!"

Gangu said, "How could I know that? You don't understand even this much."

Rama returned home, downcast. Even at this moment, if he made a clean breast of the whole affair to Jalpa, she would have taken off her bracelet and handed it over, no matter how much it would have grieved her. Rama did not have enough courage for this. He could not bring himself to deliver such a blow to her tender heart by telling her the true state of his financial difficulties.

There was no doubt that Rama, who received something over a hundred rupees monthly over and above his salary, could certainly have paid off at least half of what he owed the two jewellers in these eight months, if he had known how to practise economy. However, since his income was high, so were his expenses. Whatever he got was spent in outings and recreation, and the jewellers' money was held back in hopes of a one-time repayment. To make rupees out of cowries was the work of merchants. Clerical people make cowries out of rupees.

Later in the evening, Rama made the rounds of the jewellers once more. He badly wanted to talk another jeweller into giving jewellery on credit, but he did not succeed anywhere. News travels by wireless in the *bazar*.

Rama could not sleep the whole night. If someone had written him a note for a thousand and given him even five hundred that day, he would have been content, but trawling through his acquaintances, no such person came to mind. He had boasted and bragged to everyone in his circle, and wined and dined them, spending with an open hand. How could he now disclose his distress without losing face? He regretted having needlessly given the money to Gangu. Gangu was not going to bring charges against him. If some terrible illness had afflicted him just then, Rama would have welcomed it. At least he would have got a few days respite, but death does not come by invitation. It comes just when we are completely unprepared. By God's grace, let a telegram arrive from somewhere! He could not see any friend of his sending a false telegram to him. He was tossing and turning in the midst of these anxieties, when Jalpa's eyes opened. Rama quickly covered his face, as if he were in deep sleep. Jalpa slowly drew the sheet aside, and finding him asleep, began to gaze at him intently. She soon detected that he was awake and shook him gently and said, "Are you still awake?"

Rama said, "I don't know why I can't sleep. Lying here, I was thinking I should go away for a while to earn some money."

Jalpa said, "Will you take me along?"

Rama said, "Where all will I take you in my travels?"

"And I will live alone here! I won't stay a minute! But where will you go?"

"I have yet to decide."

Jalpa said, "So would you really go off, leaving me here? I won't be able to stay here a single day. I understand now, you don't love me. You only pretend to love me."

Rama said, "Your love keeps me tied to this place, otherwise I'd have gone by now."

Jalpa said, "You're just making it up. If you really cared for me, you wouldn't keep things from me. You're certainly thinking about something important and hiding it from me. I've noticed for several days that you're preoccupied with worry. Why don't you tell me? Where there's no trust, how can there be love?"

Rama said, "You're deceiving yourself, Jalpa. I've never kept anything from you."

Jalpa said, "So you really love me with all your heart?"

Rama said, "You will believe me when I tell you so?"

"Alright. I'm going to ask you a question now. Be on your guard. Why do you love me? Swear you'll tell me the truth."

"'You've asked a very strange and awkward question. If I were to ask you the same question, what would you say?"

"I know what I'd say."

"Tell me."

"You tell me. I'll tell you, too."

"I don't even know," said Rama. "I only know this – you are present in every single pore of my body."

Jalpa said, "Think before you speak. I know very well that I'm not an ideal wife. I haven't even come close to serving you as a wife should. Thanks to the grace of God, I haven't had to suffer any difficulties because of you. I don't know anything about housework. Whatever I learnt, I learnt here. Then, why should you love me? I'm not clever at making conversation, and I'm not that attractive, either. Do you know why I'm asking you this?'

Rama said, "How can I know? I don't understand a thing."

Jalpa said, "I'm asking so I can ensure you always love me."

Rama said, "I don't know anything, Jalpa, but I tell you truly. If you have any shortcomings or faults, I haven't noticed them yet. But what did you see in me? I'm not rich or educated or handsome. Tell me."

Jalpa said, "Shall I tell you? I'm captivated by your goodness. Why should I hide anything from you now? When I first came here, even though I considered you my husband, I still worried about whether or not you would be pleased by what I said or did. If I had married some other man, I would have behaved the same way with him, too. This is the customary relationship between husband and wife. But now I wouldn't exchange you with Krishna who loved the *gopis*! Even now, there's something concealed in your heart. You're still hiding something from me."

Rama said, "This is only your suspicion, Jalpa. I don't hide things from even my friends. And, you are the queen of my heart."

Jalpa said, "Look at me when you speak. It does not suit a man to lower his eyes." Once again, it came to Rama's mind that he should spill out all his troubles, but once again, false pride stopped his tongue.

Whenever Jalpa asked him whether or not he was paying off the jewellers, his regular reply was that he was paying them a little each month. Today, Rama's weakness aroused Jalpa's doubts. Wishing to dispel her doubts, after a little while she said, "The payment to the jewellers must be made by now?"

"There's just a little left now."

"How much is left. Do you keep a record?"

"Yes, why shouldn't I? It must be a little less than seven hundred."

"Why, that's the whole amount. You didn't use Ratan's money, did you?"

Rama had been inwardly trembling lest Jalpa suddenly ask that very question, and now she had finally asked it. Even then if Rama had gathered his courage, and confessed, his difficulties might have come to an end. Jalpa would certainly have been stunned for a moment. It is possible in a fit of anger and disappointment, a few harsh words would have escaped her lips, but then she would be calm again. By putting their heads together, they would have come up with some expedient solution. If Jalpa had revealed this secret to Ratan, she would have also agreed with them. Alas, woe is excessive self-esteem! When Rama heard Jalpa's question, he reacted as if she had given him a cruel blow. "Why would I use Ratan's money?" Rama said. "If I wanted to, I could bring three or four thousand worth of stuff today. Workmen always have a habit of delaying things. And goldsmiths can be so sour. That's all, nothing more. In ten days I'll either have her bracelet ready, or give back her money. But why do you have this doubt? How can I spend someone else's money for my own expenses?"

"It's nothing, I was just asking."

Jalpa soon went to sleep, but Rama went back to his tangle of difficulties. Where could he get the money from? If he told Ramesh Babu truthfully, he would arrange for him to borrow it from some moneylender. However, he would not be able to tell him under any circumstances. He lacked the courage.

Early in the morning he ate breakfast and set out for the office. Maybe some arrangement could be made there. Who would provide – he gave no thought to this matter. Just as a patient is satisfied by merely going to a *vaidya,* without no knowledge of whether he would get better or not, this was Rama's condition right now. There was nobody else, except a peon at the office. Rama opened up the register and began to tally the figures. For a few days, the totals were not given, but the Head Clerk had already signed. When Rama added it up, it came to two and a half thousand. All at once, he thought of something, 'Why not write two thousand in place of two and a half thousand? Who checks the receipt ledger?' Even if the theft was detected, he could always say his addition had been erroneous. However, he did not let this thought remain in his mind, for fear that his mind would be tempted, he traced over the pencilled figures with ink, put the register in the drawer, and started wandering to and fro.

Carts came by in ones and twos. The drivers saw that Babu Sahab was here today, and thought they could pay their tolls quickly and be off. For this favour, Rama took twice the usual commission, and the drivers paid it gladly, because it was market time. To wait until twelve or one o'clock for the toll house to give them clearance meant a loss of twenty-four hours. The market closed at ten or eleven o'clock, which would mean waiting until the next day. If prices dropped by even a half of a quarter rupee, there would be loss of many hundreds of rupees. So, why would they then object to the giving of five or ten rupees to avoid this?

Today, Rama learnt of this new fact. He thought, 'After all, I just sit around at home in the morning. If I were to come here instead, I might get five or ten rupees a day, and then this whole dispute would be settled in six months.' Even supposing this windfall did not occur every day, he would get five or ten, if not fifteen, on the average. If he were to get five in the morning, and that much again during the rest of the day, then he would be free of debt in five or six months. He opened the drawer and took out the register again. After thinking over these calculations, altering the accounts in the register did not seem terribly difficult. The new recruit who at first starts at the sound of a rifle, later does not panic at a shower of bullets.

Rama had closed the office and was about to go home and eat, when a peddler arrived with his cart. "I'll take the toll when I come back," said Rama. The peddler began to entreat him. He had something very urgent to do. In the end, the matter was settled for ten rupees. Rama took the toll, put the ten rupees in his pocket, and set off for home. He had received twenty-five rupees in only two or three hours. If the money averaged this amount for even a month, he would cross over the sharp edge. He was so happy that he did not go home to eat. Nor did he order anything from the *bazar*. He thought of one rupee that would be less if he spent it. Instead, he worked till the evening. He took four rupees more. As the lamps were being lit, he started for home. Much of the worry and despondency had lifted from his heart. If this fast pace lasted for ten days more, he would no longer feel the need to avoid meeting Ratan.

17

Nine days passed. Rama continued to go to the office in the morning and return home when the lamps were lit. Each day, he went with the hopes of entrapping some big game, but these hopes remained unfulfilled. Moreover, the sun of good fortune never shone again as it had on that first day. Nonetheless, he thought it no small credit to himself that he had earned a hundred rupees in nine days. He had not eaten a single paisa worth of *paan*. When Jalpa suggested going out several times, he made some excuse each time. Ah yes, but tomorrow was the last day. Tomorrow, when Ratan would ask for her bracelet, what answer would he give? He came home from the office and reflected on this, 'Wouldn't she agree to wait for one more month? If she'd keep quiet that long, then perhaps I'd be free of her debt.' He was confident that he could manage her into agreeing with his sweet talk. He decided that if she acted stubborn, he would tell her that the jeweller was not willing to return the money.

It was July, and darkness was setting in. Rama was thinking that he could go and play a few games with Ramesh Babu, but hesitated each time he saw the clouds. Just then, Ratan arrived. She was not pleased and her face looked hard set. She had come from home, ready to fight, and intended to throw courtesy and consideration to the winds.

"You've come at a good time," Jalpa said. "I'll go out with you today. These days, his workload doesn't even give him time to lift his head."

"I have to get back home right away today," said Ratan, harshly. "I've just come to remind Babuji of tomorrow."

Rama was inwardly scared at the sight of her displeased face. He wanted to please her any way he could. "Yes indeed," he answered readily, "I remember very well. I've just come from the jeweller's shop. I show up there every morning and evening for an hour, but those things take a lot of time. The price depends on the workmanship. If you look at the material quality, it's not much. Two men are working on it, but it probably won't be ready for at least another month. But it will be incomparable. You'll love it."

Ratan did not thaw even a little. "Fine," she said, flaring up, "it'll take a month more now, will it? This is such great workmanship that it wasn't finished in three months! Please tell him to give my money back. Goddesses might wear bracelets made out of expectations. I don't need them."

Rama said, "It won't take a month. I'll have it made in a hurry. I just said a month at a guess. There's only a little bit left to be done, now. It took several days to find the precious stones."

"I don't need to wear a bracelet, Brother. You just give me back my money, that's all. I've seen a lot of goldsmiths! Thanks to your kindness, I have three inlaid bracelets, but I've never seen such cheating anywhere.'

At the word 'cheating,' Rama got up, enraged. "It's not cheating. Call it my stupidity instead. What need did I have to put myself into such straits? I only gave the money you gave as advance to the jeweller to make him happy, so he'd work quickly. Now you're asking for your money. Well he can't give it back."

Ratan looking at him sharply, said, "Why won't he give back the money?'

"Because where is he going to sell the piece he made for you? It's possible he might sell it after six months or a year. Not everybody likes the same things."

Ratan scowled and said, "I don't know anything. He has delayed, so let him suffer. Either bring me my bracelet tomorrow or my money. If you're friends with the jeweller and can't say anything out of courtesy and consideration for him, then just show me his shop. Otherwise, if you're ashamed to do that, then tell me his name, and I'll find him. Wonderful! What a good joke! I'll have his shop auctioned. I'll get him sent to jail. You can't deal with these rogues without fighting."

Rama, shamefaced, stared at the ground. What an unlucky moment it had been when he had taken the money from Ratan! What disaster he had unexpectedly brought upon himself.

"That's right," said Jalpa. "Why don't you take her to the jeweller's shop? When she sees the thing with her own eyes, she'll be satisfied."

"I don't even want to take it now," said Ratan.

Trembling, Rama said, "Fine, you'll get your money tomorrow."

Ratan said, "What time?"

"I'll bring it when I come home from office."

"I'll take the whole amount. Don't try to stall by giving me only one or two hundred."

"Tomorrow you can take all your money," said Rama, and went into the gentelmen's room, where he wrote a note to Ramesh Babu. "Take this to Ramesh Babu," he told Gopi. "Bring back his answer."

Then he wrote another note and gave it to Vishvambhar to give to Manik Das and told him to return with an answer.

"It's raining," said Vishvambhar.

Rama snapped, "So, will the whole world be flooded? Run!"

Vishvambhar said, "And if I don't find him at home?"

Rama said, "You'll find him. He doesn't go anywhere at this time of day."

This was the first time in his life that Rama had asked a friend for a loan. He used all the blandishments and forceful entreaties that he could remember. It was an entirely new experience for him. He wondered, 'Will Ramesh Babu would make excuses, too? His income was large, his expenses small. If he wanted to, he could make arrangements for the money. Would he behave that kindly with me?' The two boys had not returned yet, and he started walking back and forth by the door. Ratan's car was still standing where she had left it. Just then she came out, even though she saw him there, she said nothing. She got into her car and drove off.

Where could those two boys have gone? They were probably playing somewhere, the little devils. Whatever Ramesh could give would be a windfall. He had asked for two hundred, to no purpose. Perhaps Ramesh did not have that much with him. He usually had little left after his in-laws snatched and clawed at his money. If Manik wanted to, he could give five hundred or a thousand, but he thought he ought to wait and see – this would test his friend today. He thought that if these people did not give him any money today, then he would not ask them anything. He was nobody's servant; why should he go running if they should summon him to play chess. If Rama heard the sound of footsteps, his heart would pound loudly. Finally, Vishvambhar returned. However, Manik had written: 'I am very short of money these days, and was just about to ask you for something myself.'

Rama tore up the note and threw it away. He fumed, 'That self-seeking fellow! If the Sub-Inspector had asked for it, he would seen the note and have taken the money and run to make a delivery.' Rama thought he could afford to wait. He would exact revenge when Manik's goods would require toll to be paid on them.

Just then Gopi returned. Ramesh had written: 'I've made three or four rules in my life and keep them with the greatest strictness. One of them is that I never lend or borrow money from friends. You don't have any experience of this yet, but you will after a while. If friends begin to borrow money, it doesn't take long for ill-will to appear. You are my dear friend. I don't want to make you my enemy, so please forgive me.'

Rama tore up and threw away this note, too. He sat in a chair and stared fixedly at the lamplight. It is doubtful whether he even saw the light. He would have perhaps gazed just as intently at the black, impenetrable cloud masses in the sky.

There is a state of the mind when the eyes are open and see nothing, and when the ears are intent and hear nothing.

18

Evening had come, and silence had spread throughout the compound of the Municipality Office. The office workers were leaving, one by one, and the sweepers were plying their brooms in the rooms. The peons were putting on their shoes. The peddlers were counting their daily earnings, but Rama was sitting in his chair writing in the register.

Today too, he had come here early in the morning, but once again he had not caught any big game – just the ten rupees, as usual. What means did he have to save his imaginary honour now? Rama resolved to deceive Ratan. He knew well she was impatient because she thought he had spent her money. If she knew that she could get her money immediately, then she'd be pacified. Rama wanted to allay her suspicions by showing her a bag filled with money. He was waiting for the Cashier Sahab to depart – he had deliberately stayed behind late, today. Today's receipts of eight hundred rupees were with him, and he wanted to take them home. The cashier got up right at four o'clock. What need did he have to ask for the day's receipts from Rama? He would be free of counting the money. The poor fellow's waist was aching from sitting all day long and writing in the ledger and counting money, over and over again. When Rama knew that the Cashier Sahab must have gone some distance, he closed the register and said to the peon, "Pick up the bag. Let's get these accounts closed."

"But the Cashier Babu has gone," said the peon.

"The Cashier has gone!' said Rama opening his eyes wide. 'Why didn't you tell me? How far do you think he's gone by now?"

"He must have reached as far as the corner of the street."

"How will this cash be deposited?"

"If you order me, I will call him back."

"Yes, go right ahead. Even though I haven't said so yet, now you'll go and call him back. You're a real calf's uncle, an idiot! Had too much straw today? Oh well! The money can stay right here, in this drawer. It will be your responsibility."

"No, Babu Sahab, I won't let the money be kept here. Not all the times are the same – if the money should somehow disappear, then despite my innocence, I'd be beaten. And there's not even a suitable lock here."

"So, where should I put this money?"

"*Huzur*, take it with you."

This was exactly what Rama had wanted. He had an *ekka* brought, kept the money bag in it and set off for home. As he went he thought that if Ratan could be influenced by threats, he would have no trouble with her.

He could also tell her that there were only three or four days left, at the most. She would be reassured by seeing the money in front of her.

Jalpa saw the bag and asked, "You didn't get the bracelet?"

"It's not ready yet. I thought I'd bring back the money to calm her down."

"What did the jeweller say?"

"What was there to say? He kept saying, it will be there today, tomorrow.... Ratan Devi hasn't come as yet?"

"She must be . . . she is anxious, isn't she?"

When Ratan did not come by the time the lamps were lit, Rama decided she would not come and put the money in the cupboard. He went out for a walk. Just ten minutes later, Ratan arrived and said, even as she was entering, "The bracelet must have come?"

"Yes," said Jalpa, "it has come. Put it on! The poor fellow went to the jeweller's several times. The scoundrel won't give it to him and plays his usual tricks."

"What sort of jeweller is he that he plays tricks for so many days! If I'd known there'd be such a wrangle over my money, I wouldn't have given it. I don't have either the money or the bracelet."

Ratan spoke in such a mistrustful way that Jalpa flared up. "Your money has been put aside," she said haughtily. "Take it when you want. This matter is not under my control. Ultimately, only when the jeweller gives the bracelet, only then will you take it?"

"Has he promised? By when will he give it?" asked Ratan.

"What's to be said for his promises? After all he's made hundreds of promises."

"So this means he won't make the thing?"

"Understand what you wish."

"Then give me back my money. I can do without such a bracelet."

Jalpa rose with flashing eyes, took the bag from the cupboard, and flung it down before Ratan. "This is your money," she said. "Please take it."

In reality, Ratan's impatience was caused by the reason which Rama had understood. She suspected Rama and Jalpa of having spent her money, and this was why she had been haranguing them for the bracelet. Seeing the money, her suspicions were calmed. Somewhat shamefacedly, she said, "If he promises to have it done in three or four days, then let the money be."

"I don't expect him to give it to you so soon. When the piece is ready, the money will be asked for."

"Who knows whether I'll have money then or not. When money comes you see it, when it goes, you don't. Who knows how it flies away? What's wrong with your keeping it?"

“Things are the same here,” said Jalpa. “And to keep someone else’s money in your house is dangerous, too. If there is a problem, then one will have to needlessly bear the punishment. On the fourth day after my marriage, all my jewellery was stolen. We weren’t fast asleep, but who knows when we dozed off and the thieves did their work. It was a slap worth ten thousand. If such a misfortune were to happen again, we’d be completely dishonoured.”

Ratan left. Jalpa was glad that the burden was lifted from their heads. Many a time, the severest blows are delivered by the hands of our sincerest well wishers.

When Rama returned around half past eight, Jalpa was cooking. As soon as she saw him, she said, “Ratan had come. I gave her all the money.”

The ground shifted under Rama’s feet. His eyes opened so wide that they almost touched his forehead. In a panic, he said, “What did you say? You gave Ratan the money? Who told you to give it to her?”

“You brought her money here, yourself. You were also waiting for her. As soon as you left she came and starting asking for the bracelet. I got so angry that I gave her the money.”

Rama, on his guard now, said, “She didn’t ask for the money?”

“Why wouldn’t she ask? Yes, when I gave her the money she started saying, ‘Why was I returning it to her? Keep it with you.’ I told her I didn’t keep money belonging to people who have such suspicious natures.”

“For God’s sake, don’t do anything like this in the future without asking me.”

“So what has happened now? Go and ask her for the money. But from now on, why bring trouble into your life by bringing money home?”

Rama was so dispirited that he did not possess the strength to even quarrel with Jalpa. Feeling tearful, he went downstairs and began thinking about the whole situation. It was unjust to get angry with Jalpa. When he had clearly said the money was Ratan’s, and had not hinted in the least that she should not give the money to Ratan without asking him, Jalpa was not at fault.

He thought, ‘The problem won’t be solved by getting irritated and furious.’ He needed to calm down and reflect. It was essential to get the money back from Ratan. If he had been here, when Ratan had come, how beautifully the whole difficulty would have been smoothed over. What disastrous impulse had overcome him to go for a walk! No one dies from not taking a walk for a day. Some hidden power was determined on bringing about his destruction. Ten minutes of absence has spoiled the whole game. Ratan had said to keep the money. If Jalpa had acted a little intelligently, matters would never have reached such a pass. He realised that he was thinking of things that had already happened. The problem was – how to get the money back from Ratan? He wondered why should he not go and say he had heard that she was angry because her money had been returned, and that in reality, he had not brought the money for her. He would then tell her that he had demanded it from the jeweler, so that he would finish making the piece and give it to them. It was just possible that she might be ashamed, beg his pardon, and give him the money again. He decided he ought to go there right now.

After deciding this, he glanced at his watch. It was a quarter to nine and it had grown dark. Ratan would not be able to leave home at this time. Rama got out his cycle and went off to meet her.

Today there was a big celebration at Ratan's bungalow. There was always some kind of festival or banquet or party going on here. Her lonely, dull life made her rush after these things like a thirsty person after water. There was a large crowd of children there. A swing was hanging from a mango tree, many electric lights were lit, and the children were swinging, with Ratan standing and pushing them. There was a great uproar. Vakil Sahab, wearing a woollen overcoat even in this weather, was sitting on the veranda, smoking a cigar. Rama wanted to go over to the swing and talk with Ratan, but seeing Vakil Sahab stand up, he felt too bashful to go over to her. As soon as he saw Rama, Vakil Sahab stretched forth his hand and said, "Come, Rama Babu, and tell me the news of your Municipal Board."

Rama sat down on a chair and said, "Nothing new has happened."

"When will the motion for the compulsory education of girls be passed? Several other Boards have passed it. Until the education of women is widespread, we will never progress. You wouldn't have gone to Europe? Oh! What freedom, what wealth, what life, what enthusiasm! In a word, one knows it's paradise! And the women are really goddesses! So cheerful, so independent! All this is the good outcome of female education!"

Rama, speaking according to what little he knew of conditions in these countries from the newspapers, said, "But the conduct of women over there is not very good."

"Nonsense! Each country has its own way of doing things. When you see a young woman and a young man wandering around alone together, you're aghast. You've become so dirty-minded that when you see a man and a woman together, you can't help being suspicious. But where boys and girls study together, this social division becomes relatively important. So many points of sympathy and affection are established between them that very little sexual desire remains. Understand this –the country which has more independent woman, the more civilised that country is. To keep women prisoners, or in *purdah*, or miles away from menfolk means that in our country the general public is so depraved, that it doesn't hesitate at all to insult women. There are literally thousands of subjects such as politics, religion, fine arts, literature, philosophy, history and science on whose basis, young men can build deep friendships with young women. Sexuality is the chief basis of attraction in those countries, where people's outlook is narrow. I've lived for a whole year in Europe and America. I've had many beautiful women-friends. I've played with them, even danced with them, but never a word passed my lips that would have made a young woman hang her head in shame. And then, where aren't there good and bad people?"

Rama derived no pleasure from this conversation. He was deeply plunged in worry at this moment.

Vakil Sahab spoke again, "As long as we don't let both women and men freely pursue their own mental development, we'll keep on declining. Don't bind the feet of society with fetters, don't throw chains around its neck. Push for widow remarriage, push very hard. But what I don't understand is why the newspapers make such a fuss when a middle-aged man marries a young woman. In Europe old men of eighty marry young women, and elderly women of seventy marry young men. No one says a thing. No one even hears a whisper about it. We want to kill off old people even before they die. Nonetheless, if ever a person needs companionship, it is in his old age, when he wishes to have some support all the time, when he becomes dependent."

Rama's attention was fixed on the swing. Just then, his greatest desire was to somehow get the chance to speak to her, albeit briefly. For him to just go there would be against good manners. Finally, after a little while he glanced at the swing and said, "Where have all these boys come from?"

"Ratan bai is very fond of children's company," said Vakil Sahab. "Who knows how all these boys gather here. If you're fond of children, then go on over there."

This was exactly what Rama wanted, and he reached the swing in a trice. When Ratan saw him, she smiled and said, "These little devils are leading me around by the nose. None of them ever gets tired of swinging. Come on, you do a little forced labour too, I've got tired." And she sat down on the nearby brick platform, while Rama began to push the swing. When the boys saw a new person, they all became impatient for their turn. Ratan had given them all two turns, but how could the rest of them sit looking on while some of them were getting a third turn? Whenever two got off the swing, four more got on. Rama did not have the slightest love for children, but he was trapped at this moment, so, what could he do?

Finally, after half an hour of this forced labour, he got fed up. His watch showed it was nine-thirty. How could he strike up a purposeful conversation? Ratan was so engrossed in the swinging that one might think she had completely forgotten about the money.

Suddenly, Ratan came close to the swing and said, "Babuji, I'll sit while you push, but not from underneath. Push the swing while you stand on it."

Rama had been afraid of sitting on swings since childhood. Once when some friends forcibly seated him on one, he had become dizzy. Her appeal practically forced him to get on the swing. How could he display his incompetence? Ratan sat down holding two children and sang a devotional song.

The swing has been hung from the branch of the kadam tree,

Oh Queen Radha has come to swing.

Rama stood on the swing and began to pump, but his legs were trembling, and his heart was in his throat. Whenever the swing descended, it seemed to him as if something liquid was piercing though his chest; Ratan was singing along with the children.

The swing has been hung from the branch of the kadam tree,

Oh Queen Radha has come to swing.

After a short while, Ratan said, "Push harder please, Sahab. You're hardly moving the swing."

Ashamed, Rama put more force into it, but the swing did not go any higher. He began to feel dizzy.

"You don't know how to pump it. Didn't you ever swing?"

"Yes," said Rama, shrinking with embarrassment, "but it's been ten years since I did."

"So sit down with these children on your lap, and I'll swing you. If you can't touch that branch up there, tell me." Rama grew terribly afraid. "It's very late now," he said. "I'll come again some other time."

"Oh ho, it's not late yet, it's not even ten. Don't panic. The night's hardly begun. Swing a lot and then go, please. And bring Jalpa tomorrow. We will both swing."

When Rama got off the swing, his face clearly displayed his terror. It had seemed to him each time the swing rose that he was going to fall. He wobbled towards his cycle, sat on it and fled home.

For some distance he was hardly conscious. His feet kept pushing the pedals by themselves. After going half the distance he came to himself. He turned the cycle around, went a little distance, and then got off and started thinking. What an opportunity he had let slipped because of his embarrassment. He had come away from there with nothing in hand. Why had he not been able to say a word? Ratan was not any sort of monster who would eat him up! Suddenly he remembered that the bag contained eight hundred rupees. When Jalpa had flared up and given Ratan the bag, she must not have counted the money in it, either, otherwise she would certainly have said something. Heaven forbid that the bag be given to someone else, or that more money be added to money elsewhere, that would be a disaster. Then he would be disgraced. He thought he should go right now and ask for the excess money, but it was late now – he would have to go again, tomorrow.

Even if he got those two hundred rupees back, he would still be short of six hundred. How would he arrange for that? He could manage it only if God saw him through this difficulty. If no arrangement had been made by morning, then the thought of what might happen made him tremble.

There are occasions in our lives when, there are glimpses of hope even in disappointment. Rama thought that if he visited Gangu once more, he might find him at his shop, and could beg for mercy. It was possible that Gangu might take pity on him. When he reached the jeweller's market, Gangu's shop was closed. He was just about to return when he saw Charan Das coming. As soon as he saw Rama he said, "Babuji, you've completely given up coming this way. Tell me, when am I going to get my money?"

"You'll get it very soon, Brother," said Rama, humbly. "There won't be any delay. Just see, Gangu's got his money, now it's your turn."

"I know the whole story. If Gangu hadn't been smart enough to take his money, he'd be stamping his feet in frustration like me. It's been going on a whole year. At even twelve per cent interest a year, I'd have earned eighty-four rupees. Come tomorrow and settle accounts. If not the whole amount, give me a half or a third. The employer is assured when people pay as well as take. When people turn a deaf ear to him, he begins to suspect that their intentions are bad. So when will you be coming tomorrow, please?"

"Well, I can't bring the money tomorrow, but I'll come over whenever you say. Couldn't your Sethji arrange for me to have four or five hundred rupees? I'll grease your palm, too."

"What kind of crazy talk is that, Babuji? Sethji won't give you a single paisa. He's behaved very well in not taking legal action against you. Instead, I'm forced to hear a lot of things. Do I have to speak to your Head Clerk?"

"I'm your debtor, not the Head Clerk," said Rama, flaring up. "I haven't died. I don't run away from home. Why are you so impatient?"

"A whole year has passed," said Charan, "and we haven't received a single paisa. If not patient, then what else would we be? Consider giving at least two hundred tomorrow."

"I told you I don't have it now."

"You spend money right and left every day, and still you say you don't have any money. Collect some money tomorrow. Our man will certainly come."

Rama went off without replying. He had come here to accomplish something, but in return, he had been forced to endure this harassment. He hoped the wretch would not actually send a collector to his father, or he would really be in the fire. Jalpa, too, would realise what a liar he was.

Although no tears came to Rama's eyes, every fibre of his being was weeping. What a big mistake he had made in concealing the true state of his affairs from Jalpa. She was a sensible woman. If she had known how poor her home really was, she would never have let him borrow to buy her jewellery. She had never directly asked him for anything. Rather, it was he who had been so obsessed with increasing his own importance. Why had he not been thriftier with his money, especially after taking on such a big financial burden? He could certainly have paid these two moneylenders, Gangu and Charan, half of what he owed them, but now this disaster had fallen on his head. Why did Jalpa have to go out every day with all the women of the neighbourhood? The *tonga* driver alone had probably taken hundreds, but it had been considered essential to impress him. The whole *bazar* could know that he was only an empty braggart, but not his own wife. How intelligent of him! Questions hounded him. 'Why had it been necessary to have curtains for the door? Why had he brought two lamps? Why had he brought the new tape to have the *charpais* rewoven?' As he went along, he added up all the expenses which a man of his means ought to have delayed. A healthy man does not worry about what, how much and when he eats, but when he gets sick he remembers that he had eaten *pakoris* yesterday. Victory is an extrovert, defeat, an introvert.

"Where did you go?" asked Jalpa, "Why did you take so long?"

"I had to go to Ratan's bungalow on account of you. You gave her all the money. Two hundred of it was mine."

"How could I know? You didn't say a thing. But none of that money will leave her. She'll send it to you herself."

"I agree. But I have to produce the government money tomorrow."

"Take two hundred from me tomorrow. I have it with me."

Rama did not believe her. "Suppose you don't have it? From where did you get so much money?"

"What difference does it make to you? I am saying that I'll give you two hundred."

Rama's face lit up. He began to cherish a few hopes. She would give him two hundred, he would take two hundred from Ratan, and he had a hundred, himself, so that left around three hundred. Where was that three hundred to come from? No one came to mind from whom he had any hope of getting so much. If Ratan gave back all the money, the whole mess could be straightened out. This was his only basis for hope. When he lay down after eating, Jalpa asked, "Which thoughts are you lost in today?"

"Thoughts about what? Do I look sad?"

"Yes, you're really worried about something, but aren't telling me."

"If there was something, would I hide it from you?"

"Splendid! Why would you tell me the secrets of your heart? After all, the ancient sages have not commanded it."

"I'm not one of their devotees."

"I'd know that if I sat in your heart and took a look."

"You'd see your own image there."

Jalpa had a terrible dream that night and screamed. Startled, Rama asked, 'What is it, Jalpa? What were you dreaming of?"

Glancing about wide-eyed and anxious, Jalpa said, 'My life was in great danger. I don't know what kind of dream it was."

"What did you see?"

"What should I tell you? It is difficult to say. I saw you being arrested and taken away by several policemen. How terrible they appeared!"

Rama's blood dried up. Three or four days ago, he would have laughed dismissively hearing of this dream. This time, he could not help being inwardly alarmed, though he laughed and said, "You didn't ask the police why they were taking me away?"

"You are laughing, but my heart is trembling."

A little later Rama began to babble in his sleep. "Mother, I'm telling you, you won't see my face again. I'm going to die drowning."

Jalpa had not fallen asleep yet. Frightened, she forcefully shook Rama awake and said, "You were laughing at me and now are talking nonsense yourself. My hair stood on end when I heard you. Were you dreaming?"

Feeling embarrassed Rama said, "Yes, I was. But there's no telling what I was seeing. I don't remember a thing."

"But why were you threatening Mother?" Jalpa said. "Tell me truly, what did you see?"

"I don't remember anything," said Rama, scratching his head. "I must have started babbling just like that."

"All right then," said Jalpa. "Turn on your side. People talk in their sleep when they lie on their backs."

Rama turned on his side, but it seemed as if worry and doubt were sitting on his eyes warding off sleep. He was still awake when two o'clock struck.

Suddenly Jalpa got up and drank from the water pot and said, "I was feeling so thirsty. You are still awake?"

"Yes, sleep has left me. I was thinking about how you came by two hundred rupees. It surprised me."

"I brought them from my parents' house. Some I got as a farewell gift, some, I'd put aside previously."

"Well, then you're very capable of saving money. Why haven't you done that here?"

Smiling, Jalpa said, "Now that I've got you, I don't worry about money."

"You're probably cursing your fate."

"Why would I curse my fate? Let those women bewail their fates, those whose husbands are idlers, drunkards, hoodlums or invalids, or whose husbands constantly pepper them with ridicule and quarrel with them over every little thing. If a man is good-natured, a woman will be happy with him even if she has to fast."

Feeling delighted, Rama said, "So I appeal to you?"

"You've turned out to be more than I'd hoped for," said Jalpa, proudly and affectionately. "I have three friends. Not one of them has a husband like you. One's an M.A., but always ill. The second is a scholar and rich too, but always running after prostitutes. The third is a stay-at-home and a total idler."

Rama's heart swelled with emotion. How treacherous he had been to this very image of love, this goddess of kindness. If she loved him this much in spite of his many deceptions, how blissful his life would have been if he had been honest.

19

Early next morning Rama sent his man across to Ratan. In his letter he wrote: 'I'm terribly sorry that yesterday Jalpa behaved with you in a way she shouldn't have. I never intended to return the money to you. I took the money from the jeweller to put some pressure on him. You'll get the bracelet, for sure, in three or four days. Please send the money. There were also two hundred rupees of mine in that bag. Please be so kind as to send them, too.' He left out no possible expression of modesty consistent with his own self-respect. Until his man returned, he continued to gaze distractedly along the way he had gone. Sometimes he thought she would make excuses, then, that she was not at home, or that she would promise to return the money three or four days later. Everything depended on Ratan's money. If Ratan flatly refused, then everything would be ruined. Just imagining this made Rama terribly fearful. At nine o'clock his man finally returned. Ratan had sent two hundred rupees, but she had not replied to his letter.

Rama looked despairingly toward the sky. Why had she not answered his letter? Did she not even understand common courtesy? What a hypocritical woman she was – last night she had seemed the very model of benevolence and kindliness, but the whole time her heart had been filled with revenge. In his worry about the rest of the money, Rama forgot to bathe and eat.

When the water-carrier, the *kahar*, came inside, Jalpa asked, "Is it because you've had news of some other work that you're just strolling around? It's almost ten and there's not a trace of the vegetables you're supposed to bring."

The *kahar* glanced at her angrily and said, "Do I have four arms and legs? I was busy. The Babu sent me to bring some money from the lady."

"Which lady?"

"The one that comes in the motorcar."

"So did you bring the money?"

"Why wouldn't I? She lives at the other end of the earth. My legs are aching from running there and back."

"Alright. Be quick and get the vegetables right away."

Off went the *kahar*. As soon as Rama came inside with the money, Jalpa said, "You had your money brought back from Ratan, haven't you? Now you won't be taking any from me?"

"Don't give it to me,' said Rama, sadly.

"I told you that I'll give you the money. Why did you think of asking for the money so soon? Maybe she thought that you didn't trust her even that much."

"I didn't ask for the money," said Rama, despondently. "I just wrote saying there were two hundred rupees extra in the bag. She sent them on her own."

Jalpa laughed and said, 'My money's very lucky, shall I show you? I select and keep only rupees in mint condition. All of them are from this year, see how they glitter. Take a look and your heart will be satisfied."

Just then someone below called out, "Babuji, the Seth has sent me for his money."

Dayanath was just coming inside for his bath when he saw the Seth's peon and asked, "Which Seth? What money? There is no money belonging to anyone else in my house."

"The *chote* Babu has taken some goods. A whole year has gone by and he hasn't given us even a single paisa. The Sethji said me to ensure that he gives something today."

Dayanath summoned Rama and said, "Look here, which Seth's man is this? If there's something left to pay, why don't you clear the accounts? How much is left to pay?"

Rama did not have time to say a word before the peon shot out, "Seven hundred altogether, Babuji!"

Dayanath's eyes touched his forehead in shock and he repeated, "Seven hundred! Well, Sir, he says seven hundred!"

"I don't know exactly," said Rama, intentionally stalling for time.

"Why wouldn't you know?" said the peon. "I have a note with me. You haven't paid a paisa for a year, so how could it be less?"

Rama spoke directly to the peon. "Go back to your shop. I'll come myself."

"I'm not going unless I get something, Sahab," said the peon. "You always postpone things like this, and they grumble at us."

Rama could bear being humiliated in front of the whole world, but to be humiliated before his father was no less than dying. That a man who had never in his life taken a single paisa wrongfully, who would prefer to go hungry rather than borrow for a meal, should have such a shameless and dishonourable son. Rama could not wound his father's soul so deeply. He had wanted to conceal from his father that his son was disgracing his name. "Are you still standing here?" he said to the peon in a loud, harsh voice. "Get out, or else I'll have you thrown out."

"Give us the money and I'll go. Do we wait for sweets at your door?"

"You won't go? Go tell your Lala, that he can file a complaint."

"Why are you saying such shameless things, Sir?" said Dayanath, scolding him. "When you didn't have any money in your pocket, why did you get the thing, in the first place? And when you bought it, you should have paid for it at once. When they say pay – you say file a complaint. If they file a complaint, what will be left of your reputation? Do you even care about it? Everyone in the city will be pointing fingers at you in scorn, but what do you care? What were you thinking of that you took such a heavy load upon yourself? Even if it were a wedding or some such occasion, it was still worthwhile. And what kind of woman would see her husband doing something so foolish and not forbid it? After all, what were you thinking when you took on this debt? You don't have such a big income as that."

Rama found his father's upbraiding hurtful. In his opinion, his father had no right at all to speak about this subject. Unhesitant, he spoke forth, "You're getting upset for no reason. If I come to ask you for money, then say something. I'll pay it off, little by little, from my own salary."

He thought to himself, 'This is all the result of your doing, Father. I'm atoning for your sins.'

Seeing father and son arguing back and forth, the peon left silently. Dayanath, muttering and fuming, went in to take his bath. Rama went upstairs; shame and remorse at being scolded by his father, scorching his face. The very disgrace from which he had fled hither-thither, treading warily from narrowing branch to branch and leaf to leaf, had happened, after all. Even his anxiety about the government money he had taken had vanished in the face of this humiliation. True borrowers have vast reserves of courage. An ordinarily sensible person flies into a panic when he falls into circumstances like Rama's, but experienced persons do not even get a wrinkle on their brows. Rama was not yet competent in this art. If the messenger of Yama, god of death, had come just then to seize his life, the look in his eyes would have been welcoming. 'What is going to happen?' – these words were pouring out of his entire body. 'What is going to happen?' He could not find any other words to describe his situation. This question hovered about him like an ever-present demon glaring at him. 'What is going to happen?' These words seemed like innumerable whirlwinds rising in every direction. All he could do was shut his eyes and not think about it. He felt so distressed that tears brimmed in his eyes.

"You said that there was only a little left to pay," said Jalpa, enquiringly.

Rama hung his head and said, "This wicked fellow was lying. I gave them some money."

"If you gave them some money, then why would they be pestering you about it? When your income was so small, why did you get any jewellery at all? I never insisted. And even supposing I had said something three or four times, you should have understood and acted more cautiously.

Along with you, I was also scolded. A man keeps things secret from the whole world, but not from his own wife. You've kept things even from me. If I'd known that your income was so small, would I have been so crazy as to take all the ladies of the neighbourhood out for *tonga* rides? At the very most, I would have felt unhappy from time to time, but at least I wouldn't have had to put up with this harassment from the jeweller. And if he complains, the seven hundred will become a thousand. How could I know you were playing false with me? I wasn't some prostitute who was snatching and clawing at your money to feather my own nest. I'm your partner in both good and bad times. In good times, it is alright if you are not concerned with what I say, but, in bad times, I'll cling to you."

Rama was silent. It was time to go to work and there was no time to eat. Rama dressed and left for the office. "Are you going off without eating anything?" asked his mother.

Rama did not answer her, and was about to leave the house when Jalpa rushed downstairs and called out to him. "Why don't you give the two hundred rupees I have to the jeweller?" Rama had deliberately not asked Jalpa for money, as he was leaving. He had known that if he asked she would give it, but after hearing so much from her, he was not just embarrassed to entreat her for it,· he was extremely afraid. He did not on any account want to hear another lecture – even the approaching disasters seemed a little lighter, comparatively. When Jalpa called to him, a little hope sprang up. He stopped abruptly and said, "That's fine. Give it to me."

He sat in the outer room. Jalpa ran upstairs, brought the money, rapidly counted it and put it in his bag. She thought he would not be able to contain his joy at receiving the money, but her hopes went unfulfilled. He still had three hundred rupees to worry about. Where were they to come from? A hungry man wants a meal according to his wishes – he is not satisfied with two-four *phulke.*

When he reached the street, Rama took a *tonga* and told the driver to go to Georgetown – maybe he would meet Ratan. If she wanted, she could easily arrange for three hundred rupees. Along the way he kept thinking to himself that today he would not shrink a bit. After a little while he reached Georgetown, and Ratan's bungalow came into view. She was sitting on the veranda. When Rama saw her, he waved and she waved back – then he completely lost his nerve. He could not bring himself to go inside. The *tonga* moved away. If Ratan had invited him in, he would have gone. If she had not been sitting on the veranda, he might still have gone inside. When he saw her sitting in front, he was too steeped in embarrassment to act.

When the *tonga* reached Government House, Rama awoke with a start and said, "Go to the Tolls Office." The *tonga* driver turned the horse around.

It was about eleven o'clock when Rama reached the office. His face was drawn, and his heart was pounding. The Head Clerk, Ramesh Babu, must certainly have inquired about him. He would summon him as soon as he went. He did not do any one the least favour in the office. As he was getting down from the *tonga*, he glanced in the direction of his room, and saw several people standing there looking at him. He went towards Ramesh Babu's office, instead.

"Where have you been till now, Sir?" asked Ramesh Babu. "The Cashier Sahab has been running all over looking for you! Did you meet the peon?"

"I wasn't at home," said Rama in a faltering voice. "I went to the Vakil Sahab's house. I'm trapped in a big problem."

"What kind of trouble? Everything's fine at home, isn't it?"

"Yes, everything's fine at home. Yesterday evening there was lots of work here, and I became so involved in it that I lost track of the time. When I finished it and got up to leave, the Cashier Sahab had gone. I had the day's receipts of eight hundred rupees with me. I began to think where I could keep them. There's no strongbox in my office, so I decided to take them with me. There were five hundred rupees in coins, which I put in the bag, and three hundred in notes, which I put in my pocket, and went home. I had to get a couple of things in the market. When I reached home, the notes had disappeared.'

Ramesh Babu stared at Rama in astonishment. "Three hundred rupee notes had disappeared?"

"Yes, Sir, they were in my upper coat pocket."

"And they didn't knock you down and grab the bag?"

"What can I say, Babuji? I can't begin to tell you what my state of mind has been since then. I've been running around worrying about this ever since. I was unable to arrange for the money."

"You musn't have said anything to your father?"

"You know what he's like. He'd scold me instead of giving me the money."

"So, now what will you consider?"

"I will think of something, one way or another, by this evening."

"Then you'd better do so!" said Ramesh, assuming a harsh manner. "How could you have managed to be so careless? Not a single paisa has ever fallen from my pocket. Were you walking along the street with your eyes shut or were you drunk? I don't believe what you say. Tell me the truth now. Have you spent them on this and that? Why did you ask me for money the other day?"

Rama's face turned pale. Suppose the truth were to unravel . . . "Would I spend government money?" he said, inventing excuses as he went. "That day I asked you for money because my father had a sudden need. There was no money in the house. When I read your letter to him, he laughed a lot and made other arrangements. I'm astonished myself at how those notes disappeared."

"If you're embarrassed to ask your father for money, shall I write a letter and have the money borught?"

"No, Babuji, for God's sake, don't do that, please," said Rama, putting his hands to his ears. "If that's what you want, then please, shoot me instead."

Ramesh thought for a moment, and said, "Are you sure you'll get the money by this evening?"

"Yes, I certainly hope to."

"Then deposit the money that's in the bag now, but listen, my friend, I'm telling you straight out, if you haven't brought the rest by ten o'clock tomorrow, I won't be responsible. The rules say that I should hand you over to the police this instant, but since you're still just a boy, I'll pardon you. Otherwise, you know that when it comes to government business, I don't show any sort of consideration. If my brother or son were in your place, I'd treat them the same way, or rather even more severely. Even so, I'm treating you very leniently. If I had the money, I'd give it to you, but you know my circumstances. I don't have any debts, of course. I don't lend to anyone, and I don't borrow from anyone. It'll be bad if the money doesn't appear tomorrow. Even my friendship won't save you from the clutches of the police. As a friend, I've done my duty today, or else you'd be in handcuffs right now."

Handcuffs! This word pierced Rama's chest like an arrow. He trembled from head to foot. His eyes filled with tears as he imagined this calamity. He went very slowly to his chair with his head bowed like a condemned prisoner and sat down, but that terrible word resounded again and again in his heart.

Dark heavy clouds had covered the sky, and the sun was nowhere to be seen. Was he, too, shut up in a prison of clouds? Were there handcuffs on his hands, too?

20

When Rama left the office that evening, Ramesh Babu came running after him and enjoined him to bring him the money the next day. Rama was internally convulsed with anger, 'You've become the very epitome of righteousness, have you? You damned hypocrite! If you were to be in a fix you'd run around licking other people's boots, but when it comes to me, you suddenly become an idealist. These are all toothless threats! When your time comes, may you die slowly!'

After walking a little further, he began to think he should go to Ratan once more. There was no one else from whom he had any hope of getting money. When he reached her bungalow, she was sitting on a round platform in her garden. Near her sat a Gujarati jeweller, who was showing one beautiful ornament after another kept in his trunk. When she saw Rama she was quite pleased. "Come, Babu Sahab, see what wonderful things Sethji has brought. See how beautiful this necklace is? He says it costs twelve hundred rupees."

Rama taking the necklace in his hand, looked at it and said, "Yes, it certainly seems to be a good piece."

"The price is too much," said Ratan.

"Madam," said the jeweller, "If someone gives you a necklace like this for any less than two thousand, I'll pay any penalty you like. I paid twelve hundred to have it made."

"Don't say that, Sethji," said Rama smiling. "You'll have to pay the penalty."

"Babu Sahab," said the Gujarati, "you can get a necklace exactly like this for a hundred rupees. It will probably have a greater shine than this, but you ought to judge its worth properly. I, myself, haven't bargained over this with you. One bargains with novices. Why with you? We aren't mere tradesmen, Babu Sahab, we observe people's natures. The lady here has displayed a very rich, noble nature indeed!"

"Bring the price down a little, Sethji,' said Ratan, looking at the necklace, helplessly entranced. "It's as if you've sworn not to."

"Don't even mention bringing the price down, Madam. This piece is a present for you."

"Ok," said Ratan. "Now please tell me something. What's the very least you'll take for it?"

"Twelve hundred rupees and twelve cowries, Huzur," said the jeweller, somewhat maliciously. "I swear to you. I'll sell it for fifteen hundred, right here in this city, and what's more, I'll be sure to tell you who bought it."

As he said this, the jeweller took out the case to keep the necklace. Ratan, now, was certain that he would not reduce the price. Like an impatient child, Ratan said, "You're putting away that necklace as if you're afraid the evil eye will fall on it."

"What am I supposed to do? When the worth of such a piece is not appreciated even in such a distinguished gathering, I feel quite sad."

Ratan went inside and summoned Rama saying, "Do you think he'll come down a little more?'

"In my understanding, I don't think the thing is worth more than a thousand," said Ramanath.

"O probably! I've got just six hundred rupees with me. If you can arrange for four hundred, I'll buy it. He's going to Kashi by the very next train, and he won't agree to give credit. Vakil Sahab has gone to some meeting, and won't be back before nine or ten o'clock. I'll give the money back to you tomorrow."

"Believe me, I'm completely broke," said Rama, feeling very embarrassed. "I came to ask you for some money. I need it very badly. Give me your money and I'll get some nice necklace from here, for you. I'm sure you can get one like this for seven or eight hundred."

"Go on, you're not going to take me in with your words again. You couldn't get a bracelet made in six months, and now, how will get a necklace? I've looked around in several shops, and such a piece may not turn up. Even if such a piece might turn up, you'd have to give one and half times as much, around here."

"So why don't you ask him to come here tomorrow? If he really needs to sell his things, he'll stay today."

"Alright," said Ratan. "Let's see what he says."

They both left the room and went back outside. "Why don't you come tomorrow morning at eight o'clock?' said Rama to the jeweller.

"No, Huzur. I have to meet with three or four important people in Kashi tomorrow. If I don't go today, I'll lose a lot."

"I've got six hundred with me just now," said Ratan. "Give me the necklace, please, and take the rest of the money when you get back from Kashi."

"It isn't about the money," said the jeweller. "I usually take it over a month or two. But one can't rely on me, I am from another province. We're here today and gone tomorrow; who knows when or where we'll return? Give me a thousand now and two hundred later, please."

"There won't be any deal then," said Rama.

"That's your privilege," said the jeweller. "But I can tell you this much, you won't get a deal like this again."

"If you've got the money, you can get lots of things,' said Rama.

"Sometimes, even if you've got the money, you can't find good things," said the jeweller.

Saying this, he put the necklace in its case, and began to pack up his trunk as if he did not intend to remain a moment longer.

Ratan was straining every nerve to listen, like some prisoner standing to hear the judge's decision about his fate. All the affection of her heart, all the passion of that affection, and all the impatience, longing, and effort of that passion, were centred on that necklace as if her very life lay hidden itself among the beads, as if the amassed desires of her past and future lives were hovering over it. When she saw the jeweller's trunk closing, she began to writhe like a fish out of water. She opened chests, she opened drawers, but nowhere did she find money.

All at once she heard the sound of an automobile, and looked towards the gate. Vakil Sahab was driving towards the house. He stopped the car near the veranda and came towards them. Ratan got off the platform and said, "You told me you'd be back at nine."

"The quorum was incomplete, so what would I do just sitting around? No one really wants to do any work. They all just want to earn a good reputation for free. Is this a jeweller?"

The jeweller rose and saluted him.

Vakil Sahab said to Ratan, "Well, did you find anything you liked?"

"Yes, I like a necklace. He's asking twelve hundred for it."

"Is that all? Look for something else you like. You don't have anything nice to wear on your head."

"All I want right now is the necklace. Who wears things on their heads these days?"

"Take something and keep it with you. You'll wear it sometime. If you don't, you'll see others wearing something like it and say to yourself that if you had one, you'd wear it, too."

Vakil Sahab loved Ratan like a father loves his daughter, not how a husband loves his wife. Like a doting father at a fair who brings his sons toys after asking them repeatedly what they would like, he, too, would bring toys for Ratan. She just had to voice her desire. What else did he have to please her with, besides his wealth? He needed some sort of foundation for his life – a live foundation with whose support he could stand erect in the struggle of life in his decrepit condition, much as a worshipper needs an image of his deity. Without an image, what will he strew flowers on, what will he bathe with the holy Ganges water, what will he feed delicious things to? Vakil Sahab needed a wife in exactly the same way. For him, Ratan was merely an embodied figment of his imagination with which he could quench his spiritual thirst. Perhaps, without Ratan his life would have been as empty as a face without eyes.

Ratan took the necklace from the case, showed it to Vakil Sahab and said, “He's asking for twelve hundred rupees for it.”

In the eyes of Vakil Sahab the value of money lay in its power to give pleasure. If Ratan liked the necklace, he did not care what its price was. He took out his cheque book, and looking towards the jeweller and said, “Tell me the truth, now, what figure should I write? If there's any difference between its real worth and what you're asking for, you'll know.”

The jeweller looked at the necklace as he turned it over, and said hesitatingly, “Make it eleven hundred and fifty.” Vakil Sahab wrote the cheque and gave it to him. The jeweller gave him a *salaam*, and departed.

Ratan's face was glowing with joy, now, like spring in all its natural glory. Never before had such pride, such rapture appeared on her face. It was as if she had just received all the riches of the world.

She fastened the necklace around her neck and went inside. Vakil Sahab's views and conduct were a curious mixture of the old and the new customs. He still would not take any food from anyone's hand, even a Brahmin's. Today, Ratan cooked especially nice dishes for him. How else could she show her gratitude?

Rama sat for a while, listening to Vakil Sahab singing his song in praise of Europe. At last, he grew disappointed and left.

21

If anyone had wanted to see the embodiment of the saddest, most hopeless, most worried being in the whole world just then, he should have looked at the young man pedalling his cycle in front of Alfred Park. If Rama had seen some deadly snake at that moment, he would have welcomed it with open arms and drunk its poison like nectar. He would be protected, not by nectar, but by poison. Only death could bring an end to his cares, but could death save him from infamy, too? By morning, the news would spread from house to house – he had embezzled government money, and when caught, had committed suicide. What good would it be to be free of his worries, if even after death he would bring ridicule and disgrace to his family? What other recourse did he have?

If Rama went to Jalpa and related the whole story to her, she would certainly show him some sympathy. No matter how sad Jalpa would be, she would not hesitate for even an instant to take off her jewellery and give it to him. By pawning her jewels, he could make good the government money he had taken. He would have to reveal his secrets. There was no other option left.

Rama set out for home with his mind made up, but his pace lacked the quickness which is a sign of mental enthusiasm.

When he arrived home, however, he thought that since he had to do this anyway, what was the hurry? He would ask her for them whenever he wanted to. He spent some time in casual conversation, ate and lay down. Suddenly it occurred to him that there was no reason he could not make off with something on the sly. He had done just that once before, to save the family honour. Why could he not save his own life in the same way? Perhaps he would never be able to tell Jalpa by himself the true extent of the misfortune. He would be lying here till morning, pondering whether he should or should not, and in the morning, he would not have a chance to say anything.

Then, he began to have misgivings that Jalpa might open her eyes while he was stealing something. Then he would have no other recourse than drowning himself in the Triveni. Whatever happened, he would have to make the attempt once. Slowly, he moved Jalpa's hand from off his chest and stood up. He thought that Jalpa would be roused from sleep as soon as her hand was moved, but realised this had only been a misapprehension. Now he had to remove the bunch of keys from the pocket of her jacket. There was no time to be lost. Even in sleep, some small amount of consciousness continues to work. No matter how deeply a child may be sleeping, it wakes as soon as its mother gets up from the bed. When he bent over to take out the keys, he thought he saw

Jalpa smiling. He drew back his hand abruptly, and in the feeble lamplight, gazed at her face, which seemed lost in some pleasant dream. Seeing her face suffused by the sweet dream she was having, his mind was distressed, 'Oh! Was he supposed to betray this guileless creature in such a way? Could he be so treacherous to one for whom he could give up his own life? It was as if Jalpa's pure, loving heart was outlined in her lovely face. Ah! What would her state be when she learnt that her jewels had been stolen, again? She would collapse in despair, she would tear out her hair. How could he endure her agony? What kind of comfort had he ever bestowed on her? If she would have married someone else, she'd have been loaded with jewels by now. A bad fate had brought her to his house where there was no happiness, but just the opposite, so much to cry about.'

Rama lay down on the bed again. At this moment, Jalpa's eyes opened. "Where have you been?" she asked, looking at his face. "I was having such a good dream. There was a big garden, and we two were strolling around in it. Suddenly you disappeared to God-knows-where, and a *sadhu* came and stood in front of me. He looked just like one of the gods. 'My child, I've come to grant you a boon,' he said to me. 'Ask for whatever you want.' I looked all over for you to find out what I should ask for, but you were nowhere to be seen. I searched the whole garden, I peered among the trees, but who knows where you had gone. That's it. Just then, I woke up and I didn't get to ask for my boon!"

"What would you have asked for?" said Rama, smiling.

Jalpa said, "Whatever I felt like. Why should I tell you?"

"No, tell me. Maybe you would ask for a lot of money."

"Maybe, you think money's something important? I don't think it's anything at all."

"Well, I think living poverty-stricken is worse than dying. If I could catch some God, I wouldn't let him go without getting a lot of money. I don't want to put up a golden wall, and I have no wish to become a Rockefeller or a Carnegie. I just want enough so that we won't have to suffer the lack of the ordinary necessities of life. If some God would give me just five lakhs, I wouldn't ever ask him for anything again. How many rich men, merchants and landholders are there even in our poor country who spend five lakhs in a year, or even in a month? I'm ready to live seven lifetimes on that amount, but no one gives me even this much. What would you ask for? Really nice jewellery?"

Jalpa frowned. "Why are you provoking me? Do I dote on jewels more than other women do? I've never pestered you for them. If you need them, then take them away today. I'll give them gladly."

Smiling, Rama said, "Then why aren't you telling me?"

Jalpa said, "I'd ask that my lord and master should keep on loving me forever, and never turn away from me."

Rama laughed. "Do you have doubts about that, too?"

"If you were a God, I'd have my doubts, but then, you are only a man, after all. I never met any woman who didn't have a cruel story to tell about the harshness of her husband. For a year or two, husbands show great affection, and then for no known reason they seem to lose interest in their wives. Their hearts become restless. For a woman, there's no greater calamity than this. What other boon would I ask for than to be saved from this calamity?" As she said this, Jalpa threw her arms around her husband's neck, and gazing at him with loving eyes, said, "Tell me truly. Do you still want me just like you used to want me, earlier? See that you tell me the truth, now. Speak!'

Embracing Jalpa tightly, Rama said, "Millions of times more than before!"

Jalpa laughed. "A lie! A total lie! A one hundred per cent lie!"

"You forced me to lie. How'd you find out anyway?"

"I look through my eyes, how else would I find out? You swore we'd be together at all times. But whenever I look at you, you are as quiet as a mouse. If you loved me, you'd trust me. How can you even have love without trust? You can't love someone to whom you can't tell the worst of the worst that happens to you. Oh yes, you can enjoy yourself with someone like that, play around with her. Just like you would, if you went to some prostitute. People go to prostitutes to get pleasure, not to say what's in their hearts. That's just the way it is with us. Tell me, yes or no? Why are you looking away? Don't I see that you come home, visibly upset about something these days? When we talk about things, I see that your mind is somewhere else. I see that you don't enjoy your food at all, either. You do not see whether the *dal* is thick or thin, whether there are too many or too few vegetables, or whether the rice is cooked enough. You eat like a labourer and then run off in a hurry. What all do I not see? I should see it? I'm just a plaything, that's how you see me. My work is to give you enjoyment, to play with you, to give you pleasure. What should your worries mean to me? But God didn't give me a heart like that. What can I do? I understand this now, when I have to pass my life, when I'm just an object of pleasure for you, why should I plunge myself in troubles for your sake?"

Jalpa had never opened her heart to Rama before. He would never have guessed that she was so thoughtful. In reality, he had considered her just a beautiful young woman. Like other men, he, too, saw his wife in only this aspect. He was entranced by her youthful beauty. He had never even tried to look into the essence of her soul. Perhaps he thought she did not even have a soul. However, if she had not possessed an abundance of beauty and charm, perhaps he would not even have cared to talk with her. All his attraction to her, all his devotion to her, was based on her appearance. He had thought that this was what pleased Jalpa. He had not wanted to burden her with the weight of his own worries. Today he learned that Jalpa was just as capable of reflection, as he was himself. He had an excellent opportunity to blurt out his mental torment just then, but alas, hesitation and embarrassment! He held his tongue once more. How could he speak now, about matters he had kept hidden for so long? If he did, would he not have to also accept her accusations? Yes, today the veil of confusion had been lifted from his eyes, and he had learned that trying to base love upon sexual enjoyment was his ignorance.

Lost in these thoughts, Rama finally fell asleep. It was past midnight by then. He had gone to sleep with the intention of rising early in the morning, but when he awoke, the sun's rays were streaming into the room to awaken him. He rose quickly, and without washing his hands and face, dressed, and got ready to go out. He wanted to go to Ramesh Babu's. Now he would have to tell him his story. He hoped that when Ramesh became acquainted with the whole situation, he would be prepared to help a little.

Jalpa was preparing the meal. Seeing Rama leaving like this, she gazed at him enquiringly. It was as if worry, fear, indecision and violence were etched on his face and glaring fiercely. For an instant, she was nearly beside herself with worry. With a knife in one hand and a bitter gourd in the other, she stood staring at the door. What was the matter? Why did he not tell her? Even if she could not do anything else, she could offer him sympathy. It occurred to her to call out and ask him what was wrong. She even got up and went to the door, but Rama had already gone far down the street. She noticed that he was walking very quickly, and looking neither left nor right, as if he were obsessed with something. He was walking quickly with his head bowed, bumping into passers-by, and unmindful of the pushcarts. At last she returned and began cutting vegetables again, but her mind remained fixed in the direction her husband had taken. What was the matter? Why did he hide so much from her?

When Rama reached Ramesh's house, it was past eight o'clock.

Babu Sahab was sitting on his bed, meditating. When he saw Rama he gestured towards him to sit. When his meditation finished after a good half an hour, he said, "Haven't you even washed your hands and face yet? I don't like this slackness. Whatever else you do or don't do, keep your body clean. What's happened? Have you made some arrangement for the money?"

"I am here because of this concern."

"You're a strange one. Why are you ashamed to talk to your father? This will happen – he will taunt you, but you'd be free from this trouble. Tell him everything clearly. Accidents like this happen all the time. What's there to be afraid of? If you don't want to, I'll go tell him."

"If I were going to tell him, I'd have told him by now. Can't you make some arrangement?"

"Of course I could, but I don't intend to. I don't have any sympathy for someone like you. When you can tell me, why can't you tell him? Mind what I tell you. Go tell him. If he won't give you the money, then come to me."

Rama did not have the courage to say anything further. How could people be so harsh in spite of being so close! He got up and left, but nothing came to mind. He was in the same condition as raindrops which fall from the sky into a capricious breeze. He would take ten quick steps forward, stop to think, and then take five or ten steps back. He would go down this lane and then, down that.

Suddenly something occurred to him. He could write a letter to Jalpa informing her of all his difficulties. He was unable to say anything, but he saw no difficulty in writing it down. He would write a letter, give it to her, and then go sit in the outer room. What could be simpler than this? He ran home, and immediately wrote a letter.

'Dearest one, how shall I tell you about the disaster I'm trapped in? If I can't arrange for three hundred rupees within one hour, there'll be handcuffs on my wrists. I tried hard to get a loan from somebody, but I couldn't get it from anywhere. If you'd give me one or two of your pieces of jewellery, I could pawn them and take care of things. As soon as I get some money, I'll redeem them. If I wasn't helpless, I wouldn't have troubled you. For God's sake, don't be angry. I'll redeem them quickly....'

He had not yet finished the letter, when Ramesh Babu came in smiling and sat down. He said, "Have you spoken to him?"

Rama hung his head and said, "I haven't had the chance yet."

Ramesh said, "So you'll get a chance in a few days? I'm afraid that you'll leave here empty-handed today, and a real disaster will take place."

Rama said, "When I've decided to ask him, what's the worry now!'

Ramesh said, "If you get a chance today, go and meet Ratan, please. I particularly stressed this the other day, but it seems you forgot."

"I haven't forgotten, I'm ashamed to tell her."

"You're ashamed to tell your father, too? If you weren't so bashful with your own people, why would we be in this fix today?"

When Ramesh Babu left, Rama thrust the letter in his pocket and went inside, determined to give it to Jalpa. Jalpa was about to visit a woman friend. An invitation had come only a short while before. She was wearing her most beautiful sari. The inlaid bracelet on her arm, and the *chandrahar* around her neck looked splendid. She was standing before the mirror, putting on earrings. When she saw Rama she said, "Where did you go this morning? You didn't even wash your hands and face. You stay away the whole day, you're only home in the mornings and evenings. When you're not here the house seems very empty. Just now I was thinking that if I had to go to my parents' house, should I go or not? I wouldn't enjoy it there at all."

Rama said, "You're all ready to go somewhere."

Jalpa said, "Sethaniji has invited me, I'll come back by the afternoon."

Rama's state just then was something like that of a hunter, who sees a doe frolicking with her fawns, puts his levelled rifle back on his shoulder, and becomes entranced in watching the sport of affection and motherly love.

Seeing him staring fixedly at her, Jalpa smiled and said, "Look here, don't give me the evil eye! I'm very afraid of your eyes."

In a single bound, Rama left the real world and reached the world of imagination and poetry. At a time like this, when every fibre of Jalpa's body was dancing with joy, was he going to give her his letter and crush her pleasant fancies? Was he some heartless fowler to draw a knife across the throat of a warbling songbird? Was he some crass lout to tear off a morning-flower and trample it beneath his feet? Rama was not that heartless, not that crass. He was incapable of causing such an injury to Jalpa. No matter what calamities might fall on his head, no matter how much disgrace might come to him, no matter if his very life might be crushed, he could not be so cruel. Lost in devotion, he said, "I won't cast the evil eye, I will just clasp you to my heart." With this one sentence, all his worries, and obstacles melted away. In the face of his love, he hesitated and sacrificed the last opportunity he has. In the face of this disgrace, all the other afflictions of life were insignificant. His condition just now was something like that of a child, who unable to bear the momentary pain of lancing an abscess, forgets all his fears of its bursting and becoming a running sore, and about his being bedridden for years, or perhaps, even dying.

When Jalpa started to go downstairs, Rama became so agitated that he hugged her tightly over and over again, as if he might never have this good fortune again. Who knew whether this might not be their very last embrace? He clung to her as if he were one of the thousands of silk threads of her clothing. He was like a dying miser clutching the key to his treasury in a fist closing tighter minute by minute. If his fist should be forcibly opened would he not expire on the spot?

All at once, Jalpa said, "Give me a little money, I might need some."

Rama said, "Money! I don't have any money just now."

Jalpa said, "You're making excuses. Just give me two rupees, I don't need any more!"

Saying this, she put her hand in Rama's pocket and took out some money and with it, the letter.

Reaching out, Rama tried to snatch the letter from her hand, saying, "Give me that piece of paper, it's a government document."

Jalpa said, "Whose letter is it? Are you going to tell me?"

Jalpa folded it, but then opening the scrap of paper, said, "This is a government document? Your liar! You wrote it..."

"Give it to me, why are you troubling me?" Rama tried to snatch it again, but Jalpa putting her hands behind her back, said, "I won't give it back before I read it, that's that. If you keep insisting, I'll tear it up."

"All right, tear it up."

"Then I'll read it for sure," and she took two steps backwards, opened the letter again, and began to read.

Rama made no further attempt to snatch it away. It seemed to him that the sky had split into two and some terrible creature was coming towards him to swallow him up. He thumped noisily down the stairs and left the house. Where could he hide now? His condition was that of a naked man. He was naked even though he was clothed from head to foot. Ah! Everything was out in the open! All his deception was revealed. Everything he had tried to conceal all these days – he had endured so many difficulties to keep them hidden. Today, these had smeared themselves like soot all over his face. He could not bear seeing his ruin with his own eyes. It would be easier to die rather than hear Jalpa's sobs, his father's upbraiding, and the neighbour's malicious whispering. When he was no longer alive, then what did he care, if anyone was saying anything at all. Ah! His whole life was being destroyed for a mere three hundred rupees. However, if this was God's wish, what could he do? His life would not be falling from grace in the eyes of his loved ones!

How worthless, how treacherous, how deceitful, how idly boastful he must appear to Jalpa now! How could he face her?

Was there no other place in this world where he could begin a new life? Where, he could avoid everyone and live out his days, where he could hide so that the police could never find him? Where was such a place except in the depths of the Ganges? If he was alive, he would surely be caught within a month or two. What would his state be then – he would be standing in a court, fettered and handcuffed! A group of policemen would be surrounding him. Everyone in town would come to watch the show, Jalpa and Ratan, too. His father, his relatives, his friends, intimates and strangers, would all be watching the spectacle of his misery with varying emotions. No, he would not defile his honour like that, he would not. It was far better to drown himself.

Then something occurred to him, 'Who would look after Jalpa? Dear God, he had also condemned her to drown with him. His father and mother would bear up somehow or other, but who would take care of her? Could he hide himself somewhere and live? It was possible that some day Jalpa would take pity on him, would pardon his offences. It was possible that he would also get some wealth, money, but it was impossible that he could ever stand before her and look her straight in the eye. There was no telling what state she might be in now. Perhaps she come understood the purpose of his letter. Perhaps she had learned something about his situation. Perhaps she had shown the letter to his mother, and both of them were searching for him in a panic. Perhaps she had sent the boys to call his father. She must be looking for him everywhere.' He hoped that no one would come here. Just now, he was perhaps more frightened of meeting an acquaintance, than of facing death. He kept looking ahead and behind, as he hurried along in the burning sun without any idea of where he was going. All at once, he started as he heard the whistle of a train. Goodness, had he come so far? The train was right in front of him. He was seized with an overwhelming desire to sit in it, as if, if once he would sit down, he would be freed from all his difficulties. However, he had no money in his pocket. There was a ring on his finger. Summoning one of the head coolies he said, "Can you get this ring sold somewhere? I'll give you a rupee. I've got to go by this train. I left home with some money, but it seems I dropped it somewhere. If I go back, I'll miss the train and suffer a very big loss."

The head coolie looked him up and down, took the ring, and went inside the station. Rama paced up and down by the ticket office, staring in the direction the coolie had gone. Ten minutes went by and the coolie was nowhere to be seen. It struck him that he had taken the ring, and had he disappeared? He went inside the station and began to search. He inquired about him from another coolie, who asked, "What's his name?" Rama bit his tongue. He had not even asked his name. What could he say? In the meantime, the train whistle blew, and Rama panicked. He realised that the head coolie had tricked him. He entered the train and sat down without any ticket. He decided that he would say straight out that he had no ticket. Even if he was made to get off, he would at least be five or ten miles away from here.

When the train started, Rama tearfully thought over his plight, 'Oh! He did not even know whether fate would bring him back or not. When would he ever see happy times again? Those days were gone, gone forever. One day he would die, having hidden himself away from the whole world. No one would even shed tears over his dead body. Even his own family would have shed all their tears for him and become resigned by then. Just because of a little embarrassment, he found himself in this situation. If he had told Jalpa the true state of affairs from the very beginning, he would not have been compelled to run away in disgrace today. But how could he have told her, without her feeling ill-destined? Whatever else might be the case, at least he had kept Jalpa happy for a few days. He had not allowed her longings to be destroyed – even this much was more than enough for Rama to feel satisfaction, now.

Ten minutes after the train had started, the door opened and the ticket collector entered. Rama turned pale. The collector would be with him in a moment. He would be humiliated in front of all these people. His heart began to pound. The closer the ticket collector approached, the more rapidly his pulse beat. At last, the calamity was upon him. "Your ticket?" said the official.

Rama spoke a little cautiously, "My ticket ended up with the head coolie. I gave him some money to bring my ticket, but who knows where he went?"

The collector was not convinced. "I don't know anything about that," he said, "You'll have to get off at the next station. Where are you going?'

"It's a very long journey. I have to go to Calcutta."

"Please get your ticket at the station ahead."

"That's just the problem. I had a fifty rupee note with me. There was a large crowd at the ticket window. I gave the money to the head coolie to bring me a ticket, but he disappeared and never came back. Maybe you know him. He was pretty tall with a pockmarked face."

"You can put something in writing about this, but you can't travel without a ticket."

Humbly, Rama said, "My friend, how can I hide anything from you? I don't have any more money with me. Do whatever you think is suitable."

"I'm sorry, Sir. I'm bound to follow the rules."

The travellers in the compartment began to whisper among themselves. It was a third-class compartment and most of its occupants were labourers travelling east in search of work. They were enjoying seeing a member of the white-collar class being shamed like this. If the ticket collector had thrown him out forcibly, perhaps they would have been even more pleased. Rama had never cowered so in embarrassment. He stood silently with bowed head. This new journey in his life had barely begun. Who knew what other disasters he would experience in the future, or at whose hands he would be deceived? It occurred to him to leap from the train – to die would be better than to live in this terrible mess. His eyes filled with tears, and putting his head out through the open window, he began to cry.

Suddenly, an elderly man who had been sitting next to him asked, "Where are you going to, in Calcutta, Babuji?"

Thinking that this rustic was making fun of him, Rama flared up. "What's it to you where I go?"

Paying not the slightest heed to this contempt, the old man said, "I'm going there too. You and I will go together." Then he said gently, "Take the money for the ticket from me. You can pay me back there."

Rama looked at him carefully now. He was a man of sixty or seventy, so lean that his flesh had practically melted away from his bones. His moustache and hair were shaved clean. He had no other baggage than one small suitcase.

Seeing Rama gazing at him, he spoke again, "Are you going to get down at Howrah or are you going somewhere else?"

Rama, subdued by a strong sense of gratitude, said, "Babu, I'll get down at the next stop. After I've made arrangements for money, I'll continue my trip."

"How much do you need? I'm going there myself. You can give it back when you like. Will you take five or ten rupees from me and run away? Where's your home?"

"Here. I live right here in Prayag."

The old man said reverently, "Prayag is blessed. It's blessed. I've just come back from a sacred bath at the Triveni. It's truly a city where the Gods live. So how much should I give you?"

Shrinking with embarrassment Rama said, "Please understand that I won't be able to pay you back as soon as we reach."

"Oh, Babuji" said the old man simply, "you're hardly going to take five or ten rupees from me and disappear. I've seen how the *panda*s of Prayag give money to pilgrims without keeping a record. Will ten rupees be enough for you?"

"Yes, that's more than enough," said Rama, bowing his head.

Rama gave his fare to the ticket collector and thought to himself, 'What a simple, benevolent, honest soul this old man is. How many people among those they call civilised, would come to the rescue of a traveller they do not know at all?' The other passengers, too, started looking at the old man with veneration.

From the old man's conversation Rama learnt that he was from the Khatik caste, and that he had a vegetable shop in Calcutta. Although he was originally from Bihar, he had been earning his living in Calcutta for forty years now. His name was Devidin and he had been wishing to go on a pilgrimage for a long time. He was just returning from a journey to the sacred city of Badrinath.

"You've just come from Badrinath?" asked Rama in surprise. "The mountain slopes are very steep there."

Devidin said, "If God is gracious, then everything can happen, Babuji. You just need his grace."

Rama said, "You must have children in Calcutta." Devidin gave a dry laugh and said, "All my children are in heaven. I had four sons. Two were married. All of them died. I'm left sitting by myself, even though all of them were born because of me. The farmer himself harvests the seed he's sown."

Saying this, he laughed again. After a little while he said, "The old woman is still alive. We'll see which of us goes first. She says she'll go first, I say I'll go first. We'll see who wins. If possible, I'll show you myself. She still wears her gold earrings and necklace and sits in the shop. When I said, let's go on a pilgrimage, she asked if she was supposed to ruin the business because of my pilgrimage? That's how life is. Whether she dies today or tomorrow, she's not going to leave the shop. There's no one left ahead of us and no one, behind us, there's no one to laugh or cry with us, but such is the weave of illusion. Even now, she keeps getting some piece of jewellery made. Who knows when she will get her fill of it? It's the same story in every home. Wherever you turn – Ah, jewellery! Ah, jewellery! Give up your life running after jewellery, starve the people of your household, sell the things in your home. Even sell your honour. Everyone's caught the same disease, the great and the small, the rich and the poor. Where do you work in Calcutta, Brother?"

"This is the first time I'm going," said Rama. "I'll see if I can find some work or not."

"Then stay with me. There are two rooms, a veranda in front, and a little room upstairs. If I sold the house today I'd get ten thousand. I'll let you have one room. You can get your own place when you find some work. I ran away from home fifty years ago and came to Howrah. I've seen both good times and bad times since then. Now I implore God to take me. Oh yes, and to make the old lady an immortal. Otherwise, who'll take her shop, her house, her jewellery?"

Devidin laughed again. He was so jovial, so contented that Rama was surprised. He laughed at inconsequential things. He laughed where others would cry. Rama had never seen even a young man who laughed like this. He had related his life story in this short while – how many jokes he knew, too. It seemed as if he had known Rama for years. Rama was obliged, in his turn, to tell a fabricated story about himself.

"So you've run away from home, too?" said Devidin. "I understand. There must have been a family quarrel. Your wife must have said, 'I don't have any jewellery, what a wretched fate'. Your mother and your wife probably didn't get on well, and you felt even more depressed hearing them squabble."

"Yes, Baba, that's exactly it. How did you know?"

Devidin laughed and said, "It's a very powerful magical spell and it's invoked on the skull of a *teli*. You don't have any children yet, do you?"

"No, not yet."

"You must have younger brothers."

"Yes, Dada," said Rama, astonished. "You're right. How did you know?"

Devidin jokingly said, "It's all in the spells. Your in-laws are wealthy, I think?"

"Yes, Dada. You are right."

"But they're not very bold."

"You are absolutely correct, Dada. They've very timid. They haven't even called their daughter home since the wedding."

"I have understand, Brother, that's the way of the world. People will steal and beg for their sons, but for daughters, there's nothing at all."

Rama had not slept for three days. All day he had wandered around, madly in search of money, and all night, he had lain tormented by worry. As he was talking now, he began to feel sleepy. His neck lowered and his eyes began to blink. Devidin quickly opened his bundle, took out some cotton matting, and spreading it on the seat, and said, "Lie down here, brother. I'll sit in your place."

Rama lay down. Devidin looked at him, again and again, with loving eyes as if, his his son had just returned from abroad.

22

When Rama had left the room and gone rushing down the stairs, Jalpa had not the slightest suspicion that he was running away from home. She had read the letter. She flared up and felt like telling Rama exactly what she felt. Lying and deceiving her like this – but her mood changed in a moment. She hoped that the government money had not got spent. This was it – Ratan's money had been given to the jeweller. That day, perhaps government money had been brought to give to Ratan. As soon as she thought of this, she became angry again, 'Why had he concealed so much from her? Why had he boasted so much to her? Did he think that she didn't even know that there were both rich and poor people in the world? Was every woman loaded down with jewellery? Was not wearing any jewellery a sin? When money is left over after important things are taken care of, then jewellery is made. You didn't wear jewels at the expense of your stomach and body, or at the expense of committing theft or being dishonourable! Did he think she was as desperate as that?'

She thought Rama must be in his room, so she would go and ask him which jewellery he wanted. As she guessed how terrible the situation was, fear spread in place of anger. She rushed downstairs as quickly as she could. She was convinced he must be sitting there waiting for her. When she entered the room, he was nowhere to be seen. His cycle was there, and immediately she peered out of the door. He was nowhere to be seen on the street, either. Where had he gone? Both boys had gone to school. Who could she send to call Rama? An unfamiliar apprehension began to grow in her heart. She dashed back upstairs, took off her necklace and bangles and bound them in a handkerchief. She went downstairs again, went out on to the street, took a *tonga* and told the driver, "Go to the customs office." She began to repent that she had delayed so long and not taken off her jewellery and given it to Rama right away.

On the way to the office, she kept watching attentively left and right. Could he have come so far in such a short time? Perhaps because he was late, he had taken a *tonga*, too, today, otherwise she would have surely have met him by now. She asked the driver, "Tell me, did you see a gentleman going somewhere in a *tonga* just now?"

"Yes madam," said the driver. "I saw a gentleman going in this direction a little while ago."

Jalpa was somewhat encouraged. She felt she would arrive soon after Rama did. Again and again, she told the driver to make his horse go faster. It was eleven o'clock, by the time she reached the office. Hundreds of people were hurrying here and there. She wondered whom she should ask? How was she to know where he usually sat?

Suddenly a peon appeared. Jalpa summoned him and said, "Listen, please call Ramanath Babu here."

"He's the very person I'm going to fetch," said the peon. "Have you just come from his home?"

"Yes, that's just where I've come from. He left home no more than ten minutes ago."

"He hasn't come here."

Jalpa was in a dilemma. He had not come here, she had not seen him on the way. Then where had he gone? Her heart began to pound. Her eyes filled with tears. She did not know anyone else there, except the senior clerk, Rama's boss, Ramesh. She had never had the occasion to speak to him before, but now any bashfulness vanished. Fear suppresses all other emotions. "Tell the head clerk ... No, I'll come myself," she said to the peon, "I have to talk with him."

The peon, awed by her manner and her dignity, turned around and went to the Head Clerk's office. Jalpa followed close on his heels. Ramesh Babu came out as soon as he heard the news of her arrival.

Jalpa stepped forward and said, "Please excuse me for troubling you, Babu Sahab. He left home fifteen or twenty minutes ago. Has he not reached here yet?"

Ramesh said, "Well, you're Mrs Ramanath. No, he hasn't reached here yet."

Jalpa said, "But he wasn't in the habit of strolling around during office hours." Looking pointedly at the peon, Jalpa addressed Ramesh Babu. "I have a request to make of you."

Ramesh said, "Come inside and sit down, then. You don't need to keep standing here. I'm surprised he's gone off somewhere. He's probably sitting somewhere playing chess."

Jalpa said, "No, Babuji. I'm worried that he may have gone somewhere else. He wrote a note to me only ten minutes ago." She groped in her pocket and said, "Yes, look, here's that note. You're well-disposed towards him, he doesn't hide anything from you. Hasn't he lost some government money he was responsible for?"

Surprised, Ramesh said, "What? Hasn't he told you anything?

Jalpa said, "Not a thing. He's never said one word about this."

Ramesh said, "I just don't understand. He has to give three hundred rupees today. There was some money from day before's collection that he had to give to the office. There were some bank notes. He stuck them in his pocket and left. Someone pinched the notes while he was in the *bazar.* He smiled and said, "Does he worship some other goddess besides you?"

Jalpa bowed her head in embarrassment. "If that were one of his shortcomings," she said, "then you wouldn't also escape this blame, either. Someone must have taken it from his pocket. He must not have said anything to me out of shame. If he'd said something to me, I'd have given him some money immediately, what was there in such a matter?"

Ramesh Babu said, disbelievingly, "Is there some money at home?"

"You need three hundred, don't you?' said Jalpa unhesitatingly. "I'll bring it just now."

Ramesh said, "If he has come home, send him here."

Jalpa sat in the *tonga* and told the coachman to go to the market. She had decided to sell her necklace. In fact, she had several woman friends from whom she could have got money. There is great affection among women. Unlike men, their friendship goes beyond eating *paan* and playing cards together. She did not have enough time. When she arrived in the jewellery market, she began to consider which shop she should go to. She was afraid of being cheated. She walked from one end of the market to the other, without plucking up the courage to enter any one shop. Time was passing by. At last, seeing an elderly jeweller in one shop, her hesitation diminished slightly. The jeweller was a cunning old rascal; seeing Jalpa's hesitation and vacillation, he understood that he had snared easy game.

Showing him the necklace, Jalpa asked, "Can you buy this?"

The jeweller, looking at the piece carefully from all sides, said, "If I can make a little profit on it, why wouldn't I take it? But it's not a first-rate piece."

Jalpa said, "It's not first-rate because you're buying. But if you were selling, then it would be. How much will you buy it for?"

The jeweller said, "You tell me then."

The jeweller valued it at three hundred and fifty, and gradually came to four hundred. Jalpa was already late; she took the money and left without delay. The very necklace, which she had bought so eagerly, the craving for which had been implanted in her since childhood, she now sold for half its price without the slightest regret, but rather with a feeling of pride and happiness. How pleased Rama would be when he found out that she had given the money. 'If he should go to the office, what a good joke it would be,' she thought as she arrived at the office again. "What happened? Did you meet him at home," said Ramesh Babu, looking at her.

"What? He hasn't come here yet? I didn't go home." As she said this, she held out a bundle of notes towards Ramesh Babu.

He counted the notes and said, "That's good, but where is he now? If he wasn't going to come, he could have written me a letter. I was in a great difficulty. You came in the nick of time. I'm pleased to see how sensible you are. You've done your duty like a true goddess."

When Jalpa returned to the *tonga* to go home, she felt that she had increased in stature. A strange energy was coursing through her body. She was sure that Rama must be at home, sitting and worrying. She would first go and give him a good scolding and make him duly ashamed, and after she that, she would tell him what she had done. When she arrived home, Ramanath was nowhere to be seen.

Rameshwari asked, "Where did you go in this hot sun?"

Jalpa said, "I had something to do. He didn't even eat today. There's no telling where he's gone."

Rameshwari said, "He must have gone to the office!"

"No," said Jalpa. "He didn't go there. A peon had come asking for him," She went upstairs, put the remaining money in her trunk, and began to fan herself. Her body felt aflame from the heat, but her ear was tuned to the door. Till now, she had not the slightest suspicion that Rama had set out for another part of the country.

She did not become particularly worried until four o'clock, but as the day began to draw to a close, her anxiety began to grow. Finally she climbed up to the highest part of the roof, although no one went there because of its dilapidated condition, and looked around. Rama was not to be seen anywhere. When Rama had not come home by evening, Jalpa was really alarmed. Where had he gone? He went out only after returning home from the office. If he was at some friend's house, would he have not returned by now? She did not know whether or not he had any money in his pocket. Who knew where the poor fellow might have been wandering around all day. She again repented not giving him her necklace as soon as she had read his letter. Why had she remained plunged in indecision? The unfortunate fellow must be avoiding home, out of shame. Where could she go? Who could she ask for help?

When the lamps were lit she could contain herself no longer. She thought that maybe Ratan would know something. When she went to her friend's bungalow she learned that Rama had not gone there at all that day.

Jalpa carefully searched through all the parks and grounds where she had often rambled with Rama. She returned discouraged around nine o'clock. She had been able to restrain her tears until now, but as soon as she set foot inside and realised that he had not yet come, she sat down and gave way to despair. Now her misgiving that he had fled somewhere became a certainty. Still, she had some hope that he might have come and gone while she had been out. She went and asked Rameshwari, "Did he come home, Mother?"

"He must be sitting somewhere with his cronies, gossiping," said Rameshwari. "Home is like a hotel to him. He left at ten this morning, and I still don't know where he is."

Jalpa said, "He comes home from the office before he goes out anywhere. He hasn't come home today. If you say so, I'll send Gopi Babu to go and see where he is."

Rameshwari said, "Where will the boys look for him at this hour? There's no telling where he may be. Wait a while longer, then, keep his food away. How long can one wait?"

Jalpa gave no answer to this. She said nothing about what had happened at the office. Rameshwari would have panicked and cried up a storm.

Going upstairs and lying down, she started crying over her misfortune. She was so distressed that she had the sensation that a spike was rising up through her heart. Over and over she asked herself that was if he did not come back during the night, what would she do tomorrow? Where could anyone go look for him, until there was some word of where he might have gone? Today for the first time, she accepted all this as the fruit of her own actions. It was true that she had never insisted on having ornaments, but neither had she ever dearly forbidden it. If she had not been so impatient after the theft of her jewels, this day would never have come. In her weakened state of mind, Jalpa took the greater portion of the blame upon herself. She had known that Rama took bribes, that he brought home money by hook or by crook. Even then, she had never forbidden him to do this. Why had she not stayed within her limit? Why had she thought up of excursions and outings every day? Why had she not been able to control her delight when she accepted his presents? Now she was taking the sole responsibility for this, too, upon herself. Ramanath overpowered by his love for her had done everything just to please her. Young men were like that. Then what had she done to protect him? Why had she not understood that one day they would have to suffer the consequences of spending more than their income? How many things she remembered now from which she ought to have recognised Rama's distress, but to which she had never paid attention.

Jalpa sat, drowning in these cares for some time. When the sound of the night watchmen's whistles reached her ears, she rose and went downstairs. "He hasn't come yet," she said to Rameshwari. "Please go and eat your food."

Rameashwari was sitting and nodding off. Waking with a start she said, "Where had he gone?"

Jalpa said, "He hasn't come back as yet."

Rameshwari said, "Hasn't returned till now? It must be midnight. Did he say anything to you when he was leaving?"

"Nothing at all."

"You didn't say anything to him, did you?"

"Goodness, what could I have said?"

"Should I wake up Lalaji then?"

"What will you do by waking him up now? Why don't you go eat something?"

Rameshwari said, "I won't be able to eat anything now. I've never heard of such an irresponsible boy. Has said nothing and been told nothing, who knows where he is now? At the least, he could have let us know that he won't be returning at this time."

Rameshwari lay down again, but Jalpa stayed, sitting, as she was. The whole night passed by – the night like a mountain, whose every moment dragged by like a year.

23

A week went by, and there was no word of Rama. Some people said one thing, and some said another. Ramesh Babu came several times each day to enquire. All kinds of guesses were being made. The only definite information was that Ramanath had gone in the direction of the railway station at eleven o'clock. Munshi Dayanath's opinion, although he did not express it in so many words, was that Rama had committed suicide. That is what happened in such circumstances. He had seen several examples of this with his own eyes. Her mother-in-law and father-in-law laid the whole blame on Jalpa. They said clearly that that he had lost his life because of her. She had made his life difficult. Why had she gone on outings and accepted invitations, and thrown parties on such a modest income? No one took pity on Jalpa, no one dried her tears. Only Ramesh Babu praised her promptness and keen intelligence. In Munshi Dayanath's eyes though, her action had no worth. Someone who has started a fire cannot be held innocent because he comes with water, running to put it out.

One day Dayanath returned from the library, with a sad, drawn face. Since he was habitually gloomy, his sad, downcast face made it clear to even a child that he was in a really bad mood.

"What is it?" asked Rameshwari. "Did you have an argument with someone?"

Dayanath said, "No. I'm really shocked by all this harassment for payment. Wherever I go, they come running to snatch my money. There's no telling how indebted he is. Today I told them right out, that I didn't know anything. I'm not in anyone's debt. They can go and ask the Memsahab."

Just then Jalpa passed by and chanced to overhear these words. Her face had changed so much in the past week that one could hardly recognise her. She cried so much that her eyes were swollen. Hearing these harsh words from her father-in-law, she flared up. "Yes, Sir! You please send them straight to me. I'll either give them a talking-to or pay them off."

"What can you pay them with?" asked Dayanath, sharply. "It comes to thousands. Why, just one of those jewellers is owed seven hundred. How much have you paid him?"

Jalpa said, "His jewellery is here. They've only been worn three or four times. If he comes here, please send him to me. I'll give his things back to him. At the most, he will take five or ten rupees as compensation."

She was about to go upstairs after saying this when Ratan arrived, embraced her, and asked, "You haven't heard anything as yet?"

To Jalpa these words seemed to be gushing with deep affection and sympathy. Here was someone not even related to her, but so concerned, while there were her own mother-in-law and father-in-law who were intent on blaming her. Strangers were better than these relatives. Her eyes filled with tears, and she said, “No, Sister, I haven't heard anything yet.”

Ratan said, “How did it happen? You didn't have a quarrel, did you?”

Jalpa said, “Not at all, I swear. He didn't even mention to me that he'd lost those bank notes. If he'd even hinted at it, I'd have given him the money. When he hadn't come back by afternoon, I went to the office looking for him, and that's when I found out he'd lost some bank notes. I went and paid off the money straight away.”

“I understand,” said Ratan. “He's fallen in love with someone. You'll find out in a few days. If it doesn't turn out to be true, then I'll give you whatever you ask for.”

Jalpa, taken aback, said, “Have you heard anything?”

Ratan said, “No, I haven't heard anything, but it's my guess!”

Jalpa said, “No, Ratan. I can't believe a word of it. Whatever other faults he has, he doesn't have this one. I have no reason to mistrust him.”

Ratan laughed and said, “These men are experts in this art. How would you know? You poor thing.”

“If they're experts in this art, then we are no less expert in judging their hearts,” said Jalpa resolutely. “I can't belive that. If he is my master, I'm no less his mistress.”

Ratan said, “All right, let it go. Do you wan't to go out somewhere? Come, let me take you somewhere.”

Jalpa said, “No, I'm not free just now. If so, my family here is determined to take my life, then, they won't leave me alive. Where were you thinking of going?”

“Nowhere in particular, just to the *bazar*,” said Ratan.

“What do you want to buy?”

“I wanted to look at a couple of things in a jewellery shop,” said Ratan. “I want a bracelet like yours, that's all. Your husband finally returned my money after several months. I will look for one myself.”

“What's so special about my bracelet? You can get much nicer ones in the *bazar*.”

“I want one just like it.”

“It'll be hard to find this bracelet ready made, if someone copies it, then finishing it will take several troublesome months. If you don't have the patience to wait, take mine. I'll get another one made.”

Leaping up in joy, Ratan said, “Ah! You're giving me your bracelet, then what need I say? I'm so happy that I could let everyone know by beating a drum! It cost six hundred, didn't it?'

Jalpa said, "Yes, it did, but I had to waste months in the jeweller's shop. I finally got the inlaid work done by sitting there myself. Out of consideration for you, I will give it to to you."

Jalpa took off her bracelet and put it on Ratan's wrist. Ratan's face showed an unusual radiance, as if a wretched pauper were receiving something precious. For her, it was the ultimate limit of personal joy. In a voice filled with gratitude, she said, "I'm ready to give you whatever you ask for. I don't want to take advantage of you. Is it worth any less because you gave it to me? Just one thing, though. I can't pay you the entire sum right now. Do you have any objection if I give you two hundred rupees later?"

"No objection at all," said Jalpa, resolutely. "If you feel like it, don't give me anything at all."

Ratan said, "No, I've got four hundred rupees with me which I'll give you before I go. If I keep them I'll spend them somewhere else. Money simply never stays put in my hands, what can I do? Until I spend it I feel a little worried, as if I've got a load sitting on my head." When Jalpa took out the little bracelet box to give to Ratan, she felt a pang in her heart. How happy Rama used to be when he saw this bracelet on her wrist. If he were here today, would it have left her hands like this? Then, who knew when she fated to wear a bracelet again? She made a great effort to control herself, but tears spilled out.

Ratan saw her tears and said, "Let it be for now, Sister. I'll take it later. What's the hurry?"

Jalpa extended the box towards her and said, "Why? Just because you saw my tears? I'm giving it out of consideration for you, otherwise, it was more precious to me than my life. When I see you wearing it, I'll be consoled. Be so kind as to not give this to anyone else."

Ratan said, "Why would I even think of giving it to anyone else? I'll keep it as a token from you. Today after a very long time my heart's desire has been fulfilled. I'm only sorry that your husband isn't here now. I have a feeling that he'll come back quickly. He's just run away because he's ashamed, nothing else. Vakil Sahab was sorry to hear about it, too. People say that lawyers are hardhearted, but I see that when he hears of someone having even a little difficulty, he suffers."

Jalpa smiled and said, 'Sister, can I ask you something? You won't take it otherwise? Is it possible that you're not soulmates with the Vakil Sahab?"

For a moment Ratan's pleasure-flushed happy face fell. It was as if someone had reminded her of a cherished, long-lost love for whose sake she had cried, years ago. "I have never ever thought that I'm a young woman and that he's an old man, Sister," she said. "Whatever love, whatever affection there is in my heart, I've dedicated it all to him. Affection doesn't arise because of youth, beauty or money. Affection is born from affection itself.

He's working so hard, and in his condition, just for me, who else is there? Is that a small thing? Shall we go out tomorrow? Tell me, should I come by in the evening?"

Jalpa replied, "I won't go anywhere at all, but you must certainly come. We'll entertain ourselves for a little while. Nothing seems right. My mind trips restlessly from one broken branch to another, and does not rest on a thing. I just don't understand why he was so hesitant to tell me. That's my fault, too. He must have seen something in me, which made him feel he had to keep things from me. What really makes me feel sad is that I never earned his true love. You don't keep secrets from someone you love."

When Ratan got up to leave Jalpa noticed that the bracelet box was lying on the table. "Take this with you, Sister," she said. "Why are you leaving it here?"

Ratan said, "I'll take it. What's the hurry just now? I haven't even given you all the money."

Jalpa said, "No, no, take it. I won't agree to your leaving without it."

Ratan went downstairs and left Jalpa standing with the bracelet in her hand.

A little later, Jalpa took five hundred rupees out of her trunk, and going to Dayanath, said, "Please take this money and send to that jeweller, Narayan Das. I'll give you the rest of the money very soon."

"From where did you get the money?" said he, feeling ashamed.

"I sold the bracelet to Ratan," replied Jalpa, without any embarrassment. Dayanath just stared at her face.

24

A month went by. A notice appeared regularly in Prayag's biggest daily newspaper, urging Ramanath to return home, and promising a reward of five hundred rupees to anyone who brought news of him. However, no news had come from anywhere as yet. Jalpa was wasting away from worry and grief. Seeing her condition, even Dayanath began to take pity on her. At last he wrote to Dindayal one day: 'Come and take our daughter-in-law home with you for a while.' As soon as Dindayal received the news, he came rushing over, all flustered. However, Jalpa refused to go home.

Taken aback, Dindayal said, "Do you intend to just keep lying here and die?"

"If I'm to die in this way, then who can stop it?' said Jalpa, in a solemn voice. "But I'm not going to die yet, Father, believe me. There's no place for unfortunate people like there, also."

"But what is the harm in coming? Both of your friends Shehzadi and Vasanti have come. You'll enjoy yourself laughing and talking with them."

"I can't bring myself to go and leave Father-in-law and Mother-in-law alone here. Since I'm destined to cry, I'll cry."

"What actually happened? I hear that there were debts. Some people say that government money was embezzled."

"Whoever told you that, told an out-and-out lie."

"Then why did he leave?"

"I don't know anything thing about that. I keep having doubts about that myself."

"He didn't have a fight with Lala Dayanath, did he?"

"He doesn't even raise his head around Lalaji, or even chew *paan*, so why should he quarrel with him? He was fond of going for walks. He must have thought no one would let him off just like that, so he decided to run away."

"Maybe that's just how it was," said Dindayal. "Some people have a craze for gallivanting around. Tell me clearly if you face any difficulties. Should I send you anything for your expenses?"

"I don't have any troubles, Father," said Jalpa proudly. "With your kindness, I don't lack anything."

Dayanath and Rameshwari tried to persuade her, but she would not agree to go. Then Dayanath snapped, "Well, it's better than lying around here and crying the whole day."

"Is it a different world over there?" said Jalpa. "Will I become different by going there? And why should I be afraid to cry? When I had to laugh, I laughed. When I have to cry, I cry. Even if he's gone many miles away, I see him sitting here, in front of me, every moment. He's not here in person, but he's here in every single thing in this house. If I leave this place, I'll go crazy with despair."

Dindayal realised that his proud daughter was not going to abandon her insistence on remaining. He got up and went out. When he left in the evening, he held out a fifty rupee note to Jalpa and said, "Keep this, you might need it."

Jalpa shook her head and said, "I don't need it at all, Father. But yes, I want you to bless me. It is possible that your blessing will bring me grace."

Dindayal's eyes filled with tears. Leaving the note on the bed where he had been sitting, he went outside.

The month of September was well under way. Fragments of rainless clouds could be seen scuttling across the sky from time to time. Jalpa would lie on the roof and watch the gambols of these cloud fragments. What other object is more enjoyable for beings tormented by anxiety? Cloud fragments take on many different colours, many different shapes. Sometimes they come together in love, sometimes they part in a huff, sometimes they run, sometimes they come to a dead halt. Jalpa would think to herself that Ramanath, too, must be sitting somewhere watching the same cloud-play. This fantasy gave her a strange pleasure. A sort of affection grows for these sky-travelling creatures, very similar to the feeling of kinship a gardener has for plants he has grown himself or a child for the playhouse he has made for himself. Our minds turn inwards in distress. Jalpa now began to fear that God had punished her for her misdeeds. Had Ramanath not squeezed money out of others every day, after all to bring home? No one gave him that money gladly. How happy she had been to see this money, for all her pleasure and ornaments had come from this. Now she felt incensed whenever she saw those things. They were the root cause of all her griefs – because of them her husband had had to go away. These things scratched her eyes like thorns, stabbed her heart like spikes.

At last she gathered them all up one day – velvet slippers, silk socks, all kinds of embroidery, ribbons, pins, combs, mirrors, who could have counted them all? It was a big pile. She resolved to sink this pile in the Ganges and start life afresh from now on. For the sake of these things, she was in this present condition. Today she would destroy this web of illusions, once and for all. Although the thought of throwing away so many beautiful things brought pangs of regret, these few drops of water could not begin to extinguish the raging fire of remorse and disgust. She spent half the night setting them apart one by one, as if she were preparing for some journey. Yes, it really was a journey for her – from darkness to light, from falsehood to truth. She thought to herself that if God should take pity and let Rama return home, then she would live within minimum expenses. She would not spend a single paisa unnecessarily. She would not let him bring home even a single paisa over his regular wages. Her new life would begin from today.

At four in the morning, when the sounds of people on the streets were heard, Jalpa picked up her bag, full of things, and set out to bathe in the Ganges. The bag was very heavy. It was difficult to walk even ten steps with it hanging from her hand. Again and again, she shifted it from one hand to the other. She was also scared that someone might see her. She had never had the occasion to carry such a load before. Horse-cart drivers called to her, but she paid them no attention. When her arms tired, she shifted the bag to her back and started walking again with lengthened steps. She drew the edge of her sari well across her face so that no one would recognise her.

She had nearly reached the bathing *ghat*s when faint morning light was seen. All at once, she saw Ratan in her car. She attempted to bow her head and hide her face, but Ratan recognised her even at a distance. She stopped the car and asked, "Where are you going, Sister? What's that bag on your back?"

Jalpa thrust the *sari* aside from her face and said confidently, "I'm going to bathe in the Ganges."

"I've just come back from bathing, but let's go. I'll come along with you. I'll take you home and then go home myself. Keep the bag here."

"No, no," said Jalpa. "It's not heavy. Go on, you'll be late. I will carry on."

Ratan did not agree. She got out of the car, took the bag and put it inside. "What have you filled in this? It's really heavy. May I open it and see?"

"There's nothing in it worth your looking at."

The bag had no lock. When Ratan opened it and looked, she was astonished. "Where are you going with these things?"

Jalpa sat down inside the car and said, "I'm going to sink them in the Ganges."

Even more astonished, Ratan said, "In the Ganges! You haven't gone a little mad, have you? Come on, let's go home. We'll leave the bag there and then come back."

Jalpa said firmly, "No, Ratan, I'll go after I've thrown these things in the river." "After all, why?"

"First drive on, then I'll tell you."

"No, first tell me."

"No, that won't happen. First drive on."

Defeated, Ratan had the car driven ahead, and said, "All right, now will you tell me?"

Jalpa said reproachfully, "You of all people ought to have understood. Why are you asking me? Of what use are these things to me now? Whenever I see them, I feel grief. When the one person who enjoyed seeing them has gone, what am I supposed to do with them?"

Ratan heaved a deep sigh, grasped Jalpa by the hand, and in a trembling voice, said, "You're doing a great injustice to your husband, Sister. How much delight he must have taken in bringing them for you. How pleased he must have been seeing how splendid they looked on you. Each one of them is a memory of his love. By throwing them into the Ganges you are showing him great disrespect!'

For a moment, Jalpa became lost in thought – she began to debate and grew uncertain. Almost instantly, she regained control of herself. "That's not right, Sister. My mind won't be at peace until these things are out of my sight. This love of luxury has put me in this awful situation. This is a bundle of misfortunes, not of memories of love. His love is engraved on my heart."

"Your heart is very hard, Jalpa," said Ratan. "I probably wouldn't have been able to do what you're doing.'

"But for me, these things are the root cause for all my troubles."

After a short silence, she spoke again. "He's done me a great wrong, Sister. I consider that any man who keeps things hidden from his wife does not love her. If I'd been in his place, I wouldn't have run away and abandoned everyone like this. I'd have poured out all the pains of my heart, and I'd have done everything according to his advice. How does this deceit come between man and woman?"

Ratan, smiling grimly, said, "There are probably very few men who open their hearts to a woman. When you yourself hide things in your heart, why do you have hopes that he won't conceal things from you? Can you honestly say that you didn't conceal things from him?"

"I didn't hide things from him," said Jalpa, with some embarrassment.

"You're telling a lie, a complete lie," said Ratan forcefully. "If you'd trusted him, he'd have opened up to you, too."

Jalpa was unable to counter this censure. Now she realised that the deceit between her and Rama had been begun by her.

They reached the bank of the Ganges and the car stopped. Jalpa began to take the bag, but Ratan pushed aside her hand and said, "No, I won't let you do it. Just imagine that it's already sunk in the river."

"How can I possibly imagine that?"

"Show me this much kindness for being like a sister to you."

"I could wash your feet for being like a sister, but I can't keep these thorns in my heart," said Jalpa.

"You won't agree, no matter what?" said Ratan frowning.

"Yes, no matter what."

Ratan turned her face away in aversion. Jalpa took the bag, and quickly going down the stairs of the *ghat*, reached the edge of the river where she lifted the bag and threw it into the water. Her face lit up from her victory over her weakness. She felt more joy and pride than she had ever had when first receiving these things.

Among the countless beings performing their devotional ablutions that morning, perhaps no one felt as much inner light as she, as if every particle of her body were suffused with the golden radiance of dawn.

When she had bathed and returned to the car above, Ratan asked, "Did you toss them in?"

"Yes."

"You're very ruthless,"

"It's this ruthlessness that triumphs over one's fickle mind. If I'd been ruthless some while ago, would this day have ever come?"

The car drove on.

25

It had been more than two months since Ramanath's arrival in Calcutta. He was still staying in Devidin's home. The thought of where the money would come from haunted him constantly like a recurring refrain. He formed all kinds of plans, iamagined of many kinds of things, but he never set foot outside the house. True, when it became quite dark he would always go to the neighbourhood reading room. He was always eager to read the news of his home city and province. He saw the notice that Dayanath had had published in the papers, but could not believe it. Who knew whether the police might not be practising some deception in order to arrest him? Who could possibly have paid off the money? Impossible!

One day, in the same paper, Ramanath found a letter published from Jalpa to him. In words filled with insistence and pleading, she urged him to return home. She wrote: 'Nothing is owed by you to anyone. Come home, no one will say anything to you.' Ramanath became agitated, but then it immediately occurred to him that this too was some devilry by the police. What proof was there that Jalpa had written this letter? And even if he was to believe that his family had paid off the money, how could he go home? His reputation must have been besmirched everywhere in the city, the police must also have been warned. He decided that he would not go. He· would not even think of going home until he had at least five thousand in hand. If the money had not been paid off, and the police were searching for him, why then, he would never go home, never!

Devidin's house had two small rooms and a veranda ahead. The shop was on the veranda, food was prepared in one room, and pots and pans, kept in the other. There was a small room above and a small open terrace. Rama lived in this upper portion of the house. Devidin had no special place for himself for sitting or sleeping. After the shop closed at night, this same veranda became a bedroom; both he and his wife slept there. Devidin smoked his *chilam* and spoke to people going and coming, all day. The old woman did all the work of running the shop. She bought things from the *mandi*, sent and brought things to and from the station. Devidin did not even recognise the shop's customers. He knew a little Hindi — he would sit and read the *Ramayana, The Parrot and the Mynah,* the *Rasleela,* or *The Story of the Virgin Mary.* After Rama's arrival, he developed a taste for learning English. He would sit from early morning until nine or ten o'clock studying the letters in an English primer, with Rama. There would be frequent interruptions for jokes, of which Devidin had an unending store. His wife, Jaggo, did not like the time Rama spent, sitting with him. She had made Rama into her bookkeeper and had him keep her accounts book, but she did not think it worthwhile to hire anyone for such a small amount of work. Previously, she had had her customers do this for her. Rama's staying with them affronted her, but he was so courteous, so ready to be of service, and so devout, that she could not openly object. To be sure, by ascribing it to others, and with repeated innuendos, she vented her spleen. Rama had declared himself to be a Brahmin, and he observed the religious duties of one. By becoming pious and a Brahman, he was able to gain the esteem of both husband and wife. He understood the old woman's character and behaviour very well, but what else could he do? He was powerless to be brazen. Circumstances had robbed him of his self-respect.

One day, Ramanath was sitting reading a paper in the reading room when he suddenly spotted Ratan. From her manner it seemed as if she was searching for someone. Scores of people were sitting reading books and papers. Rama's heart began to pound. He slipped out of the room with averted eyes and bowed head and stood hidden in the darkened veranda at the rear, where some old broken boxes and chairs were kept. His soul was in a fever to meet Ratan and ask her for news of home, but he could not face her because of his shame and embarrassment. Oh, there were so many things to ask, but the most important of all was, what did Jalpa think of him now? Was she not weeping over his cruelty? Was she angered at his arrogance? Did she consider him deceitful and dishonest? Had she become thin? And what were people's feelings towards him? Had his house been searched? Had a lawsuit been brought against him? He was impatient to know a thousand such things, but how could he show his face? He kept peeping out. When Ratan left and her car had moved, he revived. He did not go the reading room for a week. He did not leave the house at all.

Sometimes when he was lying around, Rama would get so perturbed that he considered going to the police and telling them the whole story. Let whatever happen, happen. One or two years of imprisonment would be far better than his lifelong imprisonment. Then he would make a new entry into life and its struggles, work more intelligently, mind his hands and feet and not go beyond his limit, even by a single grain-width. However, in a moment, his courage would fail.

Two more months passed in this way, and January arrived. Rama had no winter clothes. He had brought nothing at all from home, nor was he able to get anything made here. Till now, he had made it through the nights somehow or other by spreading a *dhoti* over himself, but without a quilt or blanket how could he get through the crackling cold of January? The poor wretch lay curled up like a bundle the whole night. When it was particularly cold, he would cover himself with the bedding. Devidin had given him an old carpet to spread on the bed. This was probably the best bedcover in the house. This class of people would have only tattered old quilts for spreading, even though they wore ten thousand rupees worth of jewellery, or spend ten thousand for a wedding. How was anyone supposed to keep warm with this rotten old carpet, but it was better than nothing at all. Rama was too diffident to be able to say anything to Devidin, and Devidin for his part, probably didn't want to spend such a lot, or perhaps, he simply did not notice it. When the day began to draw to a close, Rama would shudder as he anticipated the misery of the coming night, tearing towards him as if it were the terrible goddess of destruction, Kali. He would get up again and again in the night to open the window to see how far away morning was.

One evening as he was going to the reading room, he saw that thousands of beggars had gathered around a large mercantile building. He wondered what was going on, and why so many people had collected there. He pushed his way though the crowd to find out, and learnt that a wealthy merchant donating blankets to the poor. The blankets were shoddy, light and thin, but people were grabbing them, one by one. It occurred to Rama to take one for himself. Who knew him here? Even if anyone did, what harm would it cause? If a poor Brahmin didn't have the right to accept the gift of a blanket, then who did? An instant later his self-respect came to life. He stood and stared for a little while, and then moved on. Setting the mark on Rama's forehead, the merchant's bookkeeper took him to be a Brahmin. There were very few Brahmins among all these beggars. The religious merit of bestowing a gift on a Brahmin was much greater – the bookkeeper was secretly pleased that a sacred Brahmin had appeared. Hence when he saw Rama going, he said, "Punditji, where are you going? Please take a blanket!" Rama almost died of shame. He was only able to utter a few words, "I don't wish to." He moved ahead as he said this. The bookkeeper thought that this Brahmin might be leaving because he saw the blankets were shoddy. Probably, he had never in his whole life met a god with so much self-esteem. Some other Brahmin would have flattered him with sweet talk, and asked for a better blanket. This divine soul who was leaving without a word, must certainly be some great ascetic soul. He leaped forward, seized Rama by the hand, and said, "Won't you come, your Reverence, there's a beautiful blanket kept for you. These are for beggars." When Rama saw that he was getting something without even asking for it, and that it was being forced on him, he said, "No, no" twice more, and then accompanied the bookkeeper inside. The latter took him inside the building, seated him, and presented him with a rather good, thick blanket. Rama's contentedness made such an impression on him that he tried to give five rupees as a religious donation, but Rama refused outright to take this. The collected glory of several lifetimes had already been wounded by taking only the blanket – to stretch forth his hand for this donation became impossible for him.

Astonished, the bookkeeper said, "If you won't agree to take this gift, Sethji will be very grieved."

In a detached manner, Rama said, "I took the blanket when you insisted, but I can't take your donation. I don't need money. The gentleman at the house where I'm staying gives me meals. What will I do with more?"

"Sethji won't agree."

"Please ask for his pardon on my behalf."

"May your renunciation be blessed. It's Brahmins like you who have established the honour of our religion. If you'll please just sit for a while, Sethji must certainly be coming. He'll be very pleased at the good fortune of seeing you. He's a great devotee of Brahmins. Every evening, he says his prayers, and he reaches the bank of the Ganges at three in the morning, and then comes home to worship. At ten o'clock, religiously he reads the *Bhagavata*. At midday, as soon as he eats his meal, he comes here. Around three or four, he goes off to pray. At eight o'clock, he comes here again for a little while. At nine o'clock he goes to the temple to hear devotional hymns and after praying again, he eats another meal. He'll be here in a little while. If you'd sit for a few minutes, it would be very good of you. Where do you live?'

Rama avoided mentioning Prayag and told him that he came from Kashi. Rama dreaded staying, lest Sethji should start some religious conversation, whereupon he would be unmasked. Promising to come another day, he made his escape.

When he returned from the reading room at nine o'clock, he was afraid that Devidin would see the blanket and ask him where he had got it from. What answer would he give? He would make some excuse. He would say that he had borrowed it from the shop of an acquaintance.

As soon as he saw the blanket, Devidin asked, "Did you reach Seth Karorimal's, Maharaj?"

"Which Seth Karorimal?" asked Rama.

"Well, that person, the one who owns the big red building."

Rama was unable to make up any excuse. He said, "Yes, the bookkeeper wouldn't leave me in peace. He's a very devout soul."

Devidin smiled as he said, "A very devout soul, indeed! If he had not clutched the earth in his hands, it would have been destroyed by now."

"He acts like a devout soul," said Rama, "but only God knows what's in his mind. If you don't call someone who reads scriptures and worships all day, who busies himself with charity and fasts, a pious soul, then what else do you call him?"

"You should call him a sinner, a really bad sinner. Mercy does not even pass by where he is. He has a jute mill. You won't find the kind of cruelty he shows towards the workers in his mill anywhere else. He has people beaten with whips. He's earned hundreds of thousands by selling ghee adulterated with fat. If one of his employees is even a minute late, he cuts his wages on the spot. If he does not give away three or four thousand a year, how will he digest his wealth of sins? Really pious Brahmans don't even glance at his door. Was there any other Brahmin there besides you?"

Rama shook his head.

"Not one goes there. Yes, but greedy and useless people do. All the worshippers I've seen were like stones. By worshipping stone idols, their hearts become like stone, too. He has three very large pilgrim-houses; the point is that he's a hypocrite. Even if a man does nothing else, he ought to at least keep mercy in his heart. All the hundred religions have this in common."

After he had eaten the food kept for him, he lay down, As he spread the blanket over himself, Rama began to feel intense remorse. He had raked in thousands of rupees from bribes without feeling even a moment's remorse. One got bribes through cleverness, through skill, through effort, but spineless, inactive and and hypocrites subsisted on the basis of gifts. He thought, 'Now I am so wretched that I have to receive food and clothes through charity.' He had been staying at Devidin's house for two months, now, but he considered him a guest rather than a beggar. The feeling of charity had never entered his mind. Rama felt such a surge of agitation that he was ready to go to the police station that very instant and spill out his whole tale, and then there would be an end to this. He would get two or three years of punishment, but his life would not hang in this terrible state of anguish. 'Why not go and drown himself somewhere? Where was the advantage in living like this? Here he belonged to no home or to any place. Instead of making others' burdens lighter, he was looking to others to take care of him. Who was getting any benefit from his life? How shameful was his life,' these thoughts coursed through his mind.

Rama made a decision that tomorrow he would fearlessly go and search for work. Whatever was going to happen, he would let it happen.

26

Rama was just in the middle of washing his hands and face, when Devidin arrived with his primer and said, "Brother, this English of yours is very strange. 'S' 'i' 'r' is 'sir', then why does 'p' 'i' 't' become 'pit'? 'B' 'u''t' is 'but', then why is 'p' 'u' 't' 'put'? It must be very difficult for you, too."

Rama smiled and said, "It seemed difficult at first, but now it seems easy."

Devidin, "On the day I finish reading this primer, I'll offer Hanuman a *laddu* or two. Primer *(parai-mar)* means someone else's woman's *(parai)* death *(mar)!* I say let mine die. What pleasure would I get from the death of someone else's woman? You have children, don't you, Brother?"

"Yes, I do!" said Rama, speaking as if there were, but there might as well not be.

"Has any letter or something come?"

"No!"

"And you haven't written either? My God, you haven't sent a single letter for three months? Your people won't be worried?"

"What sort of letter am I supposed to write until I have some fixed place here?"

'Well, my good fellow, at least write to say that you're all right here. You ran away from home, so they must be very worried. Your father and mother are alive, aren't they?"

"Yes, certainly."

"Well then, Brother," Devidin entreated him, "write a letter this very day. Listen to me."

Till now Rama had concealed his true state of affairs. How many times had he wished to say something to Devidin, but it would come to his lips and go no further. He wanted to hear Devidin's criticism, wanted to know what advice he would give. This time Devidin's good nature overwhelmed him. "I ran away from home, Dada," he said.

"I know that," said Devidin, smiling behind his moustache. "Did you quarrel with your father?"

"No."

"Your mother must have said something?"

"Not that, either."

"Then there must be some trouble with your wife. She must have told you that she wants to live separately from your mother and father. You must have said you won't. Or she must have insisted on having jewellery. Made it very difficult for you. Is that so?"

Rama, embarrassed, said, "It was something like that, Dada. She wasn't especially eager for jewellery, but when she received it she liked it. Since I was carried away by my love, I didn't think about the consequences."

"You didn't spend any government money, did you?' said Devidin, as if the words came out of his mouth by themselves.

Every hair on Rama's body stood on end. His heart pounded. He had wanted to conceal the matter of government money. Devidin's question was like a surprise attack. Rama was like an expert soldier who had wanted to lead his army through mountain passes, avoiding the eyes of spies, but this sudden attack had scattered his forces in disarray. The colour left his face. All at once he found himself unable to decide what answer to give.

Sensing his state of mind, Devidin said, "Love is very strange, Brother. Adults commit blunders and you're still a boy. There are thousands of lawsuits over embezzlement every year. If you were to investigate them, you'd find one reason for all of them – jewellery. I've seen ten or twenty such incidents with my own eyes. This disease is like this. The woman says outwardly, 'Why did you bring this? Why did you bring that? Where will the money come from?' but inwardly her heart starts dancing with joy. A postal official used to live right here. The poor wretch cut his throat with a knife. I know another Muslim gentleman who got a five-year sentence and died in jail. I knew a third person, a Brahmin *pundit*, who killed himself by taking opium. It's an awful disease. But who am I to talk about others? I spent three years in jail, myself. It was when I was a young man and this old woman was in the bloom of youth. When she'd gaze at me, I'd feel as if she'd pierced my heart with an arrow. I was a postman. I distributed money orders. She was after my life for earrings! She'd say, she wanted only gold ones. Her father was a Chaudhari and had a dry-fruit shop; he had an inflated opinion of himself. I was intoxicated with love and I regularly boasted about my income. Sometimes I bought her garlands of flowers, sometimes sweets, sometimes scented oils. I was lighthearted. The times were good and whatever I asked for, the shopkeepers gave me. Finally I forged a signature on a money order and embezzled the money. It was only thirty rupees. I bought her the earrings. She was so happy; so happy that I can't describe it. But in a month's time, the theft was detected and I spent three years in jail. When I had completed my sentence got out, I ran away and came here. I never went home again. How could I show my face! Yes! I sent a letter home. As soon as this old woman got the news, she came. Even after all this happened, her craving for jewellery is unsatisfied. Whenever you look, she's having something or the other made. If she has something made today, then tomorrow, she'll have it melted to get something else made. The same old gold wire keeps on going around like this. She's found a goldsmith who'll work for vegetables he gets from the shop. My advice is to write a letter home. But the police must be searching for you. If they find out where you are, then everything will be ruined. Should I have someone write a letter and send it?"

"No, Dada!" said Rama vehemently. "Have mercy. It will be do more harm. I'm more afraid of my family than the police."

Devidin said, "Your family will come as soon as they get news of where you are. This topic will not come up. You don't have to worry about them. Only the police are to be feared."

"I'm not afraid of punishment at all," said Rama. "I didn't tell you. One day in the reading room I saw a woman I'm acquainted with. She visits our house a lot. She's a great friend of my wife, and married to an important lawyer. As soon as I saw her, I was in a panic. I was so taken aback that I didn't even have the courage to look at her. I got up quickly and went and hid in the veranda at the back. If I had talked with her a little at that time, I'd have learnt of all the news from home, and I'm sure that she wouldn't have mentioned our meeting to anyone either, not even to my wife. But I just didn't have the courage. And now, even if I wanted to meet her, I won't be able to. I don't have the slightest idea about her whereabouts.'

Devidin said, "So why don't you write a letter to her?

Rama said, "I will write no letter."

Devidin said, "So for how long are you not going to write a letter?"

"Let's see," said Rama.

Devidin said, "The police must be looking for you."

Devidin plunged into worry. Rama thought that perhaps fear of the police was making him anxious. He said, "Yes, that keeps on making me uneasy. You can see that I seldom go out during the day. I don't want to drag you down along with myself. I will definitely go, why should I get you tangled up in this? I'm thinking of going somewhere else, and living in some village, where there's not even a whiff of the police."

"Don't worry about me at all, Brother," said Devidin, lifting his head proudly. "I'm not one to be afraid of the police. Having some stranger stay in one's house is not a crime. How am I supposed to know who the police are after? That's the work of the police, and they should know. I'm not a police informer or spy. I'm not a snitch. You just keep on protecting yourself, we'll see what God does. Oh yes, don't say anything to my old woman or she'll spill the beans."

Both sat silent for a moment. Both wanted to bring the subject to a close now. All of a sudden, Devidin burst out, "Well, Brother, if you agree I'll go to your home. No one will even hear of it. I'll go around asking about all the details. I'll meet your father, explain things to your mother, and have a talk with your wife. Then you may do whatever seems proper to you."

Rama, secretly pleased, said, "But how will you manage to ask, Dada? Won't people say, what's all this to you?"

Devidin guffawed and said, "Brother, there's nothing easier. Put a garland of beads around your neck and become a Brahmin. After this, you read the palm or check the *kundli*; everything is possible.The old lady will bring offerings. On seeing her, I'll tell her that she is very troubled as her son is away; have any of your sons gone far away? On hearing this, all the occupants of the house will come out. They will come. I will read their palms. I am really confident in these things, Brother, you don't worry. You see, I'll also earn something. It's the time of *Magh Mela*. I'll bathe in the river, too."

Rama's eyes sparkled with delight. His mind travelled to the realms of sweet fancies. Jalpa would go running to Ratan. Both of them would ask Devidin all kinds of questions: "Tell us, Baba, where has he gone? He's all right, isn't he? When will he come home? Does he remember his family, sometimes? He hasn't fallen into the clutches of some fascinating woman there, has he?" They would both ask for the name of the city where he was. If his father had somehow paid off the government money, that would be so wonderful. Then only one worry would remain.

"So is that advised or not?" said Devidin.

"Where will you go, Dada?" asked Rama. "It's going to be a lot of trouble for you."

Devidin said, "I will bathe in the river, too. Without trouble, does good ever happen? I'm telling you, you come along also. I'll assess the situation there. If you see all is well, you go home peacefully. If things aren't right, you return with me."

"What are you saying, Dada? I will never leave like this," Rama laughed and said. "Suppose some policeman should grab me at the station, just as I'm getting off the train, why, it would be all over."

"Why, it's a joke. A policeman grabbing you?" said Devidin, growing serious. "Just tell me and I'd take him to Prayaraj's main police station and stand him up there. And if anyone even glanced at me sideways, why, I will shave of my moustache. There's no way that would happen! I know hundreds of murderers that live right here in Calcutta. They dine as guests of police officers, and even though the police know who they are, they can't do a thing to them. Money is very powerful, Brother."

Rama gave no answer. A question had presented itself to him. The things he had considered really very difficult because of his lack of experience, this old man had made really easy. He was no idle boaster. Whatever he said, he was capable of bringing to completion. 'Could he really go home along with Devidin? If he could get some money here, he could have a new suit made, and go in style,' he thought as he began to imagine the occasion of his arrival at home, wearing a new suit. As soon as they saw him, Gopi and Vishvambhar would run inside, shouting, "Our brother has come! Our brother has come!" His father would come out. His mother would not believe it at first, but when his father would go to her and say,

"Yes, he's come," she would start crying and come to the door. Just then, he would reach the door and fall at her feet. Jalpa wouldn't come; her self-respect would keep her where she was. Rama even began to think up the sentences with which he would convinve and placate Jalpa. Perhaps the money would not even be mentioned. Everyone would be embarrassed to say anything about this subject. When a loved one commits some misdeed, he is not made to feel unhappy by being reviled by us. We do not want him to give the least attention to what has happened, so we act in an appropriate manner. So, we display not the slightest doubt, that he should not forget it and remember, lest he feels he is being dishonoured.

"What are you thinking?" asked Devidin. "Will you go?"

"Since you are so kind, I'll go," said Rama in a subdued voice. "But you'll have to go to my home first and bring back every bit of news. If I'm not satisfied, I'll come back here."

"Agreed," said Devidin, resolutely.

"There's one more thing," said Rama, hesitantly and lowering his eyes self-consciously.

"What's that? Tell me."

"I'll have to get some clothes made."

"They'll be made."

"I'll pay you back when I get home."

"And I'll give you your guru *dakshina* right there, too."

"I have to pay you guru *dakshina*. If I've taught you a few English alphabets, you won't get any particular benefit from this. But the lessons you've taught me, I won't be able to forget my whole life. To praise someone to his face is flattery, but Dada, after my mother and father I don't love anyone else as much as I do you. You reached out and took my hand in my worst hour, when I was amidst troubles and being swept away. God knows what condition I'd be in by now, on which bank I'd have been washed ashore."

"And suppose your father won't let me enter your house?" said Devidin, mischieviously.

Rama laughed. "Father will think of you as his older brother. He'll show you so much hospitality that you'll get bored. Jalpa will drink the water she's washed your feet in, and look after you so well that you'll become young again."

"Then the old woman will burn and die of jealousy," said Devidin, laughing. "She won't agree, otherwise I'd love for the two of us to take everything, lock, stock, and barrel, and go there to Allahabad, and stretch out on our mats. I could spend the rest of my days comfortably with you, but this old witch won't leave Calcutta. So it's decided then?"

"Yes, it's decided."

"When the shop opens let's go and get some cloth. We'll give it to a tailor today for stitching."

For a long time after Devidin left, Rama sat absorbed in pleasant dreams. Today he began to frolic unrestrainedly in that bottomless, limitless ocean of imagination, whose surging feelings he had never allowed to dwell in his mind. Their depth, breadth and intensity had frightened him so much that he had never let his restless mind go wandering in their direction for fear of slipping and drowning in them. Now, he was aboard a boat and revisted that trip to the Triveni, the delights of Alfred Park, the joys of Khusro Garden, those gatherings with his friends – all these memories came, one after the other and delightfully tickled his heart. Ramesh would embrace him as soon as he saw him. His friends would ask him, "Where had you gone, Friend? Did you travel a lot?" Ratan would come running as soon as she got the news and ask, "Where did you stay, Babuji? I searched all over Calcutta for you." Then Jalpa's image came and stood before him.

All of a sudden, Devidin came and said, "It's ten o'clock, Brother. Come on let's go to the *bazar*."

A startled Rama asked, "It's ten o'clock?"

"Not ten, it's about to strike eleven."

Rama got ready to go. When he reached the door, he stopped.

"Why are you standing there?" asked Devidin.

"You go. What will I go and do?'

"What, are you feeling scared?"

"No, it's not that I'm afraid, but what's the use?"

"What am I going to do by myself?" said Devidin. "What do I know about what kind of cloth you like? Come on and choose what you like. We'll give it to the tailor right there."

"Get whatever cloth you wish. I like everything."

"What are you afraid of? The police won't do a thing to you. No one will even look at you."

"I'm not afraid, Dada. I just don't want to go."

"What else are you, if not scared? I'm telling you that no one will say a word to you. I will take the responsibility for that, but you are still so scared for your life."

Devidin tried hard to convince him, to reassure him, but Rama would not agree to go. No matter how often he denied he was not afraid, he simply did not have the courage to set foot outside the house. What could Devidin do if some policeman should get hold of him? Even supposing the policeman was an acquaintance, there was no certainty that he would allow considerations of friendship to influence him in an official matter. In the end, Devidin would be reduced to supplication and flattery, while Rama would be caught. If he should be caught, he would go to jail, instead of Prayag. At last, Devidin went by himself.

When Devidin returned after an hour, he found Rama walking up and down on the roof. "Do you have any idea what time it is? It's just about twelve. You're not going to prepare your meal? You're so happy about going home that you've given up eating and drinking?"

"I'll get it ready, Dada. What's the hurry?" said Rama, shamefacedly.

"Take a look at this, I brought some samples. Whatever you like from these I'll take to the tailor."

Devidin brought out hundreds of samples of wool and silken cloth, and put them before Rama. Not one of them was for less than five or six rupees a yard.

Rama, turning the samples over and over, asked, "Why did you bring such expensive cloth, Dada? Weren't there any cheaper ones?"

"There were cheaper ones, but the point is they were English."

"You don't wear English clothes?"

"I haven't bought any for twenty years, nor do I talk about it. The price is higher for Indian-made cloth, but the money stays right here in the country."

Feeling ashamed, Rama said, "You're very strict about your principles, Dada."

Devidin's face suddenly brightened. His dimmed eyes sparkled, and his whole body grew taut. Haughtily he said, "If you live in this country, drink its water and eat its food, and won't even do this much, then shameful is your life! I've given two young sons to this *swadesi* movement, Brother. How can I tell you what fine young men they were? Both of them were sent to keep watch on a shop selling foreign cloth. It would have taken a lot of nerve for any customer to go into that shop. Joining their hands in entreaty, beseeching, threatening, shaming; they turned everyone away. The cloth market was so desolate, that jackals could have roamed there. All the merchants went to the Commissioner and complained. When he heard what was going on, he became enraged, and sent twenty white soldiers to clear the *swadesi* sentinels from the market immediately. These whites told the two brothers to get out, but they didn't budge an inch. A crowd gathered. The whites charged on horses, but the two of them stood as firm as rocks. Finally, when they couldn't bring things under control in this way, they beat the boys with their bamboo staves. Both heroes took the blows, but didn't stir from their place. When the older brother fell, the younger came and stood in his place. If the two had taken up their own staves, then, Brother, they'd have given those soldiers a good drubbing and chased them away. But for a *swadesi* to even lift a hand would have been a big offence, when they didn't even protect their heads. In the end, the younger one, too, dropped. People lifted them up and took them to the hospital. That very night both of them departed from this life. I swear to you by touching your feet, Brother, that I felt my chest had become a yard wide; my feet didn't touch the ground. I felt so elated that if God hadn't already taken my other children, I'd have sent them, too. When the funeral procession started, there were a hundred thousand people in attendance. As soon as I'd given my boys to the care of the Ganges, I went straight to the cloth market and stood in the very same place where the dead bodies of the two heroes had fallen. Speak about customers, you couldn't see even the son of a sparrow there. I didn't leave the spot for eight days, except to go home at daybreak for half an hour to bathe and eat a little before going back. On the ninth day the shopkeepers swore that they wouldn't order foreign cloth from then on. After that the watch was lifted. And from that time on, I haven't brought even foreign matches home."

"Dada," said Rama wholeheartedly, "you're a true hero and those two boys were true warriors. Seeing you make one's eyes pure and sacred."

Devidin looked at him as if he felt that this fulsome praise was not in the least exaggerated. With the dignity of a martyr, he said, "Whatever these bigwigs do will come to nothing. All they know is how to complain. They can't do any more than to weep and wail like little girls. These grand patriots can't be at ease without their foreign liquor. Go, look at their homes. You won't find even a single Indian thing. They'll have ten or twenty kurtas made of coarse homespun cloth for show, but all the other things will be foreign. Everyone, great and small, is blindly pursuing the good life. On top of this, the contention is that they are working for the betterment of the country. What! You're going to better the country? First better yourself. Your work is robbing the poor and enriching foreigners, and that is why you were born in this country. Yes, keep on complaining, and wallow in foreign liquor, drive foreign cars, enjoy foreign jams and pickles, eat from foreign dishes, take foreign medicines, but keep on whining about the country. The point is, nothing will come from this whining. A mother feeds milk to stop the whining of her child, but a tiger doesn't leave its prey. Complain to someone merciful and righteous. What will your threats accomplish? Who is going to pay attention to a threat that has no force in it? Once there was a very big meeting here. A certain Sahab Bahadur rose and performed his antics. When he finished speaking and came down from the platform, I asked him, "Sahab, tell me the truth, when you mention self-rule, what sort of picture comes before your eyes? Like the English, you'll draw a big salary too, live in bungalows too, enjoy the mountain air, and travel around wearing English styles. How will the country benefit from this kind of self-rule? You and your friends and relations will pass your lives in great ease and comfort, but there will be no benefit to the country!" He started looking right and left. "You eat five times a day, and good stuff too, while the wretched farmer doesn't even get a single meal of dry parched grain," I said. "The government gives you official positions to suck his blood! Have you ever given him a thought? When you're so crazy about living it up now without even being in power yet, when you do get into power, you'll grind the poor and swallow them."

Rama could not bear to hear this censure of respectable society. After all, he was a part of that society, too. "It's not true that educated people don't care about the farmers, Dada," he said. "So many of them were or still are farmers themselves. If they believed that farmers could benefit from their sacrifices, and that whatever surplus resulted would be spent on farmers, then they'd cheerfully work for lower salaries. But when they see others gobbling up any surplus, they think others are to eat it up, then, why shouldn't they?"

"So when we get self-rule, won't there still be five or ten thousand officers in every province? Won't lawyers still be robbing people? And will the police stop robbing people?"

For a moment Rama was taken aback. He had never thought about this himself, but an answer quickly occurred to him. "Dada, everything will be done by vote of the majority, then. If the majority says that the office workers' salaries should be reduced, then they'll be reduced. And whatever amount is demanded for the rural masses, they'll get it. The key will remain in the hand of the majority. And even if it takes five or ten years from now, in the future, the majority will be the farmers and labourers themselves."

Devidin, smiling, said, "Brother, you understand these things, too. That's just how I had thought. God willing, I'll live a little longer. My first question will be whether there'll be a two hundred per cent duty on foreign things and a four hundred per cent duty on automobiles? All right, cook food now. We'll go give the cloth to the tailor this evening. I'll eat by then, too."

That evening Devidin came and said, "Let's go, Brother, it's dark now." Rama was sitting with his head in his hands. Sadness spread across his face. "Dada," he said, "I'm not going home."

Startled, Devidin asked, "Why? What's the matter?"

Rama's eyes filled with tears. "How can I show my face, Dada? I should have drowned myself."

As he said this, he wept loud. The anguish which had been lying dormant till now, revived on receiving these cool drops of water. His tears, as it were, pierced through Rama's whole existence. For fear of these very tears, he had not stirred up his pain, had not attempted to revive it. By deliberate forgetfulness had wanted to keep it inert, just like some harassed mother fears to wake her child, lest he immediately demand to be fed.

27

After a few days, one evening, Rama was returning from the library at about eight o'clock when he met several young men on the way, discussing a diagram of a chess problem. This diagram had been published in a local Hindi daily newspaper and a prize of fifty rupees had been promised to the person who solved it. The problem seemed almost insoluble, or at least this seemed evident from the remarks of the young men. It also seemed that many other local chess players had tried their utmost to solve it, but had failed completely. Now Rama remembered that many people had been huddled over a newspaper in the library, making copies of this diagram. Everyone who came had spent three or four minutes looking at the paper. Now he realised this was what it had been.

Rama was not acquainted with any of them, but he was so eager to see the diagram that he could not refrain from asking about it. "Do any of you have a copy of the diagram?"

When they heard this blanket-clad person asking about the diagram, the young men took him for a cunning fellow. "Yes we do," said one of them coldly. "But what could you do if you saw it, when some of the best players here are completely baffled. One gentleman who has no equal in chess, is ready to give a hundred rupees of his own to get it solved."

Another youth said, "Why don't you show it to him? Who knows whether this poor fellow might figure just it out? Perhaps he's just the person to whom the correct solution might occur."

There was no kinredness in this appeal, rather, it was fiiled with sarcasm. The hidden meaning was that we have no objection to showing it to you, or to your being satisfied by looking at it, however, a fool like you who will not even understand it, how will you find a solution?

They went into a shop they frequented, and showed Rama the diagram. He remembered at once, having seen the diagram somewhere before. He began to think, where that might have been.

One of them, poking fun at him, said, "Surely you must have worked it out?"

Another added, "If he hasn't yet, he will in a minute."

A third said, "Please tell us one or two of the moves, won't you?"

Rama, getting excited, said, "I can't say that I'll solve this, but I did solve a problem like this once, and it's possible I can solve this one, too. Please let me have pencil and paper so I can make a copy of it."

The young men's disbelief grew somewhat less. Rama received pencil and paper. He copied it in a moment, thanked them, and started to leave.

All at once he turned around and asked, “To whom should I send the answer?”

One of them answered, “To the editor of the *Praja-Mitra*.”

When Rama reached home, he began to ponder over the diagram, but instead of thinking about the moves of the chess pieces, he thought about where he had seen this diagram before. If he remembered this, he would probably think of the solution. Like others, he began to look for excuses to avoid making mental efforts, and took a vacation, as it were, on some pretext or other. He sat up half the night with the diagram spread out before him. He had played through many of the most outstanding games of chess, and he remembered all of their board diagrams, but where had he seen this one?

Suddenly it flashed before his eyes like lightning. The lost memory returned. Aha! Rajah Sahab had given him this diagram. Yes, that was right. He had cudgelled his brains for three days before solving it. Yes, that was right. He had even copied the diagram and brought it along. So now he remembered every single move, and in a moment the problem was solved. Intoxicated with joy, he pranced and jumped around, twirled his moustache in smug satisfaction, gazed at his face in the mirror, and then lay down on the bed. If he kept on getting one chess diagram like this each month, then life was made.

Devidin was just lighting the fire when Rama, beaming, came and said, “Dada, do you know where the office of the *Praja Mitra* is?”

Devidin said, “Why wouldn’t I? Is there any address of any newspaper office around here that I don’t know? The editor of the *Praja Mitra* is a lively young fellow who always has his mouth full of *paan*. If you go to meet him, he has expressive eyes and speaks little, but he’s endowed with tremendous courage. He’s been to jail twice.”

Rama said, “Could you go there today, please?”

“What will you achieve by sending me?” said Devidin, looking distressed. “I can’t go.”

Rama said, “Is it very far?”

Devidin said, “No, it’s not far.”

“Then what is the matter?”

Looking guilty as a criminal, Devidin said, “It’s really nothing, just that the old woman gets angry. I’ve promised her that I won’t get involved in this domestic versus foreign goods dispute or go into any newspaper office. I live off what she gives me, so I have to dance to her tune.”

Rama smiled. “Dada, you’re joking. I have something very important to get done. A chess problem was published in that paper, with a prize of fifty rupees. I’ve solved it. If my solution is published today I’ll get that prize. The undercover police are often there in newspaper offices. That's what I'm afraid of. Otherwise I'd go myself. But if you won't go, I'll have no alternative but to go myself. It took a lot of effort to solve this problem. I stayed up the whole night."

"It's not alright for you to go there,' said Devidin, in a worried tone.

"Then what?" said Rama perplexed. "Should I send it by post?"

Devidin thought for a moment. "No, why should you send it by post? If it goes by ordinary post, it could end up anywhere, and then your efforts would be wasted. If you register it, it'll get there some time day after tomorrow, and tomorrow is Sunday. If you send it by someone else, he'll make off with the prize. It's also possible that the newspaperman might play false, and publish your answer under his own name, and keep the money."

"I'll go myself," said Rama, uncertainly.

Devidin said, "I won't let you go. If you should get caught, that would be the end of it."

Rama replied, "I'll get caught one day, anyway. How long can I keep hiding?"

Devidin said, "So before anything has happened, why are you making such a big fuss? We'll see what happens when you do get caught. Bring it here, I'll go. I'll give the old woman some excuse. Right now, I'll be able to meet the editor, he will be in the office. Then I'll go wandering around, so I won't be back before ten o'clock."

"Then go after ten, where's the harm?" said Rama, fearfully. Devidin stood up. "By then, if some other work will come up before then, this won't get done today. I'll be back in an hour. The old woman be here later."

Devidin spread his black blanket around himself, took Rama's envelope, and set out.

Jaggo, his wife, had gone to the market for fruit and vegetables. After half an hour she returned with a small basket on her head, followed by a porter with a larger basket on his head. She was drenched in sweat. As soon as she arrived she asked, "Where has he gone? Just get this load off my head, my neck's broken."

Rama strode forward and lifted the basket off her head. It was so heavy that he was hardly able to manage it.

Jaggo asked again, "Where has he gone?"

Rama made an excuse. "I don't know. He went off this way just now."

The old woman had the porter put his basket down, sat on the ground, and waving a tattered little fan, said, "He is addicted to *charas*. Look at me, killing myself earning a living, while he sits around and spends it and smokes *charas*."

Rama knew that Devidin smoked *charas*, but to calm the old woman, said, "He smokes *charas*? I haven't seen him do it."

The old woman moved the back of her sari aside and scratched herself with the fan handle. She said, "Which intoxicant has he renounced? He'll smoke *charas*, he'll smoke *ganja*, he wants liquor, he wants *bhang*. Yes, he hasn't taken opium yet, or God knows, maybe he does, I don't keep an eye on him all the time. I keep thinking, who knows what's ahead. If you have a little money in hand, even strangers treat you like their own kin. But this fine fellow doesn't worry the slightest bit. Sometimes it's a pilgrimage, sometimes it's this, sometimes it's that." Putting her finger on her nose, she said, "I'm plagued to death by him. If God takes me away, then I'll leave his bad company behind. Then, Lalaji will remember me. Then where will he find that Jaggo who worked and worked to let him indulge himself? If he doesn't shed tears of blood then, then tell him that somebody said he would."

"How much is it?" she said to the porter.

The porter, lighting a *bidi* said, "Take a look at the load, Dai; it broke my neck."

"Yes, yes," said Jaggo, unsympathetically, "it broke your neck. You're very delicate, aren't you? Take this and come again tomorrow."

"That's very little. It won't fill my stomach," said the porter.

Jaggo gave him two more coins and a few potatoes, sent him off, and started to arrange things in the shop. Suddenly, she remembered her accounts. "Brother," she said to Rama, "would you please jot down what I spent today? It was hot as blazes in the *bazar*."

The old woman put her purchases one by one in the shop's display baskets as Rama wrote down the accounts. Potatoes, tomatoes, pumpkins, bananas, spinach, broad beans, oranges, cauliflowers – she remembered the weight and price of each one of them. After she heard Rama read everything out twice, she was satisfied. Having earned respite from all her tasks, she filled her *chilam* and seating herself on a three-legged stool began to smoke. From her manner, it was apparent that she was smoking to vent her spleen rather than to savour the tobacco. After a moment she spoke. "If I were another woman, I wouldn't put up with him for a moment, not a moment. I keep my nose to the grindstone from early morning, and then slave away sitting in the shop until ten o'clock at night. It's twelve o'clock by the time I eat and drink. Then, we get a little money. Whatever I earn, he wastes in getting intoxicated. I hide it in the most secret of places I can find, but he always finds it. He takes it out from there. Sometimes, when I get a few things or clothes made, it hurts his eyes. He constantly taunts me. It wasn't written in my fate to enjoy the company of my two boys, so what should I do? Rip open my chest and die? Even if you ask for it, death doesn't come. If it had been my fate to enjoy myself, would my young sons have died, and would I have had to suffer torment at the hands of this drunkard? He got carried away by this *swadeshi* controversy and took the lives of my darlings. Come into this room, Brother, and let me show you their exercise clubs. Both boys could swing them around five hundred times."

Going into the dark room Rama saw a pair of clubs. They were varnished and were so well kept, it was as if someone had just put them down after swinging them.

The old woman gazed at them proudly. "People said I should give these to the Brahmin who carried out the commemoration ceremonies. They said that every time I saw them I'd pine for my sons. But I told them that this pair of clubs belonged to my sons. Now, they are my two darlings."

Today, boundless respect for the old woman awoke in Rama's heart for the first time. What pure steadfastness, what immense motherly love that had granted life to these two pieces of wood. Rama had thought Jaggo was lost in greed and illusion, ready to sacrifice life for money, and bereft of any softer feelings. Today he realised how loving, tender and wise her heart was. When the old woman looked at his face, her mother's heart, for some reason, suddenly grew impatient to embrace him. Both their hearts were bound together with ties of love – on the one side, the affection of a son, on the other, the devotion of a mother. The hidden feeling of mutual dislike, which had separated them until now, was suddenly removed.

"You've washed your hands and face, haven't you, Son?" she asked. "I've brought some very sweet oranges, so take one to taste."

"From today I'm going to call you mother," said Rama, eating the orange.

Two pearl-like tears appeared in the old woman's withered, lustreless, cold, miserable eyes.

Just then, Devidin entered furtively. Flaring up, the old woman asked him, "Where did Your Highness's vehicle go so early this morning?"

Devidin smiled easily and said, "Nowhere. I had gone somewhere for a little work."

"What work was it? Could I hear about it too, or am I not worthy of hearing it?"

"I had a stomach ache,so I went to the *vaidji* to get some digestive powder."

"You're a liar. Just fool those who don't know you. Did you go looking for *charas*?"

"No, I swear by touching your feet. You're giving me a bad name for no reason."

"So where did you go then?"

"I told you. I ate a bit too much last night, so my stomach swelled up, and something sweetish ..."

“It’s a lie, a total lie! Lie, but when you do, your face clearly tells me that it’s some excuse. You went out in search of *charas*, *ganja*. I won’t believe one word. You keep thinking of getting intoxicated even in your old age, while over here I’m slowly dying. Going out first thing in the morning, he comes back at nine o’clock. It looks like he’s got some girl somewhere.”

Devidin picked up a broom and began to sweep the shop, but the old woman snatched the broom from his hand. “Where were you till now? Till you tell me, I won’t let you inside.” Devidin disconcerted, said, “What’s the good of your asking? I went to a newspaper office. Do whatever you want.”

Slapping herself on the forehead, the old woman said, “So you’ve caught hold of that craze again? You swore to me that you’d never go near the newspapers again. Tell me, was it your mouth, or someone else’s?”

“You don’t understand what’s its about, you just start getting angry.”

“I understand a lot. The newspaper people stir up trouble, and get poor wretches sent to jail. I’ve seen it for twenty years. People who hang around those offices get arrested. There are police searches every other day there. Do you want to eat bread in jail in your old age?”

Devidin gave an envelope to Ramanath and said, “This is the money, Brother, count it. See, I went to collect this money. If you don’t believe me, take half of it.” Wide-eyed, the old woman said, “Well, so now you want to drag this poor fellow down with you, too? I’ll set fire to your money. Don’t take it, Brother. You’ll lose your life if you do. When you get hold of anyone, without paying for it, then, you tempt them with greed. They will watch the *bazaar*, they will give evidence in court. Throw his money away. Take whatever money you need from me.”

When Ramanath told her the whole story the old woman calmed down. Her raised eyebrows lowered, her harsh expression softened. After driving off the rain showers, the blue sky burst out laughing. Delighted, she said, “What are you going to bring me with this, Son?”

Rama put the envelope in front of her. “It’s all yours, Mother,” he said. “Where am I going by taking this money?”

“Why don’t you send it home? It’s been so long since you’ve been here, you’ve sent nothing.”

“This is my home, Mother. I don’t have any other.”

The old woman’s heart, long deprived of affection, thrilled with ecstasy. How many days had her soul thirsted for this filial devotion. All the love gathering up in her wretched heart, like the milk collected in a mother’s breast, was impatient to pour itself out.

She counted the notes and said, “There’s fifty here, Son! Take fifty more from me. I’ve kept it in the teapot. Open a tea stall. Put out four or five stools and a table just to the side here. Sit here for two hours morning and evening, and you'll get enough to live by. Many of my customers will also drink tea."

Devidin said, "Then I'll take the money for *charas* from his shop."

Looking at him with smiling, blissful eyes, she said, "I'll keep account of every paisa. Don't be under any illusions about that."

Rama went to his room feeling gratified. He had experienced a sort of joy today that he had never experienced at home. The love naturally received in any home was what he ought to have received in his own home. The love he received here seemed to have suddenly poured from the sky.

He took a bath, put the *tilak* on his forehead, and had just sat down to carry out his pretence of worship, when the old woman came and said, "Son, you find it very troublesome to cook. I've arranged for a Brahmin woman to do it. She is very poor. She'll cook your meals. You'll eat food cooked by her. She lives by all the rules prescribed for her caste, Son, that is right. She takes loans from me, so that's why she agreed."

What deep, unlimited motherhood was sparkling in those ancient eyes, and how spotless, how pure! The question of great and small, of caste boundaries, vanished of its own accord. "When you became my mother," said Rama, "all this business of untouchability stopped. I'll eat only from your hand."

"Oh no, Son," said the old woman, biting her tongue. "I'm not going to spoil your *dharma*. You, a Brahmin and us, Khatik! Has this happened anywhere?"

"I'm going to eat in your kitchen. When the mother and father are Khatik, the son's a Khatik, too. Whoever has a great soul is a true Brahmin."

"And what would your own people say if they hear this?"

"I'm not worried about what people may hear or say, Mother. People get corrupted from wrongdoing, not from eating or drinking. Food that's given with love is pure. Even the gods eat that kind of food."

The pride of caste rose in the old woman's heart. "Son, the Khatiks are not some low caste," she said. "We don't take food even from Brahmins. And we don't even take water from Kahars. We won't touch meat or fish. A few of us drink alcohol, but secretly. This hasn't left anyone untouched, Son. And some very big, tilak-wearing persons gulp down liquor. But will you like my *rotis*?"

"*Rotis* made with love have nectar in them, Mother, whether it's made from wheat or *bajra*," said Rama, smiling.

When the old woman left, it was as though she held a treasure of joy in her arms.

28

Ratan had been very concerned about Jalpa from the time Rama had left. She wanted to keep on helping her on any pretext. Nor did she want Jalpa to know about it in any way. If it had been possible to find out Rama's whereabouts by spending some money, she would have been delighted to do so. Her heart was wrung whenever she saw Jalpa's tearful eyes. She wanted to see her looking happy. Accustomed to going to Jalpa's house when she became dispirited by her own dark, sad home, she was cheered up when they laughed and talked for a while. Now the same misfortune had cast its shadow there, too. Previously, on going there she had felt that she, too, was part of the world, that world in which there was life, longing, love and joy. Her own life had already been sacrificed on the altar of a vow, and she honoured that vow with her body and soul. Does the water kept in a pot over a Shiva-lingam have the same flow, the same waves, the same roar that a river has? It cools Shiv's forehead; that is its task, but the flow, the waves, and the roar of the river has disappeared from it.

There was no doubt that Ratan was acquainted with the most respectable and prosperous families of the city. However, where there was respectability, there was also exaggerated formality, ostentation, envy and slander. She was disinterested in being a part of a club. There was certainly enjoyment, sport and amusement, but there were also men's eager glances, restless hearts and lustful words. Though Jalpa's home had no splendour, no wealth, it also had no ostentation, no envy. Rama was young, handsome, and even if he were romantic, Ratan had had no occasion as yet to doubt him in this regard, nor was this possible with such a beauty as Jalpa around. Fed up with the crookedness and cheating of all the other shopkeepers in life's bazar, she had taken refuge in this little shop, but now, it too, had been shattered. Where would she buy the materials of life now, where would she get the real goods?

One day she brought over a gramophone and played it till evening. Another day she bought a basket of fresh fruit and left it. Whenever she came she brought some sort of special gift. Till now she had seldom met Rameshwari, but now she often came and sat with her, and talked about this and that. Sometimes she would put oil on Rameshwari's head and braid her hair. She began to feel affection for Rama's brothers, Gopi and Vishvambhar, too. Soemtimes, she would take them out for rides in her car. They would go to her bungalow as soon as they came from school and play with several other boys there. Ratan took great pleasure in their crying, shouting and quarrelling. Even Vakil Sahab began to feel some intimacy with Rama's family. He would ask over and over again, "Has any letter come from Rama Babu? Have you found out anything? His people aren't facing any difficulty, are they?"

One day, when Ratan came with a long face and bleary eyes. Jalpa asked her, "Are you not feeling well today?"

"I am well," said Ratan in a frustrated voice, "but I had to stay up the whole night. Vakil Sahab has been suffering greatly since last evening. Every winter he has an attack of asthma. The poor man takes emulsions, *Sanatogen,* and who knows what other sorts of concoctions the whole winter through, but the illness won't leave his throat. There's a well-known *vaidya* in Calcutta. We intend to get treatment from him this time. I will leave tomorrow. He doesn't want to take me along, and says there will be a lot of bother there, but my heart won't accept this. At least there ought to be someone who can speak up. I've gone there twice, and whenever I've gone, I've been sick. I don't like being there at all, but should I look after my own comfort or his sickness? Sister, sometimes I get so fed up that I feel like taking a little poison and dying. But God won't do even this much for me. If someone took everything I have, to make him well, to root out his sickness, I'd give it cheerfully."

"Haven't you sent for any *vaidya* here?" asked Jalpa, alarmed.

"I've seen all the *vaidyas* here, Sister. *Vaidyas*, doctors. I've seen them all"

"So by when will you return?"

"Nothing is certain. It depends on his sickness. I might come back in a week, or it could take a month or two, who knows for certain? But I won't come back until his sickness is rooted out."

Fate sat laughing in the starry sky. Jalpa smiled to herself. An illness, which has not been ended in youth, is not likely to be ended in old age. It was impossible not to have sympathy for Ratan's good intentions. "God willing, he'll get well soon and come back, Sister."

"If you'd come too, it would make me happy," said Ratan.

"How would I go, if I could go?" said Jalpa, compassionately. "Here at least, I keep hoping all day that some news will come. There, I'd just get more anxious."

"My heart says that Rama Babuji is in Calcutta."

"So, please search around for him. If you could somehow learn anything, let me know right away."

"You don't even have to mention it, Jalpa."

"I know. You'll keep writing, won't you?"

"Yes, certainly I will, if not every day, every other day, for sure. But you write back, too."

Jalpa started to prepare *paan*. Ratan kept staring at her face expectantly as if she wished to say something and could not bring herself to, from embarrassment. When giving Ratan the *paan*, Jalpa guessing her state of mind, asked, "What is it, Sister? What are you saying?"

"Nothing," said Ratan. "I have some money with me. You keep it. If it stays with me, it'll get spent."

Smiling, Jalpa refused and said, "And if I will spend it, then?"

"It's yours, Sister," said Ratan, joyfully, "not some stranger's."

Jalpa fixed her gaze on the floor, lost in thought and gave no answer. "You didn't answer, Sister," said Ratan reproachfully, "and I don't understand why you keep aloof from me. I want there to be not the least distance between us, but you keep running far away from me. Just suppose you spent fifty or a hundred rupees of mine, so what? Sisters don't keep count every paisa between them like this."

Looking serious, Jalpa said, "You won't get offended if I say something?"

"If it's something bad, of course I will."

"I'm not saying it to hurt your feelings, but it's possible that you will feel bad. Think about it, is compassion mixed with this sisterly feeling of yours or not? Are you taking pity on my poverty and ..."

Ratan leaped towards her, closed her mouth with both hands, and said, "Enough, let it be. Think what you like, but this feeling was never there nor will be. I know that if I am hungry, I know that I can unhesitatingly tell you, Sister, I'm hungry, give me something to eat."

Without any tenderness, Jalpa said, "You can say that now when you know that you can feed me dried fruits some other time in exchange for *rotis* or *puris* from here. But God forbid that a time come, when there's not even a piece of *roti* in your home, then, perhaps then you won't be so unhesitant."

"I wouldn't hesitate to ask you for something even then," said Ratan resolutely. "Friendship doesn't take circumstances into consideration. If it does, then don't consider it to be friendship. When you talk like this, you're shutting the door on my face. I had decided in my own mind, to spend the days of my life with you, but now you're warning me. Unfortunate people can't get love even if they beg for it."

Ratan's eyes filled with tears as she said this. Jalpa considered herself a sufferer, and those who suffer have the freedom to speak the truth mercilessly. However, Ratan's emotional distress was more agonizing than her's. Jalpa still had some hope of her husband's return. He was young, and as soon as he arrived, Jalpa would forget these terrible days. Her hopes would rise again, like the sun, and her wishes would ripen and blossom again. The future, with all it's expectations and desires, was in front of her – immense, brilliant, lovely. What was Ratan's future? Nothing – emptiness, darkness.

Wiping her eyes, Jalpa stood up. "Keep on answering my letters," she said. "Give me the money."

Ratan took a bundle of notes from her purse and put it in front of Jalpa, but there was no pleasure on her face.

Jalpa said simply, "Did you feel bad?"

"Even if I felt bad, how would it affect you?" said Ratan, sulkily.

Jalpa threw her arms around her neck. Her heart was overflowing with affection. She had never felt so much love for Ratan before. Until now she had held herself aloof from her and envied her, but today she had a glimpse of Ratan's true character.

She was really an unfortunate woman, and more unfortunate than herself.

A moment later, with eyes filled with tears and laughter, Ratan took her leave.

29

In Calcutta, Vakil Sahab already had made arrangements for a place to stay. There were no difficulties. Ratan took Maharaj and Timal Kahar along. Both were old servants of Vakil Sahab and had become almost like members of the family. The bungalow was just outside the city; they took three rooms – they did not need more space than that. The compound had many kinds of plants and flowers, and the place seemed very beautiful. There were a great many other bungalows in the neighbourhood. People from the city came there to take in the air and go back refreshed, but Ratan felt torn to pieces there. Those who are with sick people get sick themselves. Those who are sad find Paradise sad.

The trip made Vakil Sahab even more tired. For two or three days his condition was worse than it had been in Prayag, but after a few days of treatment, he became a little better. Ratan would sit on a chair near him, from morning until midnight. She did not even pay any attention to eating or bathing. If Vakil Sahab expressed a desire for her to leave him, so that he could express himself freely. To assure her, he would try his best to conceal his true condition. She would ask how he was today and he would give a wan smile, saying that he he felt very refreshed. If the poor fellow had spent the whole night tossing and turning, but if Ratan asked whether he could sleep the last night, he would say he had slept well. Ratan put some wholesome food before him, he would eat it even though he had no appetite. Ratan would think that he was getting better. She passed on this information to Dr. Kaviraj, who was pleased at the success of his treatment.

One day Vakil Sahab said to Ratan, "I'm afraid that when I get well I may have to give you some treatment."

Pleased, Ratan said, "What could be better? I beg God to give me your illness."

"Go for walks in the evenings. If you do want to get sick, then get sick after I get well."

"Where should I go? I just don't feel like going anywhere at all. I like it best of all."

Suddenly Vakil Sahab remembered Ramanath. "Go walk around in the city parks. You, perhaps, might find Ramanath."

Ratan remembered her promise. The delightful prospect of finding Rama enlivened her for a moment. If she should meet him sitting somewhere in a park she would say, "Tell me, Babuji, now where are you going to run off to?" This imaginary scene brightened her face. "I promised Jalpa that I'd look for him," she said, "but I forgot after I came here."

"Go today," said Vakil Sahab insistently. "Not just today, go out every evening for a whole hour."

Looking concerned, Ratan said, "But I'll keep on worrying."

Vakil Sahab smiled and said, "About me? I'm getting better."

"All right,' said Ratan, doubtfully. "I'll go."

Since the previous day, Ratan harboured some doubts about Vakil Sahab's assurances. In his efforts he she saw no signs of improvement. Why was his face growing paler day by day? Why were his eyes closed all the time? Why was his body wasting away? She was unable to express these doubts to Maharaj and Kahar, and she was embarrassed to ask Dr Kaviraj. If she met Rama somewhere, she would have asked him. They had been here so long; she could take him to another doctor. She had become somewhat disappointed with Dr Kaviraj.

When Ratan had gone, Vakil Sahab said to Timal, "Lift me so I can sit up, Timal. My waist is stiff from so much lying down. And give me a cup of tea. It's been many days and I have not seen a single cup. This healthy food is killing me. As soon as I see milk, I break out into a fever, but I drink it out of consideration for her. This Kaviraj's treatment doesn't seem to be doing me any good. What do you think?"

Propping up Vakil Sahab with the aid of a pillow, Timal said, "Babuji, you could consider it to be that. Just consider it. I didn't say it, because I was afraid of Bahuji."

After a silence of several minutes Vakil Sahab said, "I'm not afraid of death, Timal. Not a bit. I don't believe in heaven or hell at all. If people have to be born again according to their essential values, then I believe I'll be born into some good home. Even so, I don't feel like dying. I think, what will happen if I die?"

"Babuji, you say so, but don't say things like that, please," said Timal. "If God wills, you'll get well. Shall I fetch another doctor? You people have studied English. As you say, you don't believe in anything. I have my own doubts it's something else. Sometimes, you should listen to what villagers have to say. Let's consider it, whether you give them any credit or not, I'm going to bring an exorcist. The sorcerers and exorcists of Bengal are famous."

Vakil Sahab turned his face the other way. He had always made fun of the idea of the malevolent effects of evil spirits. He had even thrashed several sorcerers. In his opinion, all this was fraud and trickery, but just now he did not have the strength to oppose Timal's suggestion. He turned his face away.

Maharaj brought tea and said, "Master, I've brought tea."

Vakil Sahab looked at the cup of tea with hungry eyes and said, "Take it away, I won't drink it now. If she should find out, she'll be sad. Tell me, Maharaj, since I've been here, does my face look a little fresher?"

Maharaj looked towards Timal. He always looked to others' opinions before giving his own. He did not have the power of thinking for himself. If Timal said, "You're getting better," he would confirm it. Sensing his uncertainty, Timal said, "Of course, it's fresher, but, yes, certainly not as much as it ought to be."

"Yes, it's certainly somewhat fresher," said Maharaj, "but very little."

Vakil Sahab did not answer. Speaking three or four sentences had exhausted him and he lay inert peacefully for five or ten minutes. Perhaps he had realised his true condition. The shadow of death had started spreading across his face, his mind and his brain. If there was any hope, it lay, perhaps, in the weakness of his mind that exaggerated his wretched condition. Now and then, his breathlessness became worse than before. Sometimes his inward breath would remain, floating above him – he felt, now, my life leaves me. The terrible mortal agony had begun. Who knew when the obstruction would last a moment longer and end his life?

In the adjacent park, the moonlight had spread a sheet of mist and lay, sobbing quietly on the ground. It seemed as if the flowers and bushes stood with sad, bowed heads, torn between hope and fear and put their hands on his chest, touched his cold body and two tear drops fell from them – then, they looked as before.

Suddenly, Vakil Sahab opened his eyes. Tear drops were irritating corners of both his eyes.

"Timal," he cried in a feeble voice, "Has Siddhu come?"

Then embarrassed by his own question, he smiled and said, "I felt as though Siddhu might have come."

He heaved a deep sigh, fell silent, and closed his eyes.

Siddhu was his son's name; he had died as a young man. At this time, his memory was constantly recurring to Vakil Sahab. Sometimes the boy's childhood appeared before him, sometimes his death came before his sight – how clear, how full of life these images were. His memory had never been so lifelike, so vivid.

A few minutes later, he opened his eyes again and gazed here and there distractedly. It seemed to him that his mother had come and was asking him how he was feeling.

All of a sudden, he said to Timal, "Come here. Call a lawyer. Bring him here. Go quickly. Or she'll be back from her outing at any minute."

Just then the sound of a car horn was heard, and in a moment Ratan arrived. Any thought of summoning a lawyer vanished.

Vakil Sahab, looking pleased, said, "Where did you go? Did you find out anything about him?"

Putting her hand on his forehead, Ratan said, "I looked in several places. I didn't see him anywhere. In such a big city one doesn't get to know the streets quickly, so where am I likely to find him? It's time to take your medicine, isn't it?"

"Bring it, I'll take it," said Vakil Sahab, in a whisper.

Ratan took out the medicine and lifting him up gave it to him to drink. She was feeling a little frightened for some unknown reason. An unclear, unknown misgiving was weighing her heart down. "Should I send a telegram to one of those people?" she asked abruptly.

Vakil Sahab looked at her questioningly. Then grasping her intent on his own, he said, "No, no. There's no need to call anyone. I'm getting better."

After a moment, making an effort to be alert, he spoke again. "I want to have my will written out."

It was as if a cold keen arrow entered Ratan through her foot and came out through her head. It was as if every joint in her body was loosened, all her limbs scattered, and every particle of her mind blew into the winds. The earth had disappeared from under her, and the sky, above her. Now she was standing without support, without movement, without life.

"Should I call someone from home?" she said in a choked, tearful and tremulous voice. From whom could she take advice here? There was no one she could call her own.

Now Ratan was feeling impatient for her 'own' relatives and friends, for anyone at all whom she could trust, whose advice she could take. If her family came, they could scurry around and send for some other doctor. What all could she do by herself? In the end, when else could relatives to be of better use? It was in these times of distress that they were of most use. Then why did Vakil Sahab say no one was to be called?

She remembered the matter of the will again. Why had that idea occurred to him? The doctor had not said anything, had he? Dear God, what was going to happen? The word 'will' with all its associations began to tear her heart apart. She became restless to release her feelings by screaming and crying. She remembered her mother. She wished to hide her face in her lap and cry. As a child, how much satisfaction it had given her soul to weep into that love-filled hem. How quicky all her distress had been soothed. Ah! Now this support, too, no longer existed.

Maharaj came and said, "Mistress, the food is ready. Shall I serve your meal?"

Ratan gave him a hard look, and he left quietly without waiting for an answer.

A moment later, however, Ratan felt pity for him. What wrong had he done to come and ask about a meal? Was food someting that one could give up? She went into the kitchen and said to him, "You two eat, Maharaj. I'm not hungry today."

"Please eat just two *chapati*s, mistress," pleaded Maharaj.

Ratan was taken aback. There was so much kindness, so much sensitivity in his insistence that she felt slightly consoled. She realised that to think that she had no one of her own here, was an oversight. Until now, Maharaj had seen Ratan as a harsh mistress, but today the same mistress was standing in front of him begging for compassion. This released all the goodness in him, and Ratan saw a look of keen affection on his weak face.

"Well, Maharaj," she asked, "Do you think this Kaviraj's treatment is doing Babuji any good?"

Very scared and reluctantly, Maharaj repeated the same words he had spoken earlier to Vakil Sahab. "Something is happening, but not as much as ought to be."

"Are you trying to fool me too, Maharaj?" said Ratan, looking at him disbelievingly.

Maharaj's eyes overflowed with tears. "God will make everything right, Bahuji," he said. "What's there to be alarmed about? We don't have any control."

"Isn't there any astrologer to be found here?" asked Ratan. "We could ask him. Some puja and reading scriptures might do good."

"I was going to say that before, Bahuji," said Maharaj, with pleasure. "But you know Babuji's nature. How angry he gets at these things."

"You must certainly bring someone in the morning," said Ratan firmly.

"The master will be annoyed."

"I'm telling you ..."

As she said this, she entered the room, and sitting down in front of the light began to write a letter to Jalpa.

'Sister, I can't tell you what's going to happen. Today I learned that I've fallen into sweet delusions. Babuji had hidden his true condition from me before this, but today it was not in his power to do so. What can I tell you, today he was talking of getting his will made. I delayed it. I'm panicking, Sister. I feel like taking a little poison and remain sleeping. The world gives the creator titles: compassionate, kind, the friend of the poor, and who knows what other good titles. But I say, even an enemy could not be more pitiless, more cruel, more harsh than he is. The idea of past lives is just something to console our minds with. What's the worth of a punishment, when we know nothing of the reason? It's a forceful staff which can injure us for any reason it chooses. I've met only one flickering lamp along this dark, desolate, thorn-choked path of life. I hid it in the border of my sari, and thanking fate, went on my way, singing. But now this light is being snatched away from me. Where will I go in this dark, who will listen to my weeping, who will hold my arm?

Pardon me, Sister. I didn't have the leisure to find out anything about Babuji. Today I took a turn in several parks, but I didn't learn anything about him anywhere. I'll go again when I have the opportunity.

Give Mother my *pranam*.'

After writing the letter, Ratan went into the veranda. A cool breeze was wafting through the air. It was as if nature was lying on the sick bed and heaving sobs.

Just then, Vakil Sahab began to breathe very rapidly.

30

It was after three o'clock at night. Ratan had been lying in an armchair dozing off and on since midnight, when she suddenly awoke with a start on hearing deep snoring from Vakil Sahab. He was gasping for breath. She sat down at the end of his bed, lifted his head, and put it on her thigh. She had no idea how late it was, and glanced at the little clock on the table. It was just after three. There were four more hours till morning; Kaviraj would come about nine o'clock, she felt desperate when she realised this. Would this ill-fated night never depart and take its black face away? It seemed as if a whole age had passed.

A few minutes later, Vakil Sahab's breath stopped. His whole body was drenched with sweat. He gestured with his hand for Ratan to move away, and putting his head on the pillow, closed his eyes again.

All at once, in a feeble voice he said, "Ratan, it's time to say goodbye now. My offence ..."

He joined his hands together and gazed at her in abject entreaty. He wanted to say something, but no sound came out of his mouth.

Ratan screamed out, "Timal! Maharaj! Are you both dead?"

Maharaj came and said, "I had just gone to sleep, Bahuji. Is Babuji ..."

"Don't babble," Ratan scolded him. "Go and bring Kaviraj. Tell him to come right away."

Maharaj put on his old overcoat in haste, picked up his staff and set out. Ratan got up and began to light the stove, thinking that perhaps some warmth might be of use. All her panic, all her weakness, all her sorrow had vanished. In their place a powerful self reliance appeared. Stern duty made her entire being alert.

When the stove was lit, she began to warm his chest with a ball of cottonwool. After some fifteen minutes of one rapid application after another, Vakil Sahab's breath became more normal. The wheezing came under control. Placing both of Ratan's hands on his cheeks, he said, "You're suffering a lot of stress, Darling! How could I know this time would come so soon? I've done you a great wrong, love! Ah, what a great wrong! All desires remained in the mind. I've destroyed your life – forgive me."

These were the last words, which issued from his lips. This was the last formulation of his life, the last tie of affection.

Ratan looked towards the door. There was still no sign of Maharaj. To be sure, Timal was standing there, limitless darkness before him, but as if he had swooned away in the final agony of his life.

"Timal, will you heat some water?" said Ratan.

Timal standing there itself, said, "What good is it of heating water, Bahuji? Let him touch its tail and donate the cow. Sprinkle two drops of Ganges water on his face."

Ratan put her hand on her husband's chest. It was warm. She stared at the door again. Maharaj was nowhere to be seen. Even now she still thought that if Kaviraj came, perhaps Vakil Sahab's condition would stabilise. She was repenting bringing him here. Perhaps the strain of the trip and the climate had made his illness incurable. She was also regretting having gone out in the evening. Perhaps he'd caught cold precisely during her short absence. What else was life, except one long repentance?

Was it only one or two things she repented? What comfort had she brought to her husband during these last eight years of his life? He would be poring over law books until midnight, while she lay sleeping away. While he had discussed cases with his clients in the evenings, she had made excursions to the parks and the cinema, and strolled about in the bazars. What else had she considered him to be, but a money-making machine? How much he had wanted her to sit and talk with him, but she had wandered around, running here and there. She had never tried to grow close to his heart, never looked with loving eyes. She had never lighted a lamp in her own house, but had wandered around taking pleasure in the lamp-lit homes of others. She had thought of nothing else except her own amusement. A luxurious life and amusement, these had been the two goals of her life. She had been satisfied to calm her burning heart in this way. In a fit of pique, she had kicked aside her daily bread, just because she had not received better – a plate of *khir* and *malai*.

Today Ratan came to know the love which this departing soul had had for her. At that time, he had been consumed with anxiety about her. In Ratan's life, there was still some pleasure, some interest, some enthusiasm in life. What kind of happiness had there been for him in life? He had taken no pleasure in eating or drinking, nor shown any fondness for fairs and dramas. Was life one long course of austerities, whose chief goal was carrying out one's duty? Could Ratan not have made his life happy? Could she not have released him, for a single moment, from the cares of his arduous duties? Who could say whether this expiring lamp might not have glowed for some more days with rest and relaxation? However, she had never seen herself as having any duties towards her husband. There had always been a rebellion in her soul, merely because she had kept asking herself why she been, thus, associated with him. In this matter, had he been entirely guilty? Who was to say whether her poverty-stricken parents, too, might have done even worse by her? Were all young men principled? Amongst them were adulterers, hot-tempered brutes, drunkards, all kinds of them. Who could say what her condition might have been at this moment? Ratan was censuring herself with every fibre of her being now. Her head bowed over her husband's cold feet, she began to cry bitterly. All those harsh feelings, which had constantly risen in her heart, all those cutting vows that had burned her as she had voiced them, were now stinging her like hundreds of scorpions. Alas! She had behaved like this with a being who had been as deep as the sea. How much tenderness had been in his heart, how much generosity! If she had given him a *paan*, how pleased he used to be. If she ever had spoken to him with a smile, how gratified he would be. However, she could not bring herself to do even that much. Her heart was being torn apart by remembering these things, one after another. As she bowed her head over his feet she wished with all her might that she could die that very minute. Such great affection surged in her heart today as her head touched his feet, as if she would have given away the hoarded treasure of a thousand years, at this moment, with no thought of anything. Face to face with the supernatural radiance of death, all her internal disaffection, all her ill-temper, all her rebellion was obliterated.

Vakil Sahab's eyes were open, but there was no sign of any emotion on his face. Even Ratan's tumultuous emotions could not rekindle his dimming consciousness. He was free from the entanglements of happiness and grief – if anyone cried, he knew no sorrow, if anyone laughed, no happiness, either.

Timal brought Ganges water in a small ladle and sprinkled it on his face. Today Vakil Sahab presented no objection. He, who had been the enemy of hypocrites and the superstitious, was quiet now. Not because he had developed any religious belief, but rather because he no longer had any desire to do so. With this same deep sadness, he would have swallowed some poison.

How peacefully the greatest event of human life takes place. That immense part of the world, that raging sea of great ambitions, that storehouse of unending efforts, that theatre of love and hate, of joy and sorrow, that battlefield of intelligence and strength – no one knows when or where it vanishes to, no one comes to know. Not a sob, not a sigh, not a wail, comes forth. Who can tell where the sea waves end? Who knows where a sound goes to, in the wind? What else is human life but that wave, that sound? Is it any surprise that its completion, too, is so very quiet, so unseen? Devotees of the spirit ask, "Is no substance left?" A worshipper of science says a subtle radiance leaves the body. Devotees of the science of imagination say the vital essence may emerge from the eyes, from the mouth, from the top of the head. Let someone ask them, when a wave is being absorbed, is there a spark? When a sound is vanishing, does it become incarnated? This is merely a rest during that endless journey, not where the journey ends, but where it begins anew.

What a monumental change it is! Someone who could not stand the bite of a mosquito; now he can be buried in earth, or placed on a funeral pyre, and there will not even be a wrinkle of displeasure on his face.

Timal glanced at Vakil Sahab's face and said, "Bahuji, get up. Let us take him off the cot. Master has gone away."

Saying this, he sat on the ground, covered his eyes with his hands, burst into loud sobs. Today thirty years of being together had come to an end. The master who had hardly spoken two words to him, who had never summoned him rudely, was now leaving him and going away.

Ratan was still waiting for Kaviraj to come. Timal's words struck her like a blow. She rose and put her hand on her husband's chest. After sixty years of movement without rest, he was now resting. She did not have the courage to put her hand on his forehead, again. As she touched the body and stared at the dead face, she felt detachment, which was mixed with guilt. When her fingers touched the very feet on which she had rested her head and wept, she felt as though they were being cut. She had never understood that the thread of life was so delicate. The thought of death had never entered her mind. This same death had robbed her in front of her own eyes.

After a moment, Timal said, "Bahuji, what are you looking at now? Get him off the cot. What had to happen has happened."

He grasped the feet, she, the head, and together they laid the body down. Sitting there on the floor, Ratan began to weep, not because now she had no support left in the world, but rather because she had not been able to fulfil her duty to him.

Just then, the sound of a car was heard followed and Kaviraj entered.

Perhaps there was still a dying spark of hope lying in Ratan's heart. She quickly dried her eyes, adjusted the sari on her head, straightened her dishevelled hair, and stood up gazing at the door. Dawn had coloured the sky with its golden rays. Was this also the dawn of a new life for Vakil Sahab's soul?

31

The corpse was brought to Kashi that very day, and there the cremation took place. A nephew of Vakil Sahab's, who lived in Malwa, was summoned by a telegram, and he performed the cremation ceremony. Ratan thrilled with horror at the very thought of the funeral pyre – she might have fainted had she gone there.

These days Jalpa would spend nearly the whole day with Ratan. She was so distracted by grief that she gave no thought to domestic matters, nor even to eating and drinking. Every day, some memory would set her weeping for hours. If she had observed even a portion of her obligations towards her husband, she would have been consoled. When she mentioned her neglect of her duty, her harshness, her greediness for finery, she would weep so hard that she would hiccup uncontrollably. She pacified her soul by discussing Vakil Sahab's good qualities. As long as a guardian had been sitting at her door, she had had no concern for dogs and cats, thieves or robbers. Now, because there was no guardian at the door, she remained vigilant and sang praises of her husband. She and Jalpa never discussed how she was to carry on with her life, which of the servants should be dismissed, or which household expenses should be reduced – no one mentioned these matters. It was as if, to be concerned with these would be a lack of devotion to the departed spirit. It also seemed inappropriate to Ratan to eat regular meals, wear clean clothes, or read something to divert her mind. On the day of the *shraddh* ceremony, she gave all her clothes and ornaments to the officiating Brahmin. Of what use were they to her now? Would she keep these and mar her own life? On the other hand, she took care of and watched over even the smallest possessions of her husband, considering them to be remembrances of him. Her temperament became so gentle that no matter how great a damage might occur, she did not get angry. A tea set slipped and fell from Timal's hands, but Ratan face remained impassive. When the very same Timal had broken an inkwell previously, she had scolded him mercilessly and sent him out of the room. However, today when much more harm was done, she did not even open her mouth. It was as if harsh feelings feared to enter her heart, lest they be struck down. Or perhaps, she considered it a sin to allow any thoughts except his praises, or any feelings except grief, into her mind and heart.

Vakil Saheb's nephew's name was Manibhushan. He was very sociable, cheerful, and competent. In just this one month he had made hundreds of friends. Ratan had no idea of how familiar and informal he had become with all those lawyers and important men who had been acquainted with Vakil Sahab. He began to carry out all the bank business in his own name.

Vakil Sahab had twenty thousand rupees deposited in the Allahabad Bank. Manibhushan took control of this, and also began to collect the rent from Vakil Sahab's houses and the village revenues, as if none of this was connected to Ratan, in any way.

One day, Timal came and said to Ratan, "Bahuji, the one who was going has gone, now listen to some news about household affairs, too. I've heard that Bhaiyaji has had all the money in the bank put in his name."

Ratan looked at him so harshly and angrily that he never had the courage to say anything again. That very evening Manibhushan dismissed Timal, charging him with theft. Ratan was not in a position to say anything.

Now only Maharaj was left. Manibhushan plied him with so much *bhang* that he won him over. Maharaj began to sing his praises. He would say to the maidservant, "Babuji has a very noble nature. If you bring him some purchases, he never asks how much they cost. Big things happen in big houses. Bahuji used to split hairs, but this poor fellow says nothing." The maidservant had already been won over. Her youth had enticed her new master. She would wander idly in the outer sitting-room, on one pretext or another. Ratan had no inkling of the defences and traps being erected against her.

One day, Manibhushan said to her, "Kakiji, it seems useless to me to stay here now. I'm thinking of taking you home. Your bahu will take care of you there, the children will amuse you, and the expenses will be less, too. If you say so, this bungalow can be sold. We'll get a good price."

Ratan gave a start as if she had been roused from a faint, or as if someone had shaken her awake. Looking at him disconcertedly, she said, "Were you saying something to me?"

"Yes, I was. I was saying that it's useless for us to live here, now. If I were to take you away, how would that be?:

"Yes, that would be all right," said Ratan, sadly.

"If Kakaji had written a will, then please bring it and I'll take a look."

"He didn't write a will. And what was the need?" replied Ratan, just as if now she were sitting in heaven with no concern at all for earthly affairs.

Manibhushan asked again, "Perhaps he wrote it and left it somewhere?"

"I don't know anything about it. He never mentioned it."

Secretly pleased, Manibhushan said, "I'd like to have something built in his memory."

Ratan said, "Yes, yes, I'd like that, too."

Manibhushan said, "You know that the income from the villages is about three thousand a year. That's how much their yearly donation is. I saw their account book. It's not less than two hundred or two hundred and fifty a month. My advice is to leave all that just as it is."

"Yes. What else?" said Ratan, very pleased.

Manibhushan said, "Let the income from two villages be put into a religious endowment. The rent from the houses is about two hundred to two hundred and fifty a month. Let a small Sanskrit school in his name be opened with this income."

Ratan said, "That would be very good."

Manibhushan said, "And let this bungalow be sold, and the money be put into the bank."

"That would be very good," said Ratan. "What do I need money for now?"

Manibhushan said, "We're all present, ready to serve you. Shall we get rid of the car, too? If we start thinking over these issues now, then there will be some respite in two or three months."

"What's the hurry now," said Ratan, negligently. "There's some money in the bank, isn't there?"

Manibhushan replied, "There was some money in the bank, but for a whole month now, there have been expenses. There's probably five hundred or a thousand left. Here, it's as if money just blows away with the wind. I won't be able to stay in this city for even a month. We ought to get rid of the car very soon."

In answer, Ratan said the same thing again, "That would be good." She was in that state of mental frailty when even tiny tasks seem incomprehensible. Manibhushan's competence had, in a way, defeated her. Even the slightest sympathy he showed her at present, she understood it as him being her well-wisher. Grief and remorse had made her mind so fragile and soft that anyone could influence it. All her malice and aloofness had been reduced to ashes, and she regarded everyone as one of her own. She did not doubt or suspect anyone. Perhaps, even if a thief had plundered her possessions in front of her, she would have made no outcry.

32

After the last of the funeral rites, thirteen days after Vakil Sahab's death, Jalpa reduced her visits to Ratan's house. She would only go once a day for an hour or two. At home, Munshi Dayanath had had a fever for several days. How could she leave him suffering from fever? Whenever Munshiji had a touch of fever, he would rave and rant. Sometimes he sang, sometimes he cried, sometimes he would see the messengers of Yama, the god of death, dancing before him. He would set his heart on everyone in the house sitting near him, and on having all his relatives summoned so he could have his final meeting with them, because he saw no hope of surviving this illness. Yama himself was standing there in front of them with his vehicle. Rameshwari could manage everything else, but she could not stand hearing his nonsense. As soon as he began to weep, she would leave the room. She felt he was being plagued by evil spirits.

Munshiji had several files with newspapers in them in his room – he was addicted to them. When Jalpa became restless from sitting there so long, she would start flipping through these files. One day she saw a chess problem in an old paper, for whose solution some gentleman had even offered a prize. She remembered that on the same shelf where Ramanath kept his chessboard and pieces, was a notebook in which there were also several such problems. She hastily ran upstairs and took it out. The same problem was in the notebook, and not only the problem, but its solution, too. Suddenly an idea flashed in Jalpa's mind, 'How would it be if she had this problem published in some newspaper? Maybe it would catch his eye.' The problem was not so easy that it could be solved quickly. When no one in this city was his equal, then the number of people able to solve it could not be large. Whatever else might be, since he had already solved this problem, he would solve it again as soon as he saw it. Whoever would see it for the first time, would take a day or two to think it over. She would write that whoever found the solution first would receive a prize. It was certainly a gamble. Even if he did not get the money, at least it was possible that his name would be among one of those who had solved it. Then, she could learn something of his whereabouts. If nothing happened, then nothing but money would be lost. She decided the prize was ten rupees. If the prize was small, then no player of any stature would take notice. That would be to Rama's advantage, too.

In the midst of this elaborate scheme, she was unable to meet Ratan. Ratan kept waiting for her the whole day. When she had not come by evening, she could not contain herself. Today, she left the house for the first time after her mourning for her husband had begun. There was no excitement anywhere, no life anywhere, as if the whole city were grieving.

She loved to drive the car fast, but today she was going even slower than a *tonga.* Seeing an elderly woman sitting on the side of the street, she stopped the car and gave her four *anna*s. A little farther ahead, two constables were walking with a prisoner in tow. She stopped the car, summoned one of the constables, and giving him a rupee, said, "Give this prisoner some sweets to eat." The constable saluted her and took the rupee. He was happy, thinking that he had woken up, seeing the face of someone fortunate.

As soon as Jalpa saw her, she said, "Pardon me, Sister. I couldn't come today. Dadaji has had a fever for several days running."

Ratan at once stepped towards Munshiji's room, asking, "He's in here, isn't he? You didn't tell me."

Munshiji's fever had subsided somewhat. On seeing Ratan, he said, "I'm very sorry, Deviji, but this is life. Today it's one person's turn, tomorrow another's. This is the fixed movement from life to death. I'm about to go, too. I won't survive. I'm very thirsty. My chest feels as if a hot stove were being burnt in there. I'm burning up. There's no one I can call my own. Baiji, all our relationships in this world are selfish ones. One day a person stretches out his hand and dies. Alas! Alas! I had a son, and he slipped out of my hand, too. Who knows where he went? If he were here today, he' would give me a mouthful of water. My two other brats don't care at all whether I die or keep living. They just want to eat and drink three times a day, that's all. They're not good for anything else. When they sit here, they both start suffocating. What can I do? This time, I won't live."

Ratan comforted him. "This is malaria. You'll be all right in three or four days. It's nothing to get excited about."

Looking at her dejectedly, Munshiji said, "Please sit down, Bahuji. If you say that, it is your blessing, and probably, I'll be saved, but I don't have any hope. I'm completely prepared to challenge Yamaraj to a fight. I'm going to receive his hospitality now. Where will you go now to save yourself, boy? I'll chase him so much that he'll never forget. People say that the souls there live just as they do here. There are courts of law just like here, officials, kings, poor people; lectures are given and newspapers are published. Then what's there to worry about? I'll become a clerk there, too! I'll read the newspapers with pleasure."

Ratan started laughing so she could not keep standing straight. Munshiji was not saying these things in jest. His face bore the marks of serious thought. Today Ratan had laughed for the first time in one or two months, and to hide her mirth she went out of the room. Jalpa, too, came out with her.

Ratan looked at her with guilty eyes and said, "Who knows what Dadaji must have thought. He probably thinks: 'Here I am dying and she feels like laughing.' I can't go in there again, or he'll say something again and I won't be able to stop myself from laughing. Just see, how ill-timed my laughter was today."

She began to reproach herself inwardly for her lack of restraint. Jalpa, guessing her state of mind, said, "Even I usually feel like laughing at what he says, too, Sister! Just now, his fever is a little less. When it's higher, he starts saying the silliest things, and then it's hard not to laugh. This morning he was saying, 'My stomach has exploded, my stomach has exploded!' He just kept saying it over and over. Neither Mother nor I could understand what he meant. But he kept on repeating it. 'My stomach has exploded! My stomach has exploded!' Come, let's go back into the room."

Ratan said, "Won't you come with me?"

Jalpa said, "I can't come today, Sister."

"Will you come tomorrow?'

"I can't say. If Dada's condition should improve a little, I'll come."

"No, you must come. I need some advice from you."

"What advice?"

"Mani says, what's will I do by staying here? Let's go home. He says I should sell the bungalow."

Jalpa, suddenly dismayed, seized her hand and said, "You've given me very bad news, Sister. You're going to leave me in this condition and go away? I won't let you go. Tell Mani to sell the house. But until I find out something about Rama, I won't let go of you. You stayed away for a whole week, but, for me each moment was as heavy as a mountain. I didn't know that I had come to care for you so much. I might die if you go now. No, Sister, I'll fall at your feet to beg you to not even mention going away now."

Ratan's eyes, too, filled with tears. "I tell you truly, I couldn't stand it there either. I'll say I don't want to go." Jalpa, holding her hand, took her to her room upstairs, and putting her arms around her neck, said, "Do you swear upon it?"

Ratan embraced her and said, "Here, I swear I won't go, no matter what happens, even if the world turns upside down. What's there for me there? Why should I sell the bungalow? There's two hundred or two hundred fifty from the house rents. It's plenty for both of us to get by. I'll tell Mani today that I'm not going."

Suddenly she saw the chess pieces and chess problem diagrams on the floor and asked, "Who were you playing chess with?"

Jalpa told her everything about her scheme to roll the dice of her own fate on the chess diagrams. She was secretly afraid that her friend would find her proposal worthless, consider it madness, but Ratan was delighted as soon as she heard it. "Ten rupees is a very small prize," she said. 'Make it fifty. I'll give the money."

"But," said Jalpa doubtfully, "won't really good players be tempted to compete for such a large prize amount?"

"It doesn't matter," said Ratan firmly. "If Babuji Ramanath sees it, he'll certainly solve it, and I expect that his name would come first. If nothing happens, we'll certainly find out where he is! His address will turn up in the newspaper office. You've certainly thought up a good plan. My heart says it will have good results. I've become convinced of the truth of urgings of the heart. When I went to Calcutta with Vakil Sahab, my heart was telling me that going there wouldn't turn out well."

"So you have hope?"

"Full hopes. I'll bring the money tomorrow morning."

"Then I'll write the letter today. Whom should I send it to? It should be some well-known newspaper there."

"The *Praja-Mitra* was mentioned a lot there. You often see people reading it in the libraries.'

"Then I'll write to the *Praja-Mitra*," said Jalpa. "But what if they gobble up the money and don't publish the diagram?"

"What would happen? Fifty rupees would be gone. Gobbling up a trifling amount is the mark of someone no better than a dog. But that's not possible. People who go to jail for the welfare of their own countryand those who endure all kinds of threats, wouldn't stoop that low. If you come with me for half an hour, I'll give you the money right now.'

Half willing, Jalpa said, "How can I go anywhere now? I'll come tomorrow."

Just then Munshiji cried out, "Bahu! Bahu!"

Jalpa darted towards his room. As Ratan was going outside, she saw Rameshwari fanning herself. "Are you feeling hot, Mother?" she asked. "I'm shivering with cold. Oh! What's that white stuff all over your feet? Were you grinding flour?"

Looking ashamed Rameshwari said, "Yes, the *vaidya* said to feed him bread made with freshly ground flour. Where are you going to get such flour in the *bazar*? There's no woman in the neighbourhood to do it on hire. Even labourers have it ground in the *chakki*. I'm willing to give an anna for each *ser*, but no one is available."

"You are able to use the grindstone?" said Ratan, in astonishment.

Smiling abashedly, Rameshwari said, "It was nothing. A quarter kilogram lasts for two days. He hardly eats a thing. Jalpa was grinding it, but then

I have to sit with him. Given the chance, I will grind away all night, rather than sit with him for an hour."

Ratan went and stood near the hand-mill for a moment, then smiled and sat down on the stool. "Now, you must not be able to use this, Mother," she said. "Bring me a little wheat, and let's see what I can do."

Putting her hands to her ears, Rameshwari cried, "Oh no, Bahu, you're not going to grind. Come away from there."

Ratan joined her hands in respectful salutation. "I've ground flour for a long time, Mother. When I was at home, I ground it every day. Bring a little wheat, my Mother."

"Your hands will ache. You'll get blisters."

"Nothing will happen, Mother. Please bring some wheat."

Rameshwari, seizing her hand, tried to force here to get up, and said, "There's no wheat in the house. And who's going to bring it from the bazar this time of day?"

"All right, let it go. I'll take a look in your store-room. How is it possible that there is no wheat?"

All the foodstuff was kept in a room next to the kitchen. Ratan went inside and began poking around in the earthen pots. She found some wheat in one of them, and very pleased, said, "Look Mother, did it turn up or not? You were trying to fool me."

She took out a little wheat, put it into a basket, and going to the hand-mill, happily began grinding. Rameshwari went to Jalpa and said, "Bahu, she's sitting at the mill grinding wheat. When I try to make her get up, she won't. If anyone sees her, what will they say?"

Jalpa came out of Munshiji's room, and to derive some enjoyment from her mother-in-law's agitation said, "What disaster have you brought about, Mother! Really, if someone should see this, we'll certainly be disgraced. Come on, let me see."

"What can I do?" said Rameshwari, helplessly. "I tried to persuade her not to, but I failed. She just won't listen."

Jalpa went and looked. Ratan was absorbed in grinding the wheat. Her face was glowing with a natural delight. In this little while beads of perspiration had appeared on her forehead. Her sturdy hands were spinning the hand-mill like a top.

Jalpa laughed and said, "Hey you, the flour had better be finely ground, or you won't get your money." Ratan did not hear her. She smiled uncertainly like deaf people do. Jalpa spoke more loudly. "Grind the flour very fine, or you won't earn any money." Ratan laughed too and said, 'I'll grind it just as fine as you tell me to, Bahuji. I should get good money for grinding."

"Half a paisa per *ser*."

"Half a paisa is the right price!"

"Go, wash your face. Half a paisa per *ser* is what you'll get."

"I'll get up when I've ground it all. Why are you standing here?" said Ratan.

"Shall I come and join you, too?"

"I feel like singing some hand-mill song."

"You're going to sing alone?" Turning to Rameshwari, she said, "Mother, won't you go sit with Father? I'll be there very soon."

Jalpa sat down by the hand-mill, and the two of them began to sing a hand-mill song.

Where have you gone, oh yogi, now that you've bewitched the yogini?

Both of them had sweet voices. The hand-mill, whirling round and round, was accompanying them, like an instrument. When they would finish a verse and be silent for a moment, the voice of the mill, as if coloured by the echo of their singing, would become even more charming. Both their hearts were full of the natural joy of living just now – there was no burden of grief, nor the sorrow of separation. They were just like two birds twittering away, entranced by the extraordinary splendour of dawn.

33

Ramanath's tea stall had opened, but it opened only at night. It was shut during the day. Even at night, it was usually Devidin who minded the shop; still, business was good. On the very first day three rupees came in, and from the second day onwards, an average of four or five rupees. The tea was so delicious that whoever drank tea there once never went to another stall again. Rama added some things for the customers' entertainment. When he had accumulated a little money, he bought a beautiful table. After the evening lamp was lit, there was little sale of vegetables. Rama would take the baskets inside and put the table on the veranda. He would put a set of playing-cards on the table, and he also began to subscribe to two daily newspapers. The tea stall thrived. In those three or four hours, six or seven rupees would come in. After all the expenses were deducted, three or four rupees would be left.

In these three or four months of enforced austerity, Rama's craving for a life of pleasure grew even more vehement. He had been powerless as long as he had had no money in hand. As soon as he got money, he gave in to his craze for trips and outings. He remembered the movies too. Many of the ordinary things of daily life which he had postponed getting earlier now began to appear without restraint. He bought a beautiful silk sheet for Devidin. Jaggo had recurring headaches, so one day he brought her two little bottles of scented oil. Both of them were gratified. If the old woman would take some load on her head now, he would scold her. "Kakiji, now that I've begun to earn a little money, too, why are you killing yourself? If I see you putting a basket on your head again, I tell you, I'll pick up the shop and throw it away. Then you can give me any punishment you want." Hearing this son scolding her, the old woman was thrilled. Whenever she brought a load from the market, she would sneak a look to see whether Rama was in the shop or not. If he was sitting there, she would give some porter one or two paisas to put the load on his head. If he was not there she would rush to the shop, quickly lower her burden, and sit at ease, so that Rama would not know what she had done.

One day a new and wildly popular drama of Radheshyam's was being put on at the Manorma Theatre. People were reserving their seats a day before. Rama was intent upon reserving a place, too. If he could not get a ticket for the night performance, he thought he would go wild with impatience. The show was being highly praised, and seats were no longer available at even double the price. His eagerness pushed fear of the police behind him.

Surely, trouble was not so close at hand that he would be caught by the police as soon as he set foot outside the house. If day time was not a good time, then he would go out at night. However, if the police wanted to, could they not catch him at night, too? Then again, his description was no longer accurate. A turban was enough to change the appearance of his face. Persuading himself thus, he left the house at ten o'clock. Devidin had gone somewhere. The old woman asked, "Where are you going, Son?" Rama answered, "Nowhere in particular, Kaki. I'll be right back."

Once Rama reached the street, his courage melted away like snow. At every step he suspected that some constable was approaching. He believed that every policeman, even the lowest *chaukidars*, knew his description and would recognise his face at a glance. Suddenly the thought occurred to him that undercover plain-clothes policemen roamed around all over the place. Who knew, the man approaching him might be some police spy. How attentively he was looking towards him. Was he not getting suspicious of someone going along with lowered head, like this? Everyone else was looking straight ahead and walking. No one was walking along with their heads bowed. To walk along in the midst of this hurly-burly of motorcars with bowed head was to surely invite death. Anyone could take such a stroll in a park without being noticed. Here, he ought to look straight ahead. However, the man next to him was still staring in his direction; perhaps he was from the secret police. To get rid of him, Rama stopped at a shop to have some *paan*. The man continued on his way, and Rama heaved a sigh of relief.

Now he lifted his head and went forward with more courage in his heart. He knew nothing about the tram routes at this time, or he would have travelled by tram. He had gone only a short distance, when he saw three constables walking along. Rama left the street and began to walk along a footpath. Needlessly putting one's fingers into a snakehole was what kind of bravery? By great misfortune, the three constables also left the street and took the footpath. One had to repeatedly dodge the rapidly moving automobiles. Rama's heart began to pound. To take another footpath would make things look even more suspicious. There was no lane he could slink into either. By now they had come quite close. What was the matter? They were all looking towards him. How stupid he had been to put on this turban, and how useless it had been. A tiny thing like that had risen to undo him. This turban was going to get him caught. He had put it on to change his appearance, but on the contrary, it had made an even bigger spectacle of him. Yes, the three of them were staring at him. They were talking among themselves, too. It seemed to Rama that his legs had no strength. Perhaps, in their minds, they were all comparing him to his official description. Nothing could save him now. How ashamed his family would be when they got news of his arrest. Jalpa would weep her life away. He would not get less than five years punishment; his life was coming to an end today.

His imagination filled him with such terror that he lost his presence of mind completely. By the time the group of constables reached him, his face was distorted by fear, his eyes, alarmed, and his gaze, unnatural. He looked so desperately for other people, whose presence would shelter him so that he could avoid the eyes of the police that it would have been natural for even an ordinary person to be suspicious of him. So how could he escape the experienced eyes of these policemen? One of them said to his companions, "If a man is not a thief, he can easily pass in between your feet. A real thief does not have that strength." The second said, "I'm having doubts about him myself. You've said it, Pandey, he's a real thief."

The third man was a Muslim. He called out, challenging Rama, "Oh Sir, oh, Turban, come over here, what's your name?"

"What will you do ny knowing my name? Am I a thief?" said Rama, arrogantly.

"Not a thief, a saint. Why won't you tell us your name?" Rama hesitated for a moment, then said, "Hiralal."

"Where's your home?"

"Home!"

"Yes, I am asking about your home."

"Shahjahanpur."

"Which neighbourhood?"

Rama had never been to Shahjahanpur, nor did he remember any imaginary name to tell his questioner. Losing his courage he said, "You are writing my description."

"Your description has already been written," said the constable, threateningly. "You gave a false name, a false address, and when I asked for your neighbourhood you looked away. We've been looking for you for months, and today we found you. Let's go to the police station."

He seized Ramanath's hand as he said this. Rama, trying to free his hand, said, "Bring a warrant, then I'll go. Do you take me for a country bumpkin?"

"Grab his hand," said the constable to one of his companions. "You'll see the warrant at the station."

In cities, incidents like this are even more entertaining than conjurers or jugglers, and hundreds of people gathered. Just then Devidin was returning home after taking some opium, and seeing the crowd, he came to have a look too. Seeing three constables dragging Ramanath away, he stepped forward and said, "Hey, Hey! Jamadar, what are you doing? This Punditji is our guest. Where are you taking him to?"

The three constables were acquainted with Devidin. They stopped, and one of them said, "He's your guest? Since when?"

Devidin did some calculations in his head and said, "It must be a little more than four months. I met him in Prayag. That's where he lives too. He came from there with me."

The Muslim policeman, secretly pleased, said, "What's his name?"

"He must have told you his name, didn't he?" asked Devidin, taken aback.

The policeman's suspicions were confirmed. "It seems that you're with him," said Pandey, glaring threateningly. "Why aren't you telling us his name?"

"Understand, browbeating doesn't work with me, Pandey," said Devidin with ill-founded courage. "Threats are no good here!"

The Muslim constable, as if he were a mediator, said, "Old Father, you're needlessly getting upset. Why won't you tell us his name?"

Looking towards Rama in distress, Devidin said, "We call him Ramanath. We don't know whether that's his real name or not."

Glaring at Rama and lifting up his palm as if to strike, Pandey said, "Speak Punditji, what is your name? Ramanath or Hiralal? Or both? One for your family, one for your in-laws?"

The third constable addressed the onlookers. "His name is Ramanath, he says Hiralal. We've proved it." The onlookers began to whisper among themselves. It was certainly something to cause suspicion.

"It's clear that he gave both a wrong name and address."

A Marwari gentleman said, "He's a pickpocket, then?"

A *maulvi* said, "He's a wanted criminal."

Seeing the crowd was with them, the police became even more forceful. Rama now saw that his welfare lay in going quietly along with them. He bowed his head as if he did not care at all whether a stick or a sword struck it. Never before had he been so disgraced. Even suffering the rigours of jail could not give rise to this much self-humiliation.

The police station came into sight in a little while. The crowd of spectators thinned. Rama stared towards them in shame and hope. There was no trace of Devidin. A sigh escaped from Rama's lips. Had this support, too, slipped out of his grasp in this calamity?

34

In the office of the police station just then, four men were sitting at a big table. One was the Daroga, rather fair-complexioned and an enthusiast in whose large eyes there was some tenderness. Next to him was the Assistant Daroga. He was a Sikh, fond of joking, the very embodiment of liveliness, wheat-coloured in complexion, with a well-built, compact body. An orthodox Sikh, he kept long hair and wore steel bracelets, but he did not abstain from cigars. The Inspector and the Deputy Superintendent were sitting on the other side of the table. The Inspector was a middle aged, dark-complexioned man with small *cowrie*-shaped eyes, heavy cheeks, and very short in stature. The Deputy Superintendent was a tall, lean youth, very thoughtful and taciturn. His long nose and lofty forehead bore witness to his aristocratic descent.

Taking a puff from his cigar, the Deputy said, "It won't work with an external witness. We'll have to turn one of these into an 'approver'. There is no other alternative."

Looking towards the Daroga, the Inspector said, "We didn't leave anything undone, I swear it. We tried all kinds of entrapments and failed. They've all bonded together so strongly that we can't break any of them. We even tried the external witnesses, but no one would listen to us."

"We'll have to try that Marwari again," said the Deputy. "Send for his father and threaten him a lot. Maybe that will influence him."

"On my honour, that's just what we've been doing since this morning," said the Inspector. "The poor father fell at his son's feet, but nothing could make the boy agree."

For a little while, all four sat lost in thought. Finally, the Deputy said in a discouraged tone, "The case won't be heard. We'll get a bad name for nothing."

"Delay things for one more week," said the Inspector. "Maybe someone will break."

After making this decision, both the Inspector and the Deputy left along with the Assistant Daroga. The Daroga had just sent for his *hookah* when suddenly, the Muslim constable appeared and said, "Darogaji, please arrange for a reward. We've arrested a suspected criminal. He's from Allahabad and his name is Ramanath. At first, he gave a false name and residence. He's staying with Devidin Khatik, the one who lives at the corner. If you scold him a little, he'll tell everything he knows."

"You mean the Devidin whose two sons..." said the Daroga.

"Yes, Sir. The same."

In the meantime Ramanath was brought before the Daroga, who looked him over from head to foot as if he was mentally comparing to his police description. Then giving him a stern look, he said, "Well, so this is Ramanath from Allahabad. Well met, Brother. You've been giving us trouble for six months. Your police description is so clear that even a blind man could recognise you. When did you come here?"

"Tell the truth about everything, and no force will be used," the constable advised Rama.

Trying to look cheerful, Rama said, "I'm in your hands now, whether you're lenient or harsh. I was an employee of the Allahabad Municipality. Call it stupidity or bad luck, but I spent three hundred rupees of government duties. I couldn't get enough money to pay it back on time. Out of shame, I said nothing to my family· members, otherwise it wouldn't have been difficult to arrange for that much money. When everything fell apart, I ran away and came here. Every word of this is true."

"This matter is punishable," said the Daroga gravely. "Did you have a taste for liquor?"

"I will swear befor you, that no liquor ever touched my mouth."

"Robbed in the bazar of love, *Huzur*?" said the constable, in a lighthearted manner.

Rama smiled and said, "How would I have time for such gossips back there?"

"So did you gamble it away? Or throw it away on jewels for your wife?" said the Daroga.

Rama, ashamed, fell silent. A guilty smile spread over his face.

"That's good," said the Daroga. "You'll find especially large ornaments here."

All of a sudden, old Devidin came and stood there.

"What business do you have here?" said the Daroga in a harsh voice.

"I came to give you *salaams,* Huzur," said Devidin. "Look kindly on this poor wretch, Huzur, he's a very plain and simple, poor fellow."

The Daroga said, "Boy, you've been hiding a criminal wanted by the government in your home. On top of that, you've come to recommend him?"

Devidin said, "How could I recommend him, Huzur? I'm a person of no account."

"Did you know there's a warrant out on him? He's embezzled government money," said the Daroga.

"Huzur, it is humans who forget and make mistakes. He's a youth, he probably spent it."

As he said this, Devidin took out five guineas and put them on the table.

"What's this?" said the Daroga, flaring up.

"It's nothing, Huzur," said Devidin. "Just for eating some *paan*."

Daroga said, "Are you giving me a bribe? Look out, boy, or I'll have you sent in on the same charge."

Devidin said, "Send me, Sir. It will save my wife the worry of getting a shroud and wood for my funeral pyre. I'll bless you, as I sit there in jail."

"If you want to get him released," said the Daroga, "then bring fifty guineas with you. Did you know there's a five hundred rupee reward for capturing him?"

"What's a little reward like that to you people? This is a poor stranger, who'll remember you as long as he lives."

"Don't talk nonsense. I didn't come here to earn religious merit."

"I'm very hard up, Huzur. I hardly get any money from the shop."

"Go. Ask the old woman," said the constable.

"I'm the one who earns the money, Brother," said Devidin. "You know what happened to my boys. I scraped some money together by practically starving myself, so now I've just come back from a pilgrimage to the seven holy places. I'm really have very little."

"Then take your guineas," said the Daroga. "Throw him out of here."

"If that is your order, here, I'm leaving. Why will you have me pushed out?" said Devidin.

"Put him in custody," said the Daroga to the constable. "Tell the Munshi to take down his statement."

Devidin's lips were trembling in the grip of seething emotions. Rama had never seen such desperation on his face, as if some sparrow was overcome with emotion on seeing a crow forcing its way into its nest. He stayed standing at the door of the police station for a minute, then spun around and said something to a constable, then plunged toward the street and left, but returned in an instant and said to the Daroga, "Huzur, won't you give me a two-hour extension?"

Rama was still standing in the same spot. Seeing so much tender concern, he burst into tears. "Dada, don't upset yourself now. Let what's written in my fate happen. Even if my own father were here, what more could he have done? Until my dying breath, your kindness ..."

Wiping his eyes, Devidin said, "What are you talking about, Brother? When it comes to money, Devidin is not one to step back. I've lost or won this much money in gambling, in one day. If I were to sell the house just now, it'd be worth ten thousand. Shall I put it on my head and take it with me? Darogaji, don't send my brother into custody now. I'll provide for the money and come back in just a little while."

When Devidin left, the Daroga said in a voice filled with kindness, "He's a seasoned old man to be sure, but very goodhearted. What did you drug him with?"

"Everyone feels pity for the poor," said Rama.

The Daroga smiled and said, "Except the police, you should add. I'm not sure that he'll bring fifty guineas."

"Even if he does bring it, I don't want him to pay such a big penalty. Put me in custody at your pleasure," said Rama.

"When I'm getting six hundred and fifty instead of five hundred, why should I pass it up? If some other good friend of mine should get the reward for your capture, what's the harm?"

"When I have to do hard labour, then, the sooner the better," said Rama. "I had thought I could live here, escaping the attention of the police. Now I know that this apprehension and fear of being caught at any time of day or night is no less than being in jail itself."

It seemed that the Daroga had suddenly remembered something he had forgotten. He took out a file from a drawer, flipped back and forth through its pages, then in a mild tone said, "If I were to tell you some plan by which Devidin's money would be saved and there'd be no blot on your reputation either, how would that be?"

"I have no hope of any such plan," said Rama in disbelief.

"Well, Sir," said the Daroga, "God has a hundred different games to play. I can arrange it. All you have to do is just give testimony in a court case."

"It will be false testimony?"

"No. Completely true. Look at it like this. It will make a man out of you, you'll escape the clutches of the Municipality, and the government might even give you some financial support. As it is, if your case is sent up, you won't get less than five years punishment. Suppose that this time Devi manages to save you, well and fine. But how long can a nanny-goat be glad that her kid is safe? At some point.... Your life will be ruined. Understand by yourself what your gains and losses may be. I'm not trying to force you."

The Daroga related the description of a robbery. Rama had read about such cases in the newspapers. "So I'll have to become an informer and say that I was a partner of these robbers?" said Rama, hesitantly. "That would be false testimony."

"The case is completely genuine," said the Daroga. "You won't be entrapping any innocent people. Only those who ought to, will go to jail. So where's the falsehood, then? The people around here are not willing to give testimony out of fear of the robbers. That's all there is to it. I agree that you'll have to tell some lies, but considering that you'd be beginning a new life, a few lies amount to nothing. Think it over carefully, and give me an answer by evening."

These words sank deep into Rama's mind. If by lying once, he could atone for his previous misdeeds and improve his future, too, then what was there to consider? He would escape going to jail. There was no need for a lot of thought, for or against. Of course, it should be ensured that the Municipality would not press charges against him again, and that he'd get some good position. He knew the police needed him and that they would not refuse any reasonable conditions he might make. Rama spoke as if his soul was caught in the throes of moral crisis. "I'm afraid that my testimony may implicate some innocent people."

"I give you my assurance that it won't," said the Daroga.

"But if the Municipality holds me responsible, who will I call on for help?"

"Dare they! The Municipality won't utter a sound. In criminal cases, the plaintiff is the government itself. When the government pardons you, how can it bring a case against you? A written pardon will be given to you, Sahab."

"And a job?" said Ramanath.

"The government itself will arrange that. The government wants to keep people like you as its friend. If your testimony is first rate and you don't get caught in any of the traps in the other side's cross-questioning, then you'll truly be an exceptionally useful man."

The Daroga sent for a motorcar at once. He took Rama along with him and set off to meet the Deputy Superintendent Sahab. Why should he delay in displaying his skillful handling of things? He met alone with the Deputy and praised himself to the skies. He had found out about this man in this way: as soon as he had seen his face, he had, at once, guessed that he was a fugitive, and arrested him on the spot. His guess had turned out to be one hundred per cent right – after all, could his judgement be mistaken? "I recognise the eyes of a criminal, Huzur. He has absconded after embezzling money from the Allahabad Municipality. He's ready to give testimony in the case at hand. The man is educated, is decent and intelligent."

"Yes, the fellow appears to be clever," said the Deputy, doubtfully.

"But without a pardon, he won't have any confidence in us. If he should ever suspects we're playing a trick on him, he'll go back on us," said the Daroga.

"That's will happen, of course," said the Deputy. "We'll have to have a discussion with the Government about him. Telephone the Allahabad police and ask them if there's a case against this fellow. We'll have to tell the Government all this." The Daroga looked in the telephone directory, dialled the number and began talking.

"What did he say?" asked the Deputy.

The Daroga said, "He says there's no case there against a person by that name."

"I don't understand how that can be," said the Deputy.

"He didn't change his name, did he?"

"He says no one embezzled any money from the Municipality. There's no such case."

The Deputy, puzzled, said, "That's very surprising. The fellow says that he took the money and ran off. The Municipality says that no one embezzled any money. He's not crazy, is he?"

"I don't understand a thing," said the Daroga. "If we tell him there's no charge against him, he'll disappear so quickly that we won't see the dust stirred by his feet."

The Deputy said, "All right, call and enquire at the Municipality office."

The Daroga dialled another number, and another question and answer session began.

"Was there a clerk named Ramanath in your office?"

"Yes, there was."

"Did he embezzle some money and run away?"

"No. He ran away from home, but he didn't embezzle any money. Is he there with you?"

"Yes, we arrested him. He himself says that he embezzled some money. What's going on?"

"You police always have an answer for everything. Use your brains."

"Our minds aren't working here."

"Not just there, they don't work anywhere. Listen, Ramanath made a mistake in adding up the total receipts, panicked, and ran away. We learned later that there was no shortage in the deposit. Do you follow now?"

"What can we do now, Khan Sahab?" said the Deputy to the Daroga. "The bird has flown the coup."

The Daroga said, "How will it fly away, Huzur? Why should this be told to Ramanath? It's easy, just don't let anyone meet him who could acquaint him with news from outside. His family will definitely learn where he is now, and somebody or other will certainly come in search of him. Don't let anyone come to see him. Don't let anything be given to him in writing. Let him be reassured verbally. Let him be told that a report has been submitted to the Commissioner Sahab for his pardon. We should consult the Inspector Sahab, too."

While the Daroga and the Inspector were conferring with the Deputy Superintendent, Devidin had returned to the police station after an hour. The constable told him that the Daroga had gone to meet the Deputy.

"Has the Babuji been taken into custody?" asked Devidin, alarmed.

"No. He took him along," replied the constable.

Striking his head, Devidin said, "You can't trust anything that policemen say. I told him I'd be back in an hour with the money, but he didn't have even that much patience. He'll get five hundred from the government. I'm ready to give him six hundred. Yes, in the government, it's just about doing your duty, what else? They'll send him back to Prayag from there. I won't meet him, also. The old woman will cry herself to death." Saying this, Devidin sat down on the floor, right there.

"How long are you going to sit there?" said the constable.

As if stung by an insect, Devidin said, "I'll go when I've had a word or two with the Daroga. Even if I have to go to jail, I'll certainly scold him, scold him badly. After all, he has children, too. Doesn't he fear God even a little? Did you see the Babuji as he was leaving? Was he very sad?"

"He wasn't sad at all," said the constable. "He was laughing a lot. Both of them got into a motorcar and left."

"Oh yes, then, was he laughing, poor fellow?" said Devidin, disbelievingly. "Even if he was laughing on the outside, he must have been crying in his heart."

Devidin had not been sitting there an hour, when all of a sudden Jaggo arrived. Seeing Devidin sitting by the door she said, "What are you up to here? Where is Brother?"

Devidin, deeply wounded, said, "They took him to the Superintendent. No one knows if we will be able to meet him or if he'll be sent back straight to Prayag."

"The Darogaji is also so mean," said Jaggo. "So how could he say he'd take such and such amount, and where did they take him to?"

Devidin said, "That's just why I'm sitting here. When he comes I will have a word or two with him."

"Yes, scold him for sure," said Jaggo. "He is not true to his own words, so how will he be with his father? I'll tell him bluntly. What will he do to me?"

Devidin said, "Who's at the shop?"

Jaggo said, "I closed it and came here. The poor fellow hasn't even eaten anything yet. He has been hungry since morning. Let the whole show be burnt to ashes! He went to get a ticket just for that. If he hadn't gone out of the house, this calamity wouldn't have fallen on his head."

"Suppose they send him to Prayag from there, then what?" said Devidin.

Jaggo said, "Then a letter will definitely come. We'll go and see him there."

With eyes full of tears, Devidin said, "If he is sentenced?"

Jaggo said, "We will collect the bail, then how will he be sentenced? The Government will take back its own money, isn't it so?'

Devidin said, "No, you mad fool, it's not like that. Even if the stolen money is returned, the thief is not free to go."

Jaggo, realising the grimness of the situation, said, "Darogaji..."

She was not even able to finish what she was about to say when the Daroga's motorcar pulled up in front of them. The Inspector Sahab was there, too. As soon as Rama saw the two of them, he got out of the car, came to them, and looking pleased, said, "Have you been sitting here long, Dada? Come on, let's go into the room. When did you come, Mother?"

"Speak up, Chaudhuri, have you brought the money?" said the Daroga, jokingly.

Devidin said, "When I said I was coming back in a little while, you should have waited for me. Here, take your money, please."

"You must have dug it up from somewhere?" said the Daroga.

Devidin said, "By your grace, I can get five hundred to a thousand or more right now. There was no need to dig up the ground. Let's go, Brother, the old woman's been standing here quite a while. I pay off the money and come. That was the Inspector Sahab, wasn't it? He used to be in this very station."

"Well, Brother," said the Daroga, "take your money and put it back in that same pot. The advice of my superiors is that we shouldn't let him go. It's not something in my power."

The Inspector had already gone into the office. The three of them: Devidin, Rama and the Daroga went into the adjoining room.

When Devidin heard what the Daroga said, he scowled. "Darogaji," he said, "men say what they mean, I know that much. I brought the money as you told me to. You have to keep your promise. To go back on your word after you've said something is how scum behave."

The Daroga ought to have been infuriated after hearing such harsh words, but he did not mind it at all. He laughed and said, "Brother, call me scum, call me a deceiver, but we can't let him go. You don't get big game like this every day. I can't put a promise ahead of my promotion."

Devidin grew angrier on hearing the Daroga laugh. "So which side of your mouth were you speaking from?"

The Daroga said, "I spoke out of this mouth, but my mouth doesn't always stay the same at all times. I use this same mouth to abuse someone, and to praise him, too.'

Flaring up, Devidin said, "You should shave off your moustache!"

Daroga said, "I agree with great pleasure. That was my intention from the first, but I didn't do it out of shame. Now, you've strengthened my heart to do so."

Devidin said, "Don't laugh, Darogaji. When you laugh, my blood boils. I'll say something to the Captain Sahab for sure, even if I have to go to jail for it. I'm an ordinary person, but by your grace, I've got connections with very important officers."

The Daroga said, "Oh my dear friend, are you really going to complain to the Captian about me?"

Devidin thought that his threat had worked. "When you don't listen to what anyone says, when you go back on your word, then others will do what they think best," he said insolently. "The Captain's wife comes to our shop every day."

"Who, Devi?" said the Daroga. "If you make any complaint against me to the Captain or his wife, I swear to you that I'll have your house dug up and thrown away."

Devidin said, "The day my house is dug up, that turban and that badge won't stay where they are either, Huzur."

The Daroga said, "All right then, let's shake hands on it. We'll each give the other a couple of slaps, that's better."

Devidin said, "You'll be sorry, Sir, I'm telling you this, you'll be sorry."

Rama could no longer restrain himself. Till now he'd been standing and watching the spectacle of Devidin's anger as abjectly as a wet cat. Letting out a guffaw, he said, "Dada, Darogaji is provoking you. We've settled things so that I'll go free without any giving or taking, and on top of that, I'll get a position. The Sahab has given a definite promise. I'll have to stay here now."

"What's this you're saying, Brother, what are you saying?" said Devidin, like a man who has lost his way. "Have you been tricked by the police? There must be some scheme hidden here."

"I have to give testimony in a case, that's all," said Rama, confidently.

"It must be a false case," said Devidin, shaking his head sceptically.

Ramanath said, "No, Dada, it's a completely straightforward matter. I've already asked."

Devidin's doubts were not pacified. "I can't say anything more about this, Brother. Just think it over a little before you do anything. If you're worried about my money, then understand that if Devidin cared about money, he'd be a millionaire today. These hands have earned hundreds of rupees every day and thrown it all away. Which case do you have to give testimony in? Did you learn naything about it?"

The Daroga giving Rama no opportunity to reply, said, "It's that robbery case in which several poor people lost their lives. These dacoits created a disturbance through the whole province. Out of fear, no one was willing to give evidence.'

"Oh, so he's become an informer?" said Devidin, contemptuously. "So that's it. You'll have to say just what the police teach you, Brother. I'm a man that doesn't understand much, so how could I know the real truth about these things? But if I were told to become an informer, I wouldn't, even if they gave me a lakh of rupees. How can an outsider know who's guilty and who's innocent? Along with three or four criminals there'll certainly be three or four innocent people, too."

"In no way whatseoever," said the Daroga. "All of the men who were caught were seasoned dacoits."

"That's what you say, isn't it?" said Devidin. "But how do we know?"

"Why would we try to implicate innocent people?" said the Daroga. "Think about that."

"I've been through all that, Darogaji," said Devidin.· "It would be better if you would commit them to trial. They'd get a year or two in jail for the price of one guilty person escaping punishment, you wouldn't have the blood of innocent people on your head."

"I've thought a lot, Dada," said Rama timidly. "I've looked at all the papers. There are no innocent people in this case."

"Maybe, Brother," said Devidin sadly. "Life also happens to be very precious."

He said this and turned away abruptly. He was not able to express his inner feelings any more clearly than this.

Suddenly he remembered something. He turned and said, "Should I give you some money before I go?"

"What's the need?" said Rama, slightly irritated.

"He'll have to stay right here, from today," said the Daroga.

"I know that, your honour," said Devidin, in a harsh voice. Devidin said, "He will feast, he'll get a bungalow to live in, servants, a motorcar. I know all this. No one from outside will be able to meet him, nor will he be able to come and go alone. I've seen all this."

Devidin left very quickly after he said this, as if he were suffocating there. The Daroga called out to him, but he did not turn back. The pain of defeat was spread over his face.

Jaggo asked, "Isn't Brother coming?"

Devidin, staring at the street said, "Brother won't be coming now. When our own people are not with us, then strangers will remain strangers."

He left. The old woman followed him, fuming and muttering to herself.

35

In crying, there is much pleasure, peace and strength. Anyone who has not sat alone, weeping and wailing over the memory of someone or the absence of someone, has been deprived of one of the joys of life, on which hundreds of laughs have been sacrificed. Ask those that have received this good fortune about the pleasure of this sweet sorrow. After laughing, the mind becomes distressed, the soul disturbed, as if we have grown tired, been defeated. After crying, one experiences a new vigour, a new life, a new enthusiasm. When a letter from the office of the *Praja Mitra* reached Jalpa, she read it and burst into tears. Holding the letter in one hand and grasping the doorframe with the other, she wept copiously. Who can say what thoughts made her weep? Perhaps the unhoped for success of her scheme made her soul delirious, took her to the depths of joy, where water is, or to those heights where heat becomes frost. Today, after six months, this happy news had reached her. How long had she been the plaything of treacherous hopes and harsh disappointments? Ah! How many times had the urge to end this life welled up in her heart. If she had really sacrificed her life, she would never have even seen him. How hard his heart was – he had sat there for six months without writing a single letter, without even enquiring. Ultimately, he would have thought that, at the most, she would cry herself to death. When had he ever cared about her? A man would spend ten or twenty rupees on even his friends and companions. That was not love. Love was a thing of the heart, not a matter of money. As long as there had been no trace of Rama, Jalpa had taken the whole blame on her own head. Today, as soon as she had news of him, her heart suddenly hardened. All kinds of reproaches arose. What did he think he was doing sitting there? It was because he was independent, free, not eating someone else's food. If ever she had gone off like that without saying a word, how would he have behaved towards her? Perhaps he would have come with a sword and tyrannised her or perhaps he would have never have looked at her face for the rest of her life. As she stood there, Jalpa opened an office of complaints in her innermost heart.

All at once, Ramesh Babu called out from the doorway, "Gopi, Gopi, come here please." Munshiji Dayanath, lying in his room, groaned, "Who is it? Come into the room. Oh my! It's you, Ramesh Babu? Babuji, I was dying and now I've revived. I just want you to understand that I've got a new lease on life. There's no one ahead or behind. Both boys are good-for-nothings, it means nothing to them whether I live or die. Their mother is afraid as soon as she sees my face. In a word, it's my poor daughter-in-law who's saved my life. If it weren't for her, I'd have passed on by now."

Summoning false sympathy, Ramesh Babu said, "You've become this sick and I wasn't even informed. Even though I was here, you had to undergo such hardship. Your daughter-in-law didn't write to me about it, not a single note. You must have had to take leave?"

Munshi said, "I sent a request for leave, but Sahab, I didn't send a doctor's certificate. Where was I going to get sixteen rupees from? One day I went to the Civil Surgeon, but he refused to write a letter. You certainly know that he won't even speak without taking a fee. I came back and sent the request. I don't know if it was accepted or not. That's the way it is with doctors. They can see that a person is practically dying, but they won't take a step without a little present."

Ramesh Babu, looking worried, said, "You've told me some very bad news. If your leave is not approved, what will happen?"

Munshi said, "What will happen? I'll just keep sitting at home. If the Head asks, I'll tell him straight out that I went to the Surgeon and he didn't give me leave. After all, why did the Government appoint him? Simply to increase the splendour of the chair he sits in? He's willing to see me dismissed, but he won't give me a certificate. The brats have disappeared, and there's no one to even bring you some *paan*. What to do?"

Ramesh smiled and said, "Don't distress yourself over me. I haven't come to eat *paan*, I've come to fill my stomach with sweets. He called out to Jalpa. "Bahuji, I've brought some good news for you. Send for some sweets."

Jalpa placed the *paan* in front of him and said, "Tell me the news first, please. Maybe the news you think is fresh has 'gone stale'."

Ramesh said, "Well, perhaps it may not be so. I've learned where Rama is. He's in Calcutta."

Jalpa said, "I already knew that."

Munshiji sat bolt upright. It was as if his fever fled and hid itself under the cover of his eagerness. He caught hold of Ramesh's hand and said, "You've learned he's in Calcutta? Did some letter arrive?"

"It wasn't a letter," said Ramesh. "It was a police inquiry. I told them that there was no charge of any kind against him. How did you find out, Bahuji?"

Jalpa described her scheme, and showed the letter from the office of the *Praja Mitra*, too. There was a receipt for the prize along with the letter which bore Rama's signature.

"It's Rama Babu's signature all right," said Ramesh. "It's very clear. It couldn't possibly be forged. Hats off to you, Bahuji. Splendid! What a clever piece of work you pulled off. You outwitted everybody. No one else thought of it. When we think of it now, it seems such a simple thing. Someone ought to go who can save him, and drag him back here."

Ratan arrived as this conversation was going on. As soon as Jalpa saw her, she left the room, embraced her, and said, "Sister, a letter came from Calcutta. He's there."

Ratan said, "Do you swear by my life?"

Jalpa said, "Yes, I'm telling you the truth. Look at the letter, won't you."

Ratan said, "So, go this very day."

Jalpa said, "That's just what I was thinking. Will you come?"

"I'm ready to come," said Ratan, "but who will I depute to look after the empty house? Sister, I'm beginning to have some doubts about Manibhushan. His intentions don't seem to be good. There wasn't less than twenty thousand in the bank, but who knows where it has been spent? He says it was all spent for funeral expenses. When I ask for an account, he looks at me angrily. He keeps the key of the office with him, and when I ask for it, he puts me off. He's playing some legal trick on me. I'm afraid if I go away and leave him here, he'll sell everything and run off. Potential buyers are coming to look at the bungalow. I'm also thinking that I'll go live peacefully in some village. If the bungalow is sold, I'll have some ready cash in hand. If I don't stay here, maybe I won't even see that money. Take Gopi along and leave today itself. I'll make arrangements for money."

"Gopinath may not be able to go," said Jalpa. "Someone is needed here to look after Dada's medicines, too."

"I'll do that," said Ratan. "I'll come every morning, give him his medicine, and leave. I'll look in once every evening, too."

Jalpa smiled and said, "And who'll sit with him all day?"

Ratan said, "I'll sit with him a little while every day, too, but, you leave today. Who knows what condition the poor fellow may be in? So that's settled, isn't it?"

When Ratan went into Munshiji's room, Ramesh Babu stood up and said, "Please come in, Deviji. We've learned where Rama Babu is."

"Half the credit for this is mine," said Ratan.

Ramesh said, "It must have happened according to your advice. Now our concern is to bring him here."

Ratan said, "Let Jalpa go and bring him back. Gopi can go with her. Do you have any objection to this do you, Dadaji?'

Munshi Dayanath did indeed object. If he had had the strength, he would have gathered five or ten more people together to keep him company. So why would he not have objected to family members going? Such a problem had arisen, that he was unable to say anything.

Why would Gopi not have been happy on getting such a good opportunity for a trip to Calcutta? Vishvambhar felt his heart was wrenched. If the

Creator had not made him the youngest, this unjust discrimination would not have occurred today. How could Gopi possibly be considered more intelligent, for wherever he went, he always lost something or the other before he returned? Yes, Gopi was older than him. This divine enactment had rendered him, the younger brother, helpless.

By nine o'clock that night Jalpa was ready to go. She bent her head to her father- and mother-in-law's feet and took their blessing. Vishvambhar was crying; she embraced him lovingly and took her seat in the motorcar. Ratan had come to take her to the station.

As the car drove off, Jalpa said, "Sister, Calcutta must be a very big city. How will I find out where he is?"

Ratan said, "First go to the *Praja Mitra* office. You'll find out over there. And Gopi Babu is with you, after all."

"Where will I stay?"

"There are *dharmshalas*. If not, then stay in a hotel. Look, if you need money, send me a telegram, and I'll send some, one way or another. If Babuji comes, it will be a big help for me. This Manibhushan is going to ruin me."

"The hotel people won't be scoundrels, will they?"

"If they try the least little prank, give them a good thumping. Don't even ask anything. Just give them a good beating, then talk." She took out a knife from the waist of her garment and said, "Keep this with you, and hide it in your clothes. I keep it with me whenever I go out. It keeps up my courage. You can consider any man who molests a woman to be a coward from head to foot, mean and a rogue. Once he sees the gleam of your knife and your boldness, he'll be frightened to death. He'll immediately run away with his tail between his legs. But, if it should turn out that you are forced to use the knife, don't hesitate for even a moment. Take the knife and plunge it into him. Don't worry at all about what may happen, or what may not. What's going to happen, will happen."

Jalpa took the knife, but did not say a word. Her heart was growing heavy. There were so many things to think about and ask about, that just reflecting on them depressed her.

The station came into view. The coolies lifted the luggage. Gopi bought the ticket. Jalpa stood on the station platform like a stone statue, as if she had become unconscious. Before some great test, we fall silent – all our powers are involved in the preparation for the struggle.

"Be on your guard," said Ratan to Gopi.

Gopi had been doing physical exercises for several months now. While walking he would watch his arms and chest. He seemed much the same to those who saw him, but in his own eyes, he had become something more. Perhaps he was even surprised that people did not move out of his way when they saw him coming, or why they were not frightened by his shape and size. "If anyone even lets out a cheep, I'll break his bones," he said, conceitedly.

"I know that," said Ratan, smiling. "Don't go off to sleep."

"I won't even shut my eyelids for an instant. Sleep won't dare to come!" The train arrived, and Gopi entered a compartment and took control. Jalpa's eyes filled with tears. "Sister, bless me so I can find him and return safely," she said.

Her faltering heart was seeking for some support, some help, some strength now, and what else could bestow that strength on her, except blessings and prayers? These are the everlasting storehouses of that strength and peace which never disappoint anyone, which take everyone by the arm, and which ferry everyone across the river of difficulties.

The engine let out a whistle. The two friends embraced, and Jalpa sat down inside the train.

"Send letters as soon as you reach," said Ratan. Jalpa nodded.

Ratan said, "If you need me, write immediately. I'll drop everything and come.'

Jalpa gave another nod.

"Don't cry along the way."

Jalpa laughed. The train moved off.

36

Devidin closed the tea shop that very day, and all day long roamed around the court where the robbery case was going on and where Ramanath's testimony was being heard. Rama's testimony went on for three days continuously and for all three days, Devidin neither ate nor slept. Today, as before, the instant he came home he took off his kurta and began to fan himself. It was well into February and it was getting a little warm, but not enough to make one perspire or feel the need for a fan. The court officers were wearing winter clothing, but Devidin was soaked in perspiration. His face, where an honest merry old age had resided, had become as angrily irritated as if he had just returned from forced labour.

Jaggo brought him some water in a lota and said, "Shall I keep your *chilam* here for a smoke?"

She had shown him this consideration for three days now. The old woman had never before asked about bringing his *chilam*. Devidin understood the significance of this. Looking kindly at her, he said, "No, let it be. I won't smoke."

"Wash your hands and face, there's dust on you."

"I'll wash. What's the hurry?"

The old woman was eager to know today's news, but she was afraid lest Devidin get irritated. She wanted to relieve his tiredness, which pleased him. He began to narrate all the events of the day without any promting.

Jaggo said, "Eat something at least, then. You didn't eat anything this afternoon, either. Shall I bring some sweets? Here, give me the fan."

Devidin gave her the fan, and she began to wave it back and forth. After sitting for two or three minutes with his eyes closed, he said, "Brother's testimony finished today."

The old woman's hand stopped. "Then, will he come home from tomorrow?" she said.

"There's no recess yet," said Devidin. "The same declaration has to be made in the Civil Court. And now, why would he come here at all? He'll get some nice place to stay. Oh, but he's a very self-seeking person. He's implicated fifteen innocent people. Five or six of them will be hanged, and the others will get ten or twelve years each. His declaration put this case on firm ground. No matter how much he was cross-examined, he didn't hesitate at all. What nerve. Now not one of them will escape. Who did his duty; who did not, only God knows, but all of them will be ruined. And he ran away from home after embezzling government money. We've been badly deceived."

Looking at him with mild reproof, Jaggo said gently, "Our good and evil is with ourselves. The whole world is self-seeking; who dies for someone else?"

"To give poison to someone who cuts other people's throats for his own self-interest would not even be a sin," said Devidin, in a sharp tone.

Suddenly two persons came and stood before them. One was a fair, handsome boy, who could not have been older than fifteen or sixteen. The other was a middle-aged man and from his appearance seemed to be a peon.

"Who are you looking for?" said Devidin.

The peon said, "Your name is Devidin, isn't it? I've come from the office of the *Praja Mitra*. This babu is the brother of that Ramanath who received the chess prize. He came to the office looking for him, and the editor sent him to you. So I'll go now, all right?"

He left as he said this. Devidin surveyed Gopi from head to foot. His features were similar to Rama's. "Come and sit, Son," he said. "When did you come from home?"

Gopi considered sitting down at a Khatik's shop to be beneath his dignity. "I came just today," he said, continuing to stand. "My sister-in-law is with me, too. I'm staying in a *dharmshala*."

'So go and bring the bahu here," said Devidin, standing up. "Rama Babu's room is upstairs. You can stay there comfortably. Why stay at the *dharmshala*? Don't leave, I'm coming too. There's every kind of convenience here."

He gave this news to Jaggo, and telling her to sweep out the room, set off to the *dharmshala* along with Gopi. The old woman immediately swept the room, and quickly went and bought sweets and curds from a confectioner's shop. She filled an earthen pot with water and placed it upstairs. Then she washed her face and hands, took out a colourful sari, put on jewellery, and dressed and ready, awaited the bahu's arrival.

Just then a phaeton arrived. The old woman went and helped Jalpa to get out. At first, Jalpa hesitated slightly seeing a vegetable shop, but the loving welcome in the Jaggo's eyes banished her hesitation. When she went upstairs with her, she found everything laid out in its own place, as if it were her own home.

Putting water in the *lota*, Jaggo said, "Brother lived right here in this house, daughter! But now the house has been deserted for fifteen days. Wash your face and hands and eat some curds and sugar, daughter. You probably don't know Brother's situation just now, do you?"

Jalpa shook her head and said, "I don't know anything for certain. I learned from the person who publishes the newspaper that the police had arrested him."

Devidin had come upstairs, too. “They arrested him, no doubt, but now he’s become a government witness in a court case. There won’t be any case against him now in Prayag and if things work out he’ll get government service, too.”

“Did he become a government witness because he was afraid of the Prayag case?” said Jalpa proudly. “There’s no case at all against him there. Why would there be a trial?”

“Wasn’t there some affair involving some money?” said Devidin, hesitantly and fearfully.

Reacting as though she had been struck, Jalpa said, “That was no matter. As soon as we learnt that he had spent some government funds, we returned the amount. He panicked neddlessly and came here, and kept such silence that we didn’t hear a word from him.”

Devidin’s face became as radiant as if he had just been relieved of some torment. “Well, how could we have known? We tried repeatedly to persuade him to write home, they must be worrying, but he wouldn’t write because of his shame. He mistakenly believed that there had to be a case against him in Prayag. If he had known would he have become a government witness?”

The meaning of ‘government witness’ was not unknown to Jalpa. Neither was the scorn and dishonour in which it was held by society unknown to her. She knew why government witnesses were created, what kind of temptations were put before them, and how they turned into puppets of the police and strangled their very own friends. If any person becomes ashamed of his bad behaviour and moves towards the truth, pushes aside the protection of deceit and trickery, then he is truly a virtuous man. Then, however much his courage may be praised, it is always too little. However, the condition is that he is ready to bear the results of what he has done, along with his companions. That he mount the gallows laughing and joking – such a person is a true hero. If, for self protection and from fear of harsh punishment, he selfishly saves his own skin by acting treacherously, and betrays his own companions, then he is cowardly, degraded and shameless. Treachery is just as despicable among robbers and other enemies of society, as it is in any other area. Society never pardons such people, never. Jalpa understood all this very well. Here, the problem had become even more difficult and tangled. Rama had not disclosed his own misdeeds from fear of punishment, at the very least, he would have been truthful. Even if he was condemned, he would have had the one virtue of partial truthfulness. Here, other misdeeds had been revealed, which he could not possibly have had anything to do with. Suddenly Jalpa did not feel so sure of this. Surely something else had happened which had compelled Rama to become a government witness. Shrinking with embarrassment, she asked, "Did something . . . did something happen here, too?"

Aware of her mental distress, Devidin said, "Nothing at all. He came here with me straight from Prayag. Since he came here, he hasn't gone anywhere. He didn't even go outside. One day he went out and that day, the police arrested him. He saw a constable coming, got scared because he thought he was coming to arrest him and took to his heels. This made the constable suspicious, and arrested him on suspicion. I got to the police station after they did. At first the Daroga asked for a bribe, but when I returned after getting the money from home, something else had already been hatched. Who knows what the officers talked about, but they turned him into a government witness. Brother did tell me that he would not have to lie at all in this affair, and that the police had a genuine case. What objection was there to speaking out the truth? I shut up. What could I do?"

"There's no knowing what kind of narcotic they made him inhale," said Jaggo. "Brother wasn't like that. He kept calling me 'Mother, Mother' all the time. All kinds of people came to the shop, both men and women. He didn't have the impudence to look at anyone straight in the eye."

"He didn't have any badness in him," said Devidin. "I never saw a boy like him. He was deceived."

After thinking a moment, Jalpa said, "Has he finished giving evidence?"

"Yes, it went on for a whole three days. It finished today."

"So nothing can be done now," said Jalpa, anxiously. "Will I be able to meet him?"

Devidin smiled at this question of Jalpa's. "Yes, of course! Because of which the entire plot will be smashed to bits and the game, spoilt. The police are not such stupid asses. These days, they don't let anyone meet him. He's strictly guarded."

No more discussion was possible on this question just then. It was not easy to solve this knotty a problem. Jalpa summoned Gopi, who was standing on the edge of the roof watching the passing spectacle on the street. He was embarrassed and happy as if he were at his in-laws'. He came very slowly and stood by them.

"Wash your hands and face and eat something," said Jalpa. "You like curds a lot."

Gopi blushed and went out.

"He won't eat in front of us," said Devidin smiling. "We'll both leave. Tell us whatever you need, Bahuji. This is your home. We thought of Brother as our own. Who else is there with us?"

"He would eat what I made with my own hands," said Jaggo proudly. "He didn't feel any false pride."

Jalpa smiled and said, "Now you won't have to cook, Mother. I'll do the cooking."

"In our community it's forbidden to eat from the hands of other communities, Bahu," objected Jaggo. "Why should I make my community despise me for eating from your hand for even a few days?"

"Our community forbids eating others' food, too," said Jalpa.

"Who's going to come here to see you?" countered Jaggo. "And then educated people don't even consider these things. Our community is a bunch of fools."

"It doesn't feel right that you should cook and I eat," said Jalpa. "Whoever you made a bahu, you'll have to eat food cooked by her. If you were not going to do so, why did you make me your bahu?"

Giving Jaggo an approving look, Devidin said, "Bahu has said something remarkable. Think it over before you give her an answer. Come on, now, let's give these people a chance to rest a little."

When both of them had gone, Gopi came and said, "Did Brother live here at this Khatik's place? They certainly seem to be Khatiks."

"Whether they are Khatiks or Chamars, they're a hundred times better than you or I," snapped Jalpa. "They put up a stranger in their own home for six months and gave him food and drink. Do we have that much courage? Here, a guest is a burden for them. If they are lowborn, we are even more lowborn than them."

Gopi had washed his hands and face. As he ate his sweets, he said, "No one raises his status by putting someone up. No matter how much merit a Chamar may get from being generous and charitable, he'll still be a low-caste Chamar."

"I consider such a Chamar better than a Brahman *pundit* who always devours the wealth of others," said Jalpa.

Gopi went downstairs after his snack. He was very keen to roam around in the city. Jalpa did not feel like eating anything. She had a complicated problem before her – how to get Rama out of this quagmire. Just imagining the scorn and derision awaiting him was a blow to her pride. They would be disgraced in everyone's eyes forever, unable to show their faces to anyone.

Who would bear the responsibility for the blood of innocent people? No one could know who was guilty and who was innocent among the accused, or how many of them were the victims of enmity and greed. All of them would be sentenced. Perhaps three or four of them would even be hanged. On whom would the blame for their murder fall?

'No one would be blamed for murder', she thought further. Who knew whether anyone would be blamed or not, but for one's own self interest –

Oh! How contemptible! How had he ever agreed to it? Even if he'd been afraid of the Municipality bringing a case against him, it would have meant no more than three or four years of imprisonment. To stoop to such terribly low depths to avoid this!

Now, even if he learned that the Municipality could not do anything to him now, what could possibly be done now? He had already given his testimony.

Suddenly, something pierced her heart like a massive spike. 'Why could he not change his declaration? If he should learn that the Municipality could do nothing to him, perhaps he would change his declaration on his own. How could he be informed of this? Was it possible somehow?' she thought.

Impatiently, she went downstairs and gesturing for Devidin to come, said, "Tell me, Dada, couldn't we get even a letter to him? Maybe if we gave the guards a five or ten rupees, the letter might reach him."

Shaking his head, Devidin said, "It's difficult. They put very trustworthy men on guard duty. I went twice, and not one of them would allow me to even stand in front of the gate."

"What's near around the bungalow?"

"On one side, there's another bungalow, on another, an orchard of grafted mango trees, and in front, the street."

"He probably comes out in the evening to roam around?"

"Yes, he brings out a chair and sits. One or two police officers stay with him, too."

"If someone should hide in that orchard, how would it be? When he saw Rama alone, he could throw him a letter. He'd surely pick it up."

"Yes, it's certainly possible," said Devidin, surprised, "but only if you meet him alone."

When it grew a little darker, Jalpa went along with Devidin to see Ramanath's bungalow. She wrote a letter and put it in the neck of her garment. Again and again she asked Devidin how far they had yet to go. Really! Still only so much further to go? The compound here would undoubtedly be lighted. Her heart began to surge with emotion. If she should find Rama sauntering around alone, what would be better? She would wrap up the letter in a handkerchief and throw it in front of him. His expression would be bound to change.

Suddenly a doubt seized her. 'Suppose, despite reading her letter he still did not change his declaration, then what? Who knew whether he even remembered her or not? Suppose he should turn away when he saw her?' thinking so, her doubts began to frighten her. "Tell me, Dada, did he ever mention his home?"

"Never," said Devidin, shaking his head. "He never mentioned it to me. He used to stay very sad."

These words lent even greater force to Jalpa's doubts. They had come some distance out of the densely populated area of the city, and there was dead silence all around. Even the wind was taking a rest now, after blowing hard all day. In the faint light of the moon, the trees and open grounds on the side of the road seemed dejected and lifeless. It began to seem to Jalpa that her efforts would bear no fruit, and that her trip had no purpose. On this endless road, her condition was something like that of an orphan who wanders from door to door for a handful of food. He knows that at the next door he will receive no food, just curses, but he still stretches out his hand, still pleads for more. He has no support from hope – hopelessness itself is his support.

All at once, on the right side of the street the light of an electric lamp was visible.

Devidin pointed towards a bungalow and said, "This is his bungalow."

Jalpa looked fearfully towards where he had pointed, but only silence lay around them. No person was there. The gate was locked.

"No one's here," said Jalpa.

Peering inside the gate, Devidin said, "Yes, maybe they've left this bungalow."

"They must have gone out somewhere."

"If they'd gone out, they'd have left a guard at the gate. They've left this bungalow."

"So let's go back."

"No," said Devidin. "We should, at least, find out where they've gone."

On the right side of the bungalow, some light showed in the mango grove. Perhaps a Khatik was guarding the grove. Devidin went inside and called out, "Who's there? Who's leased this orchard?"

A man appeared out of a dense cluster of mango trees. "Hey, it's you, Jangli?" said Devidin recognising him. "You're leasing this orchard?"

Jangli was a short, well-built man. "Yes, Dada, I'm leasing it," he said. "But there's nothing here. So, I'll be paying a fine instead. How did you happen to come here?"

Devidin said, "No reason, really, I just came by chance. What happened to the fellow who was in the bungalow?"

Jangli looked around and then whispered, "That informer was detained in it. Everyone left today. I've heard that they'll come back in fifteen or twenty days when the case will be presented again in the High Court. Educated people are also such doublecrossers. Dada! The testimony he gave was totally false. Wonder whether he has any children or not. He wasn't even afraid of God!"

Jalpa was standing right there. Devidin did not give Jangli a chance to spew out any more poison. "So they'll come in fifteen or twenty days?" he said. "Are you sure?"

Jangli said, "Yes, that's just what the guards were saying."

Devidin said, "Do you know anything about where they went?"

Jangli said, "They went to the site where the incident took place."

Devidin started to smoke his *chilam* and Jalpa came out on to the street and began to walk up and down. Her heart had been torn to pieces hearing the scorn heaped on Rama. She felt neither anger nor shame towards him. She was impatient to pull him out of this morass with her own hands. Even if Rama should upbraid her, even if he should spurn her, she was not going to let him fall into this pit of disgrace.

As they were leaving, Jalpa asked, "You told that man to let us know when they come back, didn't you?"

Devidin said, "Yes, I told him."

37

A month passed. At first, Gopinath roamed around Calcutta for a while, but after only four or five days he got so fed up with the place that he began to repeat the refrain of home, home, home. In the end, Jalpa thought it best to send him back. Here in Calcutta, he just hid and cried and complained.

Jalpa went to Rama's bungalow several times. She knew that he had not returned yet, but she still received a strange satisfaction in doing the circuit.

When Jalpa grew tired of reading or lying around, she would go stand in front of the window for a while. One evening, while she was standing there, a procession of motorcars came into view. She became curious about where so many motorcars were going and began to look very attentively: there were six of them filled with police officers, and one was full of constables. When her gaze fell on the last car, it was as if a current of electricity coursed through her entire body. She became so obsessed that she dashed from the window towards the stairs, as if she wanted to stop the car, but in the same instant she realised that by the time she got downstairs, all the cars would have gone by. She came back to the window again. Rama's car had come directly in front of her by now, and his eyes were raised towards the window. Jalpa wanted to communicate something with a gesture, but embarrassment stopped her. It seemed as if Rama's car had slowed down. Devidin's voice could be heard, too, but the car did not stop. In an instant, it had moved on, though Rama kept looking at the window, again and again.

Jalpa went to the stairs and said, "Dada!"

Devidin came to the bottom of the stairs and said, "Brother has come. What a motorcar that was."

He came upstairs. "Did he say something to you?" said Jalpa, her eagerness overcoming her embarrassment.

"What else did he have time to say except 'Ram, Ram'? I asked how he was, and he made an encouraging gesture before he moved on. Did you see him or not?"

"Why wouldn't I have seen him?" said Jalpa, with bowed head. "I was standing right by the window."

Devidin said, "Then he must have seen you, too?"

Jalpa said, "He was staring at the window, at any rate."

Devidin said, "He must have been really perplexed."

Jalpa said, "Did you find out when the case will be presented?"

Devidin replied, “Tomorrow, for sure.”

Jalpa said, “Tomorrow? So soon? Then something has to be done. It will have to be today, itself. If he got my letter somehow, then it would work.”

Devidin gazed at her as if to say: “It won’t be as easy to do this as you think.”

Jalpa, as if reading his mind, said, “Do you doubt that that he won’t be willing to change his evidence?”

Devidin saw no way out now except to accept his misgivings. “Yes, Bahuji,” he said. “I feel very doubtful about it, and what’s more, if you ask me it’s risky. Even if he does change his testimony, he won’t escape the clutches of the police. They’ll fabricate some other charge to catch him, and then bring a new case against him.”

Jalpa gave him a look as if to tell him she was not the least bit frightened by this. Then she said, “Dada, I’m not taking the responsibility for saving him from the police. I only want to save him from disgrace, if that’s possible. I can’t see so many homes ruined through him. Even if he really were a member of a gang of robbers, I would still want him to stand by his companions, and cheerfully endure whatever fell to his lot. It would never please me to see him betray others and become an informer. But this case is totally fabricated, and I simply can’t bear for him to give false testimony to save his own skin. If he won’t change his testimony himself, then I’ll go to the court myself and expose the truth, no matter what the results may be. If he leaves me for good, or never looks at my face, I’m willing to accept it. But it cannot be that he should disgrace himself so thoroughly. I’ve written all this in my letter.”

“Now I’m sure that you’ll manage everything, Bahu,” said Devidin, gazing at her respectfully. “When you’ve made your heart so strong, you’ll be able to do everything you wish to.”

Jalpa said, “Let’s leave from here at nine o’clock, then.”

Devidin said, “Yes, I’m ready.”

38

The same Ramanath who had never gone out for fear of the police, who was spending the days of his life by hiding out at Devidin's house like a thief, had for the last two months been plunged into a life of luxury fit for a king. He had a prettily decorated bungalow to live in, a whole group of servants to attend to him, a motorcar to ride in, and a Kashmiri cook to prepare his food. Important officers hung on his every word. Before he asked for anything, it would be done. In just a few days, he had become so fastidious that it seemed he was a hereditary nobleman. Luxury had lulled his conscience to sleep. It never occurred to him to ask himself what he was doing or how much innocent blood would be on his hands. Nor was he was ever given the opportunity for solitary thought. At night he would go with officials to the cinema or theatre and in the evenings there would be trips in the motorcar. There were always new things to amuse him. The day when the magistrate committed the accused for trial in the Sessions Court, he was the happiest person around. It seemed to him that the sun of his good fortune had risen.

The police knew that there would be no such enjoyment in the court of the Sessions Judge. It so happened that he was Indian and notorious for his impartiality. Police and thieves were equal in his estimation, nor did he show favour or leniency to anyone. This was why the police had considered it important to take Rama on a trip to the sites where the incidents had taken place. They had set up quarters in the richly decorated bungalow of a landowner. They would hunt all day, and at night listen to the gramophone, play cards, or tour the river on barges. It seemed as if some young prince had come out on a hunting trip.

If Rama had any unfulfilled desire in the midst of this luxury, it was the wish that Jalpa could be there too. As long as he had been dependent and poor, it was as if all his capacities for sensuous enjoyment had faded away. Now these cool gusts had revived them. He had become enraptured by the imaginary prospect of receiving a good position as soon as the case was concluded. Then he would go, persuade Jalpa to return with him, and enjoy life's comforts in contentment. Yes, it would be a new kind of life; its standards of behaviour, its principles would be different. He would have rigorous self-control and true restraint. Now his life would have some purpose, some ideals. The business of life was not just eating, sleeping, and worrying about money. His aimless life would come to an end with this case. His feeble will had shown him this new day and was now showing him the dream of a new and perfect life. Such people, like drunkards, make vows every single day, but what is the result of these vows? New temptations keep coming forward and the time for fulfilling the vows keeps being extended. The new day never dawns.

After a month's tour in the countryside, Rama was returning to his bungalow along with his police collaborators. The route went past Devidin's house. He could see his room from some distance away, and involuntarily lifted his gaze upwards. Someone was standing in front of the window. What was Devidin doing standing there just now? He looked more attentively. It was some woman! But where had she come from? Could it be that Devidin was renting the room? He had never done that before.

As the motorcar came a little nearer, the woman's face was clearly visible. Rama stared in astonishment. It was Jalpa! Without a doubt it was Jalpa! But no, no, how could Jalpa have come here? How could she possibly know his whereabouts? Had the old man perhaps written a letter to her? It was Jalpa. The assistant Daroga was driving. "Sardar Sahab," said Rama imploringly, "please stop a moment. I'd like to have a word with Devidin." The Assistant slowed down a little, but after a little thought he drove ahead.

"You've made me a prisoner!" said Rama angrily.

Grinning with embarrassment, the other said, "You know how quickly the Deputy Sahab gets hot under the collar."

After arriving at the bungalow, Rama began to think about how he could meet Jalpa. That Jalpa was there he now had no doubt. How could his eyes deceive him? A fiery pain sprang up in his heart; what should he do? How could he go to her? He didn't even remember to change his clothes, but stood for fifteen minutes at the door of his room. No clever scheme occurred to him, and he lay down on his bed in helplessness.

After only a little while, he got up again and went out into the adjacent courtyard. The electric streetlights had come on by now.

A guard was standing at the gate. Just then Rama felt such anger that he could have shot him. If he got a good position, he'd tell them off, one after the other. He'd get them dismissed; always sticking to him like devils! 'Just look at his face! It looks like the hind end of a goat! Oh, what a wonderful turban you have! Just like some basket-carrying coolie! If a dog should bark at you right now, you'd run away with your tail between your legs, but look at you standing here right now, so firmly as if you're protecting the door of some fort!'

Another guard came and said, "The Inspector Sahab has invited you. He's sent for some new gramophone records."

"I don't have any spare time now," said Rama furiously.

Then he began to think again. How had Jalpa come here? Had she come by herself or with someone else? That slave driver hadn't given him even a moment to talk with the old man. Jalpa would certainly ask why he had run away. He'd tell her straight out, what else could he have done at the time? But this short period of troubles had solved the question of life. Now they could spend their lives in contentment. He would try and get posted in that region.

As he pondered, it occurred to him that there would be no harm if Jalpa stayed here with him. Outsiders were prohibited from meeting him, but what objection could there be to Jalpa? Right now, however, it wasn't appropriate to raise the question; he'd settle it tomorrow. What a strange creature Devidin was, too. He'd come several times before, but today he'd fallen quite silent. At least he could have come and given the news of Jalpa's arrival to him through the constable on guard duty. Then he'd see who wouldn't let Jalpa come! At first this kind of custody had been necessary, but now his test had been completed. Maybe everyone would agree willingly.

The cook brought a plate of food. There was a single kind of meat. Rama flared up as soon as he saw the plate. These days he only felt hungry when he saw appetising food. He wasn't satisfied unless there were chutnies, pickles, and four or five kinds of meat.

"What am I supposed to eat?" he said angrily. "Your head? Take the *thaali* away."

"Huzur," said the cook fearfully, "how can I prepare more things so quickly? You came just two hours ago."

Rama said, "Is two hours such a short time for you?"

The cook said, "What can I say to you, Huzur?"

Rama said, "Don't talk nonsense!"

The cook said, "Your Huzur..."

Rama cut him short, "Don't talk nonsense! Damn!"

The cook said nothing more. He brought a bottle, broke up some ice and put it in a glass, and then moved back and stood silently.

Rama felt angry enough to tear the cook into pieces. He had become very hot-tempered these days.

When the liquor began to course through him, he became even more irate. Looking at the cook with inflamed eyes he said, "I could grab you by the ear and throw you out if I want. Now! This instant! What do you think of yourself!"

Seeing his anger growing, the cook slunk silently away. Rama took the glass, and gulping down three or four mouthfuls, he went outside and began to stroll around the courtyard. He was obsessed by one overpowering thought: how could he get out of here.

All of a sudden he became aware that outside the wires of the fence, there was someone in the cover of the trees. Yes, someone was standing and staring in his direction. Perhaps he was beckoning him to approach. Rama's heart began to thud. Could it be a plot by some conspirators to take his life? He was continuously apprehensive, and hence seldom went outside at night. His instinct for self-preservation urged him to go inside. Just then a motorcar passed by on the street, and in its light Rama saw that the dark shadow was a woman: he could clearly see her sari. Then it seemed to him that she was coming towards him. He began to feel apprehensive again; could it be a man who had changed his dress to deceive him? With each step he took backwards, the apparition moved the same distance towards him, until it reached the wires and threw something at him. Rama let out a shriek and jumped back, but it was only an envelope. He calmed down a little. When he looked up again, the apparition had merged into the darkness. Rama bounded forward and picked up the envelope. He felt a mixture of fear and curiosity, but the curiosity was greater than the fear. Taking the envelope in his hand, he began to examine it. As soon as he looked at the address, his heart began to tremble with emotion. The writing was Jalpa's.

He opened the envelope in haste – it was Jalpa's writing again. He read the letter in one breath, and then heaved a deep sigh. Along with that sigh, as if by magic, there flew away all his weakness, shame, and self-reproach; all that mental suffering which had been draining away his life-blood; and that terrible load of worry which had oppressed his soul for half a year now. Never before had he felt so much enthusiasm, so much pride, and so much self-confidence. At first he was in a frenzy to go and tell the Daroga that this case was no concern of his. But then he reflected that his deposition had been recorded, and he had already received all the disgrace coming to him, so why should he wash his hands of the results now? But what a dirty trick they had all played on him! Until now they had kept him in the dark. Every last one of them had professed friendship with him, but had kept the real state of affairs concealed from him. Even now they didn't trust him. If he should change his deposition now, he would learn how hard life could be. At most, he would not get a good position. So what? At least, all their schemes would be reduced to dust and ashes. There would be retribution for this treachery. And even if none of this turned out to be true, he would still be saved from such a great disgrace. They had all play some nasty tricks, but what else could they do besides bringing a spurious charge against him? When they could not even establish that he had lived here, what offence could they charge him with? They would all be put to shame, and would not even be able to show their faces, let alone bring a case against him.

However, they had played a trick on him, so he would play the same trick on them. He would tell them that he would give evidence if he got a good position today; otherwise he would tell them straight out that the case was no concern of his. If he did not do this, then afterwards they would make him a Daroga and send him to some obscure little police station where he would rot away. He would take an inspectorship; and a warrant of appointment should reach him by ten o'clock tomorrow. He went to speak to the Daroga at once, but then stopped. He was aching to meet Jalpa once again. Never before had he felt so much devotion, so much respect for her, as if she were some divine power whom the gods had sent for his protection.

It was ten o'clock. Rama turned off the electric light, came out on to the veranda, and banged the doors shut so that it would seem to the guard that he had shut the door from the inside and gone to sleep. He stood for a minute on the darkened veranda. Then he slowly stepped off it, went up to the barbed-wire fence, and began to think how he could get through it. Maybe Jalpa was still in the mango grove, and Devidin would certainly be with her. Only the wire was blocking his way. It was impossible for him to leap over it. He decided to get out by going through the wires. He pulled his clothes tight around him, and avoiding the thorns, thrust his head and shoulders between the wires. Somehow, his clothes were entangled. When he attempted to free them, his sleeve was caught in the barbs. His dhoti was ensnared, too. Now the poor fellow was in an impasse. He could not go this way or that. If he were the least bit careless, the barbs would pierce his body.

He was past caring about clothes now. He stretched his neck still farther forward and came out the other side, tearing his clothes. All his clothes were in shreds, and his back bore some scratches too, but even if someone had come and stood right there aiming a rifle at him, he would not have retreated. He threw away his torn *kurta* on the spot. Even though the shawl around his neck was torn, it was still serviceable. He wrapped it around himself, gathered his *dhoti* around him, and began to wander around the orchard. It was deathly still. Maybe the Khatik caretaker had gone off to eat. He called Jalpa's name softly two or three times. He didn't hear a sound, but even though he was disappointed, love did not loosen its grip on him. He went under a tree and looked around. He realised that Jalpa had gone. He followed her footsteps to Devidin's house without the slightest regret. What did he care if someone should find out that he had slipped out of the bungalow; what could the police do to him? He was no prisoner, he had not been ordained to be a slave.

It was midnight. Devidin had returned half an hour ago himself, and was about to eat when he was startled by the sight of a half-naked man. Rama had fastened the shawl around his head to frighten the old man.

"Who is it?" said Devidin, fearfully.

Suddenly recognising Rama, he leaped forward, seized his hand and said, "You've really got quite a costume there, Brother! What happened to your clothes?"

Rama said, "When I was going through the fence, they caught on the barbs and got torn."

Devidin said, "Oh Lord! You didn't get cut?"

Rama replied, "Nothing really, one or two scratches. I went through very carefully."

Devidin now asked him, "You got Bahu's letter, didn't you?"

Rama said, "Yes, I got it just then. Was she with you, too?"

"She wasn't with me," corrected Devidin. "I was with her. Ever since she saw you in the motorcar, she was determined to go."

Rama said, "You didn't write any letter to her?"

Devidin replied, "I didn't write any letters or notes, Brother. When she came I was surprised myself to see how she arrived without knowing a thing. Later on she told me everything. She had sent the chess problem diagram from Prayag, and the prize came from there too."

Rama's eyes opened wide. Jalpa's cleverness astonished him. At the same time a feeling of defeat depressed him somewhat. So he had lost here, too, and badly.

The old woman had gone upstairs. Going to the foot of the stairs, Devidin called out, "Hey, what are you doing? Tell Bahu that a man has come to meet her."

Devidin grasped Rama's hand again and said, "Come on, now it's time for you to speak up in court. You've been on the run a long time. You've been arrested without a warrant. Even the police can't arrest you so easily now."

Rama's joy melted away and he was pierced by shame. What answer could he give to Jalpa's questions? The same fear that had made him flee, had followed on his heels and defeated him in the end. He would not even be able to look Jalpa straight in the eyes. He wrenched his hand away and stood by the stairs, irresolute.

"Why have you stopped?" asked Devidin.

Rama scratched his head and said, "Go on, I'm coming."

"Ask him who he is and where he's from," said the old woman from upstairs.

"He says that he'll say what he has to say to Bahu," said Devidin, cracking a joke.

Jaggo said, "Has he brought a letter?"

Devidin replied, "No!"

Everything became quiet. After a moment, Devidin asked, "Shall I tell him to go back?"

Jalpa came to the stairs and said, "I'm asking you, who is it!"

Devidin said, "He says he's come a long way."

Jalpa asked, "Where is he?"

Devidin replied, "Here he is, standing here."

Jalpa said, "All right, tell him to come upstairs."

Wrapped in his shawl, partly timid, partly ashamed, partly fearful, Rama went up the stairs. Jalpa recognised him as soon as she saw him. She quickly took two steps backwards, but if Devidin had not been there, she would have taken two steps forward.

Never had so much intoxication been in her eyes, never so much unsteadiness in her limbs, never such a glow in her cheeks, and never such a tender quivering in her heart. Today, all her sacrifices had borne fruit.

39

The night when those who have been separated meet is the same as the night when travellers make camp – one spent in talking. Both Rama and Jalpa had to tell their stories of the last six months. Rama greatly magnified the description of his difficulties to increase his glory. Jalpa never even mentioned her troubles in her narrative. She was afraid it would cause him grief. Rama, however, took special pleasure in bringing her to tears. How he had come to run away, why he had run away, in what way he had run away – he told his whole epic in heart-rending words, and Jalpa, sobbing away, listened. He wanted to impress her with his words. Till now he had had to suffer defeat in everything. What had seemed unimaginably difficult to him, Jalpa had completed in a twinkling. He could have really spiced up his account of the chess problem, but there, too, Jalpa had shown him up. So what other means did he have to satisfy his thirst for fame than to make mountains out of the molehills of his sufferings?

"You had to bear all these hardships," said Jalpa sobbing, "but you never wrote us a single letter. Why should you have written, what were we to you, anyway. Your love was false. If you cover your eyes, you can't see the mountain in front of you."

"That wasn't it, Jalpa," said Rama, regretfully. "Only the heart knows what it has to bear, but it takes some nerve to write, too. When I had to hide my face and run away from home, how could I sit and write the story of my disasters? I decided that until I earned a lot of money, I wouldn't write a word."

"That was exactly right!" said Jalpa sarcastically, her eyes brimming with tears. "Men love money the most! And I'm a lover of money. Whether you steal, rob, forge bank notes, give false testimony, or beg, just get the money any way you can. Hurrah! How well you've understood my nature. As Gosainji the saint said, "Satisfy selfish desires, and everyone will love you!"

"No, no, dear," said Rama shamefacedly. "That wasn't it. I thought to myself, 'How can I go home when I'm so down-and-out.' I'm telling the truth, I was more afraid of you than anything else. I thought how treacherous, how false, how cowardly you must consider me. Perhaps I felt that if you saw a plateful of money your heart would become a little softer."

"I might not have even touched that plate," said Jalpa, in a tortured voice. "Today I've learned how low, how selfish, how greedy you consider me to be! It's no fault of yours, the whole fault is mine. If I were a good woman, why would this day have ever come? Any woman who spends three or four rupees a day, and who is determined to wear jewellery worth a thousand or two, when her husband is a thirty-to-forty-a-month employee, is bringing about her ruin and his. If you thought I was so greedy for money, then you did nothing wrong, but I won't jump a second time into the same fire where I was burned once. During these months I've made some atonement for my sins, and I'll keep on doing so for the rest of my life. I don't say that I've had my fill of the pleasures of life, or that I'm tired of clothes and jewellery, or that I hate trips and entertainments. All these desires are much the same as before. If you can fulfill these desires through exertion, through diligence, through industry, there is nothing more to say. But even if you bring a hundred thousand rupees, if it's by making fraudulent schemes, by making your soul filthy, then I'll kick it away. When I learned that you had become a police witness, I felt so bad that I went to your bungalow right away with Dada. But you had gone away that very day, and it's just today that you have come back. I don't want the blood of so many people on my head. Tell the court clearly that you gave evidence because you were deceived by the police, and that you have nothing to do with this case."

"I've been thinking about this question ever since I got your letter," said Rama worriedly, "but I can't figure out what I should do. I don't have the courage to take back what I've already said."

Jalpa said, "But you must change your deposition."

Rama said, "But how shall I do it?"

Jalpa replied, "What's the difficulty? When you know that the Municipality can't bring a case against you, what's there to be afraid of?"

Rama said, "It's not just fear, shame is something too. It's not in me to say one thing and then turn around and say another. And then, after the case I'll get a good position. We'll spend our lives in comfort. I don't have the strength to be knocked around from one alley to the next."

Jalpa did not answer. She was thinking how great a proportion of selfishness there was in people.

Rama spoke again, insolently, "And the whole decision doesn't depend on my evidence alone. Even if I change it, the police will stand up somebody else in my place. There's no way the lives of the criminals can be saved. Yes, I'd lose out for nothing."

Jalpa glanced at him angrily and said, "What sort of shameless things are you saying, Sir? Are you so far gone that you can cut other people's throats for your own livelihood? I won't stand for this. I'm willing to perform manual labour, to die of hunger. I can let the greatest calamities in the world fall on my head. But I can't accept even the kingdom of paradise by bringing bad fortune to someone else."

Offended by this idealism, Rama said, "So do you want me to do coolies' work here?"

Jalpa said, "No, I don't want that. But it's far better than eating bread drenched in someone else's blood."

"Jalpa," said Rama calmly, "I'm not as low as you think I am. Everyone feels something bad is bad. I'm also sorry that so many people are suffering at my hands. But circumstances have made me helpless. I don't have the strength to endure any more hard blows. Nor can I quarrel with the police.

People hardly follow ideals in this world. Why do you want to make me climb to those heights which I don't have the capacity to reach?"

"Would it be surprising that a person who has the power to commit murder has no power not to commit it?" said Jalpa, in a cutting tone of voice. "And who would agree that a person who has the strength to run wouldn't have the strength to stand? When we want to do something, the strength comes by itself. If you decide to change your deposition, then all that you have to say, and the strength to say it, will also come."

Rama listened with bowed head.

"If you want to continue to cultivate this evil-doing, then you can say good bye to me here, today," said Jalpa, growing even more heated. "I'll go away in disgrace and I won't come to trouble you again. You live happily. I'll fill my stomach by labour and effort. My atonement is not finished yet; that's why this weakness hasn't left us yet. I can see that it won't go until it has destroyed us."

Rama was cut to the quick. Scratching his head he said, "I, too, want to save us from this disaster somehow or other."

Jalpa said, "Then why don't you? If you're ashamed to say anything, then I'll go with you. That would be best. I'll come along with you and tell your Superintendent Sahab the whole story in plain language."

All of Rama's perplexities vanished. He did not want to make himself so abject that his wife would go and plead for him. "It's not necessary for you to go, Jalpa," he said. "I'll let them know."

"Tell me right out," said Jalpa, with emphasis. "Are you going to change your deposition or not?"

"I tell you I'll change it," said Rama, as if he had been forced into a corner.

Jalpa asked, "Because I say so, or from your own heart?"

Rama replied, "Not because you say so, but from my heart. I hate such things myself. There was just a little hesitation, and you got rid of that."

Then they talked about other things. How had she learned that Rama had spent the money? How had it been paid off? Had other people heard the news of the embezzlement or had it been kept quiet among the family? What had happened to Ratan? Why had Gopi gone home so soon? Were both boys studying or were they roaming around like vagabonds, as before? At last, Mother and Father were mentioned.

Then plans for their life began to be made. Jalpa said, "Let's go home, buy a little land from Ratan, and do some farming in comfort." Rama said, "It would be much better to open a tea shop here." At this a debate began, and in the end Rama had to admit defeat. If they lived here, they could not take care of the home, they could not educate his brothers, and they could not serve Mother and Father. After all, they had some duties towards their family, too. Rama was silenced.

40

Rama reached his bungalow by daybreak. No one heard or suspected a thing.

After eating breakfast, Rama shaved, dressed and arrived at the Daroga's quarters. Rama was scowling. The Daroga asked, "Is everything alright? The servants haven't played any tricks on you, have they?"

Continuing to stand, Rama said, "Not the servants, you've played tricks. Your subordinates, officers, all of you together have made a fool of me."

Panicking a little, the Daroga asked, "What is this about? Won't you tell me?"

Rama said, "This is what it's all about. I won't give any testimony in this case now. I have nothing to do with it. You people deceived me, threatened me with a warrant, and forced me to give testimony. Now I know there's no case against me. It was your trickery. I no longer wish to give evidence on behalf of the police, and I'll tell this plainly to the judge today. I won't have the blood of innocent people on my head!"

The Daroga said angrily, "You admitted to embezzlement yourself."

Rama said, "It was a mistake in addition, not embezzlement. The Municipality didn't bring any case against me."

The Daroga asked, "How did you learn that?"

Rama replied, "I'm not going to argue with you about this. I won't give testimony. I'll say right out that the police deceived me and forced me to testify. On the date of the incident, I was in Allahabad. The record of my attendance is available in the Municipal Office."

Attempting to dispel this disaster with laughter, the Daroga said, "All right, Sahab, the police did indeed deceive you, but as compensation we're willing to give you a reward. You'll get a good position, you'll travel in a motorcar. If you get a position with the secret police, you'll be completely contented. Your honour and influence with the government will be greatly increased. If you do as you intend, you'll wander around in misery. You might get a clerkship in some office, but only with great difficulty. Here the door to your advancement has opened on its own. You will gain good experience, and then one day you'll become Rai Bahadur Munshi Ramanath, Deputy Superintendent. You should be grateful for our favours, and here you are, getting angry."

These temptations had no effect on Rama. "I'm willing to become a clerk," he said. "I don't want your kind of advancement. Let this good fortune be yours."

Just then the Inspector and the Deputy Superintendent arrived.

When he saw Rama, the Inspector proclaimed, "Our Babu Sahab is already sitting here ready for us. That's the sort of competence that makes one prosper."

Rama spoke as if he too understood it to be a matter of profit and loss. "Yes, Sir, today I'll settle things. I've been guided by your views all these days. Now I'll go ahead based on what I see with my own eyes."

The Inspector looked at the Daroga, the Daroga looked at the Deputy, and Deputy looked at the Inspector. What was he saying? Taken aback, the Inspector asked, "What's the matter? On my honour, you seem to be a little angry."

"I've decided that I'll change my deposition today," said Rama. "I can't shed the blood of innocent people."

Looking towards him in a kindly manner, the Inspector said, "You're not shedding the blood of innocent people; you're building the structure of your destiny. On my honour, people very seldom get opportunities like this. What happened today to make you so angry? Do you know anything, Daroga Sahab? None of our men gave him any cheek, did they? If anyone has done anything to offend you, I'll have him shot, on my honour."

"I'll go and find out right now," said the Daroga.

"Don't trouble yourself," said Rama. "I have no complaints against anyone. I can't destroy my honour for a little personal advantage."

There was dead silence for a minute. No one could think of anything to say. The Daroga was thinking up some more trickery, the Inspector another temptation. The Deputy was reflecting on something else entirely. "Rama Babu," he said harshly, "this won't turn out well."

"It won't turn out well for you," said Rama, also getting excited, "but it's the very best thing for me."

"No," said the Deputy. "Nothing could be worse for you. We won't let you off. Our case may be ruined, but we'll give you a lesson that you won't forget for the rest of your life. You'll have to give the same testimony that you gave before. If you make any trouble, if you mix anything up, then we'll treat you differently. You'll be written up in a report and sent off to jail like this". Saying so, he placed his wrists together, suggestive of handcuffs.

As he said this he glared at Rama as though he would eat him alive. Fear rose up in Rama. These terrible words shook him. If they should bring some fabricated case against him, who would protect him? He had not expected the Deputy, who had acted like the embodiment of tolerance and courtesy, to assume this fearsome appearance all at once. However, he was not so easily intimidated. "Are you going to force me to testify?" he said, heatedly.

"Yes!" said the Deputy, stamping his foot on the floor, "I'll force you."

Rama said, "That's a fine joke!"

The Deputy said, "You think it's a joke to mislead the police! Right now I can bring forward two witnesses who can prove that you've been saying seditious things. You'll get sent up for seven years. You'll get calluses on your hands from turning the hand-mill. You won't have those smooth cheeks any more."

Rama was afraid of jail. His hair stood on end just from imagining life there. He had agreed to give his testimony because of this very fear, and now this fear began to make him cowardly. The Deputy was a master of psychology. He realised how things stood. "You won't get *puris* and *halwa* there," he said. "You'll get bread made from flour mixed with dust, broth made from rotten cabbage leaves, and *arhar daal* water to eat and drink. If they put you in solitary confinement for even four months, you won't survive. You'll die right there. The warden will abuse you every time he opens his mouth, and beat you with shoes. What do you know about it?"

Rama's face grew pale. It seemed as if his blood was drying up moment by moment. He felt such disgust with his weakness that he burst into tears. "If that's what you people want," he said in a trembling voice, "then so be it! Send me to jail! I'll die for sure? Then my neck will be safe from you. Since you're prepared to go this far to ruin me, then I'm ready to die. Whatever has to be, will be."

His mind had reached that state of weakness, when the slightest sympathy, the smallest kindness, was far more effective than hundreds of threats. The Inspector quickly perceived the opportunity. "On my honour, you people don't know this man very well at all," he said to the Deputy, taking Rama's side. "You are just going on intimidating him. Any intelligent person would feel bad about giving evidence this way. It's only natural. Anyone with the least sense of honour will find it displeasing to be a puppet in the hands of the police. If I were in the Babu Sahab's place I'd do the same. But it doesn't mean that he will give evidence against us. You people go about your business. Don't worry about Babu Sahab, on my honour."

He took Rama's hand and said, "Come along with me, Babuji, I'll play some nice records for you."

Rama freed his hand like a sulky child and said, "Don't pick on me, Inspector Sahab. Now I have to die in jail."

Putting his hand on Rama's shoulder, the Inspector said, "Why do you let such things come out of your mouth, Sahab? May your enemies die in jail!"

The Deputy did not intend to leave the smallest loose end untied. Speaking in a severe tone as if he had never been acquainted with Rama, he said to the Inspector, "Sahab, generally speaking we're ready to extend every courtesy to Babu Sahab, but if he gives testimony against us, or tries to cut us off at the roots, then we'll take our own measures too, we certainly will. We can never let him go."

At that very moment the government advocate and the barrister got out of their motorcar.

41

Ratan kept encouraging Jalpa in her letters, but wrote nothing about herself. Who will tell the story of her own sufferings to someone who is suffering herself? The same Ratan, who had never grasped any facts about money, had now in a single month become a beggar, dependant on others even for her daily food. Even though her married life had not been very happy, she had at least never felt the want of anything. Even a rider who makes a journey on a half-dead horse can complete the journey if the road is good, and servants, money, food, and the like are also there. And if the horse is fast, then what is the need to ask. Ratan's circumstances were similar. Like the rider, she was slowly making her journey through life. Sometimes she must have become irritable at the horse and seeing other riders flying by, probably wished that she too could go like the wind. But she had not been sad, she had not had to bewail her fate. She was like a cow fastened by a thin tether, absorbed with the bran and oilcake in her trough. Before her are the greenest of meadows in which fragrant grasses are rippling in the wind, but she never breaks the tether to go over there. For her there's no difference between her tether and a chain of iron. Youth has less desire for love than it does for self-display. The desire for love comes later. Ratan had received all the means for self-display. Her young woman's soul had been possessed by her own adornment and display. Her life had consisted of laughter and pleasure, trips and outings, and eating and drinking, as it does for almost all of humankind. She never wished or needed to venture into deeper waters. Affluence soothes away mental sufferings to quite an extent. She had had such a variety of ways to make her forget her sorrows – there was the cinema, the theatre, long excursions, cards, pet animals and music. However, humankind has no means to forget poverty except to weep, to curse fate, or to become alienated from the world and commit suicide. Ratan's fate had been turned upside down. Her happy dream had been shattered and now the skeleton of poverty was standing and glaring at her.

And it had all been of her own doing. Vakil Sahab had been one of those creatures who never worry about death. Somehow, he had acquired the false notion that if a man of weak health lives with moderation and watchfulness, he can have a long life. He never had strayed outside the limits of that moderation and watchfulness. So what enmity did death have towards him, that it pursued him so tenaciously without rhyme or reason? The idea of writing his will had occurred to him when he was near death, but Ratan had become so grief-stricken, so fearful on hearing even the mention of a will, that Vakil Sahab had thought it proper to put it off at the time. And from then on he had never regained enough consciousness to have it written.

After his death, Ratan had become so alienated that she had lost all good sense. This was the very occasion when she should have been especially watchful. She should have remained as alert as if she had been surrounded by enemies, but she had left everything to Manibhushan. This very same Manibhushan had gradually plundered her of all her possessions. He devised such schemes and plots that the ingenuous Ratan had not even an inkling of his treacherous behaviour. When the noose had been drawn quite tight, he came to her one day and said, "The bungalow has to be emptied today. I've sold it."

"I told you that I wouldn't sell the bungalow right now," said Ratan, a little angrily.

Manibhushan threw off the veil of politeness and said, scowling at her, "You have a habit of forgetting things. I mentioned it to you in this very room, and you gave your assent. Now that I've sold it, you've begun this song and dance. The bungalow has to be emptied today and you'll have to come along with me."

Ratan said, "I still want to live right here."

Manibhushan said, "I won't let you live here."

Ratan retorted, "I'm not your servant girl."

Manibhushan said, "The burden of your care has fallen on me. I'm taking you with me to protect our family honour."

Biting her lip, Ratan said, "I can protect my own honour by myself. I don't need your help. Without my wishing it, you can't sell a single thing here."

Manibhushan threw a thunderbolt at her. "You have no rights whatsoever to either this house or to uncle's possessions. They are my possessions. You can only ask me questions about your subsistence."

Astonished, Ratan said, "You haven't eaten some *bhang*, have you?"

"I don't eat so much *bhang* that I start saying absurd things," said Manibhushan, in a harsh voice. "You're educated; you were the wife of an important lawyer. You probably know a lot about the law. In joint families a widow has no rights to the possessions of her husband. There was never any family break-up between uncle and my father. Uncle was here and we were in Indore, but that doesn't prove that we had a family split. If uncle had wanted to give his possessions to you, he would certainly have written some will, and even if something in the will had not been according to the law, we would still have honoured it. The fact that he wrote no will establishes the fact that he didn't want to place any obstacle in the way of the ordinary operation of the law. You'll have to empty the bungalow today. The motorcar and the other things will be auctioned off, too. You can come with me or stay here as you wish. A house for a rent at nine or ten rupees a month will be sufficient for you here. I've arranged for fifty rupees a month for your subsistence. After completing all the financial transactions, there's no more than this to be had."

Ratan did not answer. For a little while she sat as if she had lost her wits. Then she sent for the motorcar and spent the whole day running from one lawyer to another. Vakil Sahab had had a great many friends among lawyers. All of them expressed regret on hearing of his decease and all were amazed by his not having written a will. There was only one remedy now. That was to try to establish that there had been a split between Vakil Sahab and his brother. If this could be established, and to do so was very easy, then Ratan would be the mistress of her belongings. If she could not establish this, then she had no other recourse.

The unfortunate Ratan returned to the bungalow. She decided that she would not use any false means to gain whatever did not belong to her. Not in any way. But who had made such a law? Were women so contemptible, so worthless, so insignificant? Why?

Ratan spent the rest of the day sitting silently, plunged in worry. She had thought for so long that she was mistress of this house. What a big mistake it had been. Those who used to gaze at her husband in expectation during his life, had now become the arbiters of her fate! This frightful insult was unbearable to a self-respecting woman like Ratan. She agreed that the earnings had been Vakil Sahab's, but it was she who had bought that village, and several of the houses in it had been built right in front of her. She had never thought for even a moment that one day this property would be the basis of her subsistence – she simply had not been concerned about the future this much. She had experienced the same pleasure in purchasing, improving, and decorating this property that a mother receives in watching her offspring flourish. There was no selfishness in this, just the pride of something that was her own, the same proprietary tenderness as a mother. These children that she had taken care of, that she had embraced and sported with, had been snatched from her as soon as her husband's eyes had closed, and now she had no right whatsoever to them. Had she known that this difficult problem would confront her one day, whether she had squandered the money or whether she had given it away, this pain of lost possessions would not have pierced her breast like a spike. Had Vakil Sahab's income been so very big, after all? Could she not have gone to Simla during the hot season if she had wanted to? Could she not have kept three or four servants if she had wanted to? If she had wanted nothing but jewels, she could have made each ornament equivalent in value to each house. She had never let these things go beyond a point; and now she was left just with this dream. This dream? What else was it? Now she could not even raise her eyes to look at what had been hers only yesterday! How very costly this dream was! Yes, now she was a wretched widow. Until yesterday, she had given alms to others, but today she would have to beg for them herself. She had no other means of support. She had been a widow earlier too; she had understood herself to be mistress of the house only in error. Now she did not have the support of even that illusion.

Suddenly her thoughts took a turn in the opposite direction. Why was she thinking of herself as a helpless widow? Was she about to beg at others' doors? Hundreds of thousands of women in this world supported themselves by their own industry and labour. Was she unable to work? Could she not sew clothes? Could she not open a little shop of some kind? She could teach young boys, too. People would laugh to be sure, but why should she care about their laughter? They would not be laughing at her, but at their own society.

When evening came, several people came with their push-carts at the door. Manibhushan arrived and said, "Aunt, whatever things you tell me to, I'll have loaded and sent on. I've got a house ready for you."

"I don't need a thing," said Ratan. "And don't you arrange for a house for me. I'm not even going to touch anything I have no rights to. I came here without bringing anything from my home, and I'll go back the same way."

"Everything is yours," said Manibhushan, feeling ashamed. "How can you say you have no rights? Take a look at that house. It rents for fifteen rupees a month. I think you won't have any discomfort there, and I'll have whatever you say sent over."

Giving him a mocking look, Ratan said, "You wasted your time arranging that fifteen-rupee house for me. What will I do with such a big house? A little room you could get for two rupees is enough for me. And there's always the ground to sleep on. The smaller the load of gratitude I have to carry on my head, the better."

"What do you want, after all?" asked Manibhushan, very meekly. "Tell me, then!"

"I don't want anything," said Ratan passionately. "I won't take even a single straw from this house with me. For me, something I have no right to is just like some stranger's thing. I won't become a beggar depending on someone else's mercy. You're the one with the rights to these things; take them. I don't mind at all. Charity can neither be given nor taken forcefully. Thousands of widows in this world are supporting themselves by their own labour. I'm the same. I'll labour like them and if I can't manage it, I'll go drown myself in some ditch. If one can't even take care of one's own stomach, one has no right to keep on living as a burden to others."

Ratan left the house as she said this and went toward the gate. Manibhushan, blocking her way, said, "I won't sell the bungalow, if you don't wish me to."

Ratan looked at him with fiery eyes. Her face was flushed. Checking her rising flood of tears she said, "I told you, I have nothing to do with anything in this house. I was a hired woman. What connection does a hired woman have with this house? Who knows what sinner made this law? If God exists somewhere, and there is justice where he is, then one day I'll stand before him and ask that wretch, 'Weren't there any mothers or sisters in your home? Aren't you ashamed to have dishonoured them?' If my voice had enough power to be heard all over this country, then I'd say to all the women, 'Sisters, don't marry into any joint family, and if you do, don't sleep peacefully until you have split your house off from the rest of the family. Don't think that after your husband's gone they'll protect your honour in his home. If your husband doesn't leave you anything, it's all the same whether you live alone, or with his family! You won't be spared from insults or hard labour. If your husband leaves you something, then you can enjoy it only by living alone; if you live with his family, you'll have to give it up. His family is not a bed of flowers for you, but a bed of thorns. It's not a boat to help you cross the sea of life; it's an animal that gulps you down.'"

Evening had come. The dust-laden winds of March were gusting fine grains into the eyes of passers-by. Ratan was walking down the street managing her shawl. Several women of her acquaintance halted her on the street to question her; several stopped their cars and told her to get in. Their kindness pierced her like an arrow. She hastened to Jalpa's house; today her real life had begun.

42

Jalpa and Devidin arrived at the courthouse at ten o'clock sharp. There was a large crowd of spectators. The upper gallery was filled with them, and a great many people were standing on the veranda and in the open ground at the front. Jalpa sat in the upper gallery, while Devidin stood on the veranda.

In the courtroom, on one side of the judge, stood several police employees, on the other, the record-keeper. Outside the witness-box, in front of the judge stood the lawyers for both sides, waiting to present the case. The number of the accused was not less than fifteen. All of them were occupying the floor next to the witness box, manacled and fettered. Some were lying down, some were sitting, and some were talking among themselves. Two were arm-wrestling, while two others were arguing. All of them looked pleased. There was no sign of panic, hopelessness or grief on any face.

Just as eleven was striking, the accusation was presented. First some procedures were discussed, then a couple of police officers gave evidence. At last Rama was brought to the witness box at about three o'clock. A thrill spread through the onlookers. Some came running from the tobacco shop chewing *paan* as they came, others folded up their newspapers and thrust them into their pockets, and everyone pressed forward to fill the courtroom. Jalpa, too, stood up carefully against the balcony. She wanted Rama to raise his eyes and look at her once, but he was standing with bowed head as if he were afraid to look around. The colour had gone out of his face. He stood, half-frightened, half-confused, as if someone had fastened him there and he had nowhere to escape. Jalpa's heart was thudding as if her fate was being decided.

Rama's deposition began. When she heard the first sentence Jalpa shuddered, the second made her scowl, the third made her face grow pale, and as soon as she heard the fourth she heaved a sigh and sank into the chair behind her. Her heart was not satisfied, and leaning on the railing she began to give ear to what he was saying again. It was the same police-taught evidence whose gist she had heard from Devidin. There was dead silence in the courtroom. Jalpa coughed several times in the hope that even now Rama might lift his eyes, but his head bowed even more deeply. Who could tell whether he recognised the sound of Jalpa's coughing, or whether his self-disgust had increased. His voice had grown fainter, too.

A woman sitting next to Jalpa turned up her nose in contempt. "I'd like to shoot this rogue. To think that even in this wretched country there are such selfish people, who don't hesitate to cut the throats of innocent people out of greed for a little money or a job!"

Jalpa did not reply.

A bespectacled woman said despairingly, "God is the master of this wretched country! Lalas like this one will never become a Governor. At most, he will become a clerk somewhere. And for that he is killing his soul. This fellow seems to be some down-and-out no-good person, of low status and worthless from head to foot!"

A third woman, smiling at her, said, "He's a fashionable man and looks educated, too. Well, what would you do with him if you got him?"

"I'd cut off his nose!" said the bespectacled goddess arrogantly. "That's it. I'd make him noseless and leave him!"

"And do you know what I'd do?" asked the third lady.

"No. Maybe you'd shoot him?" replied the second lady.

"No! I wouldn't shoot him. I'd stand him up in public and have him given five hundred whacks with a shoe! May he be beaten so hard there won't be a hair left on his head!"

Another lady said, "Don't you feel even a little sorry for him?"

"Am I showing him less pity? Full punishment for him would be to push him off the top of some high mountain. If this gentleman were in America, he'd be burned alive."

"Why are you wasting your time saying these nasty things?" said an old woman scolding these young girls. "He's not worthy of hate, he's worthy of pity. Don't you see how pale his face has become, as if someone were choking him? If he saw his mother or sister, he would surely burst into tears. This man is not bad at heart. The police have threatened and abused him. It seems as if every word he says is tearing his heart."

"When a thorn is sticking in your foot, you cry out," said the bespectacled woman, sarcastically.

Jalpa could stay there no longer. Every remark, like a burning spark, raised a blister on her heart. She felt like standing up on the spot and saying, 'This gentleman is speaking total lies, lies from beginning to end, and I can prove it right now.' She suppressed this wild urge with all her might. Her own mind was cursing her for her cowardice. Could she not tell them the whole story right now? If that made the police her enemy, let it be so. At least something would come to the attention of the court. Who knows, the lives of those wretched fellows might be saved, and the public would know that this testimony was false. As she was about to speak, her voice died in her throat. Fear of the consequences seized her tongue.

Finally she thought it best to get up and leave.

Seeing her coming down the stairs, Devidin came on to the veranda and in a compassionate voice asked, "Are you going home, Bahuji?"

Stopping her flow of tears, Jalpa said, "Yes, I can't stand it here now."

Coming out of the compound, Devidin said, intending to console her, "Once the police have intoxicated someone with their promises, he can't be influenced by anything else."

"That's all for cowards," said Jalpa, with scorn.

They continued to walk in silence for some distance. Suddenly Jalpa said, "Tell me, Dada, can't there be another appeal? Will the judgement on the prisoners be made here and now?"

Devidin understood the intention behind this question. "No," he said. "An appeal is possible in the High Court."

They walked in silence again for a while. Jalpa stopped under the shade of a tree and said, "Dada, I want to meet the Judge Sahab today and tell him everything from the beginning. If I give proof, will he believe what I say?"

Staring at her, Devidin said, "The Judge Sahab!"

Meeting his eyes, Jalpa said, "Yes!"

"I can't say anything about this, Bahuji," he said doubtfully. "That's a matter for the authorities. There's no telling if it will make an impression or fall flat."

"Can't he say to the police that your evidence is manufactured, false?" said Jalpa.

Devidin said, "He can say it."

"So shall I meet him today? Does he meet people?" asked Jalpa.

"Come on, let's go find out, but it's a dangerous affair," said Devidin.

"How is it dangerous, tell me?" asked Jalpa.

"Suppose that a case is brought against Brother for giving false testimony and he receives some punishment?"

Jalpa said, "That is nothing. You reap what you sow."

Surprised at the harshness of Jalpa's words, Devidin said, "There's another thing to worry about. It's what is to be feared most."

"What's that?" said Jalpa haughtily.

"The police are great cowards," said Devidin. "Their idea of a joke is to insult someone. The Judge Sahab would certainly summon the Police Commissioner to tell him all this. The commissioner would think that this woman is ruining the whole show. Let's arrest her! If the judge were an Englishman he'd fearlessly give the police a reprimand. Our Indian brothers are afraid to make a cheep in such cases lest a charge of rebellion be brought against them. That's the thing. The Judge Sahab will certainly give the Police Commissioner an account of all this. What will happen next is not that the case will be dismissed, but rather that the truth will not be allowed to come out. Who knows, but they might arrest you? Sometimes when the witness begins to change, or when he's ready to let the cat out of the bag, the police intimidate his family members. Their powers of deception are unlimited."

Jalpa began to feel afraid. She had no fear of her own arrest, but rather of the police committing some outrage on Rama. This fear made her timid.

She felt as tired now as if she had come from a journey of hundreds of miles. Her courageous resolution melted away like snow.

After going on a little further, she asked Devidin, "Would it be possible to meet with him now?"

"Who, Brother?" asked Devidin.

"Yes," she replied.

Devidin said, "Not at all. The guard will be made even stricter. They might even leave that bungalow. And even if you could meet him now, what would be the use? There's no way he can change his deposition now. He'd be implicated in perjury."

After going a little further Jalpa said, "I think I'll go back to Allahabad. What can I do if I stay here?"

"No, Bahu," said Devidin looking at her compassionately. "I won't let you go just now. We wouldn't feel like being at home a moment without you. The old woman would weep her life away. Stay here now and see what the court decision is. I don't think Brother is such a faint-hearted man. Everyone in your caste is devoted to government service, but even if someone gave me a salary of a hundred rupees a month, I wouldn't take a government position. It's different when you earn your own living; a man never gets tired doing this. But after five or six hours in the office, your body starts getting weak, and you start yawning."

There was no more conversation along the way. Jalpa's heart was not at all willing to accept her defeat. Even though she had lost, she still could not be satisfied to watch this drama like a spectator. She was restless to be included in the drama, and to play her own part. Would there not be another meeting with Rama? There was an ocean of fiery words welling up in her heart, which she wanted to say to him. She had not the slightest compassion for Rama, not a shred of sympathy. 'Congratulations on your wealth and power,' she wanted to say to him. 'Jalpa spurns them, kicks them away. The touch of your bloody hands will bring blisters on my body. I don't consider anyone who sells his soul for money and position to be a man. You are not a man, you are not even an animal, you are a coward! A coward!'

Her lovely face became flushed. Her neck became stiff with pride. He probably thought that when she saw him wearing a tasseled turban riding on a horse, she would not be able to contain herself with joy. However, she was not that low. Forget the horse, even if he flew on the wind, he was still a murderer in her eyes, nothing but a murderer, who had cut the throats of so many men to save his own life! Had she not explained it to him along the way? Had it made no impression on him? Oh! So eager for money, so greedy! It did not matter; she was not a beggar in need of his care and protection. Deep in these heated feelings, Jalpa reached home.

43

A month passed. Jalpa had been upset for several days. Several times near-frenzies came upon her to get the whole story published in some newspaper, to expose the whole sham, to knock down all the castles in the air. All these excesses of emotion subsided. Some strength hidden in the depths of her soul kept her tongue silent. She had ejected Rama from her heart. She felt no anger toward him now, no hatred, not even pity, but only sadness. She might not have even wept if she had received news of his death. Yes, she would have been sad for a little while, considering it to be a divinely ordained drama, a heartless comedy of the illusory world, a cruel game. That bond of affectionate trust which had been placed on her for two or two-and-a-half years had broken, but its mark was still there. During this time she had seen Rama on several occasions passing by her house in a motorcar. His eyes seemed to be searching for someone. There was some shame in those eyes, and an entreaty for forgiveness, but Jalpa never even once raised her eyes towards him. Perhaps if he had come and fallen at her feet, she still would not have looked in his direction. It was as if his hateful cowardice and great selfishness had torn up her heart. Even so, the mark of that bond of affection still remained. Now and then that passionately-loved form of Rama's, the sight of which had once made her ecstatic, entered the darkness of her heart like joyless, dull, faint moon-light, and for a moment her memories wept. And then the curtain of that darkness and silence would fall again. There were no tender thoughts for her future; only the harsh, arid present, dreadful in form, stood staring at her.

That same Jalpa who had at home given herself airs at every turn, was now the very picture of service, sacrifice, and forbearance. Although Jaggo kept on forbidding it, early every morning she would sweep the whole house, clean the cooking utensils and the kitchen, knead the flour, and light the oven. All that the old woman would have to do, was to bake the *rotis*. She put all considerations of impurity or untouchability on the shelf. The old woman would keep pushing her into the kitchen and feeding her something or other. A love like that of a mother and daughter grew between them.

The entire proceedings of the case were now over. The arguments of the lawyers for both sides had been heard. All that was left was to deliver the decision, and today was the appointed date. Finishing her household chores very early on this morning, Jalpa was sitting listening intently for the cries of the vendors of the daily papers, as if today her future was to be decided. Just then Devidin brought a paper and placed it before her; she immediately began to read about the decision. And what was the decision but an imaginary story whose chief actor was Rama. The judge praised him again and again. The whole case had rested on his deposition.

"Has the decision been published?" asked Devidin.

"Yes, it has been," said Jalpa as she read.

"Who received punishment?" he asked.

"No one got off. One is to be hanged. Five have received ten years each, and eight got five years each. That same Dinesh is to be hanged."

She put the newspaper down, heaved a long sigh, and said, "Who knows what will happen to the children and families of these poor fellows!"

Ready for her question, Devidin said, "I've been finding out about all of them from the very day you told me to. Eight of them have not married yet, and their families are well off; they won't have any difficulties at all. Five of them have married, but their families are well off, too. Some of them are tradesmen, some are landowners, and some have fathers and uncles in service. I've asked several people about them. A subscription has been raised for them here too, and if their families require it, it will be given to them. Only Dinesh's family is ruined. There are two small children, his elderly mother, and his wife. He was a teacher in some school here, and lived in a rented home. He's the one who's been destroyed."

"Were you able to find out anything about his home?" asked Jalpa.

Devidin replied, "Yes, it wasn't hard to find out."

"So when will we go?" asked Jalpa entreatingly. "I'll go along with you. There's time now. Come on, let's have a look."

"Let me go take a look first," objected Devidin. "Just where are you going to go running around with me so thoughtlessly like this?"

Having no alternative, Jalpa restrained herself and said nothing. Devidin left, and Jalpa began to read the newspaper again, but her attention was fixed on Dinesh. The poor fellow would be hanged. What must have been his state when he heard the order for his hanging? His old mother and wife must have beaten their breasts when they heard this news. The poor fellow was only a schoolmaster after all, and it must have been hard enough to make a living. What other support would there be? Imagining the family's distress, she felt such a burning scorn for Rama that she could no longer continue feeling sad. She flew into such a passion that if he had come before her, she would have cursed him in a way that even he would remember. "Are you a man? Never. You're an evil demon in human form, an evil demon! You are so beneath contempt that there's no word to express it. You are so base that the lowest of the low, spits on you today. Why hasn't someone killed you already? These men's lives would have gone, but at least your name would not have been so blackened. How did you fall so low? How can someone whose father is so truthful and so honourable, be so greedy and so cowardly?'

Evening came, but Devidin had not returned. Jalpa went and stood at the window again and again, looking here and there, but he was nowhere to be seen. The time dragged on till eight o'clock struck, but he had still not returned. Suddenly a motorcar came and stopped at the door. Rama got out and hailed Jaggo. "Everything's going well, isn't it Dadi? Where has Dada gone?"

Jaggo looked at him once and then turned away her face. She said only, "He must have gone somewhere. I don't know."

Rama took out four gold bracelets from his pocket, placed them at Jaggo's feet, and said, "I brought these for you, Dadi. Put them on, they're not too loose, are they?"

Jaggo picked up the bracelets and hurled them to the ground; and glaring at him, said, "There's room for four bracelets where there is so much wickedness! By God's grace, I have worn many bracelets and I still have three or four pounds of gold around. But whatever I've eaten, or worn, has been earned through my own efforts, not through doing wrong to someone else, not through heaping up sins on my head, not through depraving my will. May the womb that gave birth to a bad son like you be burned up. You must have come to give your sinful earnings to your wife. You must have thought that she'd go wild seeing your platterful of money. You've lived so long with her and yet your greedy eyes still can't understand her. A wicked demon like you isn't worthy of a goddess like her. If you know what is good for you, go right back where you came from; why do you want to shame yourself by appearing before her? If you had come here today wounded or beaten by the police, or if you had received a sentence or been thrown in jail, then she would have worshipped you, washed your feet, and drunk the water. She's one of those women who cannot see evil done to others even if she has to perform physical labour, go hungry, or wear rags. If you were my son, I'd give you poison. Why are you standing here making me angry? Why don't you leave? I haven't taken something from you, have I?"

Rama stood silently listening with bowed head. Then in a wounded tone, he said, "Dadi, I've done something bad and I'll be ashamed of it until my dying breath. But I'm not as low as you think I am. If you knew how harshly the police treated me, how they threatened me, you wouldn't call me an evil demon."

The sounds of their conversation reached Jalpa's ears. She peered down the stairs. Ramanath was standing there with a Banarasi silk turban on his head, a nice silk coat, and gold spectacles on his eyes. In this past month his body had blossomed out, and his complexion had become even fairer. His face had never showed so much lustre before. His last words fell on Jalpa's ears. She swooped forward like a hawk, thundered down the stairs, and launching an attack on him with eyes as piercing as arrows dipped in poison, said, "If you are so intimidated by harsh treatment and threats, then you are a coward. You have no right to call yourself a man. What was the harsh treatment? May I hear? People have gone laughing to have their heads cut off, have watched their sons dying, have agreed to be crushed in a vice, but never budged an inch from truth. You're a man, too, why did you yield to a threat? Why didn't you stand up, bare your chest, tell them to take aim, but you'd never say what was untrue? Why didn't you bow your head? The soul was put inside the body for the body to protect it, not for the body to destroy it. What reward have you received for your wickedness? Let us know!"

"Nothing yet," said Rama, in a subdued voice.

"I'm very happy to hear it!" said Jalpa, hissing like a snake. "May God ensure that you get nothing, however much you disgrace yourself! This is my prayer from the bottom of my heart. But no, the police will never wish to make a wax doll like you angry. You'll get a position and perhaps a good one, but you'll never be able to escape from the net you're caught in. Giving false testimony, making a false case, and dealing in evil, these were written in your fate. Go, enjoy your life according to your wish. I told you before and today I'm telling you again, that I have no connection with you. I consider you dead. You should also consider me to be dead. That's enough, go. I'm a woman, but if someone wanted to get me to do something wicked by threatening me, if I couldn't kill him, then I'd cut my own throat. Don't you even have as much courage as a woman?"

Whining as abjectly as a beggar, Rama said, "Won't you listen to any of my explanations?"

"No!" said Jalpa, proudly.

Rama said, "So shall I leave in disgrace?"

Jalpa said, "As you wish."

Rama said, "Won't you forgive me?"

Jalpa replied, "Never! Not in any way!"

Rama stood for a moment with bowed head, then slowly coming down from the veranda, said to Jaggo, "Dadi, when Dada comes, tell him to meet me for a little while. I'll come wherever he says."

Jaggo softening a little, said, "Come here tomorrow."

Getting into the car, Rama said, "I won't come here any more, Dadi!"

When the car had gone, Jalpa in a censorious mood, said, "He came to show off the car, as if he had bought it!"

Jaggo scolded her, saying "You shouldn't have been so unrestrained, Bahu! A man can't think of anything to say when his heart is wounded."

"He's not one to feel shame, Dadi!" said Jalpa harshly. "He's sold his soul for this comfort. Why should he ever give it up? You didn't ask him what he wanted to meet Dada for. If he'd been here he would have given him such a tongue-lashing that he'd have remembered it!"

"If I'd been in your place, Bahu, I wouldn't have said such things," said Jaggo reproachfully. "You have a very hard heart. If it had been another man would he have listened so silently? I was trembling all over for fear that he would strike you a blow. But he is a very meek fellow!"

"They don't call that meekness, Dadi," said Jalpa, with the same harshness. "It's shamelessness."

"Did Brother come here?" asked Devidin, when he returned. "I saw him in the motorcar along the way."

"Yes, he did come," said Jaggo. "He said he wanted to meet you."

"I'll meet him," said Devidin sadly. "Did you talk with him at all?"

"What talk?" said Jaggo, regretfully. "First I worshipped him, and then when I shut up, Bahu did a good job of garlanding him."

Jalpa lowered her head and said, "A man must endure the results of what he does."

"He came to meet us expecting us to receive him as our own," said Jaggo.

"No one went to invite him," said Jalpa. "Did you find out anything about Dinesh, Dada?"

"Yes, everything," said Devidin. "His home is in Howrah. I know the address and everything."

"Shall we go now or some time tomorrow?" asked Jalpa, feeling some misgivings.

Devidin said, "Whatever you wish. If you like we can go right now; I'm ready."

"You must be tired," said Jalpa.

Devidin said, "I don't get tired doing things like this, Daughter."

It was eight o'clock, and there was a continuous rush of motor vehicles on the street. The footpaths on both sides of the street were full of women and men walking along all dressed up, laughing and talking. How engrossed in enjoyment the world is, thought Jalpa to herself. Whoever has to die for it, let him die, but the world will stubbornly persist in its ways. Everyone sits in his own little house of earth; if the whole country is washed away, no matter, as long as his house is saved, and there is no obstacle to his own welfare. Jalpa's innocent heart would have rejoiced to see the marketplace closed. She would have been glad to see everyone with bowed heads, scowling, frenzied, and with faces red with inner anger. She did not know that the fall of such small fry as Dinesh did not make even a ripple in this sea of people, let alone a noise.

44

When Rama left in the motorcar, he could not think of a thing. He had no idea of where he was going. Familiar routes had become unfamiliar to him. He was not angry at Jalpa, not in the least, nor was he angry at Jaggo. He was angry with his own weakness, his own greed, and his own cowardice. Surrounded by the influence of the police, his sense of moral propriety had been corrupted. The enormity of the injustice he was perpetrating had only occurred to him once, on the day when Jalpa first admonished him. Subsequently no doubts had arisen in his mind, for the police officers had diverted his thoughts by building up high hopes for him. They would tell him, "Sir, don't worry about your wife at all. When you go to meet her with an inlaid necklace, and show her a plateful of money, all of your wife's anger will vanish. You'll reach some nice place in your province and spend your life in ease. How is she going to be angry?" They gave him numerous examples of this that they had seen with their own eyes. Rama became confused. Then he had not had a chance to meet Jalpa again. The police made a deep impression on him. Today he had gone to give Jalpa the good news of his victory with an inlaid necklace in his pocket. He knew she would first turn up her nose and frown a bit, but when she saw the necklace, he was sure she would be pleased. Then, tomorrow he would be receiving a letter of appointment from the Police Commissioner under the signature of the Home Secretary of the United Provinces. After spending a few days roaming around here, he would set out for home. He wanted to take Devidin and Jaggo along with him too, how could he forget their beneficence? He had gone to Jalpa with these resolves in mind, much as some devotee might go with offerings of flowers and food to attend on a deity. The deity, rather than granting a boon, had spurned his tray of flowers, and trampled on his food offerings. He had no chance to say anything. Coming out from the poisonous atmosphere around the police today, he was able to breathe pure air, and his good sense awakened. Now that he could see his baseness in its true form — how hideous, how fiendish an image it was. He did not have the courage to gaze at himself. He thought to himself that he would go to the judge right away and tell him the whole story. He did not care if the police became his enemy, or if he was thrown in jail to rot. He would reveal the whole deception. Could the judge not change his decision? The accused were still in custody. The police would grind their teeth, and make a great fuss; maybe they would even eat him alive. Let them eat him! It was this very weakness which had blackened his name.

Jalpa's furious image came before his eyes again. Oh, how enraged she had been! If he had known how angry she would be, he would have changed his deposition even if the world had turned topsy-turvy. They'd really tricked him, those policemen. If the judge didn't listen to anything and did not acquit the accused, then Jalpa would never look at him again. How could he face her? Then, of what use was his life? For whom would he live?

He stopped the car and looked around. He had no inkling of where he was. All at once he saw a watchman, and asked for the address of the judge's house. The watchman laughed and said. "Your honour has come very far out of the way. It's at least six or seven miles from here; he lives over by Chowringhee."

Rama asked the way to Chowringhee and set off again. It was nine o'clock. He thought to himself that if he did not meet the judge, everything would be ruined. He would not go away until he met him. If he listened, everything would be fine; if not, he would speak with the High Court judges tomorrow. Surely someone would listen. If not, he would get the whole affair published in the newspapers, and then everyone's eyes would be opened.

The motorcar was going at thirty miles an hour; he reached Chowringhee in ten minutes. There was still the same hustle and bustle here, but Rama kept driving through all the uproar. Suddenly a policeman flashed a red light at him. He stopped, stuck out his head, and saw that it was that same Daroga!

"Haven't you gone to the bungalow yet?" asked the Daroga. "Don't drive so fast; you'll have an accident. Tell me, did you meet your wife? I thought she'd be with you. She must have been really happy."

Rama felt such rage that he wanted to tear out the other's moustache by its roots, but quickly inventing a story, he said, "Yes sir, she was very happy! Extremely happy!"

The Daroga said, "I told you so, didn't I? That's just the medicine for a woman's anger. You were trembling when you left."

Rama replied, "That was my stupidity."

The Daroga said, "Let's go, I'll come with you too. We'll play a game of cards and get a little drunk. The Deputy Sahab and the Inspector Sahab will come too, and we'll send for Zohra. We'll have a good time for a while. Why don't you have Mrs. Ramanath come stay at the bungalow now? She's still staying at that Khatik's house.'

Rama said, "There's something important for which I have to go the other way just now. You take the car. I'll come on foot."

The Daroga got into the car and said, "No, Sahab. I'm not in a hurry. Go wherever you like. I won't interfere in the least."

"But I'm not going to the bungalow now," said Rama getting a little irritated.

"I'm getting the picture," said the Daroga smiling, "but I won't interfere in the least. That Begum Sahab of yours..."

"No, Sir," said Rama interrupting. "That's not where I have to go."

The Daroga said, "So is there some other target? Even at the bungalow there won't be any lack of enjoyment today. Everything you need to amuse yourself will be there."

Suddenly glaring at the other furiously, Rama said, "Do you think I am that corrupt? I'm not as low as that."

"All right, Sahab," said the Daroga, a little shamefaced. "My offence, pardon me. I won't ever be so rude again. But don't think you're out of danger yet. I'm not going to let you go anywhere that I don't feel completely confident about. You don't know how many enemies you have. I'm saying this for your own good."

Biting his lips in vexation, Rama said, "It would be better if you didn't concern yourself with what's good for me. You people have destroyed me and you still won't leave me alone. Let me die in my own way. I'm fed up with this bondage. I don't want to become a little child following its mother around. You want your car; take it gladly. I've had to sacrifice fifteen men to ride in a motorcar and live in a bungalow. To get an office, I'd probably have to sacrifice fifteen hundred people, and my heart isn't that strong. Take the car please."

He got out of the car as he said this and walked quickly ahead. The Daroga called out to him several times, "Please listen, listen to what I have to say." He did not even turn around to look. Walking a little further ahead, he took a turn; it was the very street where the judge's bungalow was. He did not meet anyone on the street. Rama walked first on the footpath on this side of the street, then on the other side, reading the numbers as he went. He stopped abruptly on seeing one number. He stood for a moment, looking to see if anyone would come out so he could ask if the Sahab was there or not. He did not have the courage to go in. It occurred to him that if the judge should ask him why he had given false testimony, he would not know what answer to give. To say that the police had forced him to give testimony, that they had tempted him, and had threatened to beat him, was a shameful thing to say. What answer did he have if the judge asked where his common sense had gone when he had brought so much disgrace on his head and stooped so low as to take the lives of so many men just to save himself from a two- or three-year sentence? He would be forced to feel ashamed, and he would look like a fool. He turned back; he did not have the capacity to face such shame. Shame has always defeated heroes. Those who do not even fear death, do not not have the courage to bear shame. To jump into a fire, or to stand in front of a sword is much easier in comparison. To avoid shame and preserve honour, great kingdoms have been destroyed, rivers of blood have flowed, and lives have been utterly consumed. This same shame drove Rama's feet to turn back today; probably even a jail sentence would not have frightened him as much.

45

Rama went to sleep at midnight, so he did not wake up until nine o'clock the next morning. He was dreaming – Dinesh was going to the gallows. All at once a woman with a sword ran to the gallows and cut the rope. A commotion broke out all around. The woman was Jalpa. People wanted to surround and catch her, but she could not be caught. No one could dare to go before her. Then she leaped forward and struck Rama. He sat up in a panic and saw that the Daroga and the Inspector were standing in his room, while the Deputy was lying back in the easy-chair, smoking a cigar.

"You slept a lot today, Sahab!" said the Daroga. "When did you get back yesterday?"

Rama sat down in a chair and said, "I got back after a little while. This case will be appealed to the High Court, won't it?"

"What appeal?" said the Inspector. "It'll just be the observance of a formality. You've made the case so strong that no one can shake it even if he tries. On my honour, you've worked a miracle. You need not worry about that now. True, until the decision is made it's appropriate to look after your safety, and this is why arrangements have been made for guarding you again. As soon as the High Court makes its decision, you'll have your position."

Puffing out a cloud of smoke from his cigar, the Deputy said, "The Commissioner Sahab has given you this Departmental Order, so that you have no doubts about it. Look, here's the name of the Home Secretary of the United Provinces. As soon as you show this D.O. there, it'll get you a very good post."

"The Commissioner Sahab is very pleased with you, on my honour," said the Inspector.

"Very pleased," agreed the Deputy. "He'll also write a separate letter directly to the United Provinces. Your fortune is made." As he said this, he handed the D.O. to Rama. Rama opened the envelope, took a look, and without any warning tore it into bits. The three men stared at him in astonishment.

"Did you have a lot to drink last night?" said the Daroga. "This won't be to your advantage."

"On my honour," said the Inspector, "if the Commissioner Sahab finds out, he'll be extremely displeased."

"I don't understand this at all," said the Deputy. "What do you mean by this?"

"It means that I don't need this D.O., nor do I want a position. I'm leaving here today," said Rama.

"You can't go anywhere until the High Court gives its decision," said the Deputy.

Rama asked, "Why?"

"It's the Commissioner Sahab's order," said the Deputy.

Rama said, "I'm not anyone's slave."

"Babu Ramanath," said the Inspector, "why are you ruining a perfectly good situation? Whatever had to happen, has happened. In five or ten days the High Court's decision will be confirmed. What's best for you is to happily accept the reward you're getting and spend your life in comfort. If God wishes, some day you too will reach some high office. What advantage is there to you in making police officers angry and enduring the miseries of jail? On my honour, if these officers withdraw their favour even a little, your existence will be in question. On my honour, just one hint would bring you a ten-year sentence. What can you be thinking of? We don't want to play those nasty tricks on you, but yes, if you force us to be harsh with you, then we'll have to be harsh. Don't think being in jail is easy. May God take you to hell rather than send you to jail. Violence and abuse are ordinary punishments there. If you're forced into solitary confinement, then death has come for you. On my honour, jail is worse than hell."

"This poor fellow is helpless against his Begum Sahab," said the Daroga. "Maybe she's plotting against his life. He's cowed by her ill-will."

"What happened?" asked the Inspector. "You gave her that necklace yesterday, didn't you? Did she still not agree?"

Rama took the necklace out of his coat pocket and put it on the table. "That necklace is kept here," he said.

"Oh, so she didn't accept it," said the Inspector.

"She's some proud lady," said the Deputy.

"We probably need to give her a little dose for behaviour modification as well," said the Inspector.

"That will depend on the Babu Sahab's manners and courtesy," said the Daroga. "If you don't force our hand without rhyme or reason, we won't go after you."

"We ought to take a recognisance from that Khatik too," said the Deputy.

A new problem confronted Ramanath now, far more complicated and far more terrible than before. It was possible that he would have sacrificed himself on the altar of duty and readied himself for a three- or four-year jail sentence. Perhaps he might even have decided to surrender himself, but there was no way he could find the courage to thrust Jalpa into danger along with himself. He was caught in the clutches of the police in such a way that now he could not see any way of extracting himself honourably. He saw that he could not overcome his opponents in this struggle. The police was all-powerful, and could defeat him any which way. All the fire went out of him. Feeling powerless, he said, "What is it you people want from me?"

The Inspector looked at the Daroga and winked as if to say, "We've got him!" He said, "Nothing more than this, that you continue to be our guest, and that you leave here after the High Court settles the case. After that, we'll no longer be responsible for your protection. If you want to get some certificate, you'll get it; but the choice of taking it or not is entirely yours. If you're smart you'll take it and profit from it; if not, you'll be knocked around here and there – the proverb that sin brings no pleasure will come true for you. We don't want any more than this from you. On my honour, everything you might want will be made available to you here; but until the case is over, you can't be free."

"Will I be able to go on trips?" asked Rama, dejectedly, "or not even that?"

"No sir!" said the Inspector, as if giving an aphorism.

"You were given that freedom," said the Daroga, giving a commentary on the aphorism, "but you used it wrongly. Until it's certain whether or not you can use it appropriately, you'll be deprived of this privilege."

The Daroga looked towards the Inspector as if seeking praise for this commentary, which he was delighted to receive.

The three officers took their leave and Rama, lighting a cigar, began to ponder on this difficult situation.

46

Another month went by, and the date for the presentation of the case in the High Court was fixed. The same timidity and sycophancy as before came into Rama's habits and he danced to the officers' tunes. He drank more than before, too; it was as if sensuality had him in its grip. From time to time a prostitute, Zohra, would come to his room, and he would listen to her sing with great pleasure.

One day he said to her longingly, "I'm afraid, I might fall in love with you. What else could the result of that be, but that I'd spend the rest of my life weeping. What hope could there be of your being faithful!"

Zohra, secretly pleased, gazed at him with her big bright eyes and said, "Yes, Sahab, what would I know about being faithful? I'm a prostitute after all. How can an unfaithful prostitute ever be faithful?"

"Can there be any doubt about it?" queried Rama.

Zohra said, "No, not at all. You people bring us hearts brimming with love, but we don't place any value on this. That's the way it is, isn't it?"

Rama said, "Not a doubt."

Zohra said, "Forgive me, but you're taking the men's side. The truth is that you people come to us to divert yourselves, just to console yourselves, just to enjoy yourselves. When you're not looking for faithfulness at all, why would you receive it? But I do know this much, that if the world should learn how many of us were disillusioned by men's faithlessness and lost our peace of mind, its eyes would open wide. It's our mistake if we want faithfulness from promiscuous people; it's like looking for meat in a hawk's nest. But if a thirsty man runs towards a dried-up well, I don't think it's the well's fault."

When Zohra left that night, she gave welcome news to the Daroga. "Today His Excellency enjoyed himself a lot. If God wishes it, in three or four days he won't even mention his wife's name."

Pleased, the Daroga said, "That's just why I sent for you. It would really be a pleasure if his wife left this place. Then we wouldn't have anything to worry about. It seems that people from the independence movement have met with that woman. They're all devils of the same sort."

Zohra's comings and goings increased to the point where Rama fell into his own trap. He had wanted to establish his credibility in the officers' eyes by displaying his love for Zohra. However, just as children get involved and burst into tears even in play, so his pretence of love became a passion of love. Now Zohra appeared to him to be faithful, a veritable goddess of love. True, she wasn't as beautiful as Jalpa, but she was cleverer in conversation, more deft in manners, more cunning in the art of attraction. Completely new plans began to grow in his heart.

One day he said to her, "Zohra, the time of parting is coming. I'll have to leave the place in three or four days. Why will you remember me then?"

"I won't let you go," said Zohra. "Take up a good job here. Then you and I can live in comfort."

"Are you saying that from your heart, Zohra?" asked Rama, enamoured. "See here, swear on my head that you won't deceive me."

Zohra said, "If that's what you're afraid of, then arrange a *nikah* marriage. If that irks you, then marry me by Hindu rites. Call some pundits. What more can I do to prove my love?"

Rama became almost delirious on receiving this proof of sincere love. And the hypnotic effect of these words was all the greater for having come from Zohra's mouth. This lovely woman, to whom many wealthy men were devoted, was ready to make such a big sacrifice for him! Is not the person, who finds lumps of gold in a mine where others have found only sand, extremely fortunate? For several days a struggle had been going on in Rama's mind. How dull, how difficult his life with Jalpa would be. Her righteousness and truthfulness would tug him at every step and his life would become one long penance, a never-ending devotion to duty. A virtuous life had never been his ideal. He too, like ordinary men, wanted to have a life of luxury and enjoyment. His temperament, much attracted to sensual pleasure, was now drawn strongly away from Jalpa towards Zohra. He began to remember examples of devoted prostitutes; along with this came instances of the fickle behaviour of wives. He decided it was all a delusion. People were neither virtuous nor vicious from birth; everything depended on circumstances.

Every day, Zohra came and added yet another knot in their ties of affection. In such a situation, even a disciplined youth would have been shaken, let alone a pleasure-loving one like Rama. The only reason he had not wandered from the straight and narrow before was that he had been netted and caged as soon as his wings had unfurled. Even after being out of this cage for some days, he had not found the courage to fly. Now a new vision was before him. This was not some little cage of clay, but rather a garden of flowers swaying in the wind, where the pleasures of freedom existed even in captivity. Why should he not enjoy the delights of sporting in this garden!

47

The more Rama was caught in Zohra's love-snare, the fewer became the doubts of the group of police officials towards him. His confinement was gradually relaxed to the point where one day the Deputy took Rama with him on an evening trip in the motorcar. When the car passed in front of Devidin's shop, Rama drew his head inside so that no one might see him. He was eager to know if Jalpa was there or if she had left, but he could not bring himself to stick out his head. He still understood in his heart that the path he had chosen was not a very good one, but despite knowing this, he didn't want to leave it. Had he seen Devidin he would have bowed his head in shame; he would have been unable to prove his side of things by any argument. He thought to himself that the best course for him was to stop meeting him altogether. Aside from Devidin, Jaggo and Jalpa, he was not acquainted with anybody in this city whose criticism or scorn he feared.

The car was turning here and there as it went in the direction of the Howrah bridge, when all at once Rama saw a woman coming towards them from the steps down the river, carrying a pitcher of Ganges water on her head. Her clothes were quite dirty and she was so thin that her neck was pressed down by the weight of the pitcher. Her gait seemed rather similar to Jalpa's. 'What would Jalpa be doing here', he thought to himself. But in an instant the car had moved forward and Rama caught sight of the woman's face. His heart nearly stopped. It was Jalpa! Hiding his head to one side of the window he looked intently. There was no doubt that it was Jalpa, but how frail, as if she were an elderly widow. There was no longer that loveliness, that charm, that liveliness, that pride. Rama was not heartless; his eyes filled with tears. Jalpa in this state while he was still alive? Surely Devidin must have turned her out and she'd become a servant to support herself. No, Devidin was not so inhuman. Jalpa herself must have refused to be dependent on him. She was certainly a haughty woman. How could he find out what was going on?

The car had gone far ahead. All of Rama's playfulness, all of his enjoyment had vanished. That ill-clothed, sorrowful image of Jalpa stood before his eyes. Whom should he talk to? What should he say? Who was his own here? If he even mentioned her name to the police, they would all get a nasty shock and would stop his leaving home again. Oh! What a look of deep sorrow had been spread over her face, what hopelessness there had been in her eyes! Ah, how many sorrowful sighs, emerging from a burning heart, seemed to lament in her sunken eyes, as if they had never seen laughter, as if they had withered before their bud had ever blossomed.

After a while Zohra came, coquettish, smiling and swaying, but, today Rama was harsh and cutting even to her.

"Are you missing someone today?" she asked.

She put her round, soft, butter-smooth arms around his neck as she said this, and drew him towards her. Rama, on his part, made not the slightest effort, but kept his head on her heart, as though this was his sanctuary now.

In a voice dripping with tenderness, she asked, "Tell me the truth, why are you so sad today? Are you angry with me for something?"

In a voice shaking with emotion Rama said, "No Zohra. I'll always be obliged to you for the kindness you've shown a poor wretch like me. You took care of me when the shattered boat of my life was sinking. Those were the most fortunate days of my life and I'll always worship their memory in my heart. But difficulty draws unfortunate people towards itself over and over again. Even the ties of love can't prevent them from being pulled in that direction. The circumstances in which I saw Jalpa today are piercing my heart like spears. She was walking today dressed in torn and dirty clothes, carrying a pitcher of Ganges water on her head. My heart was shattered to see her in such a state. I've never felt so much grief in my life. Zohra, I can't say anything about what she has to bear."

"Wasn't she at the home of that wealthy old Khatik?" asked Zohra.

Rama replied, "Yes, she was, but I can't say why she left there. The Deputy was with me. I couldn't ask her a thing in front of him. I know she'd have turned away if she had seen me, and that perhaps she considers me contemptible; but at least I would have known why she's in this plight now. Zohra, whatever you may be thinking about me in your heart, I'm drowned in the thought that you love me. And we expect at least sympathy from those who love us. There's not a single other person to whom I could tell the state of my heart. Even though you were sent to make me stray off the path, you took pity on me. Maybe you thought it wasn't proper to kick a man who was down. If today you and I should quarrel for some reason, and tomorrow you saw me in distress, would you feel no sympathy for me at all? If you saw me starving, would you treat me with less kindness than a man would a dog? I would hope not. Even if sadness or indifference might enter where love has once lived, it's not possible for violent feelings to do so. Won't you show me even a little sympathy, Zohra? If you want to, you can find out everything about Jalpa – where she is, what she's doing, what she thinks of me in her heart, why she doesn't go home, and how long she intends to stay. If you can somehow persuade Jalpa to go to Prayag, Zohra, I'll be your slave for life. I can't bear to see her in this condition. Maybe I'll escape from here this very night. I don't have the slightest fear of what might happen to me. I'm not brave, I'm a very weak man. My spirit is always defeated by danger, but even my shamelessness can't endure this wound."

Zohra was a prostitute and she was well acquainted with all kinds of men, good and bad; she had a sense of discrimination about them. She saw a big difference between this young man from a different province and other individuals! At first she had come here as a slave to money, but after three or four days she found herself attached to Rama. Mature women cannot be indifferent to affection. Rama might have every fault, but he also had affection. This was the first man she had met in her life who had opened his heart to her, who had not hidden anything from her. She did not want to lose this jewel. She did not feel the slightest jealousy while listening to what he said; on the contrary, a self-interested sympathy was evoked. By pleasing this young man, so guileless concerning love, she could make him her slave for good. She had no fears about Jalpa. No matter how beautiful she might be, Zohra, with her skill in the arts and her fine manners, could make her pale in comparison. She had left more than one great beauty of the Kayasth community weeping in her wake before this. How then could Jalpa be considered noteworthy?

"So why do you grieve so much for her, my dear?" said Zohra, trying to raise his spirits. "Zohra is ready to do anything for you. I'll find out about Jalpa tomorrow, and if she wants to stay here I'll arrange everything for her comfort. If she wants to go, I'll send her by rail."

Very humbly, Rama said, "If I could meet her once, the burden would be lifted from my heart."

"That's not easy, darling," said Zohra growing worried. "Who will let you leave here?"

Rama said, "Tell me some plan."

Zohra said, "I'll leave her in a park and come here. You go there with the Deputy Sahab and meet her on some pretext. I can't come up with anything else."

Rama was about to say something when the Daroga called out, "May I join your private conference too?"

The two of them quickly recovered themselves and opened the door. In came the Daroga smiling, and sitting next to Zohra said, "How can it be so quiet here today! Is the treasury empty today? Zohra, fill me a goblet with your henna-dyed hands today. Ramanath, dear brother, don't be angry!"

"Let it be, now, Darogaji," said Rama sourly. "You seem to be drunk."

The Daroga seized Zohra's hand and said, "Just one goblet, Zohra! And another thing, accept me as your guest today!"

"Darogaji," said Rama, changing his stance, "please leave now. I can't stomach this."

"Do you have written authority?" asked the Daroga, looking at him, glassy-eyed.

"Yes Sir," said Rama, severely. "I have got written authority."

The Daroga said, "Well, your authority is rejected!"

Rama said, "I tell you, leave this place."

The Daroga said,"Indeed! That's about as impossible as a frog catching a cold. Come on, Zohra, leave him here to babble."

Saying this, he grabbed Zohra's hand and lifted her to her feet.

Rama wrenched his hand away and said, "I've already told you, leave! Zohra can't go just now. If she should go, I'll drink both her blood and yours. Zohra is mine, and as long as I'm here no one can even look in her direction."

He grasped the Daroga's hand as he said this, thrust him out the door, and shutting it forcefully, fastened the bolt. The Daroga was a strong man, but his intoxication had weakened him. Standing outside on the veranda he began to hurl abuses and kick the door.

"Tell me and I'll go shove that wretch off the veranda," said Rama. "Devil's spawn!"

Zohra said, "Let him blabber away. He'll go off by himself."

Rama said, "He's gone!"

"You did very well to throw that pig out," said Zohra, looking delighted. "He would have taken me off and harassed me. Would you really have hit him?"

Rama said, "I would have killed him. I wasn't myself then. Who knows where I got so much strength from?"

Zohra said, "And suppose he doesn't let me come from tomorrow?"

Rama replied, "If he says even the slightest unpleasant thing meanwhile, I'll shoot him. Look, there's a pistol on the shelf. You're mine now, Zohra. Everything I have is at your feet, and I can't be satisfied till I have the same from you. You're mine, and I'm yours. No third woman or man has any right to come between us – not till I die."

Zohra's eyes were sparkling. "Don't say such things, darling," she said, putting her arms around his neck.

48

For the whole day Rama wandered around in the jungles of emotional turmoil. Sometimes the pitch-dark valleys of despair came before him, sometimes the joyfully rippling greenery of hope. Had Zohra gone? She had gone, making great promises. What need did she have to do that? She would come and say they had not met. She would not deceive him, would she? If she went and told the whole story to the Deputy Sahab then disaster would befall poor Jalpa without any warning. Could Zohra's nature be so base? Never, for if she was so faithless, so deceitful, then this world was not worth staying in. The sooner one could die disgraced, the better. No, Zohra would not deceive him. He remembered those days when Jalpa would leap up, feel his pockets and take out the money as soon as he came from the office. Now that same Jalpa had turned into a paragon of truthfulness. Then she had been a thing for love; now she was on object for veneration. Jalpa! He was not worthy of her. He could not reach the heights she wanted to take him to. Even if he could, he might get dizzy and fall. Nevertheless, he would bow his head down to her feet. He knew that she had cast him out of her heart, that she was alienated from him, and that she would feel no sorrow if he sank, or joy if he swam. Perhaps even now if she heard news of his dying or being caught in some terrible crisis, tears would come to her eyes. She might come to see his dead body. Yes! Once his life ended, perhaps then he would not be so low in her esteem.

Rama was now extremely remorseful about the error he had committed by not acting on Jalpa's advice. If he had changed his deposition to the judge during the court session as she had asked him to, if he had not been frightened by threats, if he had strengthened his courage, then why would he be in this situation. Now he believed he could have endured every difficulty with Jalpa by his side. Wearing the armour of her belief and love for him, he would have been invincible. Even if he had been hanged, he would have climbed the gallows laughing and joking.

Whatever mistakes he had made previously, this time he was suffering these hardships not through some mistake but for Jalpa's sake. If he had to endure captivity, it was much better to do so cheerfully, rather than weeping and snivelling. After all, what else could he do to build up the confidence of the police officials in him? Those rascals would torment Jalpa, insult her, bring a false case against her, and get her sentenced. That situation would be even more unbearable. He was weak, he could stand all their insults, but Jalpa might even give up her life.

Today he had learned that he could not leave Jalpa; and giving up Zohra seemed almost impossible, too. Could he keep both of these beautiful women happy? Would Jalpa agree to live with him under these conditions?

Never. She might never forgive him. Even if she should learn that he was going through these torments for her alone, she would not forgive him. She would say, "Why did you stain your soul for me? I could have taken care of myself."

He remained plunged in these perplexities the whole day. His eyes were glued to the street. The time for bathing came and went, the time for eating came and went, but he paid no heed to anything else. He attempted to divert himself with a newspaper, he sat down with a novel, but he could not apply his mind to anything. Nor did the Daroga come today. He was either ashamed of last night's incident or offended by it, or perhaps he had gone out somewhere. Rama did not ask anybody about it.

Like all weak humans, Rama too was embarrassed by yesterday's lapse. When he sat alone, he felt bad about his condition – why was his tendency towards a life of sensuality so strong? He was not so devoid of conscience that his downward progress pleased him, but as soon as other people came, a bottle of liquor appeared, Zohra sat before him, all his wisdom and sense of morality was vitiated.

It was ten o'clock in the evening, but Zohra was nowhere to be seen. The gate was shut. Rama no longer expected her to come, but even so he remained alert. What was going on? Did Jalpa not meet her, or had she not even gone? If she didn't come by tomorrow, he intended to send someone to her house. He dozed off a few times, and then it was morning. The same distress began again. He ought to send someone to her house to summon her; at least he would know whether she was at home or not.

He went to the Daroga and said, "You weren't in your right senses last night."

"That wasn't it," said the Daroga, concealing his spite. "I was only teasing you."

Rama said, "Zohra didn't come here last night. Please send someone to find out what's going on. I hope she's not angry."

"She'll come by herself if she wants to," said the Daroga, heartlessly. "There's no need to send anyone."

Rama did not insist a second time. He understood that he was not in a good mood. He went quietly away. Whom should he talk to now? It seemed shameful to talk to everyone about this. People would think that this gentleman had turned out to be a really dissolute fellow. At least he had become a little intimate with the Daroga.

He did not see Zohra for a week, and had lost all hope of her coming. In the end she had proven to be untrustworthy, Rama thought. It had been a big mistake to expect anything from her. Or was it possible that police officials might have forbidden her coming? At least she could have written him a letter. How she had deceived him! He'd poured out his heart to her for nothing. If she should say anything to these policemen, he'd be caught in a tangled mess of his own making. But Zohra could not be treacherous; his own inner soul bore witness to that, and would not accept this possibility. To be sure, she had tried to arouse him in the first few days, but then her behaviour had begun to change all on its own. Why had she said to him, again and again, with tearful eyes, "You won't forget me, will you, Babuji?" Memories of many such longings that she had expressed recurred to him and drove out suspicions of her deceit from his heart. Surely something unanticipated had happened. When he sat by himself and thought of Zohra, he would weep like a child. He came to have an aversion to liquor. The Daroga would come, the Inspector would come, but Rama found it disagreeable to sit with them for even five or ten minutes. He did not want anyone to tease him or to speak with him. He would scold the cook when he came to call him to eat. He had not the slightest wish to wander about or go on an outing. No one here was sympathetic to him, no one was his friend; he found solace only in sitting here by himself, repressing his feelings. Even his memories held no pleasure for him now. No, it was as if even those memories had been erased from his heart. A sort of indifference settled over his spirits.

It was eight o'clock on the seventh day. A very good new film was to begin showing today, a love story. When the Daroga came and told Rama about it, he got ready to go. He was just changing his clothes when Zohra arrived. Rama gave her one glance, and then began to comb his hair before the mirror. He did not say a word. To be sure, he was a little surprised to see her appearance so plain and unadorned. She was wearing only a white sari and there was not a single piece of jewellery on her. Her lips were faded, and in place of the usual flirtatiousness, her face shone with passionate seriousness.

She stood for a minute, and then going up to Rama said, "Are you angry with me? Even though I am blameless, and without even asking me about it?"

Rama did not answer, but began to put on his shoes. Seizing his hand Zohra said, "Are you displeased because I didn't come for so long?"

"Even if you hadn't come now, what right would I have had to say anything?" asked Rama, coldly. "You went out of your own kindness."

As he said this, he realised that he was wronging her, and he gazed at her ashamed.

"This is a good joke!" said Zohra, smiling. "You yourself entrusted me to do something, and now that I've done it and come back, you're getting angry. Did you think it would be so easy that it could all be done in the twinkling of an eye? You sent me to receive a boon from that goddess who is like a flower on the outside, but a rock on the inside, who is so strong even though she's so delicate."

"Where is she? What is she doing?" said Rama dejectedly.

Zohra said, "She's at Dinesh's home, the same one who was sentenced to be hanged. He has two children and there's his wife and his mother. All day long she amuses the children, brings water from the river for the old woman, does all the household tasks, and goes around collecting funds for them from important people. There was no property and no money in Dinesh's household, and his family was in great distress. They had no supporter to encourage them, and every last one of their friends turned their backs on them. They had gone without food several times; Jalpa saved their lives by going."

All of Rama's dejection vanished. He left off putting on his shoes, sat down on the chair, and said, "Why are you standing? Tell me everything from the beginning; you started in the middle. Don't leave out a single thing. How did you reach her to start with? How did you find out where she was?"

"It was nothing," said Zohra. "First of all I went to that Devidin Khatik. He gave me Dinesh's address. I went there as fast as I could."

Rama said, "Did you call her when you got there? Wasn't she startled when she saw you? She must certainly have hesitated!"

"I didn't look like this," said Zohra, smiling. "I went home from Devidin's and dressed to play the part of a Brahmo Samaj lady. I don't know what it is about me that lets others know right away who I am or what I am. When I see Brahmo ladies, no one even looks in their direction. But when my dress is the same, when I'm not wearing anything flashy or any excessive jewellery, everybody still stares at me. I can't hide what I really am. I was afraid that Jalpa would see right through me, so I cleaned my teeth thoroughly so there wasn't even a trace of *paan*. I went there looking as if I were some lady college-teacher. I disguised myself so well that no one, let alone Jalpa, could guess who I was. The curtain was drawn. I told Dinesh's mother that I was studying in a university here, and that my home was in Munger. I took sweets for the children; I went to play the part of a sympathiser, and in my opinion I played it very well. Both of those poor women started crying, and I wasn't able to control myself either. I promised to keep on visiting them from time to time. Just then Jalpa arrived, bringing water from the Ganges. Speaking in Bengali I asked Dinesh's mother, 'Is she a water-carrier from the Kahar caste?' She replied, 'No, she's come like you to share our grief. Her husband's a clerk in some office. I don't know anything else. She comes every morning and takes the children to play. I used to bring water from the river myself; she put a stop to that and brings it herself. She's given us our lives back. There was no one else around to help us. The children were suffering badly. Ever since she has come, our troubles have ceased. I don't know what good *karma* brought us this gift.'

"There's a small park in front of their house, and children from all over the neighbourhood play there. It was evening, and Jalpa Devi took both children along with her to the park. The grandmother gave each child one sweet from those I had brought, and they both began to leap and dance around. Seeing how happy they were, I felt like crying. Eating the sweets, they left with Jalpa. Once the children were playing in the park I began to talk to her."

Rama pulled his chair closer and leaned forward. "How did you begin?" he asked.

Zohra said, "I was just telling you. I asked her, Jalpa Devi, where do you live? After hearing those two women sing your praises, I've fallen in love with you."

Rama asked, "You used those words!"

Zohra replied, "Yes, I thought I'd make a little joke. She looked at me with surprise and said, 'You don't seem to be a Bengali. No Bengali speaks such clear Hindi'. I said, 'I live in Munger and I spend a lot of time with Muslim women there. I would like to meet you sometimes. Where do you live? I could come for an hour or so now and then. By sitting with you for a while, I too will learn some compassion!'

"Looking embarrassed, Jalpa said, 'You're making fun of me. Why, you're studying in college and I'm just an uneducated village woman. In fact, I'd become civilised by associating with you. Come here whenever you like; you can think of this as my home.'"

Zohra continued, "I said, 'Your lord and master has given you a lot of freedom. He must be a man of very liberal opinions. Which office does he work in?' Jalpa looked at her nails and said, 'He's a candidate for a police post.'

'He's a policeman and he gives you the freedom to come here?' I asked with surprise.

"Jalpa did not seem to be prepared for this question. A little startled, she said, 'He doesn't say anything to me… I didn't tell him about coming here... He seldom comes home. He lives right there with the police.'"

"She had given three answers at once," said Zohra. "Even so, she was having misgivings about their credibility. She stared in another direction, looking a little disconcerted.

"I asked her, 'Could you speak to your husband and somehow arrange a meeting for me with that informer who gave evidence against the prisoners?'"

Rama's eyes opened wide and his heart began to thump.

"When Jalpa heard this," Zohra said, "she looked at me piercingly and asked, 'What would you gain by meeting him?'

"I said, 'Can you arrange a meeting or not? I want to ask him what he got by incriminating so many men. I'd like to see what answer he gives.'

"Jalpa's face grew stern. 'He could say that he did it for his own benefit!' she said. 'Everyone thinks about their own benefit. I did, too. When no one asks hundreds of policemen this question, why would he be asked? There's nothing to gain from it.'

"I said, 'Well, suppose your husband had turned informer like this, what would you have done?'

"She looked at me in a frightened way and said, 'Why do you ask me this question? Why don't you look for the answer in your own heart?'

"I said, 'I'd never speak to him or look at his face again.'

"Reflecting deeply, Jalpa said, 'Maybe I would think the same way—or maybe I wouldn't—I can't say. After all, police officers have women folk in their homes too. Why don't they say something to their men? It's possible that my heart may become like theirs, just as theirs have become like their men's.'

"By now it had become dark. Jalpa Devi said, 'I'm getting late and the children are with me. Please come meet me again tomorrow if it's possible. I get a lot of pleasure from your conversation.'

"As I started to leave, she spoke again to me as she was leaving. 'Please come for sure. I'll meet you right here. I'll wait for you.'

"But after only ten steps more she stopped again and said, 'I didn't even ask your name. I haven't got my fill of talking with you yet. If you're not getting late then come and let's talk a little longer.'

"That was just what I wanted. I told her my name was Zohra."

"Really!" exclaimed Rama.

Zohra said, "Yes, what was the harm. At first even Jalpa was a little surprised, but it didn't matter. She understood that I was probably a Bengali Muslim. We both went back to the house; who knows how she even sits in that little wooden box. There wasn't even space for a sesame seed. Clay pots here, water there, a bed over here, bedding over there. The dampness and bad smell practically tear your nose apart. The food was ready; Dinesh's wife was washing the pots and pans. Jalpa made her get up. 'Go feed the children and put them to bed,' she said. 'I'll do the washing up.' And she started to scour them herself. Seeing this service had such an effect on my heart that I sat down on the spot and began to wash the pots which had been scoured. Jalpa told me to move from there, but I didn't. I kept on washing the dishes. Then she moved the water container to one side and said, 'I won't give you any water. Get up now. I'm ashamed. I beg you to move; you've been punished for coming here. You must never have had to do such work in your whole life.' I said, 'Nor you, either. When you're doing it, what's the harm in my doing it?'

"'It's different for me,' she said."

"'Why?' I asked. 'Whatever it is for you, it's the same for me. Why don't you keep a servant?'

"'Servants ask for eight rupees a month,' she said.

"'I'll give you eight rupees each month,' said I.

"Jalpa gave me a look full of true love, true joy, and true blessing. That look! Ah! How pure it was, how purifying! How low, how hateful my life seemed to me, compared to this unselfish service of hers. I can't describe how much pleasure I received from washing those pots and pans.

"When she got up after washing the dishes, she sat to massage the feet of the old woman. I stood silently. 'If you're getting late, then go and come again tomorrow,' she said to me.

"'No,' said I. 'I'll take you home and leave from there.'

"In fact we left there after nine o'clock. On the way I said, 'Jalpa, you're really a goddess.'

"'Zohra, don't say that,' she blurted out. 'I'm not performing service, I'm doing penance for my sins. I feel very sad. There's probably not a more unfortunate woman in the whole world than me.'

"I asked as if I didn't know, 'I don't understand what you mean.'

"Staring straight ahead, she said, 'You'll understand some day. My penance won't be finished in this life. It will take several lives for that.'

"I said, 'You're perplexing me, Sister! I don't understand a thing. I won't let go of you until you explain yourself.'

"Jalpa heaved a sigh and said, 'Zohra, rather than keeping something to oneself, it is easier to burden others with it.'

"In an injured tone I said, 'All right, if you don't have much confidence in me during our first meeting, I won't fault you; but sooner or later you'll have to confide in me. I won't leave you.'

"The two of us walked some distance in silence. All at once Jalpa said in a trembling voice, 'Zohra, if just now you learned who I am, you might turn away from me in hatred and run far away even from my shadow.'

"I don't know what magic there was in those words but I felt a thrill all through my being. This was a cry from a heart filled with grief and shame and it brought the outlines of my ruined life right before me. My eyes filled with tears. I felt like ending my act and revealing who I was. I can't say why being with her affected me like this. I've made duffers out of many a police officer and many a cunning rogue, but in front of her I was as timid as a wet cat. Somehow or other I curbed my feelings.

"When I spoke my voice was choked too. 'You're wrong, Devi. Perhaps I'll fall at your feet then. To be ashamed of one's defects or the defects of those close to one is the action of a true-hearted person.'

"Jalpa said, 'But what good would it do you to know my situation? Just consider me to be a poor wretched woman who takes pleasure in spending time with poor wretches like herself.'

"She put me off like this again and again, but I wouldn't let go. Finally she let it out."

"Not like that, you'll have to tell me everything," said Rama.

"How can I tell you a story that might go on half the night? It'll take hours," said Zohra. "When I'd kept after her a long time, she finally told me, 'I'm the unlucky wife of that informer who has caused such suffering to these prisoners.' Saying this, she burst into tears. Then bringing her voice under control she said, ''We used to live in Allahabad. Something happened which forced him to run away. He just fled without saying a thing to anybody. After several months we learned he was here.'"

"There's a story behind that, too," said Rama. "I will tell you someday. Nobody else but Jalpa could have thought of it."

"I learned all that the next day," said Zohra. "Now I'm thoroughly acquainted with the very core of your being. Jalpa is my friend. It's hardly likely that she's hidden anything from me."

"'Zohra,' she said to me, 'I'm trapped in a terrible predicament. On one side is the life of a man and the ruin of several families; on the other is my own destruction. I can save all these prisoners' lives today if I wish. I can give the court proof of a sort which will remove all credibility from the informer's testimony, but I won't be able to save the informer from punishment. Sister, I'm suffering the torments of hell in this dilemma that's befallen me. I can't let these people die, and I can't toss Rama into the fire!' She burst into tears as she said this and continued, 'Sister, I'll die before any harm comes to him from me. I can't offer him up to justice. I'll see what the decision is. I can't say what action I'll take then. Maybe I'll tell the whole story right there in the High Court, or maybe I'll take poison and die.'

"By then we reached Devidin's house and took our leave of each other. Jalpa earnestly insisted that I return at the same time the next day, because she had no leisure for conversation all day long, but was only free in the evenings. She wanted to raise at least enough money to save Dinesh's family from any distress. She'd already raised over two hundred rupees and I, too, gave five rupees. Once or twice I mentioned that she should stay out of these disputes and go home, but I tell you plainly that I never emphasised it. Whenever I hinted at it, she'd make a face as if to say she didn't even want to hear of it. I was never able to finish saying it. There is one thing, though. Shall I tell you?"

"What is it?" asked Rama, as if his attention was elsewhere.

Zohra said, "If I speak to the Deputy, he'll have Jalpa taken to Allahabad. She won't suffer any inconvenience. There'll be two women to escort her to the station while chatting with her. The train will be ready and they'll see that she's seated in it. Or you think up some other arrangement."

Rama looked her in the eye. "Would that be proper?"

"No, it wouldn't," said Zohra looking ashamed.

Hastily putting on his shoes, Rama asked, “She’s staying at Devidin’s house, isn’t she?”

“Are you going right now?” asked Zohra, getting up and standing in front of him.

Rama said, “Yes, Zohra, I’m going right now. I’ll just have a few words with her and then go where I ought to have gone long ago.”

Zohra said, “But think a little about the result.”

“I’ve thought it all through,” said Rama. “At most it’ll be three or four years of imprisonment for the offence of giving false evidence. Enough, let me leave! Don’t forget me, Zohra; we may meet again, someday.”

Rama came down from the veranda into the courtyard and was outside the gate in an instant. “Has Your Honour informed the Daroga?” asked the watchman.

“There’s no need to,” said Rama.

The guard said, “I’ll just go ask him. Why are you taking away my living, Sir?”

Rama did not answer, but went quickly out into the street. Zohra stood motionless, looking at him with sorrowful eyes. She had never felt such a love—such an apprehensive love—for him before, like some heroic young woman watching her beloved set out for the battlefield, unable to contain herself for pride.

The watchman rushed to tell the Daroga. That poor fellow had just lain down after eating. He rushed out in a panic and ran after Rama. “Babu Sahab,” he cried out, “just listen please, stop for a moment, what’s the use of this? May I know where you’re going?” In the end the poor man tripped and fell. Rama came back, lifted him up, and asked, “You didn’t hurt yourself, did you?”

“It’s nothing really,” said the Daroga. “I just stumbled a little. Where are you going at this time? Please think about what the consequences of this will be.”

Rama said, “I’ll come back in an hour. Jalpa may have been incited by the other side to file a petition with the High Court. I’m going to straighten her out.”

The Daroga asked, “How did you learn about this?”

“Zohra heard it somewhere and came to tell me,” said Rama.

“She’s a very treacherous woman!” said the Daroga. “A woman like that ought to have her head cut off.”

Rama said, “That’s just why I’m going. Either I’ll send her to the station right now or I’ll deal with her so severely that she’ll always remember it. There’s not much time to talk with her. Please let me out of this captivity for the night.”

The Daroga said, "I'll come too, wait a little."

Rama said, "No, you'll spoil the whole thing. I'll just be back."

The Daroga was rendered speechless. He stood in thought for a minute, then returned; and set off towards the police station talking to Zohra. For his part Rama quickened his pace, took a *tonga* and arrived at Devidin's house.

Jalpa had returned from Dinesh's home and was sitting and chatting with Jaggo and Devidin. These days she ate just once a day. Just then Rama called out from below. Devidin recognised his voice and said, "Perhaps it's Brother."

"Ask him what he's come here for," said Jalpa. "Tell him to go back there."

"No, Daughter," said Devidin. "I'll just ask him what he has to say. How did he get permission to go out at this time?"

"It must be to give me a lecture, what else!" said Jalpa. "But don't hope for anything!"

Devidin opened the door. "Dada, you must be surprised to see me here at this time," said Rama coming inside. "I got permission to come for an hour. I have to beg your pardon for the many bad things I've done. Is Jalpa upstairs?"

"Yes, she is," said Devidin. "She's just come. Sit down. I'll bring you something to eat."

"No, I've already eaten," said Rama. "I just want to say a few things to Jalpa."

"If she doesn't agree, you'll be needlessly humiliated," said Devidin. "She's not a woman to do what she's told."

Rama said, "Will she talk a little while with me, or doesn't she even want to see my face? Please go and ask."

"What's there to ask?" said Devidin. "They're both just sitting there. Go on. It's still your house, just like it was before."

Rama said, "No, Dada, ask her. I won't go just like that."

Devidin went upstairs and said, "He wants to say something to you, Bahu."

Jalpa hung her head and said, "So why doesn't he say it? Have I locked up his tongue?" She said this so loudly that Rama could hear her even from downstairs. What harshness! It was as if all her eagerness to meet him had fled. "If she doesn't want to speak to me, I won't force myself on her," said Rama standing below all the while. "I've decided to tell the Judge Sahab the whole story. That's the reason I've come at this time. I'm very sorry that Jalpa had to face these troubles because of me. My good sense was clouded over. Selfishness made me blind. Love of my own life and fear of suffering robbed me of my understanding. Some evil spirit had me in its grip, but her actions have pacified it. I'll probably have to enjoy the government's hospitality for three or four years. I'm not afraid, and if I live we'll meet again. If not, forgive my weakness and forget me. You too, Devidin Dada and Dadi, please pardon my faults. I won't forget your kindness until my dying breath. If I return alive, perhaps I'll be able to do something for you. My life has been completely ruined, both in this world and the next. I also have to tell you that it was I who had stolen her jewellery. There was no money to give the jeweller, so it was necessary to give back the jewellery. That's why I had to take such a wicked action. I'm still suffering the consequences today and I'll probably be suffering them till the day I die. If I had told her the whole story straight out right then, even though she would have taken it badly, this calamity wouldn't have come upon us. I deceived you too, Dada. I'm not a Brahman, I'm a Kayasth. I played a trick on a godlike person like you. Who knows what my punishment will be for this. Pardon me for everything. That's all, that's what I came to say."

Rama stepped down from the veranda and strode off quickly. Jalpa came down from the room above, but by the time she reached the lower storey Rama was nowhere to be seen. Stepping off the veranda she asked Devidin, "Where has he gone, Dada?"

"I didn't see, Bahu. My eyes were filled with tears," said Devidin. "You won't find him now. He was practically running when he left."

Jalpa stood almost motionless on the street for several minutes. How could she stop him? How sad he must be now, how despairing! What had possessed her not to call him to her? Who could know what things would be like in the future or when they might meet again? Never in their three years of married life had her heart been so shaken by love. When she had been concerned just with sensuous pleasure, she had only been able to see the outer surface of love, but now that she had become self-sacrificing, she could see its true form. How delightful it was, how pure, how grand, how glorious! While self-indulgent, she had been content just to see the doors of the garden of love. After becoming self-denying she had reached the interior of this garden – what a lovely scene, how sweet-scented, how picturesque, how full of blooms. Its fragrance, its loveliness, were filled with divinity. When love reaches its highest elevation, it mingles with the divine. Now that she had found this love, Jalpa had no doubts that she would remain blessed in this life and in the lives to come. This love had freed her from the fears of separation, circumstances, and death – and given her the boon of fearlessness. The whole world and its unlimited abundance seemed trifling in the face of this love.

Just then Zohra arrived. Seeing Jalpa standing on the footpath, she said, "What are you standing here for, Sister? I couldn't come earlier today. Come on, I have to tell you a lot of things today."

They both went upstairs.

49

Was the Daroga likely to have any peace of mind? He waited an hour for Rama after his departure, and then went to Devidin's house on horseback. There he learned that Rama had left more than half an hour back. He returned to the police station, but there was no word of Rama here. He began to feel that Devidin had deceived him. He must have hidden Rama somewhere. He drove his motorcycle as fast as he could back to Devidin's and began to threaten him. "If you don't believe me, search the house; what else can you do?" said Devidin. "It's not even very big – one room downstairs, one upstairs."

"Why won't you tell me where he's gone?" asked the Daroga, getting off his motorcycle.

"If I knew anything I'd tell you, Sahab!" said Devidin. "He came here, quarrelled with his wife, and left."

Daroga asked, "When is she going to Allahabad?"

Devidin replied, "Rama didn't say anything about her going to Allahabad. She's not leaving here until the High Court makes its decision."

"I'm not convinced of what you're saying," said the Daroga. Saying this, he went into the downstairs room and scrutinised every single thing. Then he went upstairs and was startled to see the three women. It came to Zohra's mind to play a trick, so she pulled the edge of her sari far over her face and hid her hands. The Daroga was suspicious. Maybe that rascal Rama had changed into this costume and was sitting right here!

"Who's this third woman?" he asked Devidin.

"I don't know her," Devidin replied. "She comes to meet Rama's wife from time to time."

The Daroga said, "Watch out if you try to fool me! You're trying to hide a culprit by dressing him up in a sari! Which one of these is Jalpa Devi? Tell her to please go downstairs. Let the other woman stay."

When Jalpa withdrew, the Daroga went up to Zohra and said, "Well, Sir, pulling these stunts on me! You came here on one pretext and when you got here you started having fun. All your anger vanished into thin air. Now take off this disguise and come along with me. It's getting late."

He removed the sari from Zohra's head as he said this. She let out a guffaw. The Daroga looked as if he had slipped and fallen into an ocean of amazement. "Oh! It's you, Zohra?" he said. "What are you doing here?"

Zohra replied, "I'm carrying out my duty."

"And where did Ramanath go?" he asked. "You must certainly know."

Zohra said, "He had gone well before I got here. Then I sat here and talked to Jalpa Devi."

The Daroga said, "All right, come along with me. We have to find out where he is."

"Hasn't he reached the bungalow yet?" asked Zohra, with feigned curiosity.

The Daroga replied, "No! There's no telling where he's got to."

On the way, the Daroga asked, "When is Jalpa leaving?"

"I gave her a good talking-to," said Zohra. "There's no need for her to leave now. She'll probably come around. Ramanath scolded her badly, and she's become frightened by his threats."

The Daroga asked, "Are you sure she won't be up to any mischief now?"

Zohra replied, "Yes, that's just what I think."

"So where did he go?" said the Daroga.

Zohra replied, "I can't say."

The Daroga said, "I'll have to report him. It's important to inform the Inspector Sahab and the Deputy Sahab. He hadn't drunk too much, had he?"

"Well, he was drunk," said Zohra.

"Then he must have collapsed somewhere," said the Daroga. "He's been a great nuisance. I'm just going over to the police station. Shall I drop you at your house?'

Zohra said, "That would be very kind of you."

The Daroga seated Zohra on his motorcycle and in a little while let her off at the door of her house. But even in this short time, his mind had shifted. "I don't feel like going now, Zohra," he said. "Come on, let's chitchat today. I haven't had a kind look from you in days."

Zohra took one step up the stairs and said, "Go inform the Inspector Sahab first. This is no time for chitchat."

"No, I won't go now, Zohra!" said the Daroga, getting off his motorcycle. "We'll see about it in the morning. I'm coming too."

Zohra said, "You don't listen. The Deputy Sahab may be coming. He sent word to me today."

The Daroga said, "You aren't playing a trick on me, are you Zohra? Look here, it's not nice to be so unfaithful."

Zohra went up the stairs, shut the door, and putting her head out of the upstairs window, said, "*Aadaab arz*!"

50

The Daroga went home to bed about eleven o'clock. When he woke up it was eight o'clock. He had just got up when he was called to the phone. It was the Deputy Sahab. "This Ramanath has made a big mess. We'll have to keep him someplace else, and send all his stuff to the Commissioner Sahab. Did he spend the night at the bungalow?"

"No sir," said the Daroga. "He made some excuse last night and went off to his wife."

"Why did you let him go?" said the Deputy. "We're afraid that he's told everything to the judge. The case will have to be tried again. You've made a very grave blunder. All our efforts have been ruined. You should have stopped him by force."

"Had he gone to the Judge, then?" asked the Daroga.

"Yes, Sahab, that's just where he went, and the judge has overturned the case. He'll have the case heard again, and Rama will change his declaration. There's no doubt of it now. And it's all your bungling. We'll all be swept away in this flood. Zohra betrayed us, too."

The Daroga immediately took Rama's things and left for the Police Commissioner's bungalow. He was feeling so angry at Rama that he could have swallowed him whole! How often had he explained things to the rogue, how well he had taken care of him, but he had still acted treacherously. Zohra was in the thick of the plot, too. Scolding his wife had been nothing but a ploy. He would haul Zohra Begum over the coals this very day. Where could she go? He'd have some words with Devidin too.

It is not even necessary to mention the commotion that went on for a week among the police. They went round and round day and night in anxiety about the case. More than the case, they were worried about themselves. The Daroga was in the biggest panic of all. He couldn't see any hope of saving himself. Both the Inspector and the Deputy threw all the responsibility on his head and completely distanced themselves from him.

The rumour that the case would be heard again began to spread through the whole city. This event was completely unprecedented in the history of English law; nothing like it had ever happened before. The lawyers had legal wrangles over it. Could the Judge even do something like this? However, he was unyielding. The police made great efforts, and the Police Commissioner even went so far as to say the whole Police Department would have its reputation ruined. But the judge paid no heed to any of this. To be responsible for ruining the lives of fifteen people on the basis of false testimony was intolerable to his soul. He notified both the High Court and the government.

The police now scurried back and forth night and day searching for Rama, but somehow or other Rama had hidden himself away without a trace.

Government officials carried on a correspondence for weeks. Reams and reams of paper were covered with ink. The newspapers took up a steady critical commentary on the matter. One journalist met Jalpa and published her account of things. Another published Zohra's. Their descriptions revealed all the secrets of the police. Zohra revealed that she had received fifty rupees a day to divert Ramanath and to see that he had no opportunity to think and reflect. The police ground their teeth when they read these accounts. Both Zohra and Jalpa had dropped out of sight or the police would certainly have taken them to task.

Finally after two months a decision was made, and a member of the Civil Service was appointed to the case. The deliberations were begun in a bungalow outside the city where, it was hoped, there would not be too large a crowd. Nevertheless a crowd of ten or twelve thousand people gathered there every day. The police went head over heels trying to make one of the accused turn informer, but their efforts bore no fruit. If the Daroga wanted, he could have produced new witnesses; but he was so distressed by the selfishness of his superior officers, that he did nothing but watch the whole spectacle from a distance. When superiors get all the glory, and subordinates, all the disgrace, what interest could the Daroga have in racking his brains in anxiety for new witnesses? His superiors saddled him with all the blame in this matter: it was because of his carelessness that Rama had escaped their clutches; if he had been kept under strict surveillance, how could Jalpa have written a letter to him, and how could he have met her at night?

Under these circumstances what else was there to do except dismiss the case? The tables were turned, and the misfortune intended for others fell on the heads of the police. The Daroga was demoted, and the Assistant Daroga was given an undesirable transfer to the *tarai*.

Half the city turned out to welcome the accused on the day of their release. Even though the police released them at ten o'clock at night, the spectators had assembled. People dragged Jalpa along too, and Devidin followed. Flowers rained down on her and the skies echoed with cries of "Victory, to Jalpa Devi!"

Ramanath's trials were not yet over. It was decided that charges of perjury would be brought against him.

51

The case began at ten o'clock sharp in the very same bungalow. The August showers had begun. Calcutta was becoming a swamp, but an enormous multitude of spectators was standing in the open area in front of the bungalow; Dinesh's wife and mother were among the women. Ten or fifteen minutes before the hearing began, Jalpa and Zohra arrived in closed vehicles. The women received permission to enter the courtroom.

The police began to give their evidence. The Deputy Superintendent, the Inspector, the Daroga, the Assistant Daroga – all gave their depositions. The lawyers from both sides cross-questioned them but there was nothing noteworthy in these proceedings. The formalities were being duly observed. After this came Ramanath's declaration, but it contained nothing special either. He gave a complete description of his life during the past year, concealing nothing. On being questioned by the lawyers, he said, "Jalpa's self-sacrifice, devotion, and love of truth opened my eyes, and even more than this, Zohra's kindness and sincerity. I consider it my good fortune to have received light from the very direction where others receive darkness. In the midst of poison, I received nectar."

After this came declarations for the defence from Devidin, Jalpa, and Zohra. The lawyers questioned them too, but truthful testimony can hardly be discredited. Zohra's declaration made a particularly strong impression. She saw that the soul she had been sent to fasten in chains, was writhing with pain and needed his wounds dressed, not chains. He needed a helping hand, not the shock of a blow. "When I saw his faith, his unshakable confidence in Jalpa Devi, I forgot about myself," she said. "I felt ashamed of my meanness and my selfish blindness. It dawned on me then how wretched, how degraded my life was, and when I met Jalpa and saw her unselfish service and her ardent penance, the few remaining moral standards in my mind melted away too. I came to hate my wanton life, and I decided that I, too, would take refuge with her."

Even more remarkable was Jalpa's declaration. Tears came to the eyes of the spectators as they listened. These were her final words: "My husband is guiltless, not only in the eyes of God, but in the eyes of the law too. It was written in his fate that he would have to atone for my obsession with a life of luxury, and he did so. He fled from the marketplace hiding his head in shame. If he transgressed against me at all, it was in constantly contriving ways to fulfill my wishes. He never hesitated to take the greatest of burdens on himself to please me, to keep me happy. He forgot that a luxurious lifestyle doesn't know how to be satisfied. He encouraged me where it would have been proper to stop me, and even now I'm sure that only the threat of action against me has stopped his mouth. If there is any offender, it's me, for whom he's had to suffer so many difficulties. I agree that I forced him to change his declaration. If I believed that he had taken part in those robberies, I'd have been the first to censure him. I couldn't bear for him to build his own prosperity on the corpses of innocent people. On the days when those robberies occurred my husband was in Prayag. If the court desires, it can verify this by telephone. If necessary, a declaration can be taken from officers of the Municipal Board. In circumstances like this my duty could be no other than what I did."

"Was any report requested from Prayag concerning this matter?" the court asked the government lawyer for the prosecution.

"Yes sir," said the lawyer, "but we are not disputing this matter."

"It is clearly established from this that the accused had no part in the robberies," said the lawyer for the defence. "There only remains the matter of why he became an informer."

"For his own selfish ends, what else?" said the prosecuting lawyer.

"And I tell you that he was deceived, and when he learned that the fear which had made him agree to be a puppet in the hands of the police was his own misapprehension, he was threatened by them," said the defending lawyer.

No witnesses for the defence remained now, and the prosecuting lawyer began the debate. "Your Honour, today an accusation has been presented to you of a kind that fortunately very seldom occurs. You are familiar with the Janakpur robberies. In several villages in the vicinity of Janakpur, robberies took place constantly, and the police began to search for the robbers. For months, police officers courageously tried to find the bandits. At last their efforts succeeded and they received information of the bandits' whereabouts. They were all found sitting inside a single house, and the police captured them all simultaneously. But you know how difficult it is to produce proof for the courts in such matters. The public is so frightened of these people that for fear of their life it's not prepared to give testimony. This goes so far that even those whose homes were robbed vanished when their time to testify came.

"My honourable listeners, just when the police were caught in this tangle, along comes a young man and claims to be the leader of these robbers. He gives such a vivid, such an authoritative description of them that the police are taken in. Finding such a person at such a time seems like divine aid to the police. The young man had fled from Allahabad and reached here half-starving. Meeting with such a favourable opportunity to make his fortune, he decided to realise his selfish objectives. Having turned informer, he had no fear of punishment; he was confident that he would get a good job through the recommendations of the police. The police treated him with great respect and hospitality and made him their agent. It was very likely that the police would have dropped the case against these culprits and released them for lack of any evidence, but falling victim to this young man's trickery they decided to proceed with the accusation. Whatever his other qualities may be, there's no denying the keenness of his powers of invention. He gave such an accurate description of the robberies that not a single link in the chain of events was missing. He conjured up everything from the first bud to the last fruit. The police went ahead with their case.

"But it seems that in the meanwhile he got an even better opportunity to improve his lot! It's quite possible that organisations which oppose the government may have offered enticements to him, and that these enticements suggested a new way to fulfill his selfish aims, which would give him not only wealth, but fame, public applause, and the pride of patriotism. He can do anything for his own self-interest, whether cutting somebody's throat, or donning the garb of a sadhu. This is the goal of his life. We're glad that his judgement finally got the better of him, whether or not he'll get any benefit from it. It's just as objectionable for the police to punish the innocent as it is for them to release the guilty. They don't start such cases just to show their skillfulness. Nor is the government so devoid of legal principles that it would be beguiled by the police into proceeding with a groundless case. But who is responsible for the bad reputation the police have acquired through the trickery of this young man, and for the thousands of rupees of government money spent? Such a person ought to receive an exemplary punishment so that no one will have the courage to play such tricks again. For a person who creates such a world of falsehood, no route should be left open to let him cheat society further. The most suitable place for him just now is one where he will have an opportunity to reflect deeply for some days. Perhaps he will undergo an inner awakening in the solitude there. You should consider only whether or not he deceived the police. There no longer remains any doubt that he did deceive them. If threats were made, he could have retracted his deposition after the first court session during the second session with the judge. But even then he did not do so. This makes it clear that accusations of police threats are false. Whatever he did, he did of his own free will. If such a person does not receive punishment, then he'll be bold enough to carry out his wicked acts again, and his violent tendencies will become even stronger."

Then the lawyer for the defence gave his rebuttal. "This case is unprecedented not only in the history of English law, but perhaps also in the worldwide history of law. Ramanath is an ordinary young man, and his education too is very ordinary. He's not a man of lofty opinions. He's an employee of the Allahabad Municipal Office, where his work is to collect duties on produce. He takes bribes from merchants according to the usual custom, and he spends extravagantly without paying attention to his income. Finally one day when there's a mistake in the total, he fears that he's misspent some of it. He panics so much that he runs away from home without saying a word to anyone. His office then becomes suspicious of him, and his accounts are checked. It then becomes apparent that he hasn't embezzled anything, but has only made a mistake in his accounts."

Then mentioning how Ramanath fell into the clutches of the police, how he became an informer, and how he gave testimony, he said, "Now a new change comes into Ramanath's life, a change which turns a pleasure-loving promotion-greedy youth into a devout and conscientious one. His wife Jalpa, whom it is no exaggeration to call a goddess, comes here from Prayag in search of him, and when she learns that Rama has become a police informer in a lawsuit, she comes to meet him secretly. Rama is staying comfortably in his bungalow, and a sentry is on guard at the gate. Jalpa does not succeed in meeting her husband, so she writes a letter, throws it in front of him, and goes off to Devidin's house. Rama reads this letter, and the curtain falls from his eyes. He secretly goes to meet Jalpa. She tells him the whole story, and urges him strongly to change his declaration. Rama at first expresses misgivings but later agrees and returns to his bungalow. There he tells the police officers straight out that he's going to change his declaration. The officers offer him many inducements, but when these have no effect on Rama and when they learn that there's no embezzlement case against him, they threaten to arrest Jalpa. Rama's courage breaks. He knows the police can do whatever they want, so he changes his plans and reaffirms his previous declaration in the judge's court session. The defence did not cross-question Rama in the lower court. In the higher court he was cross-questioned, but even though he had nothing to do with this case, he answered the questions in such a way that even the judge could not doubt his testimony and the accused were sentenced. The police began to show even more regard to Ramanath. They gave him a letter of recommendation, and may have even recommended him to the government of U.P.

"Then Jalpa Devi resolved to talk care of the children of Dinesh, the accused sentenced to hang. She took care of the necessities of life for them by asking for contributions all over the place, she did their housework with her own hands, and took their children to play.

"One day, while taking a trip in a motorcar, Ramanath sees Jalpa with a water jar on her head. His sense of self-respect is awakened. Zohra has been appointed by police officials for Ramanath's amusement. Moved by seeing the young man's mental agony, she goes off with the intention of bringing him all the news about Jalpa. She meets Jalpa at Dinesh's house, and when she sees Jalpa's self-sacrifice, service, and devoted labour, this prostitute's heart is so influenced that she becomes ashamed of her own life and a feeling of sisterhood grows up between the two of them. After a whole week, she goes to Ramanath and tells him the entire story. He immediately leaves his quarters and after a few words with Jalpa goes straight to the judge's bungalow. Whatever happened after that is here before us.

"I won't say that he didn't give false testimony, but if you take note of the circumstances and the temptations, the degree of this offence is greatly reduced. If the result of this false testimony had been that an innocent person had been punished, it would be a different matter. On this occasion, the lives of fifteen young men were saved. Is he still a perjurer? He himself has admitted to his perjury. Should he be punished for this? His simplicity and goodness so enchanted even a prostitute that instead of diverting and misleading him, she lit up the right path for him. Does Jalpa Devi's conscientiousness deserve to be punished? It is Jalpa and no other who is the heroine of this drama. Her true devotion, her unaffected love, her devoutness, her adoration of her husband, her selflessness, her dedication to service – which of her virtues shall we praise! If she had not come forward today, fifteen families would have lost their sons. She knew how bright her worldly prospects would become by siding with the police, and how many of life's worries this would free her from. It was possible that she, too, might have had a motorcar, servants, a fine house, and costly jewellery. Are these joys of no value to the heart of a beautiful young woman? But she was prepared to bear great suffering. Will she be rewarded for her devotion to righteousness by being forced to stumble down the path of life deprived of her husband? Isn't so much devotion, so much sacrifice, so much deliberation—in an ordinary woman who hasn't received any higher education—an indication of some divine impulse? Is it of no importance that a fallen woman became her companion in such activities? I, for one, consider it important. Accusations like this don't present themselves everyday. Perhaps you will never again have an opportunity to hear one like this. You are sitting here to make a decision about an accusation, but outside this court is another greater court, where your judgement will be weighed. Your decision about Jalpa will be made with an impartiality which that greater court will accept – a court that is not concerned with those niceties of the law in which we get entangled, in whose complexities we are caught, so that we usually stray from the path, and usually fail to distinguish the good from the bad and the bad from the good. If you determine anyone to be a criminal for telling the truth after repenting for lying, for passing his life in difficult circumstances after spurning a life of ease and pleasure, then you will not be presenting the world with a very high ideal of justice."

In giving his rebuttal, the prosecuting lawyer said, "Righteousness and ideals are things worthy of great respect in their rightful places, but a man who knowingly gave false testimony has surely committed a crime, and ought to be punished for it. It's true that he didn't embezzle anything in Prayag and that he was merely under a misapprehension about this. But in such conditions an honest person was obliged to clear himself when he was arrested. Why did he deceive the police by giving false testimony out of fear of punishment? This is something to consider. If you think that he did something improper, then you should certainly punish him."

Now it was the time for the decision of the court to be heard. Everyone had grown sympathetic to Rama, but they were also convinced that he would receive a sentence. It remained to be seen what that sentence would be. People drew closer together in great eagerness to hear the decision, pulled their chairs ahead, and even stopped their whispering.

"The only matter of concern is this: to protect himself, a young man sought the support of the police, and when he learned the very fear for which he was seeking support was totally baseless, he retracted his deposition. If Ramanath had been a truthful person, why would he have taken refuge with the police? But there is no doubt that the police suggested this means of protecting himself by giving false testimony and tempted him with it. I am unable to agree that the proposal to give testimony in this affair originated in his mind. He was tempted, and he agreed from fear of punishment. Moreover, he must certainly have been assured that the people against whom he was being prepared to give testimony were really criminals, because Ramanath is as devoted to the law as he is fearful of punishment. He is not one of those professional witnesses who don't even hesitate to incriminate innocent people for their own selfish reasons. If this were not so, then he would never have agreed to his wife's insistence on changing his deposition. It's true that he learned there was no case of embezzlement against him after the first court session and that he could have retracted his deposition in the subsequent judge's court. He certainly expressed this intention at that time, but the threats of the police overcame him. It was natural for the police to threaten him on this occasion to save their reputation, because they had no doubt about the accused being criminals. Ramanath succumbed to threats, which certainly demonstrates his weakness, but is excusable given the circumstances. I therefore acquit Ramanath."

52

For happiness and peace, can any place be better than the banks of the Ganges on a cool, pleasant, brisk April evening by a grove of banyan trees bending to the wind, with cows and sheep tied up beneath them, with the leafy vines of pumpkins and bottle-gourds rippling on the thatched roofs of clay huts, and no turmoil and tumult? Below, the golden Ganges, sparkling in red, black and green veils, singing in deep voices, here rushing forward and there shrinking back, here volatile and there solemn, flows on into endless darkness as if she is going forward into the anxiety-ridden, struggle-filled, darkling future while playing the multi-coloured games of childhood memories in the lap of pleasure. It was here, near Prayag, that Devi and Rama had come and taken refuge.

Three years had passed. Devidin had purchased land, planted an orchard, started farming, bought cows and buffaloes, and was experiencing happiness, satisfaction, and peace in continous labour and unceasing effort. That paleness, those wrinkles, longer lined his face, and instead a new vigour, a new lustre, was shining forth.

It was dusk, and the cows and buffaloes had returned from the grazing ground. Jaggo fastened them to their stakes, brought a little hay, and placed it before them. Just then Devidin and Gopi arrived in an ox-cart loaded with grain stalks. Dayanath had cleared away the ground beneath the banyan tree, and there the stalks were unloaded; this was the threshing-floor of the little settlement. Dayanath had been dismissed from his position and was now Devidin's assistant. Even now he had the same fondness for newspapers; several papers came every day, and in the evenings when he had leisure, Munshiji would read them out loud and explain their meaning. Among his listeners were usually several people from the nearby villages, forming a little daily assembly.

Rama had become so attached to this life that he would not have dreamed of moving back to the city even if he had received the superintendentship of a police station or the inspectorship of the customs office itself. Early every morning he would rise to bathe in the Ganges, and after some exercise he would drink some milk. As the sun rose, he would take out his chest of medicines and sit down. He had studied several books on Ayurvedic medicine and gave out remedies for minor illnesses. A number of patients came each day, and his reputation grew steadily. As soon as he had a respite from this work, he would walk around his garden where various vegetables had been planted along with fruit trees, flowering trees, and medicinal roots and herbs. Just now the garden produced only vegetables, but a good yield of limes, guavas, jujubes, oranges, mangoes, bananas, gooseberries, jackfruit, wood apples, and other fruits was expected in three or four years.

Devidin unfastened the bullocks from the carts, tied them to their stakes, and said to Dayanath, "Hasn't Brother come back yet?"

Gathering up the grain stalks, Dayanath said, "He hasn't come back yet. I don't have hopes of her getting well now. Times have changed. How happily she used to live. She had a carriage, a motorcar, a bungalow and dozens of servants. Now she's come to this. Everything was available; Vakil Sahab left a fine estate, but his relatives gobbled it up."

"Brother used to say that if she'd gone to court she would have got everything," said Devidin, "but she says she won't lie in court. She's a very high-minded woman."

All at once Rameshwari came out of a hut carrying an infant in her arms, and putting the child on Dayanath's lap, said to Devidin, "Brother, please go take a look at Ratan. Who knows how things are going with her? Zohra and Jalpa are both crying. Now where has that child got to?"

"Let's go see, Lala," said Devidin to Dayanath.

"What good will it do for him to go?" said Rameshwari. "Seeing a sick person frightens him to death."

Devidin went to Ratan's little room. She was lying on a bamboo bed. Her body had wasted away. Her face which had been as radiant as a sunflower had faded and become pale. Those colours which had given her living picture a throbbing vitality had fled; only her form had been left behind. It was as if that melodious, life-giving music, flooded with beauty and joy, had been absorbed into the heavens, and only its faint, sad echo remained. Zohra was bent over her, watching her with a gaze that combined tenderness, distress, despair, and longing. For a whole year she had not known the difference between day and night in her devoted service to Ratan. How could she not feel gratitude for the love Ratan had showed her, for the sisterly affection she unreservedly maintained for her in an atmosphere of distrust and exile? The empathy she had not got even from Jalpa, Ratan had bestowed on her. Sorrow and arduous labour had brought them together, and their souls were joined. This deep love was a new experience for her, one she had never even imagined. In this friendship her deprived heart found both the love of a husband and the affection of a son.

Devidin looked towards Ratan's face with anxious eyes, then took her pulse and asked, "How long has it been since she stopped speaking?"

"She was speaking just now," said Jalpa, wiping her eyes. "All of a sudden her eyes rolled up and she became unconscious. Haven't you brought the vaidya yet?"

"He has no remedy for her," said Devidin, and taking a few ashes passed his hand over Ratan's head, muttered something, and applied a pinch to her forehead. "Open your eyes, Ratan beti," he called to her.

"My motorcar came, didn't it?" said Ratan, opening her eyes and looking around disconcertedly. "Where has that man gone? Tell him to bring it a little later. Zohra, today I'll take you for a stroll through my garden. We'll both have a swing."

Zohra began to cry again; Jalpa too could not stem the flow of her tears. Ratan stared at the ceiling for a moment, and then as if her memory had suddenly awakened, she asked with a sad, embarrassed smile, "Was I dreaming, Dada?"

As a curtain of darkness fell across the blood-red sky, at the same time death brought down the curtains on Ratan's life.

When Ramanath returned with the vaidya later that evening, the silence of death reigned. The sorrow of Ratan's death was not that sorrow which makes us wail and groan, but rather that sorrow which makes us weep silently, whose memory never leaves us, and whose load never lifts from our hearts.

After Ratan's passing, Zohra was left alone. The two of them had slept together, sat together, and worked together. Now that she was alone, Zohra took no pleasure in any task. Sometimes she would go to the bank of the river to remember Ratan and weep, and sometimes go and stand for hours among the mango seedlings which the two of them had planted, as if she had become a widow. Jalpa did not have much leisure from tending the child and preparing food to spend a lot of time with her, and when she did, they would start talking of Ratan, and Zohra would begin to weep.

It was August and war had broken out between earth and water. The armies of the latter had descended on the vehicle of the wind and were raining down shafts from the heavens. Its land forces were wreaking havoc on the earth. The Ganges was gulping down villages and towns. Village after village was washed away. Zohra watched the spectacle from the river bank. She could never have guessed how huge the slender-limbed Ganges could become. Her waves thundered in frenzy, hands of foam were leaping out of their mouths, and changing their stances like cunning fencers. Now they would move forward a step, then fall back, and then turn around and leap forward again. Now a hut would come sweeping by, rolling as it went, as if some drunkard was running; now a tree would go swimming by with its branches and leaves dripping and rising like some stone-age creature. Cows and buffaloes, beds and seats passed before one's eyes like enchanted pictures.

Suddenly a boat came into view. Several men and women were clinging to, rather than sitting in it, as the craft sometimes rose and sometimes fell.

It seemed about to turn topsy-turvy at any time, but how wonderful their courage! All of them were still calling out, "Victory to Mother Ganges!" The women were still singing songs in praise of the river. And who might be watching this life and death struggle? People were standing on both sides, standing and repressing their feelings in this tense situation. When the boat rolled to one side or the other, their hearts would leap into their mouths. Attempts were made to throw ropes, but every rope fell short. All at once, the boat turned over and all those living beings sank into the waves. For a moment a few men and women were seen to go down and come up again, but then they vanished from view. Only one whitish thing was moving towards the bank. A strong current brought it within twenty yards of the edge. From close up it became apparent that it was a woman. Zohra, Jalpa, and Rama were all standing there. A child could be seen in the woman's embrace. The three of them were in great distress to pull the two victims out, but it was not easy to swim the twenty yards towards them. Moreover, Rama was not very skillful at swimming; once he was swept off his feet by the force of the waves, there would be no stopping anywhere before the Bay of Bengal.

"I'm going," said Zohra.

"I'm ready to go," said Rama, shamefacedly, "but I doubt I can even reach there. How fast it's going!"

Taking a step into the water Zohra said, "No, I'll bring them out very soon."

She went into the water up to her waist. "Why are you risking your life uselessly?" asked Rama, becoming alarmed. "Perhaps there's a steep drop. I was about to go."

Making a gesture of refusal with her hands, Zohra said, "No, no. Swear you won't come. I'll bring them back very soon. I know how to swim."

"It's just a dead body," said Jalpa.

"Maybe there's still life," said Rama.

"Good!" said Jaipa. "Then Zohra can swim out and bring them back whenever she has the courage."

Looking anxiously towards Zohra, Rama said, "Yes, she knows something about swimming. May God see that she returns. I'm ashamed of my own cowardice."

"What's there to be ashamed of?" said Jalpa brazenly. "What's the good of putting your own life in danger for a dead body? If she were alive, then I'd tell you myself to go bring her."

"Who can know from here whether she's alive or not?" said Rama, reproaching himself,. "It's true. A a man with children becomes a coward. I stood here and Zohra went."

Without warning a powerful wave came and pushed the corpse back into the main current. Zohra had reached the body and was about to seize hold and pull it when the wave moved it away. Zohra herself was washed some little distance into the flow of the river by its force. She recovered herself, but a second wave gave her another blow.

Distraught, Rama leaped into the water and called out with all his might, "Zohra! Zohra! I'm coming."

But Zohra no longer had the strength to struggle with the waves. She was being swept away with great speed by the current, close to the corpse. Her hands and feet stopped moving.

Suddenly a surge came and swallowed them both up. After a moment, Zohra's dark hair could be seen. Just for an instant! This was their last glimpse of her, and then she was no longer visible.

Rama made about a hundred yards, thrashing his arms and legs mightily, but the impetuous flow of the waves exhausted him in even this short distance. Where to go now? There was no trace of Zohra anywhere. His last glimpse of her was still before his eyes.

Jalpa was standing on the bank crying out, so distressed that she too hurled herself into the water. Rama was now unable to keep going. One force pulled him forward, another backward. In the force ahead was affection, despair and sacrifice; behind him lay duty, love and obligation. Obligation stopped him, and he turned back.

Rama and Jalpa stood up to their knees in the water for several minutes staring in the direction where Zohra had disappeared. Rama was speechless from self-reproach, Jalpa from sorrow and shame.

At last Rama said, "Why are you standing in the water? You'll catch a cold."

Jalpa came out of the water and stood on the bank, but said not a word – the shock of death had defeated her. This event today had once again demonstrated before her very eyes how uncertain life was. She had feared for Ratan's life well before her death; it had been apparent that she would be a guest in this world only a short while longer. However, Zohra's death had been like a thunderbolt! Just a little while back the three of them had happily set out to watch the play of the waters. Who had suspected that they would have to watch such a terrible play of death?

In these last four years, Zohra had enchanted everyone with her service, self-sacrifice, and straightforward nature. What other means did she have to wipe out her past, to wash out her former stains? All her lustful desires, all her passions, had dissolved in her service. In Calcutta she had been an object of sensuous pleasure and amusement. A respectable man would probably not have even let her enter his home. Here everyone had treated her like a member of the household. Dayanath and Rameshwari had been pacified by telling them that she was Devidin's widowed daughter-in-law. In Calcutta, Zohra had begged Jalpa just to let her live with her. She had come to hate her own life. Jalpa's trustful nobility had put her on the path to self-purification, and Ratan's pure disinterested life had continually encouraged her.

After a little while, Rama, too, came out of the water and set out for home plunged in grief. He and Jalpa would often come and sit on the river bank and gaze for hours towards the place where Zohra had drowned. For several days they continued to hope that perhaps Zohra had survived, and that she would come back from somewhere or other. But gradually this feeble hope too was swallowed up in sorrow. Still, even now Zohra's form would revolve before their eyes. The seedlings she had planted, the cat she had cared for, the clothes she had sewn, her room – all these were her memorials, and whenever Rama went near them, Zohra's likeness would stand before his eyes.

Glossary

Translator's Note: This glossary is meant for non-Hindi-speaking Western readers who may not be acquainted with most of the Hindi terms I have not translated. The glossary also includes two or three lesser- known names of places, and some English words used in an unfamiliar way.

In numerous cases, I have borrowed definitions from R.S. McGregor's The Oxford Hindi-English Dictionary (Delhi, 1993), though frequently modifying or supplementing them. In other cases I have used my own definitions.

I have deliberately not attempted to give a systematic scholarly transliteration of any of the Hindi terms, knowing that Indian or Western readers familiar with Hindi do not need it, and that Western readers are not familiar with Hindi probably do not want it.

Aadaab arz	Muslim expression of courtesy appropriate for both arrivals and departures; in its one occurrence in the novel it is used ironically
Ajii	Expression used to call someone's attention without using his or her name
Anna	Obsolete (as of 1957) coin equal to one-sixteenth of a rupee
Approver	Accused person who testifies against others in turn for immunity from punishment, and for monetary or other rewards
Arhar dal	Type of pulse or lentil
Babu	Title of respectful address; also, in a transferred sense, a clerk or government servant
Babu Sahib	A still more respectful variant of babu
Babuji	Another still more respectful variant of babu
Bahu	Term of reference and of address for a daughter-in-law or for a young bride or wife
Bahuji	More respectful variant of bahu
Baiji	Respectful term of address for a woman
Barfi	Usually rectangular sweet made from thickened milk and sugar, sometimes with the addition of nuts, etc.
Begum	Title of Turkish origin for a lady of rank, or a queen; more loosely, a respectful or sometimes ironic term of reference or address for a woman, especially a wife
Begum Sahib	More elaborate version of begum

Beti	Literally, daughter; also an affectionate term of address from an older person to a younger woman
Bhagavata Purana	Sanskrit work of 18,000 stanzas dealing with aspects of ancient Indian mythology, legend, history, and theology, especially known for its treatment of the childhood and youth of Krishna
Bhai	Term of address meaning 'friend' or 'brother'
Bhaiya	Term of address and reference meaning 'friend' or 'brother'; in this novel it is the term which Devidin usually uses to address or to refer to Ramanath, and becomes something very like a proper name
Bhang	The hemp plant, especially its crushed or ground leaves, eaten or mixed into drinks for its narcotic effects
Bidi	Hand-rolled Indian cigarette made from a twist of tobacco rolled up in a tobacco leaf
Brahmo Samaj	Religious movement founded in Calcutta by Ram Mohun Roy in 1828 to reform Hinduism from within
Chamar	A very numerous community of very low ranking in the Hindu caste system, traditionally associated with leatherwork
Chandrahar	Special kind of necklace made of circular and semi-circular pieces of precious materials
Chapatti	Thin, soft, round, unleavened baked wheat cake; a staple item in the north Indian diet
Charas	Sticky or waxy gum or resin found on the hemp plant, smoked like ganja, and like ganja more intoxicating than bhang
Charhao/charava	Collection of jewellery or clothes given as a present by the bridegroom to the bride
Charpai	Four-legged bed consisting of a wooden frame and a loosely woven mesh of fabric or heavy twine
Chaudari	Honorific title; also a term for the headman of a village, or the leader of a community
Chilam	Clay bowl with or without a stem in which tobacco, etc. is smoked
Chote Babu	The junior or younger babu; in its only occurrence in the novel it refers to Ramanath as opposed to his father
Chowkidar	Watchman, guard, or local policeman

Daal	Split lentils or pulses; raw, or cooked and spiced
Dada	Elder brother or paternal grandfather; also a respectful term of address or reference for an older man. It may also be used to address non-relatives as a sign of affection and respect; Ramanath frequently addresses Devidin in this way
Dadi	Paternal grandmother; also a respectful form of address to an older woman. It may also be used to address non-relatives as a sign of affection and respect; Ramanath frequently addresses Jaggo in this way
Dai	Elder sister or mother
Daroga	Police inspector or superintendent; the police officer in charge of a police station
Darogaji	Respectful term of address or reference for daroga
Deodar	Species of deciduous tree; deodar pine or cedar (Cedrus deodara)
Devi	Literally, 'goddess' or 'lady'; a respectful term of address or reference for a woman
Deviji	A still more respectful from of devi
Dhaak	Species of deciduous tree; butea frondosa
Dharma	An almost untranslatable Hindu term including: moral or religious duty, the proper performance of one's social and religious role, fulfilling prescribed customary religious observances, religion, way of life, etc.
Dharmshala	Rest-house for travellers and pilgrims, built as an act of religious merit
Dhoti	Garment worn around the lower body consisting of a single piece of cloth, one end of which passes between the legs and is tucked in behind
Dwarchar	Marriage rite performed at the door of the bride's house
Ekka	One-horse vehicle
Ganja	Buds or flowers of the hemp plant, usually smoked like tobacco in a chilam and like charas more intoxicating than bhang
Golgappa	Very small pastry of wheat flour, made in the form of a hollow sphere, and filled with a savoury liquid; a popular street snack

Gopi	Wife of a cowherd; specifically, any of those in love with the legendary deity Krishna as described in the Bhagavata Purana
Gulli-danda	Children's game in which a smaller stick is lifted and hurled with a larger stick
Guluband	Type of close-fitting necklace
Gur	Unrefined dark reddish-brown sugar made by boiling down sugarcane juice
Halwa	Soft sweet made with ghee (clarified butter), sugar or syrup, and spices combined with a basic ingredient which may be semolina, carrots, etc.
Huzur	Old-fashioned term of address for a person of high social standing, meaning something like 'Your Highness'; often used jokingly or ironically
Jalli	Affectionate nickname for the novel's female character, Jalpa
Janwasa	Living quarters of the bridegroom's party at a wedding
Jiijaa	Term of reference for an older sister's husband
Kadam	Species of tree (Nauelea cadamba)
Kahar	Community of low rank in the Hindu caste system whose traditional tasks included fetching water and carrying palanquins
Kajli	Special type of song sung in Savan (July–August), the fifth month of the Hindu calendar
Kakaji	Term of reference and address for a father's younger brother, or more generally, for an elder male relative. It may also be used to address non-relatives as a sign of affection and respect; Ramanath occasionally addresses Devidin in this way. Manibhushan also uses this term to refer to Vakil Sahab
Kakiji	Term of reference and address for a father's younger brother's wife, or more generally, for an elder female relative. It may also be used to address non-relatives as a sign of affection and respect; Ramanath occasionally addresses Jaggo in this way. Manibhushan also uses this term to address Ratan on occasion
Kaleva	Particular meal taken by the bridegroom and his party in the bride's house
Karun	Legendary person of fabulous wealth

Kashi	Alternative name for Banaras or Varanasi
Kathak	Particular style of north Indian dance
Katora	Shallow metal cup or bowl used in cooking, and for serving meals on a thaali
Katori	smaller version of a Katora
Kayasth	Community of medium rank in the Hindu caste system associated with Hindu culture and language, whose traditional occupation was writing, under British rule, disproportionately represented in government service
Khatik	Community of a low rank in Hindu caste system, traditionally sellers of fruits and vegetable, and also distillers of alcoholic beverages
Khatri	Hindu community of merchants and traders; of medium rank in the caste syetem
Khichari	Mixture of rice and lentils cooked together with ghee (clarified butter) and spices
Khir	Liquid sweet of rice, milk, and spices; often eaten on special occasions
Kiranta	Derogatory term for a Christian
Kurta	Long-sleeved, collarless garment worn over a lower garment by men
Laddu	Large round sweet whose basic ingredients are usually chick-pea flour or thickened milk, sugar, and spices
Lathi	Long staff, usually of bamboo
Lingam	Phallic image, one of the most common forms in which the great Hindu God Shiva is worshipped
Lota	Small round pot, usually made from copper or brass for water or other drinkable fluids
Maharaj	Literally, great king or emperor; often used as a term of address to a brahman (especially as a cook) or to a supenor
Mahashaya	Gentleman; also a respectful term of reference or address meaning something like 'Sir'
Mahatma	Literally 'great soul'; a saint or saintly person used ironically in the text
Majum	Spiced sweet or drink made with bhang
Malai	Cream, clotted cream, or the skimming from boiled milk

Mardana	The men's or public part of a house
Marwari	Hindu business community from the region of Marwar in Rajasthan
Maulvi Sahab	Respectful term of reference or address for a scholar or teacher, especially of Muslim law, Persian, or Arabic
Memsahib	Term of reference for a European woman; also a humorous or ironic term for a wife; in this novel it is used to refer to both Ratan and Jalpa
Munshi	Title of respect for an educated man; also, a writer Or a teacher or tutor, especially of Persian Or Urdu
Nagpanchami	Hindu festival falling on the fifth day of the light half of the month of Savan (July-August) when women worship snakes to obtain blessings for their children
Namaskar	Formal expression of courtesy among Hindus, appropriate for both arrival and departure
Nayab Daroga	Assistant daroga
Paan	Popular Indian concoction of areca-nut, lime, spices, and various other ingredients wrapped in a betel leaf and slowly chewed in the mouth as a sort of combination of snack and digestive aid
Paandaan	Container for holding the ingredients of paan
Paisa	Money; also, historically, one-fourth of an anna or one sixty-fourth of a rupee, and now, one-hundredth of a rupee
Pakora	Small piece of vegetable, fruit, or even meat, dipped in a spicy batter of chick-pea flour and deep-fried
Panda	Community of Brahmans whose traditional duties involve superintending places of pilgrimage or temples, and serving as registrars for genealogies
Patidev	Literally, 'husband-god'; a traditional respectful term for husband
Pranaam	Formal respectful greeting
Prasad	Food offered to someone of higher spiritual status, or more frequently, to the image of a deity, and then, its nature having changed by contact with something higher, eaten by the worshipper or shared with friends and family
Prayag	A variant name for Allahabad

Puri	Round, soft, unleavened, deep-fried wheat cake; regarded as more special than a chapati
Ram Ram	The repeated name of Rama, hero of the Ramayana, used as a greeting among Hindus
Rai bahadur	High-ranking title given to Indians during British rule
Ramayan	The epic poem whose earliest version is in Sanskrit, glorifying the deeds of the deity Rama
Rasleela	Folk dance drama of north India based on scenes from the life of Krishna. In its one occurrence in the novel, it seems to refer to a written version of such a drama
Roti	Generic term for several kinds of bread-cake, including chapaatis and puris
Sadhu	Wandering holy man or ascetic
Saheb	Title for a prominent person, an officer, or (historically) a European used as both a term of reference and address; roughly translatable as 'sir'
Sahab Bahadur	During British rule, a title for a European official or for an Indian receiving British patronage
Sardar Sahab	Respectful term of address or reference for a Sikh
Sarkar	Term of address meaning something like 'Sir' or 'Your honour'
Seth	Title of respect used as both a term of reference and address for merchants, bankers, etc.
Sethaniji	Similar title for the wife of a seth
Shishphul	A still more respectful variant of seth Woman's head ornament
Shraddh	Hindu ceremony benefiting and honouring deceased relatives in which libations and offerings of food are made to the deceased and food and gifts are given to the officiating Brahmans and to relatives
Swadeshi	Literally, belonging to one's own country; historically, the name of a movement to ban the importation of foreign goods, especially cloth, into India
Tarai	Low-lying land, especially that at the foot of the Himalayas. In the context of the novel, the Assistant Daroga's transfer to the tarai represents a hardship assignment to an undesirable location because of its isolation and unhealthy climate

Tasla	Brass or iron vessel with steep sides used to boil rice, knead dough, etc.
The Parrot and the Mynah	The title of a collection of stories well-known in India
Teli	Community of low rank in the Hindu caste system whose traditional occupation was oil-milling and selling oil; also a pejorative, implying an unclean or dirty person
Thaali	Flat metal plate with a vertical rim widely used to serve meals in north India
Tilak	Sectarian mark made (with saffron, sandalwood, ete.) on the forehead. In the one occurrence of this word in the novel, Ramanath puts a tilak on his forehead to maintain his pretence of being a Brahman
Tola	Measure of weight, approximately equal to thirteen grams
Tonga	Horse-carriage; usually drawn by a single horse
Triveni	The conjunction of three sacred rivers – the Ganges, the Yamuna, and the mythical subterranean Saraswati – at Prayag (Allahabad), and one of the holiest sites of Hinduism
Tu	The most informal of the Hindi pronouns for 'you': used to express great intimacy between equals, or to express social distance between master and servant, parent and child, etc.
Upanishads	Collective title for some of the oldest mystical sacred writings of Hinduism
Vaidji	Respectful term of address or reference for a vaidya, Ayurvedic doctor
Vakil	Lawyer, pleader, or advocate
Zamindari	Landed estate; the whole system of collecting land revenue through zamindars (landholders or landowners who played the role of tax-farmers)